VEGAS DIE

A QUEST MURDER MYSTERY

Special 15th Anniversary Edition

S.P. GROGAN

VEGAS DIE

A QUEST MURDER MYSTERY

Addison & Highsmith

Addison & Highsmith Publishers

Las Vegas ◊ Oxford ◊ Palm Beach

Published in the United States of America by
Histria Books, a division of Histria LLC
7181 N. Hualapai Way
Las Vegas, NV 89166 USA
HistriaBooks.com

Addison & Highsmith is an imprint of Histria Books. Titles published under the imprints of Histria Books are distributed worldwide exclusively by the Casemate Group.

Library of Congress Control Number: 2020934254

ISBN 978-1-59211-042-1 (hardcover)
ISBN 978-1-59211-045-2 (softbound)
ISBN 978-1-59211-070-4 (ebook)

Table of Contents

Again, to Pamela

*We are standing in a boat on dry land, a boat with wheels;
party hats on our heads. You are holding me while I raise a
burning torch in the starry night. A shooting star arcs the
heavens. We are looking forward, seeking; our mutual quest
in motion.*

Artist: Cynthia Breusch *Dreams & Journeys: Out Amongst the Stars*

Part I

I have set my life upon a cast
And I will stand the hazard of the die

— Richard III, Act V, Scene 4

Bugsy Siegel monument at the Flamingo

1. Gray Memories

July, Twenty-two years ago.

Smart plan, bad destiny.

Cassandra Jewelry Emporium, corner of Eastern Avenue and Mt. Charleston Boulevard. Ten minutes, in and out. Store Manager, two clerks, and two customers led into the back office and told to lick the floor and keep their eyes shut, or else. Quick drying epoxy immobilized the alarm buttons. Phone cords severed. Surveillance cameras sprayed black. The one cell phone removed from a floor hugger.

The four gunmen operated with military precision. Jewelry from the counter displays rifled; from the safe they scooped up unmounted gem stones, pirate-era coins, rare casino chips, grab bag prizes with the most valuable dumped into brief cases. A professional job, arriving in suit and tie attire, the ski masks pulled on at the last minute. Their calling card was smash-and-grab, smashing the display glass, ruthlessness to their capabilities. They grabbed the most expensive jewelry, skipped the factory-colored stones. With their home closets full of boosted Hong Kong replica watches, 8-track tapes, and bootleg porno beta, this year, genuine shit only had been the gang's mantra.

The shattering glass freaked a woman clerk to believe this was the last day of her life, as it almost was. She scurried like a startled rabbit from the floor and bolted, screaming, a full panic attack of blind emotions. She almost made the front door before one of the robbers, a fat man, round-housed her with his gloved fist and sent her sprawling. As her arms and hands tried protecting her body, he beat her with the butt of his revolver; downward strokes, deliberate in his enjoyment. He could have killed her. He had killed before. Here, he was just pissed. Another of the heist team had to pull him away as they exited into the daylight, masks removed.

Their car, driven by the fifth gang member, pulled away from the curb, no hurry. Masks removed, once again innocuous businessmen on a work day. Several blocks later they split up, three of them driving off to establish alibis, while the two remaining, one being the crazed fat thief, took another car, but not before all the briefcases were emptied into a large athletic bag, a pro tennis racket carrier of green-red tartan design. A small Yale lock with metallic green coloring attached, snapped securely.

The two men said very little as they drove to the closed casino, pleased silence. Police cars screamed in the distance.

The fat one smirked. "This was the big score."

The other man's grimace carved his narrow face. His eyes darted in all directions causing his black bushy eyebrows to bounce like caterpillars barely clinging to their perch. His pencil-thin moustache twisted when he spoke.

"Yeah, but I don't know if I like what we're doing next,"

The fat man dismissed any other notion except his.

"Considering the heat coming down this is pretty smart. They get the stuff in Chicago today, and we get cash right back. No middleman except our VIP courier who doesn't know shit. You're pissed because you didn't think of it."

"If he only knew."

"Fuckin' rich, that's us."

As they approached the shuttered El Morocco Oasis Hotel & Casino, for over two years silent as the proverbial tomb except for clandestine meetings such as this sanctioned by the new owner, the two gangsters had no idea they would never again see the product of their aggravated larceny or profit from it.

Late in the same day, a sleek black limousine stopped in front of the Executive Jet Terminal. Arrivals and departures bustled. Several private jets on the tarmac sat fueled; pilots checked instruments awaiting their passengers.

A father and his young daughter, followed by a nurse, exited the limo and entered the terminal. The nurse slow walked the girl who bore obvious pain. A preteen youngster; her paleness blended against her white skirt and t-shirt outfit, ghost-like against the sunlight's brilliance. Their driver followed carrying three pieces of luggage, including golf clubs and an encased tennis racket attached to a red-green tartan bag, locked secure with a combination Master lock. Police officers, edgy and suspicious, hands on their side arms, stared with menacing intent at all those arriving at the jet terminal. They paid little notice to the family entourage on their way to the waiting aircraft.

Two men, joking between themselves, fiddled with last minute adjustments to their golf bags before handing them over to the copilot who stored them in the plane's cargo belly along with the luggage from the limo driver.

The father said his good-bye.

"Don't go," begged his daughter, a plea, tears welling in her eyes.

"Only three nights in Chicago."

"Don't go."

"Honey, I know you're not feeling well. I wish I could stay, but this trip is part business, and important." He pointed to the nurse nearby.

"Doris will take good care of you." He paused. "And there's your mom to help."

"No, my Mother can't help." The girl snapped. The father nodded a silent understanding. His wife existed in a hazy world of morning Screwdrivers and evening Cosmopolitans.

The father withdrew from his coat pocket a small rectangular box covered in ivory wrapping paper and tied with pink ribbon.

"This is for you. Open it after I'm gone. When we meet again it will be in the Garden of Allah."

He kissed her. She hugged back with sobs, clinging for long moments before he gently broke free. She watched him shake hands with his friends, jovial, as they all boarded the private jet. He turned and waved to her.

A minute later, as the girl watched, the plane exploded.

2. Sputtering Torch

Present Day

What day was this? Yes, he knew. The reporter would return to-morrow with the manuscript. He had been asked to read what the reporter had written, proof his stories. The best time would not be in his cell, but when they took him to the clinic for dialysis. Usually, he just lay there and read crap historical romance novels. Bodice-rippers. French tickler trash.

With no kidney function he was trapped within two prisons, one self-made from a life of excess. Both would hold him close until he gave up this mortal coil and they shipped his wrinkled husk to some medical school; where when they'd weigh his brain, and the professor would ask his students, "How could this brain create so much evil?"

At least his steady addiction to showgirls and double shot booze had not taken his liver or he'd be dead by now. The kidneys went instead. The price of life required cleaning his blood three times a week.

He found himself in the exercise yard. He started his ritual walk, an easy pace, to keep his heart strong, his legs from atrophy of prison confinement. As usual he found himself left alone. No fun for them to hassle a hunch-shouldered ill, old man. He had his stories if any wanted to hear, but none did, until the reporter came with his tape recorder. He tried to remember. Almost four months ago. At first he didn't want to talk, but the distraction of a visitor drew him in and the reporter seemed to have clout to give him more time for his recol-lections. He sensed his memory slipping away; he noted his oral his-tory lost a few facts here and there and he had started mixing up names. The reporter bore saintly patience and they went over the sto-ries several times, which he enjoyed retelling. The reporter had this cockiness, like he himself strutted in the old days. The reporter said his stories would be the crux of a best seller. So he told his stories glossing over the incriminating, skipping the damning.

Vagueness descended about his last showgirl, the bitch, as a sob sister on the witness stand, caused his incarceration. He did not want to admit aloud to a damn reporter, or even to himself, his last years had been downward, booze and pimping a stable of has-been line dancers turning tricks. He shouldn't have kept beating her. She was stiffing him, doing freebies behind his back. Horribly mangled, she lived. Why did they have to throw the book at him? He knew. Because he ran with a bad crowd and they never could tie him to the robberies, especially to the Cassandra heist. Can't get him on that score, so crucify him on beating up a hooker!

He didn't care about the future. Today, sunny weather lay in the forecast. His body flowed with cleansed blood. The reporter would arrive in the afternoon and he could see on paper what stories he had told best.

Someone blocked his path.

"Gotta moment, pops?"

He didn't recognize the inmate. The Hispanic accent and tattoos gave him away as East L.A. Probably one of those Barrio Locos gang members. A lot of those spic beaners were cutting into the Bloods crack trade in Vegas. The justice system juked the stupido ones who got caught. He tried to stay invisible. Ignore the prison culture, let the gangs strut and fight for their few yards of celled-in turf.

"I gotta letter for you."

"What?"

The gangsta mailman flashed a small envelope from his pants.

"Padrino. Came from the outside for you personally. Look at it over here."

He knew few people who could have sent messages or had the juice to smuggle him gifts, some hooch. Until the reporter, and two of his old comrades two weeks ago, no one came.

Like a curious mutt he followed the Hispanic inmate over to a side wall .

"Sit here, old man. I'll give you some shade." A white plastic chair they used over at the weight training area was shoved under his butt. He did not like to be called 'old'. All his stories to the reporter were of vigor and youth, of screwing and drinking. Rough times with no crap taken.

Placed in his hands, he opened the envelope to find a typed letter, no signature, no address.

Taking out reading glasses the first sentence began, 'You may not remember, but let me tell you a story…" He liked stories.

Midway through the short letter, his expression changed, darkened, and he started to say, "What the…" He tried to struggle up, but hands pushed him down.

"Finish the letter, Pops." At the last sentence, the last word, shadows circled him. Two other men stood to his side, each etched with identical tattoos as the prison mailman's. Out came a hand painted cardboard sign, with a string rope, like a placard, and one of them slipped it over the elderly man's head.

Confused, letter in hand, he read the placard. 'Guess who?' it read, ink-drawn names with empty spaces. Like that game show: industry pioneers theme, last name is, so first name is, _____ Hughes, _____ Dolittle. Fill in the blank. This was all about one of his stories, one that he did not tell, and never would. A story he had made himself forget, until now. The letter and sign brought it all back, so vivid. He could fill in the blank, and in a whispered cough, uttered the name unspoken after all these years.

He relived that story, a crazed thrill long protected by *omerta*, a code of silence. He knew who had sent the message. His question as to why, why now, to what conclusion came too quick. The gang leader stuffed the letter in the old man's mouth. As he gagged for air they pulled out hidden plastic soda drink bottles and poured the contents over him. One of the Barrio Locos lit a match.

The guards in the tower, those in the yard, became alert to a staggering fiery torch. Inmates backed away but stared with sick wonder. For a few brief moments the old man screamed, but his cries went unheard, silenced by the paper-gagged death warrant.

3. Slice of Life

The heavyset man stared at the immobile face of the statue and the unblinking bronze eyes. He cursed at what made him come to this particular place when he turned to see a gun pointed at his bloated belly. The gun leveled at him was his reality check. He had been suckered, simple as that.

Too many years of honest work made him rusty, like his arthritic knee that buckled in needles of pain as he fell, shoved to the ground. Damn grass stains. Somebody would pay, he winced. Being tied up, he noticed that the gun, a .22, not a good sign, lay out of his reach on the pedestal of the statue, like a reverent offering to a violent god. The rope thrown around him tightened and constricted his chest. He wondered if the angina would set his heart muscles into spasm.

"When my guys show up, any minute, you're dead meat, asshole."

Silence. He had no "guys" left he could count on. He knew that. Times had changed.

"Money, is that it? Take my wallet. Five bills."

Silence.

"What the hell do you want?"

His captor removed the face mask disguise. The old man stared with the sunlight in his eyes seeking recognition. Not a familiar face. He sputtered in surprise when he saw an ornate knife appear. He recognized the design, a type of silver dagger, similar to a knockoff brand he used to sell at his store for wall ornaments, mass-produced Persian kitsch.

Not this. This dagger was the real thing: a miniature scimitar, embellished on its polished scabbard with Farsi scrollwork, the hilt choked with semiprecious colored stones, highlighted by scattered sun-winking diamonds. He knew his antiques, a penchant for jewelry, his genetic desire to possess the beautiful, the unobtainable. Such a search brought him this day to the garden.

The knife slipped effortless from its silver sheath, glinting, blinding in the sunlight. The blade flashed razor sharp. Thrusting the dagger toward the old man, swiping the air in unknown magical designs, his captor spewed out words in lava-slow guttural anger.

"What the hell I want--is *you* to feel what *my* hell has been like!"

A past of ignoble deeds had prepared the old man his entire adult life for just such a moment, to be ready to accept without fear his own death. He steeled himself to handle the swift, merciful bullet, having always expected in all his years that gunshots by perpetrators unknown would be the impetus of his obituary. Not like this. Before the first slice, he prayed for the sudden heart attack he had always prayed not to have. At each incision of pain his captor told the story of why he was going to die. As his flesh parted in delicate butterfly flaying, his eyes widened in recognition of the tale and he started begging for his life, realizing all the while his sin weighed too great for earthly forgiveness.

"I've no idea what your job will be."

The official words to Owen McCombs on this first day at the new work site.

The all-night drive from Biloxi hauling his sparse personal belongings left him drained. He cleaned up his road warrior skank appearance in a restaurant bathroom near the University of Nevada at Las Vegas, UNLV. Go Rebels!

Owen scoured the daily newspaper to get a flavor of the city. News of the day spoke of urban growth and oddity crime. Roadway construction and detour announcements meant the town could not keep up with the incoming population. A third page story Owen found amusing. A graffiti artist had been caught, rather 'exposed'. Some unknown assailant – the newspaper used the term 'vigilante' – handcuffed a juvenile to a streetlight pole, pulled down his pants, and spray painted the kid's buttocks the same color as the graffiti found on the cinderblock walls of a nearby grocery store. The article reported that anonymous calls went out to the television stations to film the youth's public embarrassment. Police arrested the graffiti culprit, but Owen read where the local ACLU issued a statement saying the police should expend greater manpower trying to catch 'an obvious pervert'. What a city.

He went digging in the apartments-for-rent ads. His attempt at securing an apartment before his arrival turned into a fiasco when he hit town. Some homeless derelict had been crashing in his reserved business suite. The place reeked with unsavory street odors. He demanded an immediate cancellation of his lease. Gaining limited satis-faction, his protested results meant no roof to cover his spent body. In the classifieds, housing choices abounded, page after page. What was he even looking for? Exhaustion heavy on his eyelids kept him glanc-ing at ads offering one bedroom apartments or condos as soon as pos-sible, He rattled the paper hoping a solution would fall out. Where in Las Vegas did he want to live?

A few minutes before 2:00 p.m. found him at the Magnum Casino Hotel construction gate; his rental truck pulling his tarp-covered prized, 1970 Corvette, a prime sports car, cherry red with black inte-rior. The front gate guard frowned, jotted down the license plate num-ber and waved him in. Owen hadn't been asked for any identification. They must be expecting him.

Workers and vehicles rushed everywhere like a heavy machinery road rally. Front end loaders gouged deep holes in the ground. Dump trucks chugged the dirt out through the gates. Water sprayers kept the dust minimal. Concrete mixer trucks lumbered in, idling impa-tiently to empty their wet loads. The steel skeleton of the hotel base-ment took form in a mammoth half circle, riveted and pounded by hundreds of rampant workers.

Owen searched for a parking space only to have one of those stop-slow traffic regulators in a dust mask direct him to a spot in the brutal Nevada sun. He realized all the high-ranking employee cars found priority shade in the parking garage next to the boarded up casino, called the El Morocco. Both casino and garage formed a T shape. No shade welcome for the newly arrived.

He took in what was to be his new home. Spread out, a mini town of construction trailers, lined up like white piano keys, about twenty or so, each marked with a sign and work function. He located the trailer spray-stenciled: Magnum Marketing Department.

"I've no idea why you're here," she repeated once more, as if to wake him from his glass-eyed stare.

He had been ushered into the stark office of the Magnum Casino Marketing Manager, Ms. Melissa Steele, the Ms. annunciated with obvious emphasis. Her comment came out stiff and no nonsense in the midst of their handshake introduction.

"They gave me a week to arrive, told me I was to work on the casino opening. More details to follow," Owen tried to sound self-assured, never one of his strong traits.

On the other side of the desk, Ms. Steele, an attractive woman, seemed styled to challenge the world. In his career travels, he discovered that most people who face the public on behalf of casinos have a charisma they create by dress code. Ms. Steele wore dark slacks, a tight creased designer brand that complimented her flower print short sleeve blouse, and her figure-- a slim, tapered form, packaged, as Owen considered, alluring but stiff, muted by professionalism.

She wore, or rather did not wear, he noted, a wedding band, but her jewelry adornments reflected expensive taste. She seemed, he guessed, around his own age. He wondered if she used her dress-for-success fashion to hide a stretched budget. His own sluff outfit of today, khaki pants with a light tan blazer, off-white shirt and no tie, seemed to pass her uniform inspection.

"I've heard about you," said Ms. Steele, a thin file folder received a once over glance. "Your background is governmental affairs, advertising, and marketing." The last word snapped out like a flipped wet towel.

He tensed, wondering if he was there to be her underling or her boss. Be nice.

"My last job as you might've heard was advertising, not marketing, at the Magnum Casino in Biloxi, Mississippi. Before that I did a stint as governmental liaison officer with Magnum Central City in Colorado."

He found it strange in his first job, and thereafter, that all his Magnum business cards never bore a title, as if the higher-ups considered him one of two ways, flexible or expendable. Who was he to wonder or question? They paid him well enough, though more would be better. Owen felt that as a fledgling executive they, or Mr. Jackson Flynn, owner of the Magnum Casino Hotel chain, must be grooming him for something better. That's what drove him: a steady paycheck and expectations.

"In Biloxi, weren't you the one who coined the phrase, 'JuJu at our Bayou'?"

Owen looked at her in a different light. She either held a more extensive dossier on him secreted in her desk or she did read her intercompany newsletter. Yes, his idea. He could salve his ego, impress her, or be a company man.

"Team effort. We sought something catchy."

"I hear that phrase is everywhere down there. Like we have 'What Happens in Vegas, Stays in Vegas." She glanced down at the closed folder. "Before your Magnum career, you were a reporter for *The Denver Post*. Sounds impressive."

"I guess."

"What sort of reporting did you do?"

"Two years writing a society page column; before that I was a police reporter."

"Police reporter?"

"Five years of sneaking under crime scene tape."

Ms. Steele drummed on the file, ignoring his levity.

"Seems like your career jumps around." Her comment hit home. He did feel like a corporate nomad, never enjoying the comfort of certainty. From her it came out sounding critical, a put-down.

"I'm sure my job assignment will come down from the top," he parried her inquisition. "Mr. Flynn, he's here in town?"

Ms. Steele placed the file in her desk drawer and swiveled her chair, her back to him. Owen accepted in this initial meeting he had been mentally dismissed as harmless, ordinary. He knew he came across in other such meetings as a non-threatening bug, inept and slow, a candidate for squishing if office politics went into play. He would have future trouble with Ms. Steele. He knew it.

"Mr. Flynn's staying in the Frederick Orr Penthouse on top of the old El Morocco casino hotel building." He followed her glance out the window across the construction site to the garage, three stories of car park attached to the five story building, time stamped as an obsolete antiquity. Two bottom floor windows of the casino were boarded shut. The floors above hid behind closed blinds and curtains. Jackson Flynn stood at the career apex, one of the most powerful men in the gaming industry, a mogul in the mode of the genius reclusive Howard Hughes. The casino owner lived and worked behind these curtains on the penthouse floor strapped to a wheelchair, crippled by a drunk driver who killed his wife and one of his two children. Owen McCombs had never laid eyes on Jackson Flynn, nor expected to, his boss more myth than flesh-and-blood.

"If Mr. Flynn wants anything he communicates through his lawyers or we all get emails sent by one of his personal secretaries. If you see a guy wandering around, an African-American fellow always dressed dapper in suit and tie, even in this blister weather, that's Mr. Flynn's personal assistant, Derek Shelly. I think he doubles as a bodyguard. He seldom talks, just stares."

"Does Magnum Las Vegas have a General Manager yet?" Owen wondered who would be his direct boss.

"No. They're looking to interview internally. It better be soon, we've got to start ramping up to get competitive. The town is on notice a Magnum Casino will be opening next year and they're all nervous. Our push to wine and dine foreign whales has begun in earnest. Magnum has enlarged their Singapore and Hong Kong marketing offices." Whales, Owen knew the industry lingo, were the high rollers that could play $25,000 a hand at baccarat or blackjack, drop a couple a million dollars per night and sleep like babies. Competition for these limited players was fierce.

"Do they have an Advertising Manager in place?"

"Right now, they're using an outside agency to create the long term campaign."

"Maybe that's where they want me."

She ignored his personal issues.

"You have your housing in order?" she asked, more as a checkoff in the required conversation than sincere concern. "Quality hotel rooms are tough to come by. There's a computer convention in town, place is sold out. I could call around."

"I'll grab a cheap motel room tonight and start looking after work this week." Owen thought it wise not to tell her about 'Homeless Bob', the hobo squatter discovered eating out of his new tenant snack basket. No, he could not see Ms. Steele invoking sympathy to his job transfer hardships.

"As to your job description and title, all I know is I'm supposed to help you get oriented to the project. I assume you listened to your travel tapes?" Magnum Human Resources had supplied an 8 disc CD package for corporate employee orientation, outlining a general history on Las Vegas, listing available community services, even Best of Vegas discount tourist spots.

"Yes. They are more for the first-time hire who hadn't read a company employee manual. A lot of Vegas history and nothing about what's going on here at the construction site, what Magnum Las Vegas will look like on completion."

"I'm assigned to get you situated. Three weeks ago, I was planning slot tournaments at Magnum Cherokee." One of three American Indian casinos contracted to use Magnum management teams. "But I'm here today to give you and the Mayor a tour of what Magnum Casinos is building in Vegas."

"The Mayor?"

5. X out the Ex

Before she received the call to meet up with her new partner to cover a construction accident at the Magnum Casino building site, Detective Chase Taggart went about orchestrating the arrest of her ex-husband.

No one in the Las Vegas Metropolitan Police Department knew of her unfolding plan. She kept her secrets close. For that matter her superiors or the Personnel Department would not have guessed her baptismal name should have been recorded on all agency paperwork as Chastity Tempest Taggart, named after her grandmother, decades ago a topless showgirl in the Folies Bergere at the Tropicana. She answered to Chase Taggart, though accepting from friends the moniker, C.T., someone teasing it stood for "Constant Trouble." Being all cop she kinda liked the implication.

She parked her private car, a well-traveled and dinged Dodge Caravan, under the minimal shade protection of a Chinese Pistache tree in the planned community 15 Palm Deuces,watching the house at 5-6-7 N. Stephanie. From this vantage point she would see the drug bust go down.

For Las Vegas, the homes in this upper crust neighborhood were in the million dollar plus range. Gated on the premise that crime would stay outside wrought-iron enclosures. Not necessarily so. They scheduled the raid for 3:30 p.m. sharp based on the tipster's information. Exactly 3:30 p.m., not sooner, nor later, if you want to catch the bad guy in the act. Chase knew this to be so since she was the anonymous source who called in the tip.

A knock came to her window. The lead detective from Narcotics. She rolled down her van window to his perturbed look.

"Aren't you a little out of your territory, Detective Taggart?"

"Wanted to see you boys in action. Plus, I'm cleaning up some of my old burglary files and I heard there could be stolen goods on the premises. When I left Burglary we were having a B&E spike in the suburbs." She knew the bad guy inside had stolen property. Marital property. Hers!

"So, what is it? How long in Homicide?"

"Just finished my two week anniversary. They partnered me up with Ray Washington."

"That old war horse? Thought he'd retired?"

"End of this year."

"Learn from him. He has the history. Knows where the holes in the desert are." The Narc laughed at his own joke. "Bet it beats being a desk jockey over in Burglary."

"Yeah, new horizons. Now I get to go out and work on my tan, see how you street crime fighters save the day." Truth of the matter she felt butt glued in Homicide. All file review work, no field action. Two weeks on a new job, a career jump, and she felt stifling invisible walls. She had the talent, Chase affirmed her mantra to herself. She just needed a break to shine.

She glanced over to the armored truck and thought about the sweating SWAT personnel inside, antsy for action. Narcotics didn't need to make a major production out of this, but what the hell. Make the bastard shit in his pants.

The Narc's hand held radio crackled at low volume. A car drove up. A small dark blue Toyota. The car honked and a minute later a little boy ran out lugging a back pack. The car pulled away with its passenger.

"No," said the Narc detective into the radio. "Just get the license. That looks more like a carpool than a distribution run. I mean, hell it's a little ol' lady and a kid, for Cris'sake."

The detective glanced at his watch.

"Would you believe it, inside is a real estate agent, a guy named Kinkaid. Ought to make a good living, but thinks he could do better selling recreational drugs in the clubs. That's what we heard."

That's what she had told them, masking her voice, calling from a casino, whispering above the noise of the slot action. A poor party girl, said she the informant, and sold some bad XTC. I'm coming off the ride with bad tremors. Yes, she knew it could kill. She knew the dealer, where he lived. He would be packaging up his bad shit at 3:30 p.m. sharp.

3:25 p.m.

"Well, good luck with your promotion. Tell Ray hello for me." The narcotics detective walked off and she knew he had critical decisions on his mind. Drugs made people crazy, and breaking down doors could set off explosions inside a druggie's destroyed cortex. Her ex was not certifiable, but he did have a mean streak.

Detective Ray Washington certainly might not approve of what his new partner was up to. They were not fully bonded with their innermost private secrets. Being assigned to him brought out the internal office squabbles she saw coming at her. Everyone had their tribal clique. No one liked the idea of virgin transfer out of Burglary over to Homicide, especially since there had been structural consolidation in the ranks based on an outsider consulting report recommendation to raise caseload on parity with other departments. She faced a blue wall of male pricking egos, plus cackling hen jealousies from the few women homicide detectives. Ray, to her relief, acted different. Waiting out his last six months toward retirement he told her that he was not there to mentor, just to leave the department alive and with his pension. She told him to get her up to speed and she'd sink or swim on her own. He said he liked her attitude. Like she had balls.

3:30 p.m. Efficient, macho and surgical, with the yell of 'police', the ram splintered the front door. The four person SWAT squad charged in, full metal jacket, followed by two narcotics detectives, guns drawn, prepared. Chase stretched from her van, leaning with attitude against the door, felt the immediate metal sun-stove heat to her rear end. She waited in silence and watched the aftermath, noting the curious neighbors peeking from windows or standing in their doorways.

A few minutes later, one contingent of police left the home with two handcuffed prisoners, female and male. The young woman, college age, wore a man's robe flapping open to reveal skimpy black underwear, bra and panties. She was bawling. Wrong place, wrong man, thought Chase. Following her walked the real estate man with two police officers to either side of him, vise grips to his arms. Realtor Kinkaid wore expressions of disbelief and anger, his offended mutterings of protest, which Chase could not hear, would be the normal excuses of innocence. A detective followed with a large trash bag, full. Elicit contraband, the evidence.

Just before he was thrust in the back of a black and white police cruiser, he glanced around. Was he embarrassed at who in the neighborhood might see his predicament, think socially less of him? His eyes met hers. She could see him register a moment of recognition, his ex wife. She could see his rabid swearing, knowing she had been cursed as his eternal enemy.

The police car departed. "Bastard removal," her dry observation.

The tactical raid team exchanged banter in the front yard, as the home search by the remaining detectives continued. They might think this would be a slam-dunk conviction, felony possession of Schedule 1, controlled substances. Chase knew otherwise; she knew the man, his devious evil.

She could have let him believe an unknown buyer or competitor ratted him out. But now, the message was clear: any time you put my son at risk you are dead fucking meat.

This latest incident in a litany of betrayal unfolded when Eric, her nine year old son, brought home the pills from his dad's house in an unmarked plastic bottle. He asked her if his dad was terminally sick since his father had a guestroom closet full of this medicine. Eric too afraid to ask his father outright. Chase lasted three years in this ill-starred marriage, doomed from the start, made worse by using the bundle of joy baby as the hope of reconciliation. After the divorce, anything suspicious with Roger 'the Dodger' Kinkaid probably had validity. For example, Chase using her detective curiosity, questioned her ex-husband's real estate commissions. Were they so outstanding as to allow him to buy the new house in North Las Vegas? She knew 'the Dodger', derisively named for his erratic child support payments, to be too lazy even in a Vegas real estate boom of new house construction. Wads of cash and no sold home commissions to boast about. She had to act quickly when the police lab found the drugs Eric had given to her were hallucinogens: Ecstasy: MDMA (3-4-Methylenedioxymethamphetamine), known on the street as XTC, Clarity or Lover's

Speed. No one, she swore, would put her son into an unsafe environment, especially not his father, who should never had had joint custody, who was never around to be a father, too busy with the night scene and screwing bimbos.

Thank the heavens Nanna picked up Eric at the exact time Chase requested, no questions asked.

Chase's cell phone buzzed. Her partner, Ray Washington.

"Where are you? Fetters went around my back. Talked the Captain into having us make a run on some construction site accident on the Strip. Can I pick you up?"

"I'm off E. Cheyenne and Star Horn but close to 95. Say, I'll meet you at the Sahara off ramp on 15. We'll go in your car. I've got the Mommy Wagon. Less than five minutes, barring road construction." Vegas bi-ways many times crawled stop and go, an orange cone sort of town.

His call on a fatal accident breathed of fresh air. This would be her first in-field assignment. The last two weeks she felt invisible chains bind her, assigned to old cold case files. Learning, so they said, how files in Homicide and case paperwork differed from her stint in Burglary. But she knew the cases thrown at her were smudged with the unseen fingerprints of hazing, led by one particular police officer. From her first day on the job, for reasons unknown but to himself, she had become an obsession of Detective Michael Fetters, subject to his subtle taunts and harassments. As if reading her silence, Washington responded.

"Fetters always slithers in for the glory blood-lettings. Ten to one he finagled our rotation for us to cover some worker run over by a dump truck."

"Probably." She hedged her excitement. Homicide detectives can be loaned out as a matter of policy to unusual fatalities as investigative back up. She could care less about the impending mountain of accident paperwork. Action is still action.

"He has a special history?"

"You wouldn't read this in your Employee Indoctrination Package."

Melissa Steele leaned over the desk toward Owen. He caught her nuances, the way she flipped her hair back behind the ear, a whiff of her perfume, vanilla-orange tones, enhanced his senses. Bright, emerald green eyes seared him. She whispered in a conspiratorial tone. "'Hiz Honor', Wilford Aurelius Stokes, better known as Mayor Goodfella, was one of the top defense attorneys in town. All the high profile cases came his way: murder, robbery, and corruption — a lot of his clients had last names ending in vowels. In their wisdom, the people of Las Vegas elected a mob lawyer to run the town. Go figure. 'Goodfella' is his nickname used by friend or foe. His enemies mock him like in that Hollywood gangster movie. They speak his nickname in derisive ridicule. He has a long list of enemies.

"And don't look at us. The Mayor asked for this tour. He's facing a tough political election next year, most likely against the District Attorney. If I were to guess, I would say he's out making key new friends, or better said, trolling early for large political contributions. He may have met his match. Mr. Flynn is equal if not a genius at maneuvering for advantage."

As if on cue, Melissa's secretary announced the arrival of the Mayor of Las Vegas.

The Mayor rushed in going eye-to-eye with Owen, before his glance took in the fashion conscious Ms. Steele. He gentlemanly shook hands with her in a double grip and then pumped Owen's hand as quick introductions were made.

"All this steel going up in my city and I don't know if I'll like the finished product. Mr. Flynn should have forewarned me that he was moving in." He laughed when he saw the two Magnum executives confused to whether he was serious or not.

Owen's first impression of Melissa Steele as the corporate stuffy bitch type gave way to acknowledging her marketing efficiency as she handed the men Magnum Casino hardhats, each stenciled with their names. Melissa donned her own plastic protective hat, baby pink, her name and title in a larger calligraphy script, for all to see who was who.

For only being in town three weeks she had the tour of the Magnum construction site down pat, rattling off statistics like a docent pro.

"The casino will be approximately twenty-five hundred slots and eighty-five table games; the hotel will have three thousand rooms; and there will be a planned one thousand rooms of future condos. The estimated cost of the entire project is $2.2 billion." Owen marveled at the scope. Mr. Flynn would ride the building boom like all the other Big Boys: Harrah's, Phil Ruffin, Kerkorian's MGM-Mirage, Addelson's Venetian, and the scandalous Wynn.

The Magnum Marketing Manager laced her data with light humor that kept the Mayor enthralled. "All casinos have wedding chapels. Magnum will have the only Memorial Gardens with in-house crematorium. Your burnt remains will be left in ashtray like depositories next to your favorite slot." She paused. "Just kidding."

The men laughed, but Owen wondered if the joke was a real trial balloon. Why not offer the ultimate exit strategy for a loyal gaming patron?

Owen soaked in what he could. He felt his travel exhaustion gaining on him as he hiked the construction site in the broiling afternoon sun, careful to avoid loose rebar and the chugging concrete trucks. He jumped, barely escaping one truck's gearing onslaught. He groused to himself; where was that construction traffic cop when one needed safety? On perpetual break by the water cooler, most probably.

He sized up Mayor Goodfella as they walked the site. The Mayor asked sensible questions. He was in his late sixties, Owen guessed. His gray hair thinning. Hard lines furrowed his face like a folding Chinese fan, but he looked healthy walking with a forward pitch, a slight John Wayne swagger. He annunciated any comment with demonstrative waving, sentences emphasized with gesticulating hands; brown liver spots on the Mayor's fingers, the constant sun most likely the culprit. Many politicians, after the exercise of running for office, slip into paunchy lassitude. The Mayor's physique spiffed out with trim grace in a custom tailored suit, the apparel badge of driven men. Like how a high-rate billing attorney might look.

Ms. Steele, in severe formality, ended her statistical presentation with an appropriate political statement that "we," meaning Magnum Casino and Resort Las Vegas, "will be one of the—if not the – largest single employers within the city limits." Owen could guess the Mayor's grinning smile affixed to this tax base future.

"What's your 'hook'?" asked the Mayor. "This town has sharks, white tigers, magicians, impersonators, and mysterioso people in masks climbing poles or diving into a stage full of water. I hear Magnum Casinos is doing something with cars?"

Melissa gave Mayor and Owen a devilish curl of her lip.

"Your Honor...." began Ms. Steele.

"No, Mayor Goodfella is fine. Everyone calls me that nowadays."

"Mayor Goodfella, Mr. Flynn personally asked me to give you, as one of the key people in town, the inside scoop before the press gets it." Owen knew telling a politician a secret meant indirectly telling the press. He could see her strategy working. Tease the media by slipping them tidbits through leaks. If the leak dribbled from a top muckety-muck, reporters would fight each other bloody, clawing to expose the whole story. Flynn was priming the rumor mill. Owen loved to see a pro at work. Maybe that's why I'm here, he considered, to politically work with the press.

Ms. Steele led them to another trailer. Inside, hidden under a velvet cloth, was the entire Magnum property to scale, laid out in detailed magnificence. Owen whistled. The Mayor's eyes widened.

"Mr. Flynn proposes several unique attractions." She used a laser pointer to highlight each area as she spoke. "First, Magnum will have one of the top theaters in the country showcasing the world's premier entertainers and musical groups. Second, the Magnum Resort & Casino will be spotlighting the progress of mankind as expressed in the development of transportation. Cars, trains, planes, every conceivable motorized machine. Finally, we will have an outside water feature to carry the transportation theme to boats and submarines, available for tourist rides, in a presentation designed to knock the socks off of everyone."

She was so full of enthusiasm in the best Magnum team rah-rah that Owen caught the company spirit.

"Everyone will walk down the street to see the Magnum and leave the other places mortuary quiet." Even as he spoke he saw that he had blown it. Melissa Steele considered this room sacred and herself the high priestess, protector of all within. Owen reeled against her unpleasant glare.

The Mayor did not catch Owen's suicidal flop as he formed his own thoughts. "I saw where the New York Times editorialized against Mr. Flynn's project saying 'another sleazy carnival attraction for Sin City'. They knew about this car thing...."

"They made an assumption," she cut the Mayor off. "It's well-known Mr. Flynn's hobby is classic antique cars. We are considering the marquee something like 'Progress through Transportation'. Media pundits are just guessing."

"What did the writer call this casino?" The Mayor looked directly at the Director of Marketing.

She hesitated. "Yes, I saw it." She 'fessed up. 'Temple of Zoom'."

"I like that," said the Mayor. "Temple of Zoom'. It's catchy."

The Director of Marketing winced. Obviously, the Magnum Casino seeking an elite presence on The Strip did not wish this nickname to become fashionable. Owen could understand the concern. 'Temple of Zoom' rhymed with 'doom'.

The highlight of the tour was the gift for the Mayor, only for special VIPs. Inside a large gift box was a toy replica of the future Magnum casino. Precision craftsmanship manifested itself in intricate hard steel mechanical detail. The historical cars, trucks, planes, boats--a cornucopia of transportation. This shiny, brightly colored steel enamel 'toy', Owen guessed, had to cost a minimum $1,000.

"The grandkids won't touch this. It goes in the Mayor's office for everyone to see." Without placing a neon sign in the Mayor's office flashing, "I'm a Magnum supporter", Mr. Flynn finessed his presence to all mayoral visitors. Owen grew impressed with his unseen boss.

With the tour presentation concluded, and not feeling any more conversation with Ms. Steele would be productive or pleasant, Owen offered to carry the toy casino inside its gigantic shipping box to the Mayor's car.

In the few steps to the garage, Owen could feel the box grow heavier. The day in languid decline beat down on him, the hot, dry air sucking moisture from his lungs with each breath.

The Mayor had parked his car, a white Mercedes sedan, away from the other cars, down the ramp, probably to avoid unforeseen dents. The Mayor opened the side door and Owen tried setting the enormous box on the back seat, but the sizing didn't work.

"If it doesn't fit in your trunk, I'll bring it to your office." Owen smiled, proud of himself, hoping the Mayor saw this gesture as the standard of Magnum customer services. It never could hurt.

The Mayor with his key chain remotely clicked the trunk open. Owen started to put the box inside. Blocking his attempt was a body, a bulky body, bloodied, dead, as in not breathing ever again.

A corpse in the Mayor's car. In the next five seconds of shocked silence, they gazed at the body and back at each other. Owen's mind flashed a warning about the man standing next to him. A mob lawyer?

The Mayor pulled a cell phone from his pocket and punched three buttons: 9-1-1.

"No," Owen yelped, startled at his own brusque voice. He put down the box and pulled out his own cell phone. "It will be better coming from me. You may not want this kind of publicity."

The Mayor paused and studied Owen McCombs.

From his pocket, Owen pulled out a card of important Magnum telephone numbers that Ms. Steele had entrusted to him. First call was to Magnum Security.

"We have an accident at the construction site, in the parking garage." He stared at the man in the trunk who did not move. "Possible fatality."

Owen explained to the Mayor. "The first call should come from our people. They will call the police and paramedics." His Honor nodded. Owen, it seemed, had a game plan. The Mayor put away his cell phone.

Owen's second call was to Melissa Steele. "Are you also handling public relations?"

"They haven't brought that person on board yet," she said. "Like for advertising, they're using an agency."

"Then, you place a call to the executive office, wherever that is. Tell them we have a sensitive situation. They will hear about it in approximately two minutes or less from our security people. They need to set the wheels in motion. And you will have to write a statement for the press."

"What's going on?" she snapped.

"Unnatural death," then he hung up. To himself, Owen muttered, "Once again, I stumbled into the shit hitting the fan."

"Good God," blurted the Mayor. He had been staring at the dead man. "This is Charles DiManna. Everyone way back called him 'Chunky D', but not to his face. This man was a client of mine some twenty years ago!"

"Good God," Owen echoed.

He could hear feet running into the parking garage bringing security rent-a-cops toward them. "Mayor, stand by the passenger side of the car."

"Oh, I better not forget this." The Mayor opened up the back seat car door and pulled out a tan briefcase, highlighted with alligator leather strips. "Don't expect we should let the police see the cash I've stuffed in here." The Mayor winked.

What was Owen to think? Was this politician serious or not, and at a time like this? All he could do was put his plan into play, and hope he was protecting the innocent. Slowly, he lowered the trunk, not locking it, and walked to the driver's side door.

At least the security guards did not arrive with drawn weapons.

"What's going on and who are you?"

Owen hated people trying to stake their power territory. It meant he'd have to match the game. He walked toward them, and the Mayor slowly followed.

"I'm Owen McCombs, Senior Executive at Magnum." Well, some day he hoped to be senior. "You both know the Mayor?" Owen's deliberate walk suggested he'd been the car's driver. Like the lid on Dracula's coffin, Owen slowly raised the trunk lid. "I discovered this…dead man. I don't know how this body got here."

"Jeez Louise!" said one. Both guards in open mouth gasps clicked at their walkie-talkies in a rush for their own help, shaking and mumbling, apparently unaccustomed to violent death. Owen's earlier call had initiated the proper first responders, and he could hear sirens in the background, emergency vehicles looking for a construction accident.

"The Mayor's going over to the Marketing Office," Owen said to the guards, "It's been quite a shock. I'll stay here and talk to the police when they arrive." He pushed the Mayor, who toted his briefcase, toward the temporary safety of Ms. Steele's office and walked a few yards with him.

"When you get there…" Owen held the Mayor's arm and spoke in a low voice. "Start making your calls, but use our phones. No calls to anyone where it'll look like favoritism or special treatment. Some police investigator is going to pull our phone logs. Call your office and your wife. Don't tell anyone who you think is in the trunk."

The Mayor gave Owen a conspiratorial nod. Owen figured the Mayor's long dormant defense attorney brain cells were kicking in. Owen cautioned. "Tell Ms. Steele the basics, no more. She's sharp enough to handle the first wave of press piranhas." Owen used to be one of these working flesh eaters and knew the blood lust smell of the developing front page news story.

"Do you do this sort of 'clean up' often?" the Mayor asked. "I could have used you in the old days."

Owen could not tell if he were joking or serious.

The Mayor fast-paced up the parking garage ramp and disappeared as the Las Vegas Fire Department rescue truck, siren blaring, drove into the construction site followed by two black-and-white police cruisers. One of the security guards waved them over to the garage.

It did not occur to Owen until later, when the police started their prodding questions, to consider that the Mayor might have placed the body in the trunk himself and forgot it was there.

"Refresh my memory on the El." Chase broke the silence in their short drive over to the Magnum. Her partner, Detective, Lieutenant grade, Ray Washington was at the wheel.

"You want the way-back history or current events? The police blotter background or the sanitized press releases? I go way back with the El." Locals called the El Morocco Hotel & Casino, 'the El', pronounced 'L.'

Chase's new partner had at least twenty-five years on her. The harshness of late hours, bad fast food and the closeness with death left visible marks. A black man with a wide face, basset hound jowls in the making, a crushed nose and one ear pounded flat against his skull, gave his head a lean-to look. On top of his chiseled face dotted with childhood pox marks, Detective Washington allowed the barber to short crop his wiry hair. Like badges of honor he left the few grey hair strands around his ears to multiply.

"Give me the abbreviated history," said Chase. "I'm not really into casinos." In her mind being a single Mom drained her police salary to basic staples of living. No need to feed one arm bandits. She did not have her late grandmother's beanpole body or strutting talent to follow as a showgirl in the family tradition.

"Hey, in this town, everyone's got a casino connection."

"Not if I can help it."

Ray shifted in his seat, turned the air up to full blast, receiving less than tolerable warm-cool currents, and began his recollections.

"The El Morocco Oasis went from a 1950s dude ranch spliced together by add-on additions into a flashy North African themed casino. Its heyday was the late 60s to the end of the 70s. Yeah, the mob was around then. The El had the unsavory distinction of being controlled by the Detroit Gambino crime family. Their front man was Frederick Orr as General Manager. Orr's real name was Frederico Bandini, a West Coast enforcer, a protégé of gangster Bugsy Siegel. Frederico had to leave L.A. because, as the rumors go, he had this bad habit of removing competitors by oil drum dumping. In Vegas he sort of went legit, denied the past and for years, prospered. He kept the El flashy, even after skimming. Bandini received his own comeuppance in 1980 overseeing a late night private craps game at the El. Two .38 garlic jacketed slugs, one in the chest, the coup de grace between the eyes, all shots fired in a smoky crowded backroom where no one saw a thing. You gotta love this town's idea of important history."

"But the place shut down. The Feds get them?"

She listened as Washington told her how the U.S. Attorney's Office and the Nevada Gaming Commission in 1982 closed the casino for a variety of legal failings, including the skimming, and the building deteriorated as it sat vacant. In 1984 a local wealthy Realtor, Donald G. Grayson, bought the property and sought the funds to reopen the casino hotel, expanded and modernized.

"Sounds like you know a great deal." Washington threw a testy stare. He relaxed immediately when he saw her smile like a serious pupil absorbing the teacher's lesson.

"A little. I joined the force from the Army, served in the Military Police. So, in 1986, an airplane accident killed Grayson, survived by a wife and kid. I know that because as a street rookie I had to stand guard duty at the airport as they swept up the body parts."

"Yuck," Chase said. She was hearing oral history from a person on the scene. Las Vegas was not that old of a town, just a few generations. Washington told her around the time Grayson died there were rumors the mob sought to make a comeback into the Nevada casino industry through Grayson's reopening.

"How did the plane crash?"

"Blew up on takeoff. FAA never determined a cause, but suggested a fuel leak and a spark. Boom."

"When did Jackson Flynn come onto the scene?" Only last week a People Magazine spread on him appeared on the newsstands headlining his gaming empire, intruding into his private tragedies. Chase did not buy a copy though read a few paragraphs while standing in the grocery check-out line.

Washington continued, "From what I've heard he faked a lot of people out. Bought the El and all its acreage quietly from the Grayson Trust under a dummy corporation, announced to everyone this straw company would be putting up condos. Part of the Manhattanization of Vegas. Poof, one day his architect bounces into City Planning and changes the plan from 'Condo Time Share' to a 50-story 'Casino-Hotel'.

"The kingpins here don't like Mr. Flynn because he's a rags-to-riches story, a private company, not beholden to snoopy shareholders. There's jealousy if not fear that the new kid on the Vegas Strip may just come in and do a price gouge on the old guys."

Chase knew a little of Flynn's background, who didn't? He had one of the largest casino companies in the country, twenty casinos, all styled like mini Wal-Marts, dominant in their locations by beating up their competition with extreme discounting to capture players.

Chase brought her questions full circle. "A construction death at your casino can't be helpful?" She wondered at the ramifications, bad luck and all. Gamblers, she knew, were a superstitious lot. Was that true of casino owners? What would Jackson Flynn be doing about this 'incident'? Would he even care?

Before Washington could give his best guess, his cell phone chimed out a jazz riff and he answered. A minute later he let out a, "Holy shit", with a laugh attached.

Call completed he gave Chase the news.

"Seems the accident we are now approaching has been re-labeled a 'possible homicide'. They have trunk music, a body in a car trunk. Woo-whee, lookout and be prepared that your best new buddy, Detective Fetters, will be crapping bricks that he ever let this call get out of his grubby mitts."

"What about Fetters? I've spent two weeks trying to be nice to everyone, including him. What's his problem, except for zipper fantasy?"

"Yeah, he gets to be a real pain. Thinks he's God's gift to crime fighting and the answer to all female desires. He messes up a lot. That's why he partners alone. A while back he was police liaison to the City's Motion Picture and TV Commission, a pet project of Mayor Goodfella. The Mayor wants Vegas to be the desert Hollywood. Stars cavorting and fornicating to keep the media mentioning the party town is 'Vegas, baby'. The Commission promotes Vegas for films and TV series. Metro assists in site selection and sees that off duty police are hired for security work. Fetters showed up on movie sets as the tactical assistant for Metro, did that for a few months until the word got out he was being his usual obnoxious self and hitting on the female stand-ins. He couldn't screw the real stars so he had to settle for porking look-alike stunt doubles. The Mayor yanked him from that cushy job. If you ever want to rile Fetters just mention the Mayor's name."

Washington looked at his new partner. "He gives you shit and I'll back you."

"I can handle the scum of the earth, that's why I'm here: to serve and protect."

The Metro Police SUV pulled into the construction site.

Washington stared around, "Look how fuckin' big this place is going to be. Look at that hole in the ground. It's going to be the largest fuckin' thing in town."

"Over there," Chase pointed, "is where it's happening."

Owen stood at the top of the parking ramp among the angry curious, dusty construction workers who smelled like sweaty gym socks, justifiably steamed they could not leave the worksite at shift end. The gates shut and guarded by the police subject to further notice. Standing in the frying heat did not help attitudes. The crowd swung between riot mutiny and aww shucks wonderment, wondering if one of their own went postal and snuffed out a supervisor.

He watched as the two newly arrived officers, he guessed them to be the homicide detectives, along with various police snoops and technicians working the crime scene. Finally, brains clicked and one of them got around to running a background on the car's license plates. Thankfully, the Mayor did not promote his own vanity with something like "Vegas One."

When the identity came back the black detective turned to a police sergeant, who yelled at the first cop on the scene, who snapped at the security personnel to final musical chairs, so that the group of befuddled law enforcement officers stared at Owen McCombs. His 'Who me?' routine fell flat. He found himself escorted by one of the police officers, somewhat pushed, toward a self-appointed kangaroo court.

"And who're you?" demanded the black detective. Owen knew his innocent expression would not work here.

"Owen McCombs with Magnum Casino Resorts." Back to his simple but true status.

"And is this your car?" Owen could see the body of Chunky D. The corpse had bulk, large flabby arms. He saw half moon slices on the dead man's cheek, slivers of skin missing. "No, as I told the security guards on their arrival, I'd found the body in the car when I opened the trunk."

"But you know whose car this is, since you opened the trunk?" A leading question if there ever was one, implying: what was Owen doing opening someone else's car, an expensive vehicle owned by a very important *Number One* citizen?

Truth will out most of it, anyway. "I carried a gift package for the Mayor to put in his trunk," pointing to the discarded box on the ground, against the parking garage wall. "Once I opened the trunk and saw the body, I made the call to our security people and directed the Mayor to go up to our Marketing Department office and wait for the police, in the air conditioning, out of the heat."

General surprise. The Mayor was here, on premises.

Someone standing nearby had made a comment and the plain clothes officer responded to "Detective Washington." Owen identified his questioner's obvious traits. A military countenance in his stance, his orders to the uniforms sought discipline, to bring order to crime scene chaos. The way he pounded his fists suggested he would take no BS. Sunglasses perched on his weathered pock-marked face, this Detective Washington came off like *Top Cop*.

"Did you touch anything?" queried the detective, harsh in tone, that subtle fist pounding, as if he missed the good ol' days of backrooms and rubber hose interrogations. Having been in similar situations before--a flashback he did not relish pinballed through his brain--Owen knew the drill, be alert and specific. Say nothing that could be misconstrued or manipulated to someone's own creative theory of reconstructed events.

"Only the car trunk and perhaps the front driver's door."

A woman's jabbing voice: "Why, the driver's door if you're not the car owner and just carrying a package to the trunk?"

Owen turned to go face to face with the lady detective. As a former news reporter, he had developed an intuitive art for noticing details. Readers complimented him on that, whether describing the smell of blood droplets at a crime scene, or listing the Harry Winston carats dangling among ample décolletage at a fashion benefit. He had to shake awake those little gray cells. See and be the scene.

The lady detective received his first snap evaluation. She was easy on the eyes in a police state sort of fashion. She stood slightly under his height, short blondish-brown hair, straight with ends curling, cut above her shoulders. Her face showed scattered freckles, no makeup. That was her beauty; she did not advertise her gift, maybe oblivious to what she had. No, Owen reconsidered in his mili-second appraisal, she might be downplaying her features, the smart move in this man's uniformed jungle. Owen absorbed her stare. Watch out. Around women on first acquaintance he judged by sexual interpretation, a stupid male animal habit. Not now, not today. Think sharp.

"I went to see if someone had broken into the car to get to the trunk. The car was unlocked but nothing looked amiss." If he had the chance later Owen would have to ask the Mayor: Why did you leave your car unlocked? Or did he? Damn, a simple small detail not recalled.

"Do you know who this is?" A thumb stabbed the direction of the deceased. In his fourth view of the body today, now cognizant, he took a few seconds to move from his initial shock to what he really did see inside the vehicle. Techies shot flash photos. Several moments passed.

"No." Owen felt his stomach acid spike — my first lie in Vegas and a semi whopper. "I just drove into town this morning." That caught them off guard. Owen realized his mistake. So they now believe I am the traveling hit man on the road to perdition.

The police Crime Scene Investigator made his observations and perhaps should not have included Owen, but the casino executive looked more official than suspect.

"This is interesting. Prelim, of course. Victim seems to have multiple stab wounds; no, let me correct that, more razor type slices, skin peeled back or altogether removed. Pre-mortem, by the looks of it."

"What are those cuts on his face?" asked Detective Washington.

"Weird is what it is. Five slashes to each side of the face. More design than random. There are two deeper slashes to each arm near the armpit."

"Time of death?"

" He'll have to be posted to confirm. Still warm. Two hours, maybe."

"Knife killed him?"

"Entry wound behind the ear. Small caliber, I'm guessing .22. Execution style except for the knife; a knife's very personal."

"Tortured then shot," summarized the lady detective.

Owen looked to the open trunk, fifth glance of the day which made it like old home week, and blabbed without thinking. "But do you see blood pooling in the trunk? He wasn't killed in the trunk. But was he loaded up here? Where are the drag marks? And could only one guy lift him into the trunk? No blood smearing on the bumper. No droplets on the ground. You would expect some trace mess if one person shoved the body in. And this cutting would require time."

The investigative party gave Owen the wide eye stare, a few with open mouths of 'who is this guy'? Suspects don't enter into small talk on how the crime was committed. Owen saw Detective Washington do a quick glance at the car trunk before catching himself in the gotcha. Owen figured gangster Chunky D came to the trunk very dead. To lift a heavy corpse two people were probably involved. Did his murder happen here at the Magnum construction site or somewhere else with the Mayor the unsuspecting transport agent? Or was the body brought here in another vehicle and transferred into the Mayor's car? The Magnum employee side of him had to root for the murder being an off property event. *Keep us out of this.*

They did not need his opinions. The detectives led him out of the garage. The senior detective whose first name came across as "Ray" sent the waiting police officers, a growing number, to interview the disgruntled workers trying to get home. Detective Ray Washington entered the Marketing trailer leaving Owen outside in the scorching heat to be questioned by the lady detective. The two of them found lukewarm shade against the trailer. Owen saw their tactic, divide and confess time.

She peppered him with questions and wrote into a pocket note-pad. Owen with nowhere to go and no job to do took deliberate time in his answers. He studied his interrogator. There was something about her, a coolness in her demeanor, not frigid in that sense. Questions came from her, not meant to trip him up yet intelligent in their construction, prying with practicality. She was a 'Miss' with no wedding band though he spied an old skin indentation on her left hand ring finger. Once, during the prodding, when she adjusted her sunglasses Owen could see her eyes were grey-blue. Eyes with intent can tell you a lot.

All his answers were not untruths just modified and condensed facts. When asked about his whereabouts for the last twelve hours he pointed out the rental truck baking away. He had driven all night. Had a flat in Phobosville, outside of Houston. Hit a hailstorm at Truth and Consequences, New Mexico. Indeed, he pleaded, he was a new arrival and a stranger. He did not appreciate her dry wit, more accusation than humor, when she said, "You could bring a body to the site unseen with a truck like that."

Before he could begin his vehement denial, she interjected, "What's the car under the tarp?" He told her about his collector Corvette and then said, "Anytime you want to take a spin."

Coolness. "Are you being flip?"

"I'm being exhausted. My wall of tolerance crumbles at a lack of sleep. I arrived today. First, my apartment lease falls through. Next, I discover a murdered hoodlum in a car trunk. This was not a Welcome Wagon kinda day."

"What made you say, 'hoodlum'?

Oops. Time to tap dance.

"I assumed all Vegas citizens found in car trunks with bullets in their brains work in seamy, nefarious occupations."

Whether she believed his weak response or not, Detective Taggart joined her interviewee in a stare down, their eyes locking. Owen felt her serious penetrating once-over. She broke eye contact to make scribbles. When she wasn't looking he palmed a pill to his mouth and dry swallowed. Stress could elevate what he called his 'blue funk'.

"If I think of anything else, how do I contact you?" he said. Owen knew enough of cop minds that it would be wiser if he tried to be a 'cooperating' witness-suspect.

Chase reached for a card case in her shoulder purse.

"Also, put down your cell phone number," he said. "Calling through an agency switchboard like a police department can be frustrating." He took her card and read aloud, "Homicide Division, Detective C. T. Taggart, 229-3521, extension 714."

"Call the main number, they'll find me if it's important."

"And the 'C' stands for?"

"Detective Taggart will do."

"Well," Owen offered, "Write down my cell phone number if you have more questions. But let me get a good night's sleep. In the morning the facts will bear out my story."

He watched as she wrote in her notepad. (228) 634-5789.

"Are these all the facts?" she asked. "Now would be the time, Mr. McCombs, to amend your statement."

He changed topics. "Where's the safest place in Vegas to live?" One would think, he mused, this policewoman would know the local crime statistics and not respond with blue-green icicle eyes.

A black Chevy sedan pulled in fast, dirt clouds swirling, braking right at the Marketing Department door. Two dark suited men rushed into the trailer. After some garbled yelling, the Mayor exited, not a happy camper, followed by Detective Ray Washington, the two official garbed strangers. Standing back at the doorway were Ms. Steele and a man wearing dust caked work clothes and a beaten in hard hat.

Owen saw the double-take in Ms. Steele's face as she noticed him idling nearby with this other woman. Her facial curiosity evaporated when she saw the badge pinned to the woman's dress belt. Detective C. T. Taggart returned the glance-over. Everyone would be suspect today or was this just a woman thing.

The Mayor yelled at the two men, definitely government types, one in particular received the politician's wrath. "Don't you even think it! Whatever happened, I had nothing to do with anything. Don't even go there." He looked around, walked over and grabbed Owen's arm, dragging him off.

"We can get you a limo," called out Ms. Steele, ever helpful.

"No, I'll be fine. Mr. McCombs will drive me."

Owen noted a surprise to everyone's face, including his. Who was this guy the Mayor singled out? As he followed obediently, Owen heard the construction man arguing with Detective Ray saying that shutting down the building site was not an option. They were under contract pressure to keep on schedule, the builder pleaded. Owen didn't hear the cop reply. Murder is most inconvenient.

Another vehicle rushed in. Same fleet style as Washington's and Taggart's, and Owen could see the two detectives assume defensive tense postures. Ah, more plain clothes officialdom, the plot thickens. The start of a new argument ensued the tenor and substance fading as the Mayor and Owen reached his truck. He felt stares aimed at his vulnerable back. The Mayor continued his rant.

"Damn Feds. They think this is their miracle chance from heaven to crucify me. I'm sure they'll form some sort of task force. Forty years representing my clients and never once did anyone discover anything out of propriety or illegal in the way I handled my cases. Don't believe certain government hacks didn't try, with wire taps, undercover stings. Now this. Let's get out of here."

"Damn," came Owen's response. Walking around the truck he saw where someone halfway pulled up the truck's cargo door. He had taken off the lock when he thought he was going to be unloading at the apartment complex. Owen raised the door further. Everything looked in order. Sole possessions crammed in and filled to the gills. The sound system and speakers hidden up front in the cargo bay lay protected under couches and mattresses.

"Your whole world in there? Anything taken?"

"No, it looks fine, the cheap quality scared them away."

"Want to report it to the authorities? You have your choice of several branches here." No thank you, no more today; they nodded with mutual accord.

"Hey, what's the fuckin' Mayor doing here?" Detective Fetters called out as he approached Ray and Chase. The Feds wandered over to the crime scene. The Magnum people dove back into their respective fan swirling trailers.

"And what the hell are you doing here?" snapped Washington.

"Heard you had a stuffer and thought you might need extra help."

"I think we have this under control. Go see if a loser dove the Hoover."

Chase enjoyed the banter where her partner took no lip, holding his turf. This was a cherry case, and certainly Detective Mikey, as she had started calling him, only to herself, could smell it, probably heard the radio chatter, grasped his boffo mistake. His practical joke of assigning them a simple accident had backfired and he now scrambled for a little of the choice action. Chase did not like to deal with him. She found him gagging repulsive what with his beefcake muscles and grease backed hair, primping himself to all women as a primadonna lothario. A love life substantiated only by his boasting habits of telling dirty jokes belittling his supposed conquests. Chase saw Fetters and her ex cut from the same cloth. She felt any woman in the morning after a tryst would be appalled these men's self infatuated personalities rose from crusty underpants, not a personality of depth. Men who sought the center of attention turned Chase off. Worse, Fetters had this annoying foul habit of pulling his nose hairs in the middle of meetings.

Two television camera trucks pulled up outside the gate, and two media helicopters buzzed the site.

"What's going on here, Ray? Share, ol' buddy."

Chase saw her partner hold a curse on his tongue. The potential problem existed where Detective Fetters might be right, though he wouldn't know why. Anyone in this town long enough could see a high profile case rearing its ugly head. Washington changed his mood, acting generous. Fetters could view the crime scene on the commitment he would pick up a list of all construction employees, any check-in lists at the gate, and talk to the construction manager. "Wayne Hollister is the guy's name", said Ray. Chase knew Ray enjoyed giving interloping Fetters that tidbit. Hollister, the project construction manager, would soon be yelling his frustrated wrath at Mikey. Fetters wandered off, jibing back at Chase, giving a dipsy impression of a guard bull strutting the night shift in a women's cellblock, hoisting his belt and trousers, eyeing his prey to take.

Washington turned to her. "I have to get back to Commander Stevens ASAP, and lock us into this case as the leads. I know Fetters is going to try an end run. Meanwhile, you baby sit the crime scene until our wonder boy and the Field Service team leave. Make sure we keep an officer posted here overnight."

"I assume you'll interview the Mayor?" She hoped he would invite her to that Q & A.

"Afraid the bosses high up are going to tell me how to handle His Honor." Washington appraised his partner.

"Okay, Taggart, it would've been better first time out if you got a domestic dispute shooting, but I'm afraid you're going to cut your teeth on a big mother mucker. Watch your back-side, this is the type of case that could make or break a career."

"How about if I do some follow up on the other witness," she looked to her notes, but knew his name, "Owen McCombs."

"Yeah, sure. That friend of the Mayor. Too brassy for me — a regular smart ass."

"I agree. There's something about him, though. Like a big kid."

"Precocious like momma's sweetest angel?"

"Naw, more like a kid you know is hiding the truth. Maybe even with a hand in the cookie jar."

Half an hour later, Chase, while working with several police officers in checking out cars in the parking garage, noticed a black town car drive past the restricted front gate. The police officers at the gate should have kept everyone out of the crime scene area. Was this perhaps owner Jackson Flynn? She gave the interloper close watch. A strange thing happened. Detective Fetters walked over to greet the car. The window rolled down and the occupant and the police detective exchanged conversation she could not hear at that distance. She did recognize the passenger. Who would not? Next to the Mayor and his style of attracting scene-stealing headlines, the next in line for seeking and receiving the most favorable black ink of media exposure, the city's self-appointed Crime Punisher, the District Attorney of Las Vegas, Arthur Lattimore. Chase could observe but reached no conclusions. She turned a focused mind back to her first murder case. She wished for such a challenge. Failure was not an option.

On their drive to the old downtown area, Owen gained insight into the Mayor's controversial nature. At a street corner they paused for a stoplight near the Bonanza Gift Shop, "World's Largest", where the walking tourists could go down to the Fremont Street Experience with its overhead light show canopy and three blocks of casino mall, or the other direction, begin the hike going South along The Strip thoroughfare.

The Mayor rolled down the truck window yelling at a homeless person sitting on the ground with his cardboard sign scrawled crudely, displaying a two word bio on his Vietnam service history, crayon scratches intoning a thank you for the Deity, and a dollar sign requesting generosity. As a scraggly wretch, if he was begging on the driver's side of the truck, Owen might have tendered a sympathetic dollar or two.

"Billie, come off it, move on, get a real life. Go cash a savings bond!" The homeless man lost his hopelessness, without-purpose look and flipped off the politician. The window rolled back up and when the Mayor caught Owen's dumbfounded look. The politician's face creased to somber.

"Vegas is a great place. This city represents all parts of society. There are those who live only to take advantage of the weak and stupid. Homeless people can give the tourists a hard time. The tourists want escapism, not to be confronted on what they see on their own streets. Many of these people like Billie are sober alkies and fakes. It's a two edge sword for an old urban liberal like me."

Trying to find common ground, Owen said: "I met Lonesome Bob today."

"Ah," reflected the Mayor. "I know of him, one of the connoisseurs of the flimflam."

After a prolonged silence mulling over how to be articulate with a learned man, Owen pointed to a building, a trashed wall of indecipherable scribbling. "The graffiti delinquents seem to be getting publicity, but bad for them, what with taggers caught with their pants down, so to speak."

Owen expected the Mayor to smile at his joke. As with the homeless issue the politician's face held a stone countenance.

"These so called graffiti artists are no artists, simply visual polluters. Gangbanger wannabes. Last year, it cost Las Vegas and its businesses $30 million of time and effort to clean up the mess, money that could've been spent on the truly needy. The State Legislature needs to wake up and allow spray can defacers to be prosecuted as felons instead of us hand-slapping them."

"Maybe this Graffiti Vigilante can raise their consciousness level."

The Mayor pointed out a parking spot.

"Who knows what stirs legislators to honest action."

They hadn't driven to the Mayor's office at City Hall. The Mayor directed Owen to pull into a no park zone next to the Four Queens Casino. His rental truck and car carryall would not fit anywhere else. The Mayor stuck his business card on the rental truck's windshield, as if that would bring meter maid absolution.

Through the smoke maze of the Four Queens and its hammering clinking slots they walked through the casino and descended to a restaurant and bar called Hugos's Cellar. Owen's eyes adjusted to the dark wood catacomb. Old Vegas. Late afternoon, before the dinner trade arrived, the place held riff-raff bar flies, an assortment of regulars killing time. Owen had stepped back fifty years in time, and so did the Mayor. He smiled at his favorite waiter, ordered his favorite drink, and slid into his reserved corner booth to hold court with his cronies. Owen was odd man out: a stranger among Vegans.

"People, we have a problem," the Mayor emphasized the seriousness of the crises. In five quick sentences the Mayor highlighted the grisly discovery at the Magnum construction site, naming Chunky D as the corpse of record. He grumbled about the arrival of the FBI. Pointed to his driver, late of Mississippi, and said, "Mr. McCombs has been very helpful." Owen warmed inside, a rare treat of recognition.

The Mayor made introductions.

"This is my son, Claiborne, short to 'Clay'. An excellent attorney. My other son, Lawrence, lives in Virginia with his wife and family. That's where my two grandkids are. Clay is the lone wolf in the family, not for long, shortly prayers may be answered."

"My Father is referring to my current lady friend, and no, it's so far a status that we are just good friends. To keep the record straight, my name is Stokes, Clay Stokes. It is not Clay Goodfella." A strong grip was extended in welcome.

"Frieda Montoya is my executive secretary, my right arm, from my past attorney days. She followed me to the 10th floor at the Municipal Building. Habla Español? In this town it's an advantage." She shook Owen's hand and gave a smile, a wary one with an expression unsaid: 'what's going on'?

"I cleared off the rest of the day," she informed the group. "There were no calls from the press." Overseeing the Mayor's schedule really put her in control. A mistake for anyone to think this short, bell-shaped, red-haired Hispanic as a mere office functionary. Owen knew his politics, creating a mental post-it note to develop this relationship. He immediately realized he was thinking in terms of political bonding, a Magnum habit engrained deep.

"It's early for the Fifth Estate scum to surface, but come tomorrow, expect the deluge." With a gruff voice he introduced himself. "Byron Kane."

From his past as a police reporter Owen could spot an ex cop, cop eyes, cement stare, a jaded attitude of grit and piss. Kane did not look like he had ever been happy. Owen could guess that Kane as alumni of law enforcement came with the baggage where he saw the general populace as the unappreciative 'enemy'.

"Mr. Kane is our law firm's private investigator," explained Clay. "It seems appropriate he be with us from the start."

"I didn't catch what you do for Magnum Casinos?" Kane practicing his job.

"A senior executive position. Mr. Flynn's defining my responsibilities as we speak." Owen wished that were true.

The last person in the introductions, Harmon Hartley, the Mayor's past and future campaign manager, looked like a throw-back to the vote buying days of backroom deals and cigar smoke. To that fact, an unlit cigar hung from his mouth, chewed wet in a constant nervous twitch. Owen sensed this electioneering operative moved whichever way the political winds blew, shrewd to position himself with a proven winner. Where Kane had the police attitude, suspicious and intolerant, Hartley feigned gentility puffed like a pink skinned Pillsbury Doughboy. His eyes bulged from their sockets, white milky, like candy, or in angry twinges, like those stern orbs of killer Chuckie of *Child's Play*.

No naivety sat at this table, here now resided the constituted power elite of Mayor "Goodfella" and his behind-the-scene Kitchen Cabinet counselors. But why was Owen here? The reason arrived.

"Well, Mr. McCombs," intoned the Mayor, sipping on what one took to be a version of salt rimmed cough syrup, a color beyond sea blue, two shades short of deep purple. "What's our next step?"

Owen gauged his audience. All suspicious or hostile with blank faces. He swallowed hard to wake his confidence.

"First, the political damage control. Distance yourself from the crime before the press barrage begins. Second, find out where this Mr. DiManna came from. You could leave that to the police and even your federal friends. Not a good idea. I sense they will be falling all over themselves to make the Mayor the number one suspect. Third, push the police to secure the construction site cameras soon as possible. I saw two of them, one at the gate, one for the interior yard pointed at the trailers. Maybe a third one in the garage; at least, I saw some sort of box fixed on the ceiling. Considering the building's age, it may be obsolete. Those cameras would provide our alibis and better yet spot the killer entering and exiting."

The Mayor smiled to his cronies. "See why I brought him to the party?"

"The Feds will certainly be gunning for the Mayor," affirmed Freida. "They won't forget the Luttece prosecution disaster."

She noticed Owen's expressed ignorance.

"A government sting that went *podrido*. The Mayor, a defense attorney at the time, left them with egg all over their faces. Feds came off petty and vindictive in the newspapers. Local prosecutors filed trumped up charges and got caught, their cojones handed to them."

Hartley knew the political value of the story. "Especially one junior assistant district attorney, our buddy Lattimore. The gaffes he made are taught today in law school of what not to do.

"What do we have on Chunky D?" The Mayor sipped his drink with satisfying 'ahs'. "I haven't talked to that man in two decades. Not my ideal client."

Investigator Kane pulled out a file. So, noted Owen, there had been some earlier pre conversations about the dead man. Had Kane kept an old file or just created one?

Kane summarized his findings. "Chunky D, over the last decade, led a quiet, non-criminal life. Owns — owned — a high-end furniture store up in Downtown Summerlin. Crestview Furniture. It's doing financially well, not bad for a retired sub-sub capo."

"Chunky D could be a warning to you," said the Mayor's son. "Maybe nothing to do with his past. How about one of your other legal cases? Revenge."

Frieda speculated. "They're giving you a hint of what's coming. We better have some protection for you."

"Nonsense," the Mayor shrugged. "Somebody wants to tap me, they call the press for my day's schedule and whack me at some groundbreaking. No, this is something more."

"Let's put some of our clerks on to reviewing your old case files to see if there were ever any angry words or death threats," Clay sought to mask his concern, but family love apparent.

"I think most of my clients thought I did the best job possible." Neither a boast nor smug attitude. A stated fact. When Owen found time he would like to read up on the Mayor's career and his win to loss ratio in the court room. If more a winner than not, no wonder his enemies might include prosecutors and certain federal agents.

"Whatever, this does not look good from a public relations standpoint," observed Mr. Hartley, cigar chomping. "We should prepare a statement."

"You do that, Harmon," smirked the Mayor with a laugh. "But I want to see how you phrase the fact there was a goomba corpse in my car."

The son looked to his father. "This time, for once, you need to say very little." Owen could tell by their laughs that silence and Mayor Goodfella were not synonymous.

"If I wrote a press response," offered Owen, "I would do two of them."

"Two?" snorted Kane, the investigator.

"You don't know yet whether the police will uncover Mr. Di-Manna's identity before the morning paper deadlines. One pocket press release expresses the Mayor's shock, directing all questions to the police department. The second, with Chunky D named, has to distance the Mayor from his past representation of DiManna. What I see is a celebrity case, the public skeptical of any truths."

He caught nods of consideration and agreement around the table with the exception of Kane's objectionable frown. The Mayor turned to his political guru. "Harmon, make it happen."

The conversation turned to the political ramifications, shop talk of which newspaper columnists would be on the spurious attack. Owen heard the name Westin Pegler of the *Review Journal* mentioned.

The other topic arose on who would take political advantage of the Mayor's predicament. Consensus favored District Attorney Lattimore as a low life ambulance chaser with loftier ambitions, the Mayor's office a logical choice. Around the table the insiders gossiped like spin doctors after a presidential debate.

The conversation shifted back to the murder at hand. Hartley looked as if he were racking his brain. He asked, "Did they ever recover the jewelry from the last crime spree Chunky D's crew went on?"

Kane knew the story without referring to his file folder.

"They had about fifteen major robberies and home invasions under their belts. The press nicknamed them the 'Wrecking Crew'. They liked smashing the jewelry cases as their signature. 1986. Their biggest score. The Cassandra Diamond Emporium. All previous heists were converted to fenced cash and went into their party life. Cassandra broke the mold, and the gang. $5 million in jewels and rare collectibles stolen, none of it ever came on the market. Fell off the face of the earth. After that and the various police busts, DiManna and his buddies went low profile."

"From the Wrecking Crew's past crimes, they'd have a fence in place," said the Mayor. "Maybe for the last jobs, especially the Cassandra heist, they went to a new fence, and the guy stiffed them."

Kane, the ex-cop, refreshed them with the story of the twenty plus year old robbery at the Cassandra Jewelry Emporium.

Owen listened, fascinated. He closed his eyes to visualize the times and the crimes.

Owen opened his eyes to an angel's beatific face. She shook his arm, less a shake, more a rub caress. One of the most heavenly women he had ever seen. From her delicate mouth he thought might spring flowery verse instead, this angel of beauty said, "That little snore of yours had us all giggling."

He had been asleep! He shrunk with embarrassment.

The Mayor added his joke to the discomfort.

"When you were asleep we divided up the spoils of the city. I suppose you want to know what your cut was? He laughed and the others followed suit. Kane, the investigator, issued a snarf grunt.

Beauty smiled and sat down next to Clay and air kissed the attorney. She gave a flirty pout to father and son.

"Have you both forgotten? We have the Andre Agassi charity banquet tonight. Both your cells are off as if this meeting was so hush-hush important. I had to track you down. Luckily, Clay dear, your hideouts are usually the same as your dad's."

"That's right," said Frieda. "You'll have to be there by 7:30 p.m."

"Cocktail hour first; that cannot be ignored," said the Mayor, licking at the last violet drop from his margarita glass. "Civic duty calls."

Clay made the introduction of his girlfriend, although Owen sensed such a slotted position as 'girlfriend' maligned her character. Her attractiveness fit a businesswoman executive style, more so than he had seen in Melissa Steele earlier in the afternoon. This woman radiated glamour. She defined Rodeo Drive couture, immaculate with coiffed blonde hair. He pegged her age a few years older than he, held youthful and stunning by sublime grace.

"Kathleen Sawyer."

"Yes, I guess we should shove off," agreed Clay, "First, we have to take Mr. McCombs home."

"Home?"

The Mayor explained. "You told me your story about Homeless Bob. And you're now homeless in Vegas. We can't have that. I have rental property nearby in the Scotch Eighties neighborhood. On the corner of Birch and Silver. Three bedroom ranch style. I've two of the bedrooms rented out. You can stay in the third. It's even the master."

"The Mayor, of course, wants you to consider a core city residence," laughed his son. "He's behind a rejuvenation plan for the inner city. Encourages urban pioneering. It may be safer down in that area. Lately, there's been a rash of robberies in the suburbs. Kathleen even became a statistic when she arrived in town."

"Clay, please, it's old news. A broken window, nothing stolen."

The Mayor ignored his son and turned to Owen.

"Feel free to stay there until you find your own place. No charge, and it's my pleasure."

What could he say? Rude to decline such generosity. Saving money made him nod acceptance.

Owen, in his cumbersome truck, followed Clay Stokes in his BMW, who himself tried to keep up with the speedster Lexus of Kathleen Sawyer. The destination of truck and towed car was close to downtown, just beyond the freeway, I-15, west side. The landscape, to Owen's surprise, shifted from desert dryness, red rocky soil, cacti, and buzzing neon city into a Midwest type neighborhood, a gated community, with tree lined parkway streets, landscaped xeriscape rock gardens, homes tinged with real mowed grass.

The driveway of No. 24-25-6 Silver Avenue had plenty of driveway for both truck and car trailer beside the three car garage. A high cinder block wall, white painted masonry went around the property with sliding entry gates. The front door and windows had burglar bars, expected sacrifices to urban metro living. The house seemed a throwback to the seventies but it was a home, not a condo apartment. A bed awaiting.

"This was very kind of the Mayor," said Ms. Sawyer.

"Just for a night or two, then I'll find my own place."

"Yes, that would be appropriate." The social snob tone of her voice reminded him of sitting at charity tables in his rented tux with his newspaper underwriting his $200 per plate ticket cost. In the one-upmanship struggle of the new money classes he had never made the grade, never reached acceptability. Some day.

Clay unlocked the front door and gave the tour, while his society girlfriend, strolled outside with mild impatience, a gold cigarette case pulled from her Gucci shoulder purse. The master bedroom was expansive and more than adequate. Even with a worn rug, mirrored closets, and a lime green tile bathroom. This would do just fine. He felt that exhaustion zombie creeping back strong. As he walked back outside, he noticed two other bedrooms, shut doors, one with a heavy padlock.

"I don't know much about your housemates. Dad didn't fill me in. You'll find a garage door opener and a house key on the dresser. Make yourself at home. Dad seems to get these metaphysical revelations about people, likes to help where he can."

"Like stray cats?" Owen replied and then to himself thought, 'Quid pro quo'. As the Mayor gave, so would there be a reciprocal trade down the road due in kind. The son seemed to read his mind.

"Father has his power base by his generous nature. He's a political animal. We all are in a way. Aren't friendships based on mutual assistance pacts?"

"Are you going to follow in your father's political footsteps?"

"No, I'm happy in the defense against injustice. Father's one of a kind. Las Vegas needs showmanship and he provides entertainment for those who take government too seriously. Don't mistake his publicity antics for not having smarts."

"I agree," said Owen. "He's shrewd." Shrewd for a politician versus saying the man was smart was the far better compliment.

They walked back outside where Clay joined Kathleen, the perfect happy couple. She talked to Clay about tonight's event, how without the Mayor's car, they would have to do the driving or rent a limo. Owen opened the back of the rental truck to pull out a couple of suitcases. The crash broke through the neighborhood. Chairs and packing boxes had shifted, and with an avalanching crunch, loose furniture and cardboard boxes tumbled from the van. Owen cursed. He picked up a chair to put back in, the boxes to be next, when he heard Kathleen speak to him.

"Is this yours?"

He turned to see her holding a jewel encrusted scabbard of a small dagger, Middle Eastern in design. She slid the knife easy from its sheath, blade down, the hilt with her finger tips. It was not his knife. The three of them stared. Owen saw by the orange glint of the sun's final rays, brown looking rust adhering to the sharp blade. Dried blood.

Before her evening fell apart, before the annoying office interruption, Chase experienced a domestic crisis caused by multitasking forgetfulness. Her first active field case made her space out that tonight Nanna was going to a movie with her buddy, Mrs. Herbst, who lived across the townhome walkway. A romantic comedy with actor Hugh Grant stuttering his way into the hearts of still yearning women of all ages. Since Nanna seldom took time off from watching Eric or helping around the house, Chase was more than happy to say, 'go for it. Let me get home and settled.'

When she arrived later than she expected, Nanna passed by scurrying out the door, "Food's heating on the stove. Be back at 11:00 p.m. unless I get lucky on nickel slots after the movie."

Spaghetti and garlic bread wafted warm smells through their cozy townhome. She felt a type of calming bliss. Tonight, after the meal and the cleaning up, there would be quality time helping Eric with studies. His school in summer recess, Chase had the goal to prevent Eric from being held back a year. She had signed him up for several audit courses, purchasing home tutorial study programs. His ADHD malady created her son's ongoing struggle at concentration. Eric seldom complained, eager himself to prevail. Beyond this mild home study work, as long as he could doodle in his free time the drawings and sketches of his fantasies, he remained a happy kid.

She gave him kisses, cleared his plates from his earlier munching, and left him alone in his room reading through Manga comic books. A creative mind seeking self-control, he enjoyed his time alone where his imaginary worlds and playmates saw no reason to hassle him for his nervous energy or his failure to hold sequential thoughts.

She ate dinner absorbing the silence as refreshing. She glanced at newspaper headlines, ignoring world events, focusing on the Local Section, studying the crime stories: drive-bys, armed robberies, testimonies at high profile trials. One story where prison officials would not release the name of the inmate immolated last week in the prison yard until they completed their full investigation. Sipping sun-made ice tea as her post dinner cordial, Chase reviewed the end meeting of the day with Detective Washington. The good news filtered down that they would retain lead position in the case they caught. The bad news, Detective Fetters joined the team.

In her contribution to the meeting, Chase gave her report on the Mayor's calendar schedule of the day his office faxed over. She did not see how the politician could have any time to commit the killing. His day had been crammed with city council committee meetings interspersed with civic handshaking photo ops.

It was after Washington had left for the day that things became interesting. She ran a Codis search on Owen McCombs.

What she soon found left her puzzled. No arrest record. She Googled to discover, in his past, her suspect rated high marks as a police reporter. She scribbled into her notes the journalistic award received, *The Dunning Prize for Crime Reporting*. Of his job with Magnum Casinos she could find nothing mentioned. No press release covering promotions, no by-lines of further stories written. Odd. From newspaperman to unknown executive, like disappearing into some corporate, anonymous black hole. Munching on an almond cookie she reread her notes on McCombs.

Description of individual: close to 6 ft, maybe 5'11". Medium build. His shoulder physique suggested muscular strength, enough to shove a body in the back of a Mercedes. His Mississippi driver's license put him at twenty-nine years old, three years older than herself, though she felt her age plus some. Mr. McCombs did not strike her as a hottie, no primp sheen, neither magazine model nor beefy cheesecake. Solid fair looks summed his descriptive features. In a bar situation, to a woman's eyes, the classification would be a casual, he's okay, acceptable, no standout. The word 'unassuming' came to mind. A notion just out of reach left her analysis incomplete, a curiosity to define his character as he spoke, as he acted. Something lay hidden behind his obscurity. She needed another crack at him.

The phone rang. Could it not wait until tomorrow? No, relayed the night duty officer, the man calling said 'evidence retrieval'. The day's tiredness vanished. This guy McCombs as a probable suspect did intrigue her. She copied down the address. Curious once more. Owen McCombs in a classy neighborhood with a suspected murder weapon.

She faced a dilemma. She could not sit at home and throw this great bone to Washington, nor did she want to give anything up to the detectives on night shift rotation. No, she must go. Where could she find an emergency babysitter?

When Chase called him back about his *knife-of-death* news, her surly attitude conveyed the underlying unspoken accusation: 'I knew you had it all the time.' All right, she snapped in blatant exasperation, a patrol car would be over to secure the scene. Yes, she and her partner would make an appearance. "Go nowhere, touch nothing," commanded the lady detective.

As they awaited the arrival of the police, Clay said "Do you have a dollar? Let me have a dollar."

"Sure, I guess." And Owen dug into his wallet and handed over a crumpled bill.

"You have hired me as your legal counsel. I can now speak for you, and kindly tell you to shut up if their questioning gets too invasive."

Owen thought the siren out of place in this saccharine styled Ward and June Cleaver neighborhood. What's normal in Vegas? A few neighbors pulled back window curtains. A door across the street cracked open, shadowed eyes peering out. Owen felt uneasy. Kathleen Sawyer glanced at her watch and lit up a long stem cigarette.

A black-and-white pulled up. Two patrol officers stomped around, gave the evil eye, and stared at the knife resting on the back cargo bed of the rental truck. Early evening with red hues streaking the sky cast shades into the neighborhood, grays deepening to blues. No coolness followed the setting sun. Ten minutes followed and a brown, decade old Cadillac appeared with Detective Ray Washington behind the wheel, casual, in slacks and golf shirt. Moments later another vehicle pulled up. Detective Taggart in a Dodge Caravan, a side door dinged-up. She parked several houses down, away from the crime scene. He let his ex-reporter sleuth mind wander. Detective C. T. Taggart, he concluded earlier, is divorced. Her personal mode of transportation says she has children. She drove the type of road monster that made the carpool runs to school and soccer games. The two super cops were back. The casino executive, new to town, did not appreciate once again being the center of their attention.

Owen directed both detectives to the knife and introduced them to 'my attorney'. Clay Stokes in turn introduced Ms. Kathleen Sawyer. Amazing. Mannerisms in the police shifted in deference that the names of Stokes and Sawyer must command in the community.

Sequential events of the day were relayed to the detectives, including the news that his truck at been broken into at the construction site.

"Why didn't you come back over and report it," Detective Taggart asked.

'Because the Mayor and I don't like you guys', he wished to blurt out. He didn't say that, instead, "Because I saw nothing missing, and the Mayor had a meeting to attend."

"Are all your possessions here? You haven't off loaded any items elsewhere?" He heard obvious doubt from Detective Washington.

"Yes, as far as I can tell. And no, nowhere else. I was planning on spending the night here."

"And whose house is this?"

Owen's newly hired attorney stepped in.

"It belongs to the Mayor and his wife. They have it as a rental investment. Do you have any more questions of my client?"

Owen knew having his own attorney make a sudden appearance did not score positive points with the police. Nor suggest innocence. He saw it in faces approaching a boiling point, most notably, Detective Washington. The detective strained his speech. "Do you have a problem if we search the back of the truck, the cab, and the car under the tarp?" Washington looked first to his 'person of interest' and then to Owen's new advocate.

"I have no problem with my truck as long as it gets back in some semblance of order." It would be an improvement. He never packed with order in mind.

"How about the house?"

"No," said attorney Stokes, formal and final. "There are other tenants with property inside. The house is not in Mr. McComb's name, nor my name. I only opened the front door and showed Mr. McCombs the living room, kitchen, and bedroom. I saw him carry nothing inside. You'd need a detailed warrant of particulars if we went in that direction. Besides, we called the moment we discovered the knife as an accommodation to your investigation. If this is the weapon of any alleged crime."

"There's also the missing small caliber. Want to tell us, Mr. McCombs, where that might be?" Detective Taggart's voice angry, surprising Owen. He did not answer her. Absent, today's earlier repartee of give and take. Owen could see a complicated woman before him. That interested him, heightened, by a simple action. When she did her walk around the truck to investigate, as if to put her in the spotlight, the sensors feeling early evening enfolding clicked on, arc lights in the driveway sweeping her face with a blue-orange glow.

No soft tones in Detective Washington's face. "We'll work with what we have been invited to look into. Anything else, we'll certainly be back." All assumed he knew how much street law he could push for tonight, and ransacking Owen's rental van and clothes and furniture suited him fine.

"Clay, dear, we do have the Agassi benefit." Ms. Sawyer's whine was priceless, almost Bryn Mawr East Coast. Hepburn in *Philadelphia Story*. Owen felt he'd heard another put-on act for the evening to move things along. He jumped to the suggestion.

"I'm going inside, to bed direct. I'll leave a lock for the truck." Let them do their worst. What were they going to do, steal his J.C. Penney's bedroom ensemble?

14. Son of a Cop

Chase's strategy finessed well. To arrive at this extension of the Magnum crime scene, put things into motion, and exit as soon as possible. Detective Washington delegated the truck inspection to a set of rookie patrolmen, instructing them to put on evidence gloves for carting out the truck's contents.

With the truck search proceeding, she did not expect other bodies stuffed under mattresses, and so Chase begged off for the evening. Detective Washington gave her the nod, remarking, "About this McCombs? Keep after him."

"I grant you, he seems vague, mind and body. Doesn't carry himself like a criminal or a gunslinger."

"Yeah, and the BTK killer attended church. Keep a hard court press on his background. I know something is wrong with that guy."

"How do you figure?"

He pointed to a box on the ground. "If you look close, you'll see fingerprint kit residue." He wiped his finger across the lid confirming his statement. "Cops somewhere, I assume in Mississippi, already have been looking at this guy. Maybe the guy in the trunk carpooled up from the South."

Chase watched as crime scene techs trash out the rental truck. With nothing incriminating falling to the pavement, her assignment over, she walked to her van. A light blinked and moved within.

"How goes your drawing?" Eric lay on the back seat, wearing a miner type plastic hat with an attached Sharper Image small high intensity lamp. Bringing your son to a potential crime scene where anything might go wrong was unacceptable, except if you had no choice. She rationalized her guilt away. She parked away from the house and drive, away from her partner's car. The windows fully down and a lunchbox size battery fan circulating air.

Chase started the van and pulled from the curb.

"I thought you were using those drawing pencils I bought."

"Naw, I got a cool pen, it has three colors in the same pen. You rotate the handle."

"Where'd you get that?" Silence for the moment and she repeated the question, a little more Mother Superior in firmness.

"From that guy."

"What 'guy'?" Her hands tightened on the steering wheel.

"The one you were talking to who lives in that house. He came over, I saw him coming. He saw my work, said my space fighters were better than George Lucas. I showed him my battle cruisers. He said Electronic Arts could use drawings like these to make their computer games. Wouldn't that be rad to the X?"

She let him ramble in his excitement. At a stoplight, she asked to see his new gift. An expensive pen embossed in gold script: *Magnum Casinos*.

"Are we going back over there some time? I can show him the Inner Earth monsters I did. He'd like them. He's a nice guy, Mom."

Shit. Here was Eric, saying in his subliminal innocence: go get a life, Mom. Meet new people.

"I don't think we'll be going back there. This was official business."

"Is he a cop, too? He thought you were nice."

"What?"

"He said I had a cool Mom." She saw his wide smile in the rear-view mirror. "I told him, yeah, my dad thinks so too. He doesn't live with us but he wants us all to get back together." Eric went back to creating galactic fighters saving the universe.

Jesus H---- Out of the mouths of babes. Her son manipulated by two men — both evil!

15. Heavenly Sideburns

Through the night's blackness Owen tossed, unsettled, in a fog floating between dreams and reality. At a time where the darkness edged closer to morning Owen, with listless eyes, focused to the bedroom door. Hadn't he closed it? A beam of hall light fell across his bedroom floor onto his bed. An apparition stood in the doorway, the glare concealing the face. Owen knew by the garish clothes.

Elvis.

Elvis looked at him for a moment and quietly closed his door. He could hear Elvis walk down the hall, enter another bedroom, shut the door and heard sounds in the bathroom, faucet running, toilet flushing, silence.

He fell back asleep, fitful, hallucinating the absurd.

Don't die in the bathroom, Elvis. It's the Mayor's house. A dead Elvis would be too much for all of us.

16. Nymph Arousal

His cell ringtone annoyed him awake, motowning Temptations: *'Get Ready'… 'cause here I come.'*

"I assume you're almost out the door."

Owen recognized the tepid voice of Magnum's Director of Marketing, Melissa Steele.

"Yes, I'm leaving as we speak." A tongue dried voice betrayed him. A glance at the clock, 8:45 am, elicited a silent "oh, shit." Late for work and only the second day on the job.

"Well, slow down and have breakfast and read the paper. You don't have to come in today."

"I don't? But—"

"The word came down from the mountain top, they're sending someone around to pick you up in an hour. Just follow instructions."

"What's this all about?"

"Maybe you're heading over to the police for a formal statement. Hey, I didn't even know the body in the Mayor's car was a well-known gangster, a friend of the Mayor's." The word is out; the fan is turning, here comes the crap. "Did you know?"

"Not until late last night when I heard the name. A former client of the Mayor's, so I heard. From years ago." He heard himself being the Mayor's apologist, surprised he felt no guilt in doing so. "Was it in the newspaper this morning?"

"No, a police reporter got wind of it and called for Magnum's reaction." That's what rattled her chain, an ambitious woman forced to give plausible denial, upset for being left out of the loop. In times past,

Owen dated workaholic, striving women just like her, ravenous for responsibility and achievement. Not unlike himself.

"It will be on the afternoon wire services, and on all the evening news channels."

"You do come in tomorrow. You're scheduled to give a tour."

"What? You were magnificent yesterday. Not me."

Her response warmed up a degree or two.

"I have meetings. You don't and upper management wants certain people to have the background of the project. These guests will be perfect for your debut presentation."

"What? Who are they?"

"A Chinese government delegation. Our Mr. Flynn is entertaining gaming officials from Macau. Maybe someday there'll be a Magnum Macau to compete in the Far East against Stanley Ho, Wynn, and Addelson. I'll send over the fact sheets on the construction and casino hotel. Have a wonderful night memorizing. And don't try to wing it."

Great, he thought, shaking his head of sleep. First, a dead body, next an international incident as the newly-arrived casino executive offends an entire foreign government. The house lay quiet. No rampant Elvis on the loose.

Owen showered and dressed slack casual, raided the refrigerator for orange juice and snagged a banana for sustenance. A morning newspaper lay on the driveway. He wandered into the back yard and parked himself on a cushioned lawn chair shaded under a palmyra thatch canopy next to the sizable swimming pool. The backyard surrounded by vegetation, offered a green wall of privacy. Hidden, he liked that. The morning smoldered toward scorching. From under the eaves of the house the timer kicked on the water line mister. A congenial Outdoor Living atmosphere all things considered, like yesterday never happened.

Except... He began to peruse the morning newspaper. On page four a three inch summary digested out of the police report of a death at the construction site at the new Magnum Casino.

Flipping pages Owen read the society section and the photos on the Andre Agassi Foundation event, a fundraiser for underprivileged, at risk kids. He spied a photo of the Mayor and his wife, the portrait of a happy couple of many years. Standing beside the Mayor's wife her son, Claiborne, Owen's attorney, and next to him his date. The caption read: 'Kathleen Grayson Sawyer beams exquisite in her Oscar De La Renta gown accented by a yellow diamond necklace'. She invokes pedigree. Now he understood. She must be a Grayson of that real estate family, historic ancestry he recalled from his Vegas press clipping packet. 'Sawyer' must be a previous married name. A wealthy woman in her own right. That's why the Mayor teased about a lasting relationship for his son. A Grayson-Sawyer-Stokes (aka Goodfella) wedding would be a socioeconomic coup, certainly a benefit to the Mayor's stature. And here is a Grayson of the Grayson fortune which sold the land for the Magnum Casino. This town is too small.

His eyes strayed from the newspaper to a young woman walking from the house past him toward the pool. She said nothing, did not seem to notice him sitting there so obvious. He kept his hello silent. At the edge of the pool she dropped her bathrobe, her back to Owen. Her skin radiated a light gold sheen, a mild tan, not deep bronze. No tan marks. Naked. Entering the pool, she started a lap regime, and with each stroke her breasts, her tight ass, the sleek curve of thigh sliced through the water like a shark fin in silent precision ripples. Owen stared, his eyes peering above and around his newspaper. No complete paragraph read thereafter.

Twenty long laps is a good aerobic workout. He counted each lap. She stepped out, dried off, and wrapped herself in her robe of black silk, a back design of boxing gloves with the stenciled words, "Kid Galahad". This casualness with her body, oblivious to his gawking. Was she teasing or totally ambivalent?

"Hi. I'm Casey. And you must be Mr. McCombs? Frieda called and put us on notice you'd be staying awhile."

"Us?"

"Theodore, our other roommate." She pointed back to the house, and his eyes followed. A white lace curtain at one of the bedrooms was falling back into place. Theodore watching the water show. How many days did she work out like this? Theodore ever present as a degenerate peeping Tom? A peeping Ted.

"I thought maybe before I go to work tonight, Theodore and I could take you out for dinner. You or Magnum pays of course. We'll give you insider scoops on the real party side of Vegas. You need to know or you're going to be standing for hours in line to get into a club and you'll miss the private parties. We're on different lists so we're wired to the scene."

Casey was young, really young, observed Owen. If clubbing, at least twenty-one, though a fake I.D. not out of the question. Owen knew the casino industry's zero tolerance for underage drinking even for their nightlife. Beyond her nudity, which he mentally photographed, he saw her acne free skin, a svelte tight body, no tattoos on her ankle or ass, commonplace adornment these days. Her hair dyed deep black and cut short up off the collar, right above the ears, a girl looking boyish imp. She picked up the newspaper's Entertainment section.

"I'm interested in what conventions are coming to town," she said, shaking her wet hair, ignoring the stare she received, or maybe not.

Owen sought to clear his wandering mind. He glanced back at his newspaper, reading anything, avoiding being tongue-tied, trying to portray himself as interesting. Worldly.

"The newspaper says Vegas has a new crime fighter: 'The Grafitti Vigilante'." He leaned over to show her a grainy photo showing a paint branded naked butt. "Probably a turf war between graffiti artists. Most graffiti is gang related, initiation rituals, or staking their territory, like dogs peeing on bushes."

She kept her head buried in her own reading while responding.

"You'd think gang members would beat the snot out of each other, not catching guys and leaving them to public ridicule."

"Still, it's a crazy kook pulling a gun on kids spraying walls."

She turned a page. "A stun gun, is what I heard. Hardly lethal. Believe it or not, the Grafitti Vigilante has a public following of fans. People are tired of the mess. It's not art, it's crap pollution."

Editorial dictum heard earlier, from the Mayor.

Casey gave him an intent look, one suggesting he better appreciate she had a mind sitting on her shoulders, above her curves. She turned another page of the newspaper, folding it over, and her robe fell open. The doorbell saved Owen from his rising carnal thoughts.

He retreated to the front door to meet his ride and learn his destination.

Mayor Goodfella.

"My wife dropped me off. We're taking your car. I assume it works. I'd like the top down if we could," His Honor's verve turned up and revved on full rat-a-tat-tat motion. "We're going to pay our respect to the Widow DiManna."

Detective Taggart felt the celebrity case blowing in like a sandstorm, stinging grit in all pores, sucking air out of the room, leaving those thirsty for information. Like a gossip clearinghouse long before she saw any written report, the news filtered out from the Coroner's office. The prints from the dead man identified him as one Charles DiManna, aka Chunky D. Circulating like bad breath in a stuffed elevator the word spread about the vic, Chunky D, a known hoodlum, since 'retired'. In the 1980s he ran a heist gang known as the 'Wrecking Crew.' Commander Stevens relayed the buzz.

"Chunky D was a bad boy of many years. Graduated out of the Meyer Lansky Miami School of Mayhem. Was the muscle in Florida on loan shark operations, but kept under the Fed radar with petty crime convictions. They questioned him on the 1958 Gus Greenbaum slayings in Phoenix. Gus, a casino boss at the Flamingo then the Riv, pissed off the mob bosses. Killers, as rumors go, said to be from the Miami area. Nothing ever came out of it, certainly it'd been his style. They beat Gus's wife unconscious then slit her throat, same as Gus. Anyway, Chunky gravitated to Vegas, hooked up with Lorenzo Corallo, a second story man, for Nick Cavella's outfit out of Kansas City. They both settled down, if you can call it that, into extortion and armed robbery as a local gang."

Ray Washington knew about Chunky D.

"I really wouldn't have recognized him," said Washington finding the chair next to Chase's desk.

"In the trunk, I never looked at his face up close. Those artsy slices and dices hid his looks. Besides, that was twenty years ago when his gang operated. I knew him only from mug shots and grainy news photos. Retirement from a life of crime treated him well; added more weight." Ray leaned in with a secret grin. "Guess who was one of his most able lawyers? Our famed, high-flying Mayor."

Washington gave his opinion that the Mayor and this McCombs jerk were his 'number one' suspects, though he emphasized all leads had to be followed and documented.

Detective Michael Fetters wandered the floor, muttering to whomever he corralled. "No shit, damn Mafia hit. I knew it when I saw the body. We found the murder weapon at the Mayor's home." Not actually true but Chase held her tongue as Fetters ranted. "Mayor probably knows what went down, sanctioned the hit as Consigliore. Here comes the impeachment. Jail time for Hiz Dizhonor."

Washington, for the day's work load, hyped the task he planned for Fetters. Could Detective Fetters visit with the Feds in the Organized Crime Detail, follow the mob trail, check up on Chunky D's rap sheet: who were his enemies, where was he last seen? Pay a visit to his next of kin. Fetters threw a cocky leer Chase's direction as if these were plum assignments, his expected due. Chase saw his chest puffing with self-importance. It amazed her that he ignored her own flagrant body language: *Not a chance, loser.*

Washington picked the prime task to coordinate the Mayor's formal interview and designated himself to be a mute, highly visible puppet behind Sheriff Phillips and his anticipated televised press conference.

Taggart got the leg work, a return to yesterday's inferno, the Magnum site. Yes, her partner granted, she could stay on top of McCombs's background check. He needed her back at the crime scene to do the formal release and turn the property back to the construction people. The project G.M. phoned twice this morning shouting for the police to stop checking every vehicle entering the gate, and to let his employees have the valued shaded parking in the garage.

Paying the dues, doing the drudge, she returned to the Magnum garage. With the yellow tape removed the first level had already filled, except for the traffic cones still marking off limits the Mayor's vacant parking stall. The Mercedes sedan resided at the police impound garage being micro combed and blue lighted for particle evidence, dusted, and taped for fingerprints.

Included in her tasked assignments Detective Taggart picked up digital recordings from the two or three surveillance cameras. Very smart of someone to catch the camera angle. Their locations guarded against theft and to document the building as it climbed skyward. Now, they might reveal a killer. Appropriate legal paperwork generated and faxed over to the Magnum offices requested all the camera recordings on the construction site. They, Miss Steele said, would be happy to cooperate. Chase bet they would first dub duplicate copies for themselves.

At the elevators, in the shadows at the back of the garage's slanting lower level, she walked through an exit door that led to a covered pathway leading from the garage to the old casino building. *I wonder if Jackson Flynn would be required to make a statement. What a rush it would be to meet him in person.*

The walkway to the casino building dissected a garden courtyard, out of place in desert Vegas. The dense bushes and trees created pastoral, reflective calmness. A small sign defined the location as "The Garden of Allah." It would be sad when this garden retreat was ripped out to dig a hole for the planned artificial lake. Tourist trap progress, she grumbled. At the center of the garden in a small clearing sat a bronze bust frowning atop a granite pedestal. Around the base a raked flower bed awaited new plantings. The plaque attached to the base read: "Frederick Orr, 1922-1980. General Manager of the El Morocco Casino Hotel. Visionary and Leader".

The garden foliage, the high stucco walls, and the buildings with their storied facade muted the noise, even the nearby construction traffic seemed distant. Sounds came to her as hollow echoes. She glanced down at the grass. It looked like a blight fungus. *Curious. Not fungus. Blood splatter.* She noticed a very sparse trail of blood drippings and she used a pencil to poke in the empty flower bed around the statue, uncovering small darkly-bonded dirt clods. Someone had tilled the dirt for concealment purposes. *The killing ground.*

She felt her hand sliding to her side, slow tapping her holstered .38 Colt Ruger. Reassured, she walked to the four corners of the garden, observing, twisting behind trees, edging around bushes. In the farthest corner next to the L casino building she came to a plastic Tuff Shed. With a tighter grip to her weapon and a deep breath, she flung the shed door open. Gardening tools, a small lawnmower, and a hand push cart loaded with clay pots. The empty flower pots sat on a torn and paint spattered drop cloth. From her purse she tugged on evidence gloves. She removed the clay pots and pulled the flatbed cart out into the sunlight, flipping the tarp over to find dried blood blotches. A coil of rope lay beneath. More dried droplets.

She punched a mobile call to Washington.

"We need to shut down the garage again. Well, I found where Chunky D was killed. Right. In the garden near the office building. We were misled. By Owen McCombs, that's who. He kept us thinking the killer and the crime occurred up out of the garage, off premises, that the body might have come in and dumped. We jumped to a premise the body might have been driven in using the Mayor's car. Hey, I bought off on it. By my scenario, he's tapped on the premises, here, and one person could have done the deed. There's a gardener's cart. I think the body could've been leveraged on and carted up to the car, under a tarp, then rolled into the trunk. Yeah, I'll wait 'til forensics show up."

Anything else she missed? She walked to the office building. The glass door was locked on the inside by a wrapped chain. She sat on a stone bench, upset at herself. Investigative failure. Her own. She knew she had to bird dog Washington around as his homicide apprentice, still the police, the detectives — she and Ray — should have discovered the murder scene yesterday.

McCombs slipped back into her mind. Could he be involved? Hell, thought Chase, Scott Peterson and Ted Bundy were good looking men too, with pleasant personalities and smooth lines of patter until their hands went around the neck, or their teeth sank into skin.

McCombs became her next priority: *Numero Uno.*

18. Grieving for Chunky

As they drove up to valet, at the front entrance of the Carnivale Casino, Owen saw Investigator Byron Kane waiting. Kane gave a formal hello to the Mayor and ignored Owen. As Owen figured it, Kane opened a new classified dossier labeled, "McCombs", whether or not the Mayor or his attorney requested it.

The former cop went through his check off list. Outside of death notification by phone, the police questioning of Mrs. DiManna not yet scheduled though a priority. Her son, Pauli DiManna, nicknamed Pauli D, worked at the Carnivale as the Slot Manager. He identified his father's body first thing this morning. Kane informed them Mrs. DiManna will talk only briefly, only doing so because she knew the Mayor kept her husband out of jail, not that he didn't deserve it, she said.

The Mayor gave an eco-geo tour of where they were. Owen listened politely though he had seen this environment before, repetitive now in a hundred national locations, many with Magnum Casino branding.

The Carnivale Casino, one of those midsize casinos, explained the Mayor, encircled the metropolitan areas of Las Vegas, North Las Vegas, and Henderson. Tagged as a locals' hangout, these places were not small. Up to date techno they boasted anywhere from 500 to 2,000 gaming machines. Casinos like the Carnivale catered to customers via a different style of casino marketing, relying on using player tracking cards and coupons with point systems measuring coin in play. Not how much you win or lose, though those stats are available, the only essential one is an active player. The casinos believe that in the end they will be the ultimate winners. In constant competition they can't lose their local base. They are the experts in frenzied promotional enticement. As a perfect example, a door greeter in Mardi Gras costume sought to sign them up for a card club membership the minute they crossed the threshold.

The Mayor led the way, as usual, with Investigator Kane fast behind reading from his work up file.

"Initial review of your past cases, which Clay's secretaries are still sifting through, haven't turned up any client bearing a homicidal grudge. There's a waiting list, however, of prosecutors, police officers, and Federal agents who do not wish you the best of health." Owen blinked a surprise at Kane's attempt at humor. He didn't think the guy had it in him.

"Would you then assume," questioned the Mayor in quick-step stride, "that events in Chunky D's life should be our main focus?"

"Until another direction surfaces," agreed the lanky investigator. He still ignored Owen's presence.

"How many of his crime buddies are still out there kicking? It has to be over twenty years since their jewelry heist crime wave rolled through town." The Mayor waved to several senior citizen ladies who recognized him. Other slot players turned to see the distraction and then noting the Mayor's familiar mug, they smiled and turned back to their games, their player card leashes clipped to their clothing and plugged into their machines, their cigarette smells being sucked into the ceiling's smoke eaters, their hands tapping away at the Spin or Deal buttons in methodical repetitions, trance like.

The investigator juggled his file while walking, stepping around people as the three men threaded their way past the noisy canyons of metal moneymakers. Fused neon the light of play.

"There were five in the crew," stated Kane, paraphrasing from his notes. "Two of them dead, both recently, now three with Chunky D wasted. Mario "The Torch" Scarpeitti died only a week ago in prison. I don't have the details. Bobby Campi cashed in his chips about a month ago. Heart condition. Rumor has it he was being serviced by an escort pro and his adulation and heart climaxed at the same time." Owen wanted to say Mr. Campi went out with a bang, staying silent instead, expecting Kane's cold stare would cut him quick.

"The other current living are Morris "Sweets" Bluestein. He swiped the getaway vehicles. Got his nickname from the candy he always sucked. Never smoked and still got lung cancer. Figure that. Spending his last days at the Temple Emmanuel Hospice. And Lorenzo Corallo who is…"

"I know Larry. Used to own 'Corallo's'." The Mayor savored a memory. "Great Italian eatery over on Maryland Parkway, near the Hard Rock. The Osso Buco, unbelievable. His son comes along and converts the place to a titty-ass bar. The restaurant is still there with a new name. 'Gabriella's', I think. An era of class ended. The son, what's his name, Angelo, is raking in the sleaze coin."

"Lorenzo Corallo indicted several times, convicted only once."

"Yes, I know." The Mayor stopped his promenade. His mood changed to fit the solemn occasion.

"Lois," intoned the Mayor. "I'm so sorry for your loss."

"Aurie," said the grieving widow, "can you flag down a damn slot tech? My money keeps jamming in this frickin' bill acceptor."

Mrs. Charles DiManna, Lois, sat on a casino stool slamming the buttons on a video poker machine, slapping the metal in rapid hand movement. A burning cigarette in her mouth had long been ignored, dangling a grey ash finger of burned tobacco. An empty cocktail glass awaited a waitress's refill and not yet lunch time. Widow DiManna, painted and rebuilt, held her own in the looks department. Blonde bouffant hairdo, close to a beehive like a B-52 band member, streaked with strawberry tint. Heavy gemstone jewelry draped her neck, and faux diamond bracelets encircled her arms like writhing glass snakes. Wrinkles surgically tightened. Apparent that ten to fifteen years in age separated the couple. No doubt Chunky D at his prime stalked the better Vegas hot spots and clubs with this eye candy on his arm. So this is where bimbos end up, thought Owen.

The slot tech came and went. Lois played as she talked, her eyes on the glass slot screen. Owen noticed the credits on her machine. This lady was no nickel player. This was a dollar play machine and she had about $3,500 on the credit meter. Why was she putting money into the machine? She could have played off the credits all afternoon. Owen saw her Carnivale player card slotted registering game play.

"What can I tell you, Aurie? As far as I know everything seemed to be going well. Our furniture store sells to the new housing boom and the show homes. You know, I don't see him a lot. Like we're living together under the same roof, but after the last time he spent out of circulation, he came back more into himself. The fires died off. We went our separate ways."

Yeah, Owen mused, Chunky D probably got his kicks selling sofas to the young suburban housewives or trendy female interior designers, praying for some bored desperate housewife or closet nympho willing to exchange favors to gain a steep discount on an Ethan Allen armoire.

Owen noted that those who knew the Mayor from the early days, when he was the successful defense attorney, referred to him by 'Aurie', slang off his first name "Aurelius" Stokes.

"Lois, did Charles ever bring up any enemies from the old times, did he talk about me in anyway, angry like?"

"No, not at all, Aurie." Her eyes locked as musical riffs signaled a win, the machine zapping colored lines, credits going to the bottom line. $850 win and she didn't even hoop and holler. Odd, even for a steady customer.

"Charlie always had the highest respect for you," the widow said. "He even voted for you, and told all his friends that they'd better do the same thing."

"Do you know who his enemies were?" asked Kane. "Any unusual phone calls? Anything that might make him worry?"

She didn't look away from her game. "Most of those who were jealous of him are dead. Any Fed or prosecutor S.O.B. would have retired by now and gone fishing on my tax dollars. Unusual, I guess, he started calling his old friends recently, the ones still breathing. Started after Bobby C passed away. Balling some hooker and his ticker stopped cold. Tony Scarpettii died last week. Charlie did get agitated about that. Walked the house upset, saying things like, 'What's going on? Why?' I tried to tell him that his buddies were wearing out, they're over seventy, for God's sake."

"Any recent interest in his old business career?" Kane asked. Mrs. DiManna took a two second pause in her game.

"I don't know. I heard him one night on the phone with Larry Corallo. Maybe they had lunch, I'm not sure. After Tony's death he paid a visit to Sugar. Morris Bluestein. Poor bastard, he's on death's door. I burn a candle for him. He's Pauli's, our son's Godfather. Ain't that a kick, a Catholic kid has a Jew Godfather, promising the Church he'll be raised in the faith. Morrie always sent Pauli cash for his birthday. Still does. Nothing chincy, either." More bells and whistles as she scored to enter a bonus round. A wheel spun to land on $250. Not bad. This lady, marveled Owen, was lucky, more so than her hubby.

"Yeah, the more I think about it, I guess he did seem a little excited the last couple of days," said the winning widow DiManna. "But his excitement never came my way, if you get my meaning."

Owen took his own shot at insight, from something Harmon Hartley had mentioned.

"Did they ever recover any of the merchandise from the Cassandra jewelry robbery?" He was trolling for a reaction.

Mrs. DiManna paused more than two seconds, the first rest she had had since they arrived, and turned to Owen. She appraised him, like one would do with some fancy bauble, or a boy toy.

"Charlie DiManna was never in that racket. He was a rough guy and he knew some wise guys. But for the Cassandra job he had been set up by some snitch trying to catch a break on sentencing and the Feds were trying anything legal or not to get a conviction. Aurie proved that on appeal. Got him a new trial. And, Charlie never did anything vicious. I mean somebody beat up that poor Cassandra saleslady. Do you think I would be sitting here if I believed Charlie did something so despicable?"

Owen thought she meant she would walk out on a violent criminal who beats victims. Not so.

"He would have fenced the stuff and bought me real stones instead of this junk." She rattled her arms. "And I'd be over there in the high roller action."

A deep bass, angry voice spit from behind.

"Wha'd you doing here? Can't you see Mom's going through a personal tragedy!" Yeah, Owen thought to himself, she's going to get hospitalized with tendonitis from the repetitive button pounding.

The speaker grimaced his displeasure. A stocky build stuffed in a black suit and black thin tie, his close cropped haircut gave him no help. He did look a lot like his Father. The inverted triangle physique of large men, leaning to the plump side. Pauli DiManna's eyes were bloodshot. Owen assumed he had been boozing at the parental loss. Owen couldn't see him shedding heartfelt tears. The young DiManna didn't seem the maudlin type. Quickly, Owen extended his hand said he was from the Magnum Casino, and as part of the new competitors in town, he had to stop in and look around. Hesitant, Pauli DiManna returned the grip. He spotted the Mayor and pulled back his anger. He knew the Mayor and nodded. Kane made no move to introduce himself.

"We're paying our respects," said the Mayor. "Your father was an old client of mine."

Young Chunky Junior cracked his knuckles.

"My Mother and I can't tell you why this happened. He is—". Pauli held back a forced choke in his voice—"he was an innocent man in all things he did. Please leave us alone and let us have a chance to bear our private pain."

Mom's pain translated into a victorious 'Yes!' as she hit another video gaming winner. Pauli ignored her and her good fortune. To Owen, as a casino exec, that seemed odd.

"But your mom said your father did seem agitated in the last few days," Owen put out his old reporter antenna feelers and changed 'excited' to a more anguished verb. "And she said he had started to

talk to his old 'friends'. I wonder what those friends could tell us."
Owen emphasized the word 'friends'.

Chunky Junior gave a bitter look. "I never heard him say anything about the old days, or his friends. If I were you, Mayor, I would
have your police force start looking at your own friends for who killed
my father. If I find that person before the cops do..."

Just as the Mayor was opening his mouth to deliver a response, a
ruckus erupted at one of the nearby blackjack tables. Two undercover
casino security people had surrounded some young bearded fellow,
grabbing at each arm and hustling him down the casino floor out a
side exit. The bearded man was yelling loudly, protesting that he had
done nothing wrong, throwing out words like 'Gestapo!' Investigator
Kane gave his verdict with a sniff. "They're eighty-sixing a card counter." Owen noticed the culprit wore a Colorado Avalanche hockey
cap. Go Avs.

"It's time," the Mayor said in cathedral baritone, "Let's let Mrs.
DiManna deal with her sorrow in her own way." And the Mayor
made a grand gesture exit, courteously nodding to Paulio DiManna.
Meanwhile the widow scoring another noisy win did not notice their
departure.

Waiting for valet, Owen couldn't keep the secret any longer.

"I know one thing certain. Mom's scamming the casino with Junior's help."

Owen had finally figured it out.

Kane and the Mayor looked at him.

"She was having *too much* luck on that slot machine. Casinos are just starting to install the latest technology in machines with downloadable programs, systems the Slot Manager can control from his desk."

"And in English, what's that?" asked the Mayor.

"The young DiManna must've found a glitch in the programming sequence. With the old slots the computer chip in the game machines have algorithm formulas to determine the odds of a hit sequence. You put the e-prom chip in the machine on the gaming floor. With downloadable games, the payouts are in the central computer. Pauli gained some inside information, maybe bribed a tech to dummy up a progam interface.

"He lets Mom know which particular video machine to play. They keep each winning play under $1,199 so they don't trigger an IRS filing report. She not only wins but she builds player club points. Those points, leading to casino freebies like free drinks and buffets, room discounts, can make her winning percentage way above a 100% return. Maybe to avoid detection, after awhile Junior in the security of his office, moves the gaffed downloadable program to another machine and Momma DiManna moves over. No one the wiser."

"Criminal heredity moves into the next generation," said the Mayor.

"I'll run a background on Pauli DiManna," said Kane "See if he has any police record. But if he did, he wouldn't be working in a casino, so my guess he has a clean sheet."

"How about notifying The Gaming Control Board about DiManna's larceny fraud?"

The Mayor and Kane exchanged glances, both pondering, crafting a reply.

"I could make a call." Kane's response as Owen decided would be glory for Kane himself.

"No, let me handle it." The Mayor studied Owen. "Your sharp observation needs to land in front of the right people. The Nevada Gaming Control Board takes machine tampering very serious but timing is important. Yes, I have some ideas on who needs to get the word, and the timing." Owen felt the Mayor wanted a few brownie points, since it certainly sounded like he needed more friends within the government hierarchy.

"Meanwhile, Byron, why don't you get Mr. McCombs here a printout on what you have on Chunky D and his old wise guy buddies. See if he reads any link."

Owen doubted Investigator Kane wanted a second opinion, especially his. To the Mayor's reluctance at informing the authorities, he could see the politician's wisdom, slow caution, to maximize actions for reciprocal value.

Owen returned to his assignment in chauffeuring the Mayor. His mind muddled. Was Jackson Flynn trying to score brownie points, using him as a go-fer, his time without value? That train of thought left the station with building doubts as to his worthiness. His silent funk boarded as a passenger. Owen had forgotten this morning to take one of his prescribed pills.

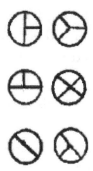

When it came her turn to chime in at the late morning conference Chase rattled off the employment highlights on Owen McCombs. Washington interrupted and gave his interpretation of the man's resume.

"I find his being a former police reporter interesting. Maybe at the DiManna crime scene he manipulated our inquiries."

Her partner shuffled papers, edgy. His comment bothered her, like a silent reprimand that maybe Owen McCombs had manipulated the police, meaning her. She knew pressure, not part of a retirement scenario, came to rest on her partner's shoulders. The press had Chunky D's name as the trunk guest and were whirling like a drought prairie sage fire. With each question the Mayor's name kept popping up.

Chase went on to say the Codis search revealed McCombs filing a police report on a break-in of his apartment, 221B Baker Avenue, in Biloxi, a couple of days before he left that State. A supplemental filing; the day he left, gunfire reported in the same neighborhood, vagueness to a shooting. Keep after McCombs, stressed Washington. He's mixed up, somehow.

Washington highlighted the autopsy report and the workup on the knife. The bullet of course killed him. Chunky D could have survived the knife wounds, scarred for life, his cut arms useless. Forensics on the Mercedes not yet complete, explained Washington, early assumptions held, the shooting did not take place in the auto. CSI confirmed what Chase uncovered in the El garden and were still at the scene processing.

Detective Fetters, pulling on his nose, arrived late, cursing under his breath

"Damn the Mayor. I track down Mrs. DiManna. She was playing slots at the Carnivale Casino."

"Widows in this town have a short mourning period," joked Washington.

"She didn't identify the body this morning. It was her son, Pauli. He's the Slot Manager at the Carnivale. Anyway, the Mayor is leaving just as I go in. And, fuck, if he hadn't gotten there first, and she says, with Pauli hanging over her, that they're not talking to the police unless their attorney is present. Bet fuckin' Super Bowl tickets that the Mayor whispered some free legal advice. He's stonewalling our investigation already. Hours old and he's fucking with us. And by the way, your buddy Byron Kane was escorting the Mayor."

Ray Washington turned and gave Chase the quick scoop about that. "Kane's ex-cop. Department fired him. Too many IAD investigations where he liked to beat the criminals before bringing them in. Then, on a slam-dunk case, paroled career criminal arrested, Kane goes out and finds exonerating evidence. Guy walks. Point of the story: Mayor Goodfella, defense attorney back then, liked that sort of ethics, brought Kane on board as their law firm's investigator."

"A fuckin' traitor," cursed Fetters.

Washington continued. "It was Detective Fetters's first high profile case in homicide. Kane brought the real suspect in, victim's DNA all over him. Of course, the suspect arrived in bad condition, teeth missing and a broken arm. That, and some vindictiveness on some people's part, led to Kane's firing." Ray and Mike exchanged stares.

"I wouldn't put it past our Mob Mayor to have his private dick do the hit. Yeah, that's something we need to look into."

"Mike," said Washington. Chase sensed sudden tension in the air. "The Mayor as suspect is not for you to play cowboy on. The Sheriff is handling this with kid gloves. What with a Mayoral election in a year, along with the Sheriff's own re-election at stake. It's not our call. Focus on ferreting out evidence. Anything else, Detective Fetters?"

Little Mikey's expression swore without words.

"Well, here's what I've got," said Detective Washington. "I had archives pull up the history of the Wrecking Crew. Made copies you all can read later. I want to divide up names and do background. The dead ones didn't kill Chunky D, but who knows where it leads." Chase sighed in relief that she wasn't going to be given all the library research.

"There were five in the gang. DiManna. Bobby Campi deceased. Had a heart attack. Fetters, Campi is yours. "Then there's Morris Bluestein. He's on his last gasp with emphysema. In a hospice over off St. Rose Parkway. Detective Taggart, all yours. Next, Lorenzo Corallo, he's still alive..."

"Larry Corallo." Fetters perked up. "Yeah, his son Angel, Angelo Corallo, owns the strip club Pussy Galore. Larry, the Father's a greeter, got a permanent booth there in their restaurant, Italian steakhouse called Gabriella's after Angel's sister. I used to moonlight there for security when I worked patrol."

Chase shook her head to the well-known axiom: For locals, Vegas is a small town.

"Well, you got some history there," said Washington, "unless you have an inside track, I better handle the Corallos. Add to your list Mario 'The Torch' Scarpetti. I remember him. When he wasn't running with the Wrecking Crew doing jewelry store heists, he had a string of prostitutes and a side job of insurance scams. Buying cheap buildings, heavy insurance, and the mysterious firebug job."

"Where's he now?" asked Fetters.

"Ashes to Ashes."

"Dead?"

"More like toast. He was in Big Max on an aggravated assault conviction when he burned up. Middle of the day. Right in front of guards and prisoners. Caught fire. Became a Crispy Critter."

"When was this?" Chase edged closer, curious.

"Six or seven days ago. It's under an internal investigation probe at the prison."

"Jeez," said Chase and thought aloud for all of them. "We have two of the old-timers, members of the same gang, cashing in their chips less than a week apart, both under violent and mysterious circumstances. What would you call that?"

"Croaking for justice," came Little Mikey's read of the timeline.

Civic responsibilities brought the Mayor back to his schedule. The Corvette sped along the Summerlin Parkway toward the Red Rock Mall shopping center dedication.

Their arrival in a flaming red Corvette fit the moment and played out as a grand entrance. A high school band gave them a rousing Sousa welcome. Owen saw a swirling miniature amusement park and a goat, donkey, duck petting zoo. Balloons hovered, strained in nets, for the proper timed release. People applauded their entrance and Owen parked near as he could to where two fake pillars were lashed together by a flimsy bright pink ribbon and bow. Gigantic gold speckled scissors awaited the Mayor's proclamation and public obligations of ribbon snipping.

Owen eased to the background as the dignitaries whisked the Mayor to his appointed chair for the ceremonies. He found himself caught up in the festivities and wandered among the food concessions and the arcade games. The crowds flowed happy, carefree. For the first time he accepted that Las Vegas would be his new home. Not just a casino but a neighborhood, a town. Time to make new friends, he considered, and ironically, with that thought in mind, Owen saw a face in the crowd he recognized.

"How is your artwork going? It's Eric, isn't it?"

The boy took a moment. "Yeah, great, thanks again for the pen. Do you have another? I bet I run out of ink in a week," the boy motor mouthed, excited.

"That was a special pen. One of a kind, but I'll look around."

Owen turned to the older lady standing with the boy and introduced himself with his first name only, and no description as to his job. "I met Eric recently…with his mom."

"I'm Eric's grandmother. This is a great event for a kid to have clean fun. They've torn down Water World and the Putt-Putt Golf to put up condos. Poor kids are going to be forced into casino arcades for entertainment. A pity."

Owen smiled in sympathy. Not the turf discussion he wanted to tread.

"Well, Eric sure seems to be into drawing. I saw some of his work."

The boy grinned, his eyes bouncing at all the carnival games and amusement rides.

"Guess what he said I could do when I grow up? Design computer games. Wouldn't that be awesome?" Eric begged ticket coupons from his grandmother, running off to stand in line at the Wild Spyder ride. Owen accepted that smart adults avoided a whip flinging machine run by road gypsies.

Assuming Owen a family friend, Eric's grandmother introduced herself as "Nanna" and proceeded to babble away. Owen gleaned important gossip. Chase, he learned her first name, was a divorced single mom who had just been promoted to Homicide Division from Robbery/Burglary. That Nanna lived with Chase and Eric, and not the detective's mother but the ex-mother-in-law, raised interesting questions. Nanna chatted on, her move to a Sun City community in Arizona postponed realizing Chase could use the help with Eric. She smiled. "Important to be near your only grandchild. It's a win-win situation."

Owen didn't want to intrude. Curious, careful to be sensitive, he asked, "Eric seems to be a ball of fire. A growing kid with an imagination."

"Yes, hyper, it leads to his concentration problems," said Nanna, sensing the young man's sincerity. "The doctors have other words for it, even call it a disease. Before they had all those fancy diagnoses, back a few years, we would have just said he was a 'wild child'. These days they give kids medicine, a doctor remedy, not a parent's. Chase and I do pretty well with him. It's his school work and relationships with kids that seem to be at a critical stage. My son, Roger, takes him for a weekend each month."

A father around only once a month spoke volumes, Owen thought.

As the three of them walked the shopping center's portable amusement park, he could hear the Mayor's voice in the background: "With the opening of this center, this great city reaches a new plateau equal to the best throughout the country…I hereby dedicate and officially open…" The band blared out crescendos, balloons floated into the blue horizon. A series of aerial rockets exploded in bangs that made Owen wince. Fireworks sounded like gunfire.

He treated Eric to a grape sno-cone and Nanna to a web spin of cotton candy. She passed sticky finger bites to them. Buddy building.

They parted after a fun filled and informative hour, refreshing for Owen, something rare in his life.

Nanna said at his departure, "Now that was fun, Owen. You're new to town, let me be hospitable. Why don't you come over and visit Eric and Chase and myself one of these nights? I fix great fried chicken and Chase's specialty is a seven bean salad."

"Yeah, then you'll see all my drawings."

"With that sort of invitation how can I refuse? As long as your mom won't mind?"

"Naw," the boy said. "It's okay." Eric ran off to the next gravity defying ride.

"The sooner the better," said the grandmother.

"The sooner the better," said Owen. Each with strange twinkles in their eyes.

The Mayor secured a new ride to take him back to City Hall, his political gadfly, Harmon Hartley. As Owen edged his car through the parking lot traffic he saw Hartley and the Mayor. They were not smiling. The press had ambushed the Mayor. Harmon shot Owen the evil eye. Harmon, Owen imagined, blamed him for dragging down the Mayor's reputation. Expecting the worst, Owen turned his radio on to hear the announcer regurgitate the Sheriff's press conference. Political assassination by microphone.

It wasn't until he got back and parked his car when he spotted the Mayor's brief case stuffed behind the driver's seat in the back seat of the Corvette. The Mayor must have forgotten it. Owen would drop the case off later at his house. For the fun of it, he fiddled with the two hasp snaps. They were locked to the combination. There were four set of numbers to each clasp. These read 16-13 and 18-21. They could have been random, twirled to lock. On the other hand, most people placed lock numbers one digit off so they would not forget. Still toying, Owen set the last digits up one and down one on both locks. He repeated his method with the first digit, up one number, then down one. The lock clasps did not snap open. He placed the digits back as they were. Oh, well, harmless curiosity never hurt anyone.

Chase watched the press conference on the TV across the room while she continued her tedium of re-reading cold case files as part of her indoctrination into the homicide department.

In a foul mood, where she couldn't define the cause, a passing detective dropped a telephone message on her desk. The "To" had the detective's name scratched out and penciled in were a case file number and her name. One of the cold cases piled on her desk as part of her initiation into the homicide department. "The From" stated: Rosa Garcia, and the telephone number. The message brief: "Please call." Whoever this was, she did not recognize the name. Chase would call later, when she had time.

On the T.V., Sheriff Randall Phillips spoke to the cameras, flanked by Divisional Commander John Stevens and Detective Ray Washington. From what Chase could hear, most of the Sheriff's remarks exposed few facts. Reporter questions overwhelmed, grasping. Yes, the car's registration is to the Mayor of the City. Yes, the victim had a police record. The investigation, emphasized by the Sheriff, should be regarded in its early stages and he suggested no one jump to conclusions. Chase watched the press jump to all sorts of conclusions. Commander Stevens and Detective Washington could only say, 'We can't comment at this time'. A press conference satisfying no one.

22. Side Kicked

Owen returned to the Silver Avenue home bearing groceries. Outside his locked bedroom door, he found two large file envelopes. One, with Magnum's logo, would be Melissa Steele's educational tour package for tomorrow. The other, from the Stokes law offices, Kane's reluctant hand-over, the criminal history of the departed DiManna and his unsavory associates. He grabbed a diet Coke, some chips, and headed to the back yard with the forlorn hope to view nubile Casey taking an early evening dip. Would he be so lucky? Alone, the pool waters still, he sat down and started to open the material on DiManna when he noticed the seal torn and taped shut again. Maybe, more material added. He drank and munched and started reading about Chunky D and the Wrecking Crew.

After a good hour of read and re-reading Owen could see two main points: the Mayor had been active with the Wrecking Crew if only as their advocate for fair representation, and the multi-million dollar loot from the Cassandra store robbery never recovered. Jewelry, gems, coins, all missing.

A newspaper plopped down in front of him on the table, giving him a near heart attack. "My name's Theodore, and you are Owen McCombs. It says so here in the evening paper." He sat down at the table and pulled open a laptop computer that he had been carrying. "I seldom go anywhere without this."

Theodore resembled a scrawny Maynard G. Krebs, a beatnick from hippiedom. Thin, gangly bones, his hair to his shoulders, a dime size gold earring dangled from one ear which Owen could see when the kid shook his stringy locks. Too old to be a 'Teddy' and not old enough to be called 'Ted'. Theodore about said it all. Pale skin, dainty though not effeminate, fuzz whiskers on his chin. Elegant in a hip sort of way, he started typing on his computer with dexterity and speed. Owen felt Theodore's body at any moment might physiologically morph man to machine.

Owen looked to the late edition headlines, halfway jealous he didn't have a job on the crime news beat. As feared, the situation bad as it gets for the Mayor: "Gangster Dead in Mayor's Car!" Sub head: "Found at Magnum Casino Site." Ouch. No help to the Magnum, though not built meant no fleeing customers, a weak consolation to this new unhealthy reputation

The story revealed nothing that he did not already know except the killing site had been discovered in a garden area behind the parking garage. A telling quote on the subsequent page, not from the police who refused to give out information, a denial statement from an FBI spokesperson investigating issuing their own no comment. Why the FBI? What made this a Federal case? Had Chunky D crossed state lines and been bad again?

The Mayor's brief written quote, distributed out of his office, followed the press release style that Owen suggested yesterday. The newspaper, however, hit hard saying he refused to comment when contacted later at the Red Rock Mall opening.

Theodore rearranged the newspaper for him. "You are mentioned in the paper's second section. Above the fold." He pointed out a column in the paper penned by a columnist named West Pegler.

What's Mayor Goodfella and a Magnum exec, Owen McCombs, doing finding bodies at the new casino site? Makes you wonder what other skeletons are buried in the Magnum project, and what nefarious tie-ins we are going to uncover that reveal a casino organization known for its secret history owned by a multi-millionaire mystery man? Who's going to be *Owen* to whom? If this car casino, this Temple of Zoom, gets built, be prepared. I know there is more to this than the Mayor hauling around dead clients.

As my readers know from my previous articles, I completed the last draft of my book, *Wise Guys of Las Vegas*, the second in my omnibus on the hustling early days of Nevada and Las Vegas. Buy my book and you will understand why we don't need to return to the good old mob days of criminal violence.

Owen could not see Jackson Flynn tolerate this low heel innuendo and he did not relish reading his own name in print. No good would come of this. One day new to town he began his enemy list and put this columnist, West Pegler, at the top.

"Ah, here she is." Theodore's eyes went to gleam and his face lit in awe. Owen turned to see.

Elvis.

Casey was Elvis.

"I'm one of a kind."

To such a comment on the surface Owen could not disagree. As they drove to the restaurant, his eyes could not help but wander to this black leather nymph. He knew that she likewise observed him behind her sunglasses.

They were jammed into the Corvette, top down, the lady Elvis sitting half in the middle at an angle, her legs across Theodore. Her shoulders leaning against Owen. Casey looked less the King's image and more like a motorcycle gang chick. Her show paraphernalia, including her black Elvis wig and paste on sideburns, were in a worn suitcase stowed in the trunk…a trunk that he assumed would be, and was, empty of corpses.

"There're 20,000 Elvis impersonators from weekend warriors doing birthday gigs to professional show Elvi, about a thousand of them, most in Vegas. Probably just one hundred twenty-five true pros. There are only five professional female Elvis impersonators," she said proudly. "I'm the only one in Las Vegas. I work the "Stars Forever" tribute show at the Montecito Casino, 8:00 & 10:00 p.m. shows."

"She travels to compete each year at the Elvi Expo. You have to call them Elvi, so as not to tread on the filthy rich trademark owners of the Elvis brand name. Last year at the Expo she placed fifth as 'Best Suited'," Theodore bragged, obvious a loyal fan club booster.

"I've a pretty good singing voice," she went on, "I can range down to be a low baritone. I face obstacles. The judges are men and purists to the King's memory; they don't tolerate 'loose interpretation', so deviants like women, small people, or children don't make it into final rounds for the Golden Microphone Award for the Best Elvis Impersonator."

"Doesn't that just suck?" sympathized Theodore. She gave him a thanking smile and turned back to Owen, her face inches from his.

"It doesn't bother me, really. That's just one weekend a year. You gotta feed yourself the rest of the days." Her face said the real truth, that she would do almost anything to be a tribute winner at the annual Elvi Expo.

"What songs do you perform? What's your best?" Owen never in his life gave a thought to Elvis Presley. Maybe that's not true. He never switched stations during an Elvis song. Fast as possible he would switch channels at an Elvis movie.

"I can do his popular repertoire. At the Montecito Casino they only give you ten minutes, plus the finale with the ensemble. I come out in this black leather outfit for the first part, his younger years, and then the white jump suit in the second act, a little padding, not his fat period. People seem to be taken aback a woman can sing his songs."

"The men like it," said Theodore with a frown. "She unbuttons the front of her costume."

"Come on, Theodore, two buttons, nothing is falling out." Owen gave her a speed glance. Pre show, the buttons fastened to the top, a white star sequin scarf flapped around her neck. No doubt when her black hair was properly coiffed and sprayed, it hung flippant over her forehead in the image of the idolized hip grinder of the Sun Record days.

Casey flipped on the radio and punched in a rock station. Owen recognized the tune in play. A hard beat, torch song topping the Billboard charts, "Rush to Lust" by the Dell twins, better known as Hi-Jinx. They were bubble gummers trying the crossover career risk, jumping from Britney belly rings to Madonna foreplay sensuality. Casey warbled the lyrics along with the twins like a song bird, a sultry baby bird:

Take me, take me into your pounding sea,

Drown me in your arms, babe-bee

Make a bad girl out of me;

Hold me, hold me against the evil wind

Be my Rock of Ages but let my body bend

Take me, hold me – Don't stop my rush to lust."

Owen felt his own rise to lust, fortunately saved by Theodore saying, 'Turn here.' They pulled into a parking lot. Owen would be buying dinner.

He became alert. "Hold on, this isn't a restaurant, this is a strip club."

23. Bare Assets

How appropriate, a strip club called *The Pussy Galore*.

Owen remembered his reading. "This place is owned by the Corallo family."

"They have a great steakhouse, *Gabriella's*." Theodore and Casey strolled through the front door where the elegant and well endowed hostess, in black evening gown slit cut to the hip asked for I.D. and carded Casey and Theodore. Two bruiser bouncers in tuxes gave stone cold stares like gargoyles, protecting the inner sanctum. One of them displayed colorful green-red tattoos inching up above his neck collar.

The Pussy Galore shone like a feline decorated castle, unlike the East Colfax topless bars in Denver, or the Bourbon Street sex dives in New Orleans, places Owen had checked out only when invited to bachelor parties. Within this door he had entered a cornucopia of luxury and beauty, a world based on expensive drinks and the formality of culture more restricted than a church morality play. Unsatisfied fantasies were the end product of $20 lap dances and boob stage jiggling for dollar G-string stuffing. Erotica light. Owen inhaled the hormone atmosphere and let his eyes adjust to purple neon accenting the darkness. He could see six mini stages with dance poles. Ogling men at the stage rims stared at the meat market. Suggestive hit dance music allowed women to gyrate in various artistic, if that's what it was, forms of slinky undressing. The biz of bump and grind. Women not in the dance rotation were traipsing around in negligees, suggesting special adventure behind private doors in the VIP room. Wink. Wink. Only a few extra twenties.

"This way," said Casey, giggling, "and watch it, your drool is showing." They followed a hostess from tawdry cave blackness through another door to a more opulent setting, feeling of being in some zillionaire's mansion library and billiard room. The restaurant was dressed in rich mahogany and cherry wood, red velvet wallpaper, maroon chairs and booths and naked Greek statuary highlighted the seating area. The music matched the décor, easy jazz with blues riffs, where these softer subtle rhythms set the slow motion sways of one voluptuous dancer. This peroxide blonde displayed her attributes, physical anomalies, well beyond double D cup sizing. With eyes closed, expelling her cum-hither emotions, she glided around a center dance pole faking orgasms, like dancer Isadora Duncan might translate a *Cosmopolitan* magazine guide on how to please your man.

Several booths surrounded the outer perimeter and tables with white cloth sat in the inner ring near the circular elevated dance floor. It amazed Owen that the diners were a mixture of suited businessmen on expense accounts, hip couples, and country club foursomes drinking wine in hushed conversations. Owen saw four men off in a corner. They were rougher in character, not out on a convention lark. Not construction workers, not Mafioso slick. Owen gave them little thought except he sensed they had a 'police look', short-cropped haircuts and overweight, but not police.

When seated, Theodore posed the riddle.

"If you're a single man looking to connect, what's the best airline flight to take into Vegas?" Owen shrugged and Theodore quipped. "The Southwest Airline early Friday evening flights from L.A. or San Diego. College girls come in to strip and take back at least $2,000-$3,000 a weekend, maybe more depending on their talent and predilections."

Theodore pulled out his laptop. Great, thought Owen, I'm at a Bacchanalia skin fest with PowerPoint.

Theodore whispered, "Do you think old Larry Corallo snuffed out Chunky DiManna?"

"What?"

Casey, as Lady Elvis, joined in. "We know the Mayor would have nothing to do with a professional hit...."

"Or be dumb enough to leave the evidence in his car trunk," said Theodore.

"That's why we decided to come here." Casey threw smiles at the people still staring after they had followed her grand entrance in cycle leathers. Two men at the bar exchanged leering stares. Owen believed they were guessing Casey must be available for S&M tricks.

She continued. "We're trying to find out if Mr. Corallo knows anything. All three of us owe Mayor Goodfella a lot, the least of which is our basic cheap rent. We saw the TV this evening, read the newspaper, we can't let his enemies lynch him. Right?"

Owen was speechless. She did have a point. From her jacket she pulled out her Elvis sideburns and stuck them on and unzipped her leather jacket midway to show off cleavage pushed up with a black lace bustier. Owen stared and she smiled with pure innocence.

"You attract a bear with honey, a voyeur with skin," she laughed.

A minute later as if on cue. "That's a fine looking Elvis you have there." An old man, his voice gravel, turned facing them from his seat in the next booth. He sat with the blonde, the over baring dancer, now finished with her routine, mopping copious sweat off her face with a cloth napkin. Redressed in a teddy the lady resembled Jayne Mansfield impersonating Marilyn Monroe with a little bit of Dolly Parton, unencumbered.

"I try to do the Man the homage he deserves. Mr. Corallo, I bet you knew him personally."

The old man studied the three of them. Recognized as a local celebrity, Owen knew such attention feeds the ego mindset and lets down defenses. The old man gave a knowing nod.

"Several times I saw him over at the Hilton when he was entertaining. A couple of private parties. There's a photo of him and me down the hall toward the restrooms, me and Angelo when a youngster. He had those Southern traits of a gentleman you don't see in this town any more. God bless his soul."

"I bet those were the good old days. Can you give me any insights? I'm doing my best to capture the nuances." She was good. Owen couldn't believe it when old man Corallo came over to stand by their booth. He introduced his lady friend as Candy. Of course. She gave a friendly wave and stayed where she was, drinking. She winked at Owen and wet her lips with a slow tongue. He quickly saw and relaxed that Mr. Corallo missed her oral gesture.

Owen knew from personal experience in casino marketing that the best and only way to make a hangout succeed today, whether strip club, restaurant or casino, was that personal touch by the manager or owner, being on premise, available. Make the clientele feel they have a buddy, a name to drop, the ability to move to the head of the line.

Not to be outdone Owen quickly introduced everyone, all by first name, since that's as far as he had gotten himself. Corallo explained the Vegas show years of the sixties into the seventies and his personal knowledge of the guitar strumming patron saint.

Casey put the bait out in front, literally, and Owen was mulling over the best strategic approach when Theodore pointed to him.

"Mr. McCombs here, just yesterday, met a historic Las Vegas man of the Eighties, but it was quite tragic." Silence. Owen kicked Theodore's leg under the table.

"And?" Mr. Corallo, being ever so the host expected Owen to finish Theodore's statement, but, like tag team wrestling, Casey outdid herself.

"Mr. McCombs discovered Chunky DiManna's body at the old El Morocco. With Mayor Goodfella. Why do you suppose Chunky D ended up at the El Morocco?"

Tag. Theodore jumped back into the ring and spoke to no one in particular. "I wonder if it had something to do with the Cassandra jewelry heist? Did you ever hear if any of the jewelry was recovered? Close to $3 million?"

Larry Corallo, old as rock, but not dumb as rock. He played with fire all his life knowing how to fend off a few burning embers.

"I heard," Larry Corallo paused drawing in his audience, "that the jewelry and rare coins, if all recovered would probably fetch close to $7 million today. Insurance company would still be looking for it. They paid off the entire claim." He gave a harsh, beady eyed look to Owen. "Mr. McGiver, you don't happen to work for any insurance company, or any police authority?"

"It's McCombs, and no, sir, I work for Magnum Casinos. I just arrived in town to start work and made the mistake of opening the Mayor's car trunk."

"Pity about Chunky D. He could be great fun, but could get mean easily. Back when this was only a restaurant, I had to escort him out of here a coupla times. Couldn't hold the Chianti, chugged it like beer. Still, it didn't have to end that way. He is—or rather, was a good furniture salesman."

Theodore gave him a serious look.

"Back some time when he just started selling furniture, when would that be, the early 1980s? I heard he was competitive with Tony Spilatro and his Hole in the Wall gang?"

Mr. Corallo, the old gangster, studied the bent skinny kid as one would a pesky fly.

"Whatever you've heard is short of the real truth. That reporter digging right now for his book is just scratching the surface. The Hole-in-the-Wall Gang run by Spilotro and the Wrecking Crew, supposedly led by Chunky D were cut from the same fabric. This's all I hear, y'know. People come in here and tell me stuff. When you had two groups running around doing jobs there was bound to be friction, if not petty rivalry, y'know. Probably Chunky D met up with an old grudge."

"Where do you think this Cassandra loot is today?" Casey half whispered in her husky Elvis voice and gave him a love-me tender look that would make a woman swoon, a dead man ejaculate.

"I can't hear you, sweetums," said the old man, cupping his ear.

Mr. Corallo beckoned to a waiter, whispered to him and the employee departed.

"About Chunky D?" Owen asked. "What's your insight on the 'why' of his demise?"

Mr. Corallo did not answer. His eyes drifted to a young man in an impeccable business suit approaching the table. Owen recognized the family characteristics, the son: Angelo Corallo, aka Angel.

"These nice people here are asking me a lot of interesting questions about old Las Vegas history and about a guy who I used to know a long, long time ago. You know him, Angelo, our friend Chunky D. I just now find out, Mr. McGiver here found Chunky's body." Larry Corallo signaled to his lady friend, Candy, to follow him. Her exiting the booth was a show in itself.

"My word to you is have a wonderful dinner. And as to Chunky D, he probably messed where he wasn't supposed to and pissed someone off."

Casey gave her Elvis imitation, "Have a nice evening." Larry Corallo gave Casey his best toothy grin. His lady friend helped the elderly man to navigate his exit.

The son waited until his father departed before speaking. "My dad is an old man. He talks as an old man. His stories are of the past." Deep recessed eye sockets did a once over on the dinner table. "You don't look like cops?" Angel Corallo reflected Owen's image of what a wise guy should look like, black hair, finely trimmed, slicked back, a swarthy square face, dark skinned with a groomed five o'clock shadow. His suit was shark-skin sleek, expensive.

"We're just interested in history," said Casey in a straight voice trying act like a normal young woman, sensing her Elvis shtick would not play well with the younger Corallo.

"My father's retired from his restaurant business. Reliving history is a waste, and to some, uncomfortable."

Was Owen the only one getting vibes that they were not welcomed?

"Please enjoy a glass of wine on the house. Enjoy the entertainment." He motioned a waiter over as he stalked off.

Dinner went well except for one waiter who splashed a bowl of hot minestrone onto Owen's lap. The manager came over and apologized. She was a dark haired beauty who held the genes of the Corallo's, perhaps a sister or cousin. Casey said she might be the Gabriella of the restaurant name. For his wet slacks, in some sort of private joke, the attractive manager sent over a stripper to towel off Owen's lap in a slow circular fashion.

The culinary feast featured Osso Buco, the veal dish the Mayor raved about. Casey savored the shrimp linguini. Theodore vegetated through an eggplant parmigiana. Most of the table conversation concerned the murder and what Owen would do about it? Owen gave his excuses, *'Too busy. They're starting to give me job tasks at work. I'm not really involved. Maybe a little curious. I wouldn't know where to start.'*

"Then you won't mind if we tag along on your next stop?" Theodore was looking up from his laptop, "20-9-13 S. Pecos, Temple Emmanuel Hospice."

"What?"

"The evening's young. This is the residence of Mr. Morris 'Sweets' Bluestein. Outside of Mr. Corallo, he's the only other living member of the Wrecking Crew. We better hurry. I hear he's dying."

"Now how'd you find all this out?"

"Theodore is a genius, though unappreciated." Casey said. The computer geek looked to his heroine, totally smitten.

"It's simple. I went back to the Wrecking Crew's history and pulled up news stories through Google on their latest name mentions. One story on mob crime in Las Vegas by this West Pegler had an update on the Hole-in-the-Wall Gang run by Spilotro and the Wrecking Crew. The only one left in the Hole-in-the-Wall Gang is currently on the East Coast doing a book signing tour of his memoirs. With the

Wrecking Crew, only Corallo and Bluestein are alive. But there are two interesting side notes. Chunky D and Tony "The Ant" Spilotro hated each other, a constant competition battle for mob prestige. It never fell into a turf war. The mobs were making so much money in the seventies and early eighties from casino skimming and extortion shake downs, the bosses wouldn't let smash-and-grab hoods off the leash. But as it got further into the eighties it definitely was no love fest among hoods."

"You mentioned two interesting points?" Owen faced the truth; he was caught up in this murder mystery.

"The second is that the Mayor or members in his law firm also represented many of the Hole-in-the-Wall Gang. He didn't represent Spilotro; that was another criminal defense attorney named Goodman, so you don't want to get the name similarities confused. Someone from another gang pissed at Chunky D could've seen an opportunity with this hit to humiliate and tarnish the Mayor. Research so far says competing gang members are out of the scene."

Owen listened, thinking. *Someone wants to frame the Mayor. But what can I do? We are talking about entering the world where major crime syndicate figures, retired or not, have penchant for fatal violence. Perhaps I need to pass my interest back to the Mayor, his son and their investigator. Let the police investigate. It's their job. I'll safely go back to my unknown job. Just pick up my paycheck. When in doubt, defer.*

He picked up the bill, putting it on a credit card he knew to be nearly maxed.

"Let's run Casey to work and get back to the house," Owen prioritized. "I need to read through my package on Magnum construction facts and figures for tomorrow's tour with the Chinese delegation. No visit to 'Sweet' Bluestein tonight, if ever."

Not as easy as that. The valet, nervous, looking sheepish, took them to Owen's Corvette. All four tires were slashed flat and the driver side of the car keyed to the metal.

Gddmtmthrfkngsht!! Someone evil molested Owen's only true love.

24. Setting the Record Straight

Casey and Theodore departed by taxi, not before Owen pulled Theodore aside, his grip tight on the young man's arm. He knew his anger surged from the car's damage not against the young man.

"Let's get a few things straight between us," Owen made his voice sound adult tough, parental, as if that would set his seriousness. "First, I don't like being treated like an idiot. A lot of that Wrecking Crew information you wheeled out as if you are a brainiac came out of the report sent over from the Mayor meant for my-eyes-only. Second, get this straight, I have no interest in Casey whatsoever. Third, why were you card counting at the Carnivale Casino this morning in disguise with that hockey cap, a wig, and a bad beard paste on? It's more than coincidence that you were on the scene when the Mayor put in his appearance. This town might be small, but not that small."

Theodore owned up. "I check daily with Frieda on the Mayor's schedule. If he goes to a casino, I follow. I'm eighty-sixed in most of the Strip casinos for card counting and running with a count team. Smaller casinos on the fringes are better for me even if they run Biometric face recognition. With a disguise I have a better than even chance. The Mayor is flamboyant and the eye-in-the-sky junkies in Security like to send their cameras trailing after him. I cleared $1,000 this morning on blackjack, thanks to you and the Mayor. And by the way, when you get home tonight I'll have all of Mr. Kane's research scanned and on your laptop, for which by the way, I downloaded some new software, upgraded RAM for speed, better graphics.

"My laptop? That's in my room. The computer is password protected."

"Yeah," affirmed Theodore. "Where there's the will...and hey, thanks about Casey. I know it's pretty obvious and I act like a dork, but she is...marvelous."

Having sent them on their way by taxi, Owen felt his frustration mount as he waited through the process of the tow truck that would haul the sports car to a dealer to get the four new tires and an estimate on the vandalized paint scrape on the car's side. These destructive slashes came by deliberate forethought, malice direct or on order. His number one suspect was the younger Corallo. Not by his hand, better to assign one of his bouncer thugs. A malicious joke, a warning? Quit messing around where you're not wanted? Messing with what?

Standing in the hot air of early evening viewing the colored mélange of the pulsating night sounds of what he had been witness to, what he heard or read only jumbled back toward unanswered questions. What had Casey, Theodore and Owen initiated by their Three Stooges-Mickey Spillane act? Corallos', father and son, seemed alert and wary. Angel Corallo seemed tense, while his elderly father painted his stories with flourish, yet color without canvas. The one true fact; Owen sure pissed off someone.

By end of day, Detective Washington returned from upper echelon meetings with the brass. He was on a tight leash to report everything and to button down any office leakage of the investigation. The Sheriff made the DiManna affair the public's top interest. Washington called over Fetters and Chase and asked the all-important: "What's new? What do you have?"

Fetters reported, "We found DiManna's car, 2008 Lincoln. A couple blocks from the Magnum, papered in parking tickets. Nothing inside except furniture catalogues. Lab has the car for a quick look. Don't expect surprises."

"Did he just walk in the gate?" queried Washington, pushing for the big picture. "Check that out with the rent-a-guards." He turned to his partner.

"How about the videos from the construction site?"

"They're in processing," said Chase, "To see if they can be digitized, sharpen up the pixels. We should have them back by tomorrow."

"You bring the popcorn," Fetters joked. "We can have a regular film festival." Chase gave him a flat look, as if regarding the back wall by seeing through him.

Washington continued on his check off list. "Fetters, did you talk to the Feds?"

"Appointment tomorrow at their office. I don't know how cooperative they're going to be. Their hard-on for the Mayor is a mile longer than ours. I can't see them opening up all their organized crime files for us troops in the trenches."

"After you visit with them, if they don't want to share, I'll ask the Sheriff to make a call." Local police always bowed to the F.B.I. in investigative matters concerning organized crime. The Feds considered this turf their own private war. Wiretaps and snitches somewhere in place. Murder case accommodation between national and local jurisdictions would have to be sorted out and a pact of data sharing negotiated.

Washington pushed, "Anybody have background on the rest of the Wrecking Crew gang?"

Fetters led off, as if he had tenure rights. "On Scarpetti, I'm heading down to the prison tomorrow morning. They have his personal effects for me to look through. Say they have some yard camera film of Scarpetti burning up. Can't make hard I.D. of anyone. Just from his folder, he was the gang's jewelry expert, helped find the marks."

"Well, on Corallo," Washington added his report, "as you can understand I haven't had much time. I'll get to him tomorrow."

"I'll go if you're busy," offered Fetters. Chase guessed Fetters wanted to intimidate the working girls for free feelies.

"Thanks, anyway. But the more difficult assignments, I'll handle." Dry humor from her partner. Chase gave a chuckle. Fetters eyed her with contemptible malice seeking an outlet.

Washington turned to Chase asking about news on Morrice Bluestein. She had not made it over there, she reported. Washington scolded her, as she guessed, trying to be a balanced superior officer, showing Fetters his impartiality.

"Detective Taggart, go interview Bluestein. As soon as possible. We know the dead and dying didn't kill Chunky D. Anything helps, folks. And that goes for all of us. This is a very visible case. If we can't find a suspect in the next thirty six hours, it'll never be solved and it won't matter to you, because we'll all be on horse mounted patrol in 115 degree heat." Today was a moderate 105, warm.

"The best suspect I know works down in City Hall." Fetters said.

"Find answers," a curt reply from Washington. "Make sure they are the absolute correct ones. We are on the line here."

An overweight man, dripping of sweat, approached. He wore a police visitor's badge.

"Detective Chase Taggart?" Washington and Fetters pointed to her. The obese man dropped several stapled papers into her lap. "Congratulations," he muttered and strode away at no particular pace, looking around as a touring visitor.

"What's this?"

Washington shrugged. Fetters laughed.

"It looks like you've been served with a summons. Part of the job, testifying at trial."

"I don't have any trials pending."

Fetters grabbed the legal document from her hands, giving it a gleeful scan.

"This isn't a police case." He read: 'Kinkaid vs. Taggart.' He perused the paperwork as she made a grab. "Looks like your ex-husband's asking for full custody of your son."

"What?!" She snatched the papers. The thought of losing Eric in any guise brought the mother lion snarl to her throat.

Fetters gave her a mock evil eye.

"Been a delinquent mother, heh, Detective Taggart?"

Fetters did not receive her directed wrath.

"I'll kill the bastard! I'll kill him!" Only then did she realize her voice shrilled to a venomous shout, and that her fellow officers were poking their heads from their cubicles, around corners observing as detectives are taught, wondering to what truth and action the distraught woman who had lost her cool, really would go to deal with the 'alleged' bastard.

Later, when she calmed down from her legal ambush, including absorbing the financial sticker shock, realizing she would have to hire an attorney, Chase put on a fake emotional mask and placed a call, to be assured hearth and home lay secure. Nanna Lee answered. After small talk that restored her parental sanity, she got down to business.

"Sorry, Nanna, but I'll be late tonight. Have to run down a witness."

"That's fine, dear. We had a fun time today. Eric did quite well. No problems. In fact, he met up with a friend. We invited him over for dinner. You will be home tomorrow night? It's kinda special for Eric."

"Sure, it'd be nice to meet one of Eric's friends."

"But you already have…."

Chase interrupted. "Have to run. Home no later than nine. Bye."

Her distracted mind swerved here and there, and settled back on the DiManna slaying.

Owen McCombs. If Fetters had suspicions about Mayor Goodfella, her money rode on McCombs entangled with the mob, maybe the Dixie Mob. If so, likewise maybe McCombs's boss, Jackson Flynn. Pumped up from her run in with the process server and Fetter's interference, she wanted to bust someone's chops. She let her suspicions run wild. In these brief two days of in the field Homicide work she felt in her element and began the real detective work of locating Mr. Morris Bluestein. She'd solve Chunky D's murder; she'd made that pledge to herself. She'd show them. They can't take your child away from you if you're the heroine.

It was about 8:00 pm when a taxi dropped him off at the Silver Avenue house. The place lay silent. Theodore had not yet returned, and perhaps he had decided to take in the Montecito Casino's *Stars Forever* show, probably for the umpteenth time, to cheer on his star. Poor guy. Owen in his own past life experienced moments of tender emotion, even caring feelings, not lovesick goofy. Theodore probably tolerated ulcers from his wishful daydreams. Anyone could see Casey radiated an adolescent cuteness, a natural vibrancy of bounces and smiles that left even Owen wishing for his more youthful days.

A note was affixed to the front door, and as he read he shook his head at a resigned futility. "See you at 9:00 p.m. Mayor G."

The Mayor, he presumed, in his political scheduling require- ments could not break loose until all civic tasks of endless public hear- ings adjourned, adhering to the calendar as proclaimed by Frieda, the omnipotent secretary.

He had a free hour and took advantage. Owen would scan *The Magnum Casino Educational Prep Kit* enough to fake tomorrow's tour with the Chinese gaming delegation. Theodore, his new found buddy, might assist. He wrote a note asking the wunderkind to computer generate a dozen or so Magnum business cards. He still did not have a corporate title or a job description. He toyed with the idea of calling himself, "Chief Flunky" and let the Chinese figure that one out. He knew about Asian culture and essential he be somebody important by tomorrow morning, important to Magnum's image. Particular about titles, Asians assume that they should be talking to someone high up the ladder, on equal stature with their own position, or that Mr. Flynn showed great judgment in his tour director selection to give them an extension of himself. Owen liked this juxtaposition: I represent Jackson Flynn, therefore, out of his respect for them I have to be a man of influence. For his business card he had to be a Vice President or further elevated. In most business cultures outside the United States the "Managing Director" was synonymous with "President" title. First impressions are everything. What could he be?

Owen investigated the refrigerator, finding a note in feminine scrawl, Casey's writing, 'Drink only bottled water. Avoid Lake Mead H2O. Percolates,' whatever that meant. So instructed, he pulled out a bottle of artesian electrolyte water. He thought of them. Chase and Theodore were nice kids, young adults, younger to his advancing seniority of approaching thirty. Age, he knew, fueled his personal drive. He had no internal substance either in career or in relationships that could guide his destiny, make him happy. The blue funk hovered. The couch looked inviting.

The door chimed and woke him up. Damn. He had read one page of his homework assignment and then conked to the zzzzs.

"Fill me in on the Corallos while we drive over to visit Morrie in the hospice. Heard about your tire damage. I've the wife's car." He did indeed. A matching Mercedes, her car color a light blue while his was white, a clone to the one the police still had in custody. The only difference, on the dashboard jiggled a bubblehead doll of the Mayor's likeness.

"Thanks for dropping off my briefcase this afternoon. I have these brain farts from time to time."

Owen recognized the Mayor's designer briefcase, moving it to the back seat and sat in its place as a dutiful passenger. As he made the transfer he noticed the briefcase tumbler locks on each latch. One number to each lock remained the same. If he continued with his foolish game, he needed to find only two numbers, one for each lock. 1-0. Simple deduction, if the opportunity ever arose. What city secrets were held within? Pointing to the briefcase, he asked, "Do you bring your work home with you? Do you take it everywhere?"

The Mayor gave him a quizzical look then smiled.

"This town is 24/7, so a Mayor must adapt to strange hours."

Owen overflowed with other questions, unspoken. How did the Mayor know about his Corvette's damage? Was Theodore a spy? Casey? Owen looked out to the street in the belief Byron Kane lurked with binoculars in the bushes. He saw the Mayor's hands on the steering wheel. The liver spot on the man's fingers were gone. It must have been a rash. Had Owen shaken hands with him recently, was the rash contagious? The Mayor saw his blank stare and initiated a conversation.

"Learn anything at dinner?"

"To take someone else's car to an ex mobster's restaurant."

On the drive over, they talked as friends. The Mayor could not believe Angel Corallo, the son, would do something so petty as to draw a police report being filed about incidents in front of a strip club he owned.

"We were trying to show up like curious tourists. At least we weren't beaten and thrown in the gutter."

"Not during the dinner rush. A smart guy like Corallo Junior would have given you slow leaks in your tires and let you go double digit flat on the highway. More cunning."

Thank God the Mayor wasn't pissed at him, thought Owen. To think of his poor injured baby to be left alone in the repair shop brought palpable pain.

"Did you find out anything from your people, anything that helps?"

"No, except the police are a little miffed that we met with Mrs. DiManna. Seems like they were slow in getting around to their interview and she decided to clam up except to lay it on thick how Chunky D voted for me in the last election."

"I assume they met her at a Carnivale slot machine?"

"Actually, no," said the Mayor. "I think Pauli was covering his backside, keeping any law enforcement away from her preprogrammed gaming. They all met in the coffee shop. The DiMannas and Corallos aren't going to be too mouthy. That's why it's important to reach Morrie. I once gave him legal help. He should be appreciative."

Since the Mayor would say no more about a past client and his history, Owen interpreted that whatever it was between them, the Mayor as a defense attorney had prevailed for client Bluestein.

"I keep hearing about the Cassandra robbery? It's part of Chunky D's obituary. Why is it so big?"

"For the history books, the biggest armed theft of the day, a lot of newspaper ink. The Cassandra robbery in May 1986 for the Wrecking Crew hit their career apex, the most jewelry ever stolen in the history of Vegas.

"Did they get caught?"

"Eventually, the gang fell apart. The Feds had the heat on organized crime. In Vegas, the Stardust skimming scandal raked in the indictments and court cases. In 1986, a year of judgment, the year

Spilotro and his brother were bludgeoned into unrecognizable pulp and buried in an Indiana cornfield. You know, just this year the Feds get a squealer on who knocked off the Spilotro brothers. Twenty years it takes for justice. Think about that.

"Remember Kane's story. With this robbery, the police shut down the entire town. Amazing. Bus stations and airports watched, every crook went under the microscope. The day after the robbery the police had rounded up Bobby Campi and Morrey Bluestein. The others — Corallo, DiManna and Scarpetti, turned themselves in with attorneys present. But there really was no conclusive evidence. The perps wore masks and gloves. The lady sales clerk who had been savagely beaten was in a week long coma and couldn't remember anything, or didn't want to try. With all the negative publicity, because the police and prosecutors couldn't make the case, several do-gooders within the Department bent over backward trying to create any case, including fabricating evidence. DiManna was the only gang member charged and convicted."

"I assume that's where you came in. I recall hearing you represented DiManna on his appeal, and won."

"Police misconduct is the anathema to any society; it's the last barrier before anarchy."

"Even if the *alleged* victims of injustice are hoodlums?" The Mayor, as an ex-defense attorney, liked the sound of 'alleged', and Owen heard him use it to suggest criminal bums guilty as hell might not be guilty until the fat jury sang.

"When the police become their own hoodlums, then who's to say they won't go after you or me. As to my clients, I am representing the law first and foremost. The evidence will play out as to truth."

"How about — who are the others, Scarpetti, Campi, and Corallo?

"The police hounded them and the prosecutors looked for any indictment that might work. They even tried to make Scarpetti, who played loose matches and fire, the number one suspect on the rocket fuel explosion that happened at the Pepcon chemical plant in Henderson. Crazy. That's five years later. No luck. Instead, drinking, whoring, and beating up a hooker got The Torch thrown in jail. And that's curious, now that I think about it. As to Corallo, that's even a longer story."

"Did he do jail time?"

"Yes, more than the others. Extortion and loan sharking, had his restaurant wired where he conducted business. Always felt he got a bum rap." The Mayor went quiet and Owen got the feeling this might have been one of those cases the Mayor did not win.

At the Temple Emmanuel Hospice, they found themselves barred at the receptionist desk.

"It's past visiting hours," the nurse ogre told Owen. Recognizing the Mayor her grouch wrinkles relaxed.

"An old friend asked me to drop by. Morrie Bluestein," said the Mayor, his best smile in place. "We won't stay long."

"Not long please, he's had a visitor a few hours ago. More company today than in the past six months. Tired him out. He may be sleeping. If you do wake him up, take some hard candy. Sweet tooth addiction. " She dropped multi-colored wrapped candies into Owen's hand.

"If he's asleep, we won't disturb him." They signed a guest register and logged in their time of arrival. When the nurse stuck her head in a medicine cabinet, Owen pointed out to the Mayor the sign in sheet and Bluestein's late afternoon visitor: Lorenzo Corallo.

The Mayor and Owen walked the antiseptic linoleum corridor, all lights lowered for the night. They passed the quasi hospital noises, muted televisions humming out static voices, snores or moans from darkened rooms. A nurse at the end of the hall scurried away from them carrying a tray of medicines, her body bounces making the glass bottles clink like shaken marbles.

The door to Bluestein's room midway down the corridor was closed. The Mayor pushed it open and darkness poured out.

"We have to wake him," whispered the Mayor. "I don't know when I can get back."

Owen searched for a wall switch, and clicked on a blue flourescent glare.

Bluestein lay there quiet. No, that was not true. He lay there dying, in a quiet horror.

His hands duct taped to the metal sides of his hospital bed, his feet likewise bound, spread apart. His mouth taped shut. His whole face, chest, and arms were covered with red marks. Owen looked close. *Moving red marks. Fire ants.* They were feasting on the hapless Mr. Bluestein.

"Good God," said the Mayor. He ever so gently tugged off the mouth tape. Owen undid the arms and legs from their bindings. Bluestein's legs shuddered and collapsed, his bitten arms, dangling flesh withered from the cancer. Owen was sure Bluestein offered no strength to resist his attacker. No, more like to fend off his torturer.

"Good God," said Owen, pointing to the bloody pulp at what had been the man's genitalia. Sliced and diced. A knife had been used, just like DiManna.

The room was muggy with the window open. Owen thought the ants might have come in the window as an afterthought to the old man being bound, but instead, he spied a small line of black ant scouts crawling in. *Never too late to join the party for dessert. The ants march in, the ants march out.*

Most amazing of all was that Morrice Bluestein was still alive. He grasped at Owen's hand, the grip light, frantic in spasmodic clawing. The old man tried to draw him closer.

The Mayor reached for the room phone, discovering it ripped from the wall, the connector torn off.

"I'll go for help. Untie him and brush off all those damn ants."

Owen did as he was told, realizing he was contaminating the crime scene, an exchange to save the victim. Dead ants stuck to his hand and he realized they had been teased with some liquid Owen. Closer inspection to find a sticky soup of crystal cut candy, mixed, spread like molasses, in the man's groin area, across his chest. That's what drove them crazy and beckoned the black ants outside to join the party. The fire ants had been brought in, that he was now sure of since laying there on a chair were two plastic tennis ball cans out of place, empty, that seemed to be the bug carrier. Bluestein, ancient and terminally ill, made weak groaning gurgles. His body, his crotch, looked ugly like chopped liver, the welts on his skin like advanced measles and chicken pox. His depleted body immune systems could not offset strange insect toxins.

He kept pulling Owen down toward him, until he was near the dying man's mouth, with its cracked lips, a smell of rotting teeth. Owen barely heard the words in raspy grunts of exiting air.

"Ants lost my fortune…Damn site nation…C or hell… D's knife…save me."

Then, a long release of wheeze and his grip fell off Owen, and Bluestein's chest rose no more. The silence in the room ended with a shout:

"Freeze! Don't move! Slow, put your hands up behind your head."

That voice? He knew the drill and found his wrists roughly hand-cuffed and then bodily spun around to find Detective C. T. Taggart pointing her service revolver at his chest.

"I didn't do this," he said, and the confusion set in. Shouts in the hall and running feet, a doctor and two nurses rushed in with an emergency crash cart.

One of the nurses gave a choked scream, "Oh Lord, look at him!" And with her gun still pointed at the handcuffed prisoner Chase finally looked at the semi-naked man in the bed, his sheets thrown back. She, who had seen gore and blood smeared on the interstate highways, still gasped at the crawling microscopic predators, engorging themselves while others writhed, trapped in a stickiness in splotches over his body and feasted where the blood had begun to coagulate between his legs, upon his emasculation.

"What the hell is this?" Her head turned to a new voice, her gun still on McCombs.

The Mayor of Las Vegas stood there with his mouth open.

"What are you doing to my friend? He's trying to save Morrie's life."

"He died, Mayor. Just after you left," said Owen, a calm voice from one who is handcuff. What he said put the Mayor into the deceased's room before she arrived. Owen spoke, like he was reassuring her, "Detective Taggart, those two tennis cans over in the chair, that's how the killer brought in the ants. They need to be secured immediately for fingerprinting."

Shit, and double shit, Chase said to herself. She aimed her most deadly look in Owen McComb's direction. Her revolver moved perceptively down, not by much. Go ahead, she wanted to yell at him, see what you've done: *You've made my fuckin' day!*

Part II

Brass: *Were there any disturbances last night? Did you hear screams?*

Lady Heather: *It's when I don't hear screams that I start to worry.*

— "Slaves of Las Vegas" Episode, *CSI* TV Show

Las Vegas Metro Police Building

1. Pressed Hard

The three of them sat there more as pre indicted coconspirators than witnesses to a brutal murder. The investigation buzzed around them. When questioned by first detectives on the scene the Mayor laid out the circumstances of their arrival. The reception nurse corroborated. The resident doctor confirmed that the ants had been at their human nibbling for an hour. The time frame placed the Mayor presiding in council chambers before hundreds of witnesses and the local access cable channel.

Chase grumbled at being told to sit and say nothing. Taking off the casino executive's handcuffs left her harboring mixed feelings. He offered cooperation telling his story without whining. The Mayor of Las Vegas swore to Owen's innocence. Therein lay the quagmire of police policy. The decision hers to make. He might be guilty of something. If not, his reputation could be damaged by her actions. He explained the nuances of such improper detention, his voice irksome, too gentle, like admonishing a wayward child. In transferring his out of state gaming license, as he explained, denial or postponement by the Gaming Board based on mere suspicions later proven unfounded, could create financial repercussions for him. In such a scenario, the city could be held accountable. Assured he would sit there to await the detectives' investigation she made the field decision and Owen sat there unfettered. Let the next honcho up the chain of command throw him in a cell. She continued her silent rant.

His attempt at cordiality sounded flippant.

"Did you find anything else in your search of my truck?"

"Yeah. You have a lot of dirty underwear in need of double bleach." She didn't know if true or not but it shut him up. Being in his presence bothered her, an uncomfortable feeling.

This time the politician and the casino executive could not avoid the press. With the arrival of the first police car there followed a television mobile truck, sniffing the police calls for live on the spot fillers (better with violence) for the late news. The Mayor drinking coffee at a crime scene set off the media frenzy, like hungry ants drawn to sticky candy.

McCombs and Detective Taggart both responded when they saw Detective Washington enter, Owen with alacrity of another fine mess he had stumbled into, and Chase the trepidation that she might appear to Ray as a grandstander, seeking glory for her own account. The Mayor cursed under his breath when the Sheriff and his echelon staff marched through the canyon of glaring cameras.

Everyone whispered, each trying to angle a way to see the grotesque corpse and wonder as to the bizarre death. The Coroner himself wanting to be in on this latest twist roamed the scene delegating the police CSI techies as diminutive vassals. After a while of sitting on plastic chairs, the three of them were escorted into a cafeteria room, a tape recorder and camcorder set up to document, and scary in itself, the Mayor and Owen were read their legal rights. Detective Taggart found herself standing to the side, once again within the bosom of fellow officers, closing ranks behind one of their own. Owen found the police only public interview highly unorthodox. He thought the Mayor would defer to his legal expertise and refuse to make a statement, and had he done so Owen would have screamed out: 'I want my attorney Clay Stokes to be present!' That would have set the powder keg ablaze.

Mayor Aurelius Stokes, his formal name, in perhaps the calmest attitude ever seen from an 'alleged' witness/suspect, cleared his throat, and step by step went through his arrival and what events had taken place as he recalled them. Owen noted the Mayor relished his return as a defense attorney, if only to defend himself.

The Mayor took not one step beyond the facts, gave no opinion or observation as to what had occurred beyond his direct eyesight. The investigator, a police commander, probably the boss to Detectives Washington and Taggart, asked if the Mayor had seen anyone entering or leaving. Beyond the nurse at the front desk, no, he replied. What he was doing visiting Mr. Morris Bluestein, a known friend and associate of Chunky D, both convicted criminals? The Mayor gave a small smile and answered without emotion, "I had come to ask Mr. Bluestein, a former client of mine, if he had any idea who might have killed Mr. DiManna. When we discovered Mr. Bluestein had been attacked I immediately went for help. And that is all I have to say at this time, gentlemen" — and seeing Detective Taggart in a corner –"and ladies." Owen saw Detective Taggart shift her weight and look away. She wanted, he could guess, to be back in the role as a case lead detective.

It was Owen's turn. Instead of interviewing them separately, he guessed the police hierarchy needed a civilian witness to show how the Mayor had been fairly treated. No rubber hoses in backrooms. Owen knew prior to his election as Mayor, Aurelius Stokes made a lot of money winning police brutality cases. The atmosphere in the room seethed of open antagonism held in check by fear of the Mayor's rapier-like legal reputation.

Owen, following the Mayor's lead, agreed to make a statement. What could be wrong with the truth? The click turning on the tape recorder gave a jolting wake-up call, enlightenment to his risk. For Owen, his head and job lay heavy on the chopping block, more so his entire future, economic lifestyle. At this stage in his life his only driving goal, a hunger for material success, mirrored in highs and lows within his mental stability This could not be dismissed as a friendly game, one hand played, his bet pushing several minor chips into a ho-hum pot. This analogy intensified: he was all in. Likewise, the Mayor's coincidences to strange death threw the city official into major controversy. Owen sensed recall petitions were being printed somewhere by unknown opponents, ready to pounce. The Mayor's political career stood at the brink of destruction.

The ten or so police officials in the room heard Owen speak almost verbatim to the Mayor's recollection, leaving out the minor detail of a dying man's deathbed babble. The hard faces in the crowd told him the police were not looking beyond the Mayor and himself for answers. The blunt realization hit. He and he alone, knowing the truth of his own innocence, would be the only unbiased party to get to the bottom of what seemed apparent, the serial killing of old men. *Old mobsters.* Perhaps naïve, Owen felt an eagerness to see what he could develop on his own, and fortunate or not, someone else sensed that characteristic in him.

Before the Chief Investigator could start his probing, Detective Taggart blurted out, "You said Bluestein was conscious when you arrived. What did he tell you when the Mayor left the room?"

Owen hoped she made a wild guess. Had she entered the room moments earlier? Had she heard Bluestein's failing voice? He hesitated and found her eyes behind a frown, maybe one second too long on his part, hoping all in the room took that as a pause.

"Nothing."

"How long were you in the room alone with Mr. Bluestein?"

"Less than a minute."

"And he said nothing?"

"Maybe he tried, after the Mayor took off the mouth tape. He came across incoherent, delirious." Owen knew he talked too much. From a total lie to a half-truth that made it sound a worse lie. The dying man mumbled, that's exactly what he had done, so it had been nothing. Nothing discernible at all, therefore, he said nothing.

Behind Owen a voice spoke above a whisper.

"A minute or less gives you enough time to suffocate a person."

Owen wheeled in anger at the accusation to meet stonewall official faces. His breaking level tested Owen took a deep breath and thought of past meditation classes, part of his stress therapy at a rustic retreat in the mountains near a glass smooth blue lake outside Boulder, Colorado. Breathe in, hold, release. *Om. Om.*

"Neither suffocation nor ants killed Mr. Bluestein," said Owen McCombs, giving a quote that would be a lead in the news stories thereafter, "Terror killed Mr. Bluestein."

The Chief Inquisitor, a Commander Stevens, threw a few questions at both witnesses trying to trip them. Relaxed explanations dovetailed exactly to each other's account. Owen felt Detective Taggart's outburst threw off the police commander's cage rattling technique. He could see the police official give his detective subordinate a disapproving stare.

After a few more questions, the Mayor said enough is enough, and departed. Owen followed. No one held them back. No one said, "Let's go down to headquarters." Like a leaderless wolf pack, hungry but indecisive, milling, snarling, command officials bickered for consensus to the next step. The two witnesses made a swift exit, squeezing through a phalanx of police officers. Owen found himself brushing the shoulder of Detective Taggart.

"We should visit," said the detective under her breath in a quick lump of fast words. Caught off guard, Owen yanked a slight nod, and rushed through the uniforms, wishing to tell her, "Sooner than you think."

If still on for dinner, how would tomorrow night go? 'Knock. Knock. I'm here for fried chicken. Remember me? You frisked me kinda hard last night.'

Outside, the piranha of working press fomented in blood frenzy, pushing and shoving toward their prey. Under harsh lights, microphones were thrust upon the Mayor. In his element but wary.

"Ladies and Gentlemen, I will have a formal statement from my office tomorrow. Let me just say tonight that one of my former clients has passed away under very disturbing circumstances. The police, in who I am quite confident, have started their investigation and it would be improper of me to comment beyond what Metro's public relations department might want to release to the public at this time. I wish to offer my respect and condolences to Mr. Bluestein's family."

The Mayor ignored shouted questions. They elbowed through the camera crews to the Mayor's wife's car, a most unfortunate mode of travel under these circumstances. In the glare of cameras, the robin egg blue Mercedes exactly resembled the Mayor's car of Chunky D fame. The car received camera focus. Owen would see over the next few days the film shots interpreted to no good. How could he show up to a new murder with the same vehicle tied to another? The bizarre could not get any worse.

A hand stopped Owen's car door from opening and he looked up to find some stranger with a shitty attitude dressed like a reject from a Polo ad with a bow tie affixed to a checkered shirt, an obsolete madras design, and wearing a corduroy jacket with elbow patches. The rude man hid his features behind a full face beard and shoulder-length hair. These descriptive facts mattered little. Owen, on a guess, tossed him into the cesspool as another reporter.

"Did you kill Bluestein or DiManna?" So blunt, Owen halfway reeled.

"No, of course not," he stammered. "That's ridiculous."

"Are you after the Cassandra jewels?"

"What are you talking about?"

"There's too much coincidence tied to the Wrecking Crew, and I think you and the Mayor have the answers." The car horn honked by the Mayor scared the men enough for Owen to jerk open the door which hit the reporter, doubling him over, tripping him to the ground. Owen locked the car doors and they crept away from their latest crime scene. His eyes darted to the rearview mirror.

"Who was that guy, that ass?"

"Congrats, your first vapid bite from Mr. West Pegler, investigative columnist for the *R-J*. He's a crime buster extraordinaire."

"Sounds like in the past he's given you some bad ink."

"We've had our run-ins. He's just finished a manuscript on the Vegas wise guys of the olden days. A hatchet job from what I hear. He went around interviewing all the players. I refused to talk to him. My past clients and their cases remain privileged."

"Telling a reporter where to stick it, you're a braver man than I."

"He's misquoted me so many times I think the public is even numb to his spew. I ignore him. You, Owen, on the other hand, better watch your back. If he's singled you out tonight he's poised to strike. Rattlesnakes would cross a busy highway to avoid him."

"Why me?"

"I'm sure he thirsts for fresh blood to write his by-line on the front page. Don't let this bruise your ego. You may just be a doormat for Pegler to slime across to get to me, or maybe try to muddy your boss, Jackson Flynn."

His new nemesis, West Pegler, who had earlier made the first entry on his enemy list, received a star for sleaze by his name. Owen straightened his back, startled at a new significance: the Mayor called him by his first name. He appreciated the familiarity. Involved in his second murder in two days, yes, a friend would come in handy.

They talked little on the way home, each lost in impacting thoughts. The Mayor now comprehended that these recent events, two murdered gangsters with him in the immediate vicinity, had damaged him politically.

"I'm going to set up another strategy meeting to discuss all recent events. The press will be lying in wait at my office. Let's shift over to Ferraro's, a great Italian restaurant, say at 2:00 p.m."

The car stopped in front of the Gold Avenue house, the one the Mayor had opened up to Owen without expectation, placing a shelter over his head, befriending him.

"Owen, between you and I, only you and I, what did Morrey tell you?"

"Nothing coherent, nothing that made sense."

He gave the young man a nod of partial acceptance.

"Let's talk about this tomorrow."

Watching the Mayor drive off Owen wondered if he let his benefactor down. He cussed as the shock wave of tonight's events caught up with him, overwhelming. Two torturous deaths associated with knife wounds. Each victim in a way trapped, one bound with ropes to a statue, the other bound to a hospital bed. Coincidence or methodical calling cards left by killers unknown? No startling answers came to mind as he studied all the uncertain, leaning angles of data in, data out.

As he entered the darkened house to begin his cram course on the construction details at the Magnum Casino site, Owen looked up at the Stratosphere Tower, a three legged sentinel blinking multicolored lights. The 24-7 city basted in heavy heat where the hum of constant traffic provided the base noise to all other party animal cries. For a moment he felt a pastoral peace sweep over him. He inhaled aromas of rosemary shrubs and heard shrills of night Mockingbirds. Then he glimpsed a car with extinguished headlights pull around the corner and to the curb, a block away, facing him and the house. Who had the authority to get past the guard gate? Owen could guess. He had been rewarded with an official undercover babysitter for no other reason than Owen McCombs seemed to attract Death. He just hoped that he and Death didn't schedule the same meeting.

3. Not the best of days

Not a great new day to be the Mayor of Las Vegas.

Theodore woke Owen before the alarm blared to watch sunrise television news, and even gave Owen first dibs on the morning newspaper. Two murdered men, both with a past association to the Mayor brutally tortured and slain, and the Mayor both times first on the scene. Guilt by association. The stories interwove tidbits from the politician's past life as a criminal defense attorney so when crafted as a ten second sound bite or the lead headline, the tone implied corruption in high office.

Casey with worry asked, "Is he involved?"

She approached the couch from behind. The smell of coffee permeated his nostrils, and Owen found his reward in the extra mug offered from her hands. Caffeine, an addiction of which he approved. Casey slid over the couch to sit between the two men. Her morning outfit consisted of only a large Graceland Forever t-shirt that hung to mid hip. If she were to reach up on her toes, like to reach a glass from a high shelf, a small patch of dark Elvi hair between her legs would be visible. This thought braced Owen awake. Theodore's nonchalance at her closeness to both men signaled accepting Owen as noncompetitive.

"He's not guilty of anything. He's involved because some lowlife is trying to frame him."

"And we need to save him," echoed Theodore.

Owen agreed on the premise, yet unwilling to create the Three Amigo Crime-busters. "We—someone needs to find answers. Basic 'who, what, and why', or rather, 'motive, opportunity, identification', and then let the police have the rest: 'apprehension, confession and incarceration'. Unfortunately, I know how police on a high profile case think, and since they see a connection between the Mayor's presence at two crime scenes, all their manpower is on overtime connecting dots, whether they exist or not."

"Hey, there's you," chirped Casey, bouncing on the couch like a rah-rah college girl. "The camera makes you look ..." She searched for the right word. Owen laughed to himself, guessing if she made him look too good she'd end up with a cranky Theodore. Handsome, therefore, out. She instead said, "Fuzzy." Owen, on the television screen, could be seen standing behind the Mayor, out of focus. That's how Theodore probably saw him-- as a blurry nonentity. Theodore strolled to the kitchen and Casey leaned toward Owen and whispered in her Elvis voice, "Really, ma friend, you are one hunka, hunka burnin' luv. A bunch of wild-on women right now are calling the T.V. station trying to track down where you live." Owen accepted her comment as over-exuberance. Still, a compliment from a woman, a cute kid at that, resonated well within his fragile psyche.

Theodore returned just as the T.V. camera followed the Mayor and Owen to the Mercedes, and the camera panned into a close-up of the casino executive being accosted by Pegler.

"Hey, you hit him," said Theodore.

"No, the car door hit him and he tripped."

"Sure." Casey's voice snipped in mock belief.

The television reporter commented, "And the gentleman accompanying the Mayor is reported to be Mr. Owen McCombs, a high-ranking official at Magnum Casinos. Magnum, as everyone by now should be aware, is building a new mega resort on the Vegas Strip.

Only the day before yesterday the body of Charles 'Chunky D' Di-Manna was discovered at the Magnum Casino construction site, and by the Mayor and Mr. McCombs. At this time we cannot say if Mr. McCombs is an emissary of Jackson Flynn, Magnum's owner and how Magnum Casinos fits into these strange chain of events."

"Ouch." Ms. Melissa Steele was going to ream him a new asshole for endangering the casino's sacrosanct reputation.

"Hey, I wonder what Pegler wrote about you," said Theodore, tearing through the morning newspaper. He read the headline tease:

"Mayor and Mob in Deadly Embrace."

Theodore read Owen into a depression. He would need to take two pills this morning. In one paragraph, Pegler suggested that a cover-up existed, possibly tied to construction overruns at the new casino site. To Owen, a new twist.

Theodore gave emphasis as he approached the end of Pegler's column:

As most of my readers know, for the last several years I have been documenting the seamy side of the hidden criminal organizations in this city. We now have seen them reappear and rear their ugly heads with bloody vengeance. What is the truth? In my upcoming book, 'Wise Guys of Vegas', I will trace the history of mob influence in Southern Nevada. Where I thought the story had ended in the 1990's with convictions, Black Book inclusions, retirements by rub-out and natural causes of old age, perhaps I have been a little premature. Coming soon: the rest of the inside story.

"Hey, Case, here is a photo of a bunch of Elvis impersonators."

She looked over Theodore's shoulder and read the brief article. "That's the Executive Committee of Elvi International. They're in town for a midyear meeting. This year's convention is in Atlantic City. They're now scouting cities for the next convention. I hear it could be between Las Vegas and New Orleans."

Owen joined in. "I hear New Orleans is having more rough weather. Maybe that'll help Las Vegas' chances. If held here, does that give you home field advantage?"

She moped. "If only. Someday Elvis babes will rule."

Theodore asked, "Do you go to these Elvi meetings?"

"Oh, no, not the Executive Meetings. Those people are the purists who run Elvi International Expo (EIE). The big cheeses."

Owen inspected a photo montage of the nursing home crime scene and lousy shots of the Mayor and himself exiting the building. He re-read West Pegler's column in disgust.

"Hey, look at the T.V. It's national news running a story on the Graffiti Vigilante," said Theodore. "I guess besides you and the Mayor reeking mayhem last night, seems like the Vigilante struck again."

They watched a T.V. story with vague film showing faces and painted butts obscured with protective digital fuzz, as Owen saw it, to protect the 'alleged' innocent and heard the story of vandals caught, a twenty second news bite before commercials.

Casey recapped. "Two of them this time, a guy and a girl trussed up and spray painted. Local press might dismiss this, say it's a prankster, but the national tabloids will have a field day. Portray us as an armed mob. But the Vigilante guy is only defending property rights."

"This cowboy uses a stun gun to control. Expect to start seeing a copycat national craze."

"Good for the Vigilante," said Casey, "get those punks."

"Hey, some of those night riders might be my friends."

"Then, I'd watch your own butt and keep it clean." She laughed, not at Theodore, but at her own wit.

That gave Owen an idea.

He said to his roommates, "Let's play a word game. Here are some words and phrases I want you to help me with. Say I ran into a drunk, in fall down inebriation, here in Las Vegas. He was trying to tell me how to get him home, to find his address and that maybe a friend was there to meet him. The drunk said, slurring, 'The aunts lost my fortune...Damn site nation...C or hell'. "I guess the letter 'C'."

Theodore, who lived in a Playstation world, relished games. Casey liked thrills. They buzzed with questions. They made Owen write down what he was saying.

"Is he Anglo?" "Old or young?" "Was he born in Las Vegas?"

"White, very old, and a longtime resident, probably not born in Las Vegas." They gave sideways looks to each other.

He left them flipping through word association and singsong rhymes.

Owen began his first true work day. He dressed for success and arrived at the Magnum Casino construction site twenty minutes before his debut as tour guide. His prep work confidence faded when he confronted Ms. Steele, oozing with lack of charm.

"What the crap are you doing!?" She looked marvelous sans the frown.

"And by that you mean?"

"Well, other than finding a murdered man on a once a day basis since your arrival, and leaving me with all the national newspapers and TV shows that want exclusives, as well as a press room to set up their cameras for prime time, and all believing that Mr. Flynn must somehow be involved. Thank you very much, Mr. McCombs."

"None of this is of my doing."

"What comfort," the ice laid on . "That I think will calm the paparazzi and tabloids. Are they going to believe me? Not. I hope you don't have any skeletons in your own closet."

Melissa interpreted his startled frozen expression.

"Oh, I hope not. Please tell me it's not so!" And she shook her head in total defeat visualizing the mud she would be washing off the Magnum Casino corporate facade for the foreseeable future.

A horn honked outside. The Chinese delegation had arrived.

"Oh, that reminds me. They've added some more visitors to the tour group. I'm sure you'll handle it in your normal productive style."

That was not the voice of confidence.

"More Chinese?"

"Does it really matter? Go sic'em. I've got budget meetings all morning. Don't call me, please." She dismissed him with a wave of her hand, definitely the imaginary push out the door.

The Chinese guests unloaded from a mini tour bus. They came in all shapes and sizes, all dressed in business suits, though the late morning was notching up to oven mode. After they all exited, one young lady, the only one in their group, assumed the role of the assigned cultural aide from either Magnum Casino or the Las Vegas Convention and Visitor's Bureau. She approached Owen and, in English, with a slight accent, introduced herself as Miss Lydia Chan.

"Mr. McCombs? May I present officers of the Macau Gaming Authority." There were nine of them. He bowed, not deeply, a definite deep head nod, and said to them all, in choppy Cantonese, "Welcome. It is very good to meet you all." After which he repeated his greeting in Portuguese. Macau had been a former Portuguese colony. They all looked bemused, and smiled, and one gentleman clapped and another said to Owen in a thick deep South U.S. brogue, still finding it difficult to pronounce several of his consonants, "You hit home run."

Lydia Chan smiled. "The Authority members all speak English to various degrees. If you speak slow, they can comprehend. English is the business language of Asia and they are eager to practice it. Many learn from U.S. Armed Forces radio stations. I will help translations on any technical wording."

Owen, the tour guide casino host, turned to them all, speaking loud in annunciated cadence, "Thank you. As guests of Magnum Casino and Resorts, Mr. Jackson Flynn and the executive staff of Magnum Las Vegas welcome you." The group nodded with smiles. From his vest pocket came a gold brass calling card case. Owen took out business cards, created this morning by Theodore and his trusty Adobe design center. Magnum's address and telephone (702/726-5000) and a noble title: *Owen McCombs, Managing Partner, Senior Executive.* Whatever that meant, it did sound like Owen sat next to the almighty throne. With dignified aplomb, he handed each gentleman a card with his two hands as one hand might be perceived as an affront. They all dove for their own cards. This ceremony created face, and very important to do it right. Like a tea ceremony presentation. He read each card with serious intent, sought to pronounce the gentleman's name, and in one or two instances made a smiling comment of being impressed as to their important titles. Each card received went into his shiny card case. It would be rude to stuff their business cards into his coat pocket; it would imply he was discarding them as individuals.

As the exchange of pleasantries ended they were interrupted by the dusty arrival of a stretched lime green Hummer limousine. In another tradition of power politics where the Chinese are protocol punctual, V.I.P. Americans lean toward *le grande tardy* entrances. The chauffeur opened the door, and from the air-conditioned interior, the new guests exited with hiked skirts and shoulder twists to their long hair: three striking women, or rather two out of three.

The most beautiful, whose glistening smile engulfed the men of the Chinese delegation, was the girlfriend of his attorney. Kathleen Grayson Sawyer.

She walked in brisk, strutting strides to Owen, held his shoulders, kissed both cheeks, lip-stick imprints, and said, "What a beautiful day." Her closeness, her touch, her perfume overwhelmed his senses. To the Chinese, who were noticing their tour host had great joss with a beautiful woman, she gave a light yet formal bow and spoke greetings in both Mandarin and then Cantonese. To Owen, she winked and whispered, "Learned this in my early life world travels for Grayson International Real Estate." She waved her friends over. "Shall we begin? I don't know if I will like what Jackson is building on Daddy's land."

Kathleen Sawyer waved intros as she walked off holding Owen's arm as the procession began, "This is Lindsey and Sally Ann," not designating which was which. To the two women she said, "This is Owen, he's the Mayor's new best bud. Quite a dangerous fellow, aren't you Mr. McCombs?" Oh yeah, 'danger' was his middle name.

Noticing Melissa Steele glaring at him behind the window blinds of her office, he felt more heat added to that of the broiling sun.

The tour began in the mobile trailer that housed the miniature display of the Magnum Casino Las Vegas. Everyone crowded around, intrigued. Instead of taking a large group through mounds of dirt and interfering with construction workers, he wanted to keep everything under tight control. It soon became apparent that each member of the Chinese delegation exhibited themselves as a specialist on construction or casino operations or gaming regulatory affairs. From memory of last night's cheat sheets, his work in smaller Colorado casinos, and into midrange operations in Biloxi, he could cover most of their questions.

Security, he told them, would consist of over 850 cameras throughout the casino. No, 'shoulder gambling' would not be allowed. In Asian casinos where there were more bettors than gaming chairs at a table, many times people two to three deep would stand over the shoulder of the regular gambler and make side bets on the hands being played, Baccarat and Pai Gow being the most popular games. To another question he answered Magnum's concierge and casino host staff would number close to sixty people, with each employee required to know, other than English, two languages fluently. In fact, Magnum employees were called "cast members" as operations were a 24-7 performance. This was a page from the Disney World ops. Yes, there would be employee child daycare on premises; no, at this time it has not been established to have the casino workers become unionized. Yes, the other Magnum properties were nonunion. Unionism, a sticky question and Owen didn't know the ultimate answer. The Culinary Union, the most effective and powerful union in the country, would not tolerate a mega-casino to operate non-union, and as an organizer would battle at the ramparts for a toe-hold. He did not know which way Jackson Flynn would go so he hedged the bet to his listeners with 'it's under consideration'.

"What about the performing arts theatre showroom?" The question came from one of Kathleen's tagalong friends. She seemed to be in her early twenties, a slouching posture, her brown hair seemed unwashed, uncombed, her nose somewhat crooked, and an obnoxious raisin looking wart on one ear. He launched into his memorized notes on entertainment for the Magnum Casino, and concentrated on what he called 'the finest theatre stage yet created'. There would be 3,500 seats where everyone had an unobstructed view of the stage; the sound system state of the art, with the ceiling made up of baffling panels looking like flying saucer artwork, space-age science to disperse sounds even. If the venue had a smaller audience, the room could be broken into sections without losing style or sound quality. He pointed out that the Theatre Arts Showroom would be smaller than the Exposition Arena, a part of the planned Magnum Convention Center that could hold 14,000 people in concerts with a retractable half roof.

The young lady's next questions on acoustics brought his sales pitch back to the smaller showroom. He answered a few more probing questions. She asked them in an intelligent manner. He couldn't recall whether she was the Lindsey or the Sally Ann. Her compatriot, tall and rock solid, remained silent. This woman did not look but stared, intimidating, her eyes probing at the surroundings, at the tour group. That lady spent too many waking hours in the gym, Owen thought. She towered over the Chinese in muscle bulk. Her beauty lay in an Amazon physique, statuesque, ripple hard. Bemusing, he observed, when the Chinese were not considering the casino model, their stares disrobed the three women. The questioning lady ignored them and concentrated on the entertainment venues Magnum had in design. At the right moment Owen took the tour out the door to sun-walk the construction site. After about twenty minutes of pointing at vacant land being torn apart saying this is where this will be or that will be built, he was interrupted. The Chinese caucusing spoke to Ms. Chan who, in turn, deferred to one of the senior Chinese gaming officials. In all formality, with a slight head bow, and in broken English, the elder Chinese dignitary said, "We like see where gangsta killed."

Deferring to the Chinese request, and not to offend, he walked them toward the now infamous garage.

As his tour group made its way around the casino hotel's Grand Canyon sized basement, they literally bumped into another hard hat group walking toward them with architectural plans in hand. There were four of them, two in construction fatigues and the other two business suited. Owen recognized one of the hard hats and immediately introduced himself to Wayne Hollister, the project's overall Construction Manager. His greeting somehow poisoned the air, as if Hollister had opened a door and there stood Owen, a traveling salesman selling a pandemic virus.

This was the man, not a Magnum employee, who had been in the marketing trailer after Chunky D had been discovered. The builder who did not want the police to shut the site down. Owen knew his title and position as construction site General Manager, representing Carroll & Son, the overall general management contractors. Feeling the chill in the sweltering day, Owen chose not to introduce everyone to each other. Hollister said nothing so the two groups passed each other and went their separate directions. Owen gave a backward glance. The construction GM's rugged face, sun exposed, fit his personality, coarse and cracked like untreated leather. In his body language Hollister did appreciate the tour group on site.

In his hike, Owen sketched with his finger in the air where the water feature "Speed Lake" would be dug in replacing the soon to be imploded El Morocco Oasis building. His inquisitive young guest,

Kathleen's friend, made a strong request to pass by the location where the Magnum Showroom would be, and Owen offered several additional comments for her benefit, pointing out the close proximity of the Showroom to valet parking, to the center of the casino itself, and how the back entrance would allow the primary star and eventual visiting guest stars to exit and enter to assigned private suites without ever having to deal with an inquisitive public.

The summer heat was getting to everyone. The girl with the questions had sweat droplets smearing her makeup and her nose seemed to droop. It was time to shade rescue everyone. Kathleen Sawyer, during his tour, either stood with her girlfriends chattering, or hovered near Owen, leaving him awkward and uncomfortable. Her smiles were coquettish, not aggressive, merely hint teases. The tour to her seemed a game, but her antics were light, not overt to embarrass him.

They all entered the garage. Yellow crime scene tape lay torn and discarded. Association with death found all the employee cars crowded near the front of the ramp. Further down, no cars were parked, except one under a cloth protective cover. An antique automobile.

Mellisa Steele earlier suggested he pull back the car cover and talk about the 'transportation theme' of the casino. Owen felt she wanted to see if he could extemporaneously fend for himself. Owen had to wing it and did so.

"As you recall the theme of our project is Transportation, and I am pleased to let you be the first people to have a glance at one of the automobiles that will go into our casino collection."

The Chinese were impressed that they were so honored with a 'first'. He prayed this was not Ms. Steele's joke to punish him, like some casino executive had covered up his car to protect the wax finish from the outside alkaline construction dust. With a second for suspense, Owen removed the car cover.

Gorgeous was a weak description.

A maroon convertible Duesenberg.

"What year is this?" from one of the Chinese, peering in the window.

Owen's answer would have been a guess, and he felt relief that Kathleen jumped in.

"This is a Model J, 1929. It has a Le Grande body. Straight eight twin cam. Duesenberg was the only auto designer-builder to win a Grand Prix with this car." She reeled off the details. "For those who might know automobiles, this is a 110 points in the ranking classification."

Several of the Chinese nodded as if understanding. Owen could see his late night homework expand to new dimensions. To represent Mr. Flynn he would have to become a connoisseur of classic autos. Owen let the Chinese delegation take photos, nervous that one smear might devalue this metal masterpiece. After all, when casino owner Steve Wynn elbowed a hole in his Picasso, millions of dollars of value flitted away.

Escorting his tour away from such calamity, they all walked as requested to the bottom of the garage where Owen pointed out where the Mayor's Mercedes had been parked. From there they walked through doors, past a bank of parking elevators outdoors into green vegetation. A small information sign read: *The Garden of Allah*. He found himself next to Kathleen.

"How did you know about the Duesenberg?"

"Sotheby's Annual Auto Auction in Palm Beach. Sold by the Atlantis Foundation. That Duesenberg sold for $2.5 million. Set a record for that vintage. Gossip reported a private unnamed buyer. Voila! I subscribe to all sorts of auction catalogues, attend when I can. Pick up a few small art pieces now and then, nothing in Jackson's price-is-no-object league."

The second time she called Mr. Flynn, 'Jackson'. How well did she know the casino owner? Owen surmised that if Mr. Flynn ever came out in the light of day he and Kathleen would be hobnobbing in the same social strata. Owen took a deep breath. He had watched the Chinese touch and lean against a small fortune. He better go back later to the Duesenberg with a wipe cloth.

Kathleen gripped his arm, a hard squeeze not a caress.

"I don't think I can handle a murder scene. Gross."

"Oh, come on, Kath," said her short friend, scratching (or was it adjusting) her hair. "This is your crazy town, live to the max." Kathleen tried protesting while her young friend, laughing, dragged her along. Owen, as he had passed from garage to garden, eyed where he thought the camera monitor would be. Nothing remarkable stood out, just dark opaque glass covering a black painted wood box, the camera if any, hidden within. If the casino closing date was 1982, current technology had made the camera and surveillance system obsolete exponentially, stone-age old.

The Chinese contingent, observing the garden, seemed impressed. The setting had several feng shui elements including a water pond with swimming Koi and round river rocks set in formed design in raked dirt. A scalloped concrete pathway meandered between garage and casino building. A true road need not be straight. Owen saw the garden's boundaries enclosed by two fake walls on either side, between garage and casino building that went up two stories open to the sky like an atrium, so the sun hit center garden area midday allowing the building shade to offer a dry heat comfort. Vegetation included rainbow colored desert flowers, some scattered bunches of purple petunias and gold flowered sagebrush, odd sized palm and pine trees, and immaculate trimmed putting green grass. There were four pods of trees surrounded by floral accents, and tall hedges lined the sides of the buildings. In a corner, Owen observed, was a small tool shed for gardeners, and in the middle surrounded by ivy vines was the bronze head of the bumped-off Frederico Bandanni, listed as Frederick Orr, the most notorious of the General Managers of the El Morocco Oasis. The metal head sat on a granite pedestal and faced the pathway.

"Where he shot and chopped, this Chunk gangsta?" asked one of the Chinese. They must have all been studying local papers to bone up on their English and to see what the hot attractions were with the 'gansta's' homicide the most exciting venue in a real time Sin City.

Owen played along. "I believe he was killed at the base of this statue." There did seem to be an indentation where the crime scene specialists had core sampled some bloody mud. Digital cameras from the dignified tourists clicked away.

"Oh, my God!" Kathleen Sawyer stared at the wall on the other side of the walkway. Owen could see that a large chunk of concrete or stucco had been torn from the wall, and a large plaque had fallen to the ground. Kathleen rushed to the wall and Owen quickly followed.

She bent down and pushed the large brass plaque over. He saw an etched face and read aloud the inscription: "Donald Grayson, owner of Grayson Real Estate, owner of the El Morocco Oasis. Always to be remembered by family and friends. 1940-1986."

"Dad was so proud when he bought the El Morocco. Thought this would be his crowning achievement. He brought me here several times, told me fairytale stories of Ali Baba and the Forty Thieves, Aladdin and his magic lamp; he said the casino people called this the 'Garden of Allah'. He promised to rename it in my honor when the place reopened. The last time I saw him, at the airport the day he was killed, he gave me a going-away present. On the gift card he simply wrote, 'See you soon in the Garden of Allah, where wishes come true'." She swallowed a distant unpleasant memory. "I was not feeling well that week. My father, a true saint, made me smile through my tears. His plane blew up in front of me, flying wreckage injured me. For many reasons that week, I died." A tear fell on her Father's image. Owen sensed he was the first person in many years to see her vulnerability. A damaged little girl within an outward fancy shell.

"I am so sorry," Owen said, meaning it, hefting the plaque and leaning it against the wall. "It looks like stucco gave way. Building is about fifty years old. I'll have one of the workers remount it as quickly as possible."

"No, it's not necessary. I will request your Ms. Steele to send this to our offices before the building is torn down. Maybe they could do it now?" she glanced at the Chinese snapping group pictures of themselves in front of the statue bust of Bandanni—"before anything else happens." Her eyes had moistened to a goddess glisten, her smile to Owen one of warmth and he returned a smile to give her solace. His mind sparked that this garden would be a wonderful place to make love. Not a place to be tortured and slain. Kathleen Sawyer placed her hand over Owen's. "Thank you."

As the Chinese were doing group photo sessions and enjoying a cigarette break, Owen wandered the pastoral premises. He poked his head into the gardener's plastic tuff shed where there were shovels, rakes, a hand cart with empty black plastic shrub and flower buckets, assorted tools and garden chemical boxes. The casino building over-looked the garden area. He tried the doors into the casino. A door opened, a chain and lock dangling from the door handle on the inside. He proceeded no further. He accepted his position as an outsider to the Jackson Flynn inner sanctum. He did wonder. Since there were offices on the top floor, perhaps a distracted worker might have witnessed a murder in progress. Did the police question those upstairs employees? Did any detective take Jackson Flynn's statement, wher-ever he might be?

He considered the crime. One only uses torture to extract infor-mation, or perhaps for revenge. Had Chunky D blabbed a confession of sorts to stop the knife cuts? Had Bluestein? Faced with a slasher whatever answers they gave weren't enough. What had his killer re-ally been after?

His wanderings led him to his other two female guests who were in the shade leaning against the windows. He noticed the reflection of the younger one in the office building window glass. Two of the same: duality.

Then it hit. Without thinking, he said to the ugly girl, "If your face is uncomfortable, why don't you just take it off?" And Owen leaned toward her and plucked off the wart and attached ear from the plain, witchy woman who had been peppering him with questions the en-tire walk around.

Bam! Owen saw sky, felt pain. His arm had been grabbed and twisted from behind, his legs kicked from underneath.

The Amazon who had given him the kung fu demonstration stood over him with her fists clenched, ready to hand out a more merciless beating. She awaited the command. The short girl wore a surprised expression, no anger, more impish. Her smile from underneath the disguise underscored remarkable beauty. Owen knew that. The world knew that.

The Chinese delegation stared at his humbling loss of dignity, amazed at the husky woman's karate takedown. Everyone's eyes turned to the young woman unmasking like watching a butterfly emerge from the cocoon. She removed her face of flesh colored rubber epoxy. Yanking off her wig to reveal sand blonde hair she shook her head from side to side, a trademark to those who had watched she and her sister perform.

"This whole masquerade is just too damn hot."

"Dell," exclaimed one Chinese businessman. "Hi-Jinx", said another. Within a second they were all chattering and snapping their cameras. Kathleen walked over with a wide grin. She, not the steroid Godzilla, helped Owen to his feet.

The most dignified of all the Chinese businessmen could only mumble, "You Hi or Jinx?"

The Dell sisters were identical twins, probably the most famous in the world, unbelievably talented singing sensations with a few movie credits under their thin-waisted belts. They had been childhood television sitcom stars and then hit the concert stage circuit with several number one Billboard hits, "Rush to Lust" being the current Number One single. That song moved them up from preteen bubblegummers who had never caught Owen's attention, into sex kittens who everyone had to watch cavort in numerous television specials. Indeed, Owen had touched a forbidden idol. Awkward and lame, he handed back her wart and ear, which she took with a pixie laugh. She lifted her blouse to pull out some extra padding that had been applied for a hefty tummy look.

Her body guard (Owen could well attest) handed her a hair brush and picked up the mask elements and padding. Every day the story of the Dell twins blared out as documented fodder on the supermarket magazine stands. Their parents named the twins Hillary and Jennifer, stage names later born from agents and marketing reps to fit their personalities as precocious kiddies now budding screen and music legends. To thousands of shoving paparazzi, millions of adoring fans, they were known simply as Hi-Jinx.

To Kathleen Sawyer, Hi or Jinx said, "I guess we'll just have to keep trying other disguises, ones that work in this heat." And to her protector she gently said, "Okay, Blaze, turn them loose." Her bodyguard, no longer Lindsey or Alice, moved aside and the Chinese crowded closer. The super star did her super star fan stuff, shook their hands, posed for pictures, and signed autographs on ties, shirts, arms, and business cards.

"Where's her sister," Owen looked to Kathleen.

"Reading endorsement contracts back in their hotel suite. They might have lawyers and agents hovering for their percentages, but you'd be surprised how bright these girls are."

"And how do you know them?"

"Originally, through the Grayson Foundation, supporting charity functions on both coasts. Plus, in some ways we speak the same language." Owen understood this to mean how wealthy and public people are to carry the weight of their social responsibilities. Perhaps it wouldn't hurt Kathleen from time to time to sell them a Grayson investment property.

The fixated group followed half of the Dell twins out of the garden. Blaze, the bodyguard, her cell phone out and chirping, issued martial commands. By the time they reached the top of the parking garage, the hummer limo waited, air-conditioning powered up, the star's door open.

Goodbyes were handed out. Kathleen Sawyer took Owen's hand and in a gracious whisper, "Thank you. You are a sweet man." Their eyes met and silent intensity exchanged. She is a star in her own small Vegas world and she knows it.

The Dell twin beckoned Owen over to the limo. She pulled him half in and gave his cheek a kiss.

"I bet you're good. You'll be seeing more of me, Mr. McCombs."

"Disguised or uncovered?"

"Let's just see." The door slammed and half of the most popular singing group in the world spirited away. Now it came to him: The Magnum Theatre Showroom. Jackson Flynn is considering the Dell Twins as his premiere feature act. If Mr. Flynn could land them, their shows would be sold-out months in advance, as strong as those of the past: Elvis at the Hilton, Siegfried & Roy at the Mirage, Celine at Caesars. Perhaps that's why the job transfer, Jackson Flynn wanted him to handle the talent program for the Magnum Casino.

Owen McCombs basked in the limelight, a hero to the Chinese delegation. As the translations of thanks poured back to him, Owen learned that they could not wait to greet Mr. Flynn on his next trip to Macau. Mr. Flynn, on his arrival, would find instant access to the decision makers.

Translator Chan in her goodbye said, "You have done my countrymen a great honor. You have no problem that we convey to Mr. Flynn that you were quite helpful."

No problem at all. *That's 'McCombs' with one 's' and two 'c's.*

He waved them all goodbye, bowed several times to their bows. For a first try, he gave his tour effort high marks. It looked like this day would be a vast improvement over the past several. He saw Melissa Steele motioning him over to her trailer, into her web. Ready for anything, he took strong strides in her direction. He could handle this uppity brat.

5. Fettered to the Case

Detectives Washington and Taggart awaited Fetters to join them. In a shitty mood, the senior detective ranted.

"Another high profile murder. New players on stage; I've been shuffled aside for more important V.I.P.s."

"Another press conference?" she assumed.

"Yeah, on center stage, District Attorney Lattemore and the local FBI chief, a guy by the name of Auger."

"I've met the D.A. but not the FBI. I assume these people don't hold the Mayor in their high esteem."

"Lattemore is geared up to run against Stokes. If these murders fuel the public awareness, Lattemore would spin it to his advantage. Do you recall that prosecutor in the Binion murder trial gained the publicity to move to higher elected office?"

"This is turning into a shit fest. The FBI is going to start crowding in on our turf, put their faces in front of potential witnesses. Jam up the works."

Late as if planned, Detective Fetters sauntered in and up to Washington's desk, offering the smell of a bull session rather than a case update. Fetters threw out his nasty boy smile to Chase and she glanced back down at her paperwork. Little Mikey annoyed her and he knew it; she could see his pheromones surge. Chase wanted to get in his face and say: 'Instead of being in your presence I'd rather be on Fear Factor swallowing a bowl of live maggots.

"Mike, wha'd you find out of the Scarpitti torch job?"

"Wop fricassee," said Fetters. "I went down there and read through the prison's internal investigative file. They're pretty sure it's some Latino gang members. Can't focus on who or the motive. Seems they're more riled up over how the accelerant fuel was smuggled in. Think a guard might be involved. That ticks them off more than inmates offing each other."

"Nothing in his cell?"

"Nada. A little strange. In the yard after his self-barbecue, they found burned cardboard with string attached." He glanced at his note scrawls. "Names written, 'H.H. and Gen' nothing else. They're checking names of inmates for similarities. Definitely planned to cook him, some ashed out words, something like, 'all burn'. No one down there, the guard clique, has any clue how to investigate a real whodunit. Cell stabbings, sure, they're the experts."

How about the Torch's phone records, visitor log-in?" Ray and Chase were taking notes.

"Used to be a real loner. No family. Five months ago, this guy, the R-J reporter Pegler pays a visit. Four visits over a two month period. Warden says Pegler had permission to interview Scarpetti for a book he's writing. Said he was doing a chapter on the Wrecking Crew."

"Yeah," said Washington. "I saw Pegler last night at the Hospice covering Bluestein's death. Not to be trusted, especially how he'd translate your words into his quotes. What else?"

"Well, about a month ago, The Torch got a call from our trunk friend, Chunky D, and a week later from Larry Corallo. Some old beef gave the FBI sanctioned taps, but they aren't giving us squat. The warden glanced at the transcripts, said all they talked about was weather and family. Maybe code. Both DiManna and Corallo visited Scarpetti two weeks ago, on different dates."

"Can we get a copy of the recordings?" Chase jumped in.

"As I said, FBI are not in a sharing mood."

"Why are they involved at all?"

"Ancient crime-fighting vendettas," explained Ray. "FBI used to have a major office here in the 70s, beefed up after the Kefauver Hearings. Under pressure to kick the crime families out of the casino industry, they did too good of a job. Put them out of biz. My guess is, if the FBI can use these killings to make a big stink about organized crime resurfacing, they could generate more funding for their local office."

Detective Washington spoke to his partner.

"What about the Bluestein murder?"

"Prelim only. Autopsy results still pending. The Coroner thinks the ant juices and cuts were enough to cause a seizure."

"Cuts?" smirked Fetters. "Heard the guy lost his dong."

Chase had enough.

"The killer made slices in Bluestein's gonads and chopped off his penis for good measure. Sharp knife, says the Coroner." Chase let the two men do their natural male cringe. "They're going to try and match the knife striations with the DiManna knife we have. See if it was a paired set.

"The only fingerprints we lifted in the room," Chase finished, "after we eliminated the doctor and nurses, were the Mayor's and Owen McCombs's."

Fetters tried his own nasty retort.

"Heard you had that fellow in handcuffs and let him go."

Ray interceded.

"She made a wise choice. Someone else in that position might have shot McCombs on the spot."

Fetters ignored the insinuation. "Both of them are involved. I'd pull the Mayor in for a little brass knuckle talk…or this McCombs character."

"That's why they want me in charge of the investigation."

"Not if the D.A. and the Fibbies have their way."

Chase stood up to break the intensity. Ray calmed to re-exert his leadership. "I did check the sign in log at the hospice. The Mayor and McCombs signed as did Bluestein's other visitor, Larry Corallo. According to the nurse on duty at the time he arrived earlier in the day before dinner. When he left, the nurse said, Bluestein was crying but not enough to stop him griping for extra grape jell-o for his meal. Gave him candy for dessert."

"Wrong menu choice. Someone used the candy to let the ants suck him off." Fetters chortled at his own wisecrack.

"Corallo coulda come back," said Chase.

"Could have. We need to check Larry's alibi. I'll track him down."

Washington assigned Fetters to interview writer Pegler.

"He'll just spout journalistic confidences, first amendment stuff, freedom of the fuckin' press, and he'll tell us to stick it," Fetters pre-conditioned his expectations.

"First or Fifth Amendment doesn't cover the conversations of dead men," said Washington. "Mike, I made you point man with the Feds. I want to know everything they're doing."

"Yeah, I'm on it. Don't expect kisses and hugs from them."

"Chase, keep on McCombs," Washington reiterated. "Invite him down to our cozy facility for a formal, recorded talk. I'll sit in for the McCombs interview, monitor the approaching press conference, watch for the fallout impact. I'll put in a request for an interview with the Mayor." The meeting broke up with Fetters as cheerleader.

"Let's go get those bastards."

That overt bias left Chase with a bad feeling.

6. Guest a la mode

The herbed air within the townhome reminded Chase of family holidays and her mother's old country dishes, from *yakki* to *parusk*. With Nanna living with Eric and Chase, not only did they have wonderful meals savored with Irish heritage, and Nanna's addiction to watching T.V. cooking shows added culinary surprises, most tasty, others, experimental leading to carry-out. Tonight seemed unusual, more formal: bay leaf rubbed chicken and one of Chase's favorites, pumpkin ravioli with a sage butter sauce.

She hung up her dress jacket, and placed her revolver and belt into a locked metal box at the top of the closet. Parental precaution. She did have concerns about Eric's mood swings. One harassing incident at school could escalate his frustration into fist clenched rage. Calls, not frequent, still enough for concern to pick him up from school, 'please take him home to unwind'.

"Great smells. Special occasion?"

From the kitchen, Nanna replied, "I told you, Eric's friend is dropping by. You met him. You should change clothes."

"Okay, I'll relax to shorts."

"No. Wear that blue dress."

"Nanna, that's for church, or if by the fate of the gods, I ever went on a---." Chase paused. "Which of Eric's friends is this?"

"Hi, Mom." Eric stood on the stairs, wearing a fresh pressed shirt, clean jeans, and loafers. No garage band t-shirt, no grubby tennis shoes. Chase thought she caught a whiff of shampoo clean hair.

"What's going on?" She, as the detective in the family, deduced conspiracy. "Who's coming over?"

"He's kinda new. I met him twice. You've met him." Eric skipped to their dining room and began to set the table, doing a chore without asking. What? The earth stopped spinning on its axis?

"Nanna, did you set me up? Eric, this isn't one of your school buddies, is it? I want the truth now."

Truth rang the doorbell.

"Answer the door, please, Chase," Nanna called out, "My hands are a mess."

She had two yentas living with her. She would tell whoever it was she had a bad day, a bad headache; sorry, next time, rain check, maybe. She flung open the door.

"Hello, Detective," smiled Owen McCombs. "It's Chase, isn't it? Nanna said red wine would go best with dinner." He held out a wine bottle to her with of all things, a gift bow attached. "I hear Merlot is sideways out and Pinot Noir in." Eric popped his head into the doorway.

"Eric, I brought you some of those extra coloring pens."

"Great. Thanks. Come on in and see what I've done." Eric radiated eagerness. This man made her son happy. Chase recoiled at the ramifications.

Owen stepped around her, inches from her face, walking into her private castle. She shut the door, a bottle of wine in her hands. She wanted to guzzle its entire contents on the spot.

Owen helped her to her seat at the dinner table. Eric laughed and ran over to seat Nanna. So totally caught off guard, Chase's awkward silence came off as aloof, even haughty. She fumed within. He should not be here. Inappropriate. More angry at herself for not making that position firm at the front door. Her curiosity about this man, this suspect, overpowered her good sense.

With Eric hanging on their stories of adventure, Nanna and Owen found mutual interest discussing travel destinations. Cabo San Lucas. Martha's Vineyard. Middle East. Chase realized her world had been limited to college road trips, youthful indiscretions of binge drinking, boys with octopus hands; then Roger the Dodger, and weekend trips to California, following his hobby of motorcycle rallies. Less riding, more drinking to inebriation with the leather jacket, bug teeth crowd.

Eric showed enthusiasm when Owen mentioned he was driving a 1960 T-Bird. Chase likewise perked up.

"I thought your car was a Corvette?" Her only comment in the last half hour and too detective sounding, eliciting beady eye 'how rude' grimaces from her family.

"Mysterious, the car appeared today at my house. The Magnum people must have heard about my other car and gave me a loaner. What a loaner, this thing is totally restored. I'm sure it's part of the Flynn Collection. You'd think he'd have to approve. I don't know. I hate to give it back at the end of the week when I get my car out of the shop."

"What happened to your car?" asked Eric, passing the garlic mashed potatoes.

"Vandalism." He explained the destroyed tires and the paint scrape.

"I hate to believe," sympathized Nanna. "Your first week in Las Vegas, it's a disgrace. Where did it happen?"

Owen paused, and Chase took note. Thanks for asking Nanna.

"A steak house near 1757 Highland Drive, near that Rolling Smoke BBQ place." Owen fudged on the exact address, an address plucked randomly.

Chase tried to visualize the area. The tits and ass district. For all his gentlemanly behavior she concluded Mr. McCombs behaved like all other men, new to town and out for cheap sexual thrills. With that bad habit he might as well leave now. To her chagrin, he chalked up one for the good guy side.

"How goes your life, Eric?" asked the dinner guest.

Eric told about school, the classes he liked. Owen regaled them with stories of his early newspapering days in Denver. He told Eric of the art gallery openings he had attended off 3rd Avenue in the Cherry Creek shopping district. One gallery exhibit showed artists about Eric's age. This launched Eric and Owen into the world of art entertainment. Eric told him of his favorite Pixar and Dreamwork movies he liked for their animation, not just action or blowup the terrorist movies. Owen told him he had once written a review on the fantasy art of Frank Frazetta. That he had been to art showings of the storybook drawings by Richard Jesse Watson, the comic animals of artist Yuri Kutsenov, and the island surrealism of 'Tiki Shark' Parker.

"Go online and search Frazetta's works from the D.C. Comics period of the 1960s to his science fiction and fantasy works; see how the power of art can convey the story. Talent, which you have, requires hard work."

"Do you have talent?" asked Eric.

"Misplaced mine. I'll find it someday."

Chase found that an odd statement.

She found herself likewise listening. Owen did not lecture. He spoke in easy language for short attention spans, as if he understood her son's private demons. A camaraderie B.S., saying, as she saw it, in kid translation: 'Hey dude, like it, do it.'

With ease and grace that caught her off guard, he found the right moment to make his exit. He had an evening meeting, he said, and with a thank you and a reciprocal invitation for a tour of the Magnum site for Eric and Nanna (unspoken to Chase to join in if she so wished), he made his way to the door.

On the doorstep, he turned, "Thank you, Miss Taggart, you have a wonderful home and family."

At the mention of her family, private and inviolate, she stomped out the glow of the evening.

"My boss wants me to interview you tomorrow at our offices." She blurted out trying to sound officious.

"Yes, I can do that," he matched her businesslike clip. "I can be reached through Ms. Steele's office. You also have my cell number. Set the time and I will be there. Good night, Detective."

She did not mean to watch him walk away. He offered no backward glance. In observation, Owen McCombs did not come off as he looked, nondescript. Tonight, she had heard the man talk in casual conversation, viewed the inner personality. Intelligent. Even caring. She hated knowing that, at least, she told herself she did. He brought her into his world by calling her by her first name. As he drove off in his fancy prancy T-Bird loaner she thought she saw someone standing in the shadows, obscured near a wall of Oleander bushes, hidden. Wine and imagination blended poorly she decided, creating shadows among shadows. This night confused her enough.

"That was fun, wasn't it, Chase?" Nanna asked while both were putting away washed dishes, cellophane to the leftovers. "He seems to be quite interesting." There was that description, too.

"Interesting? That man has been in the vicinity of two violent crimes in the last week."

"I didn't see you handcuff him. Again. Or kick him out."

Chase considered her reply. Everything tonight must be taboo in some police policy manual.

"Well, it was an opportunity to dig behind his executive façade. Let him trip himself up."

"And did he?"

Except for his strip club foray, nothing sinister stood out. She deduced his police reporting stories might be a strategy to color him as one of the good guys. It hadn't worked for her.

Nanna finished wiping the counters.

"Let me ask you this, Chase. Have you seen or heard anything so far that leads you to believe he is guilty of something?"

"He is a suspect." Chase's voice strained.

"I don't mean you playing detective. Circumstantial this and hypothetical that. I mean your inner female intuition, the gut of your soul. Is Mr. McCombs an evil man?"

Chase gave her son's grandmother a glance of disbelief and retreated, shaking her head. Detectives have to deal with facts, hard evidence. She did admit to herself that her emotions were an ingredient in the mixture.

Eric moved to his room for reading and bed. She went up to kiss him goodnight and found him surfing the internet on the artwork of Frank Frazetta. "Isn't that great stuff?" All she could see in a quick glance were he-men with swords swinging at menacing hordes and dragon beasts, and big busted women in scanty clothes, standing shoulder to shoulder as equal warriors. "Yes, it is drawn extremely well," she offered to Eric as appeasement, not so sure her son should start drawing the sexual mores of Conan the Barbarian.

"Can we go see that casino construction? That would be rip-snazz'."

"I don't think so. Maybe you and I could play some miniature golf this weekend."

"Mr. McCombs, you don't think he's a killer?"

"I can't tell you that, Eric. Mr. McCombs seems nice, It's just best to keep him at a distance. He's involved in my investigation."

"Don't you just know when a person you're investigating is guilty? I mean, don't you get vibes?" Chase wondered if Nanna and Eric had plotted to undermine her moral compass.

"No, sometimes you can be fooled." Her unsaid example recalled was Rodger the Dodger Kinkaid, Eric's father, now out on bond. She remembered her impression of someone hiding in the night when Owen McCombs left, watching her, waiting, seeing who she was with. It would be like her ex to spy. Rodger launched his spiteful counter attack with the child custody litigation. He blamed her for his down-fall, not his own criminal actions. He wanted his day in court to use any weak evidence to destroy her publicly. Stay tough, she told her-self. She kept from Nanna and Eric the insidious depths of Rodger's plotting. She could not tell them.

Chase turned out the bedroom light, told her son sweet dreams, running up his arm, 'the itsy bitsy spider'. "Aw, Mom, I'm not a baby." She knew that, she knew.

As the house went quiet, Chase poured herself the last glass of Owen's wine gift. She curled up on the couch to unwind, to read chick lit escapism, author S.P. Grogan, a culinary mystery, "Captain Cooked', with the evildoer cooked and boiled by book's end. Just desserts. Chase tried to focus on the pages. Owen McCombs came into her thoughts. Applied female intuition worked. If she remotely felt McCombs was a killer, an evil man, he would not have gotten within five miles of her family. What gave her pause, had this evening been a real date, a dinner date without family present, without her rude and silent behavior, acting like a tongue-tied spinster, yes, she would be willing to go out with him. He was interesting. She turned another page of her book, dismissing the mental exercise of impossibilities.

When the phone rang her awake at midnight she found herself stretched out on the couch, the book in her lap.

Ray Washington didn't even say hello.

"Owen McCombs was beaten up in front of his house tonight."

She took a deep breath.

"Is he--?"

"He'll survive. Bruises. Doctors say maybe a concussion. Two perps using him as a punching bag until a good Samaritan broke up the fight. No immediate suspects." She came fully awake, tensed. Her mind pressed hard to define the shadow in the bushes.

"I went to University Hospital. He's been sedated. You and I need to see him tomorrow."

"Sure. I'll be in early."

She turned off the light and sat in the dark listening to the clock on the mantle ticking, cars growling on the street, her jumbled breathing.

7. Deja Blank

A fist coming toward his jaw sent him reeling. More punching met his body, pounding his muscles. A few swings his, wildly thrown, ineffective. On the ground, a boot kick into his shoulder. After that, wrapped in a shroud of blackness, came a painful peace.

When he had a lucid moment, Owen thought, in Vegas, luck should apply to beating the odds in the casino, not to the doctor saying, 'you're lucky to be alive'. He felt the presence of bandaged warmth, as well as drugged pain.

The nurse told him he slept through most of the day and that sleep rebuilds strength. The way he felt when he moved they could let him sleep another ten years. When the doctor on rounds asked where it hurt, Owen wondered, what part of his body did not hurt. The doctor came back with the test results and a disquieting diagnosis: "A mild concussion."

"I seem to remember bits and pieces. A fight, details sketchy."

"Skipping the medical terms, there could be short term memory loss. When the brain cells strengthen you should recapture what you can't remember."

Owen thought he told the doctor, 'To build new little gray cells, can I have more drip Percocet with a Vicodin chaser?'

When next he awoke, young and cute Casey held his hand. Theodore stood beside her. He remembered them.

"They beat the holy shit out of you," said Theodore in his factual appraisal.

"I hit some wall, something hard," Owen's voice gargled dryness, the words coming out in a disjointed hoarse whisper. "I can't remember… everything…Doctor says traumatic shock to my cranium."

"You came home before midnight. Theodore and I were watching T.V. when we heard this racket. I guess they'd been working on you for a couple of minutes. The noise came from the big black dude pounding on the two guys."

"Two guys?"

"You must have been jumped by two muggers when you got out of your car. Carjackers maybe."

"Your left leg," said Casey, quite concerned, "it's all black and blue. They must have stomped you. I saw it when they put you into bed." In his hospital gown? Like in naked, his butt flashing. What did she see?

He felt the wooze of the pain killer dripping into his arm as Theodore played out the blow-by-blows.

"Bang! Biff! Pow! This black dude is wailing on one of the creeps and nose punching the other. And he can toe point kick, too."

"Right in one guy's balls," said Casey. "Really neat, just curled him up."

"Casey called the police. I ran out when I saw your black hero going one way and the two creeps stumbling to their car and driving off. Real Mortal Kombat. You just laying there motionless. I got a pillow and blanket. The cops arrived really quick, like they were around the corner, and then two suits in a government car right after that, and the ambulance whisked you off and we followed."

Owen's attempt at pillow adjusting brought quick pain everywhere but he could move, thankfully not crippled or debilitated. Fingers and toes wiggled, a good sign that his synapses were snapping.

"Isn't it ironic," commented Theodore. "You both are going to be here tomorrow at the same hospital. Casey is having some work done."

Casey blushed, "Theodore, you didn't have to mention that, especially right now. It's nothing."

"What's going on?"

"For some time I've felt I didn't have a real Elvis look. Something was missing. So tomorrow, I'm going to have some outpatient surgery, that's all."

"Tell him, don't get him worried."

"Just having my lips puffed up. I can't do the lip quiver that he used on women in the audience. I want to be as true to the King as I can. They'll be giving me some injections."

The thought of needles in his lips brought sharp tingles in waves across Owen's body. With all his own problems, he felt sympathy pains for his young friend.

Casey gave his hand a gentle squeeze.

"Have you forgotten everything?"

"Yesterday is foggy at best. I know I was to have a meeting with the Mayor and his cronies yesterday afternoon. Nothing. Last I remember there was a meeting with Melissa Steele at her construction trailer."

Casey eased her touch. "Certainly, you'd remember that."

"Racking my brain, nothing solid. I have a vision of the construction manager, Wayne Hollister, being with her." Casey returned the warm pressure of her hand. He pushed his thoughts hard.

"And nothing of the fight?" Theodore wanted to rehash the action.

"Time is missing, replaced by muscle hurt. Even as you asked, I'm starting to remember a blur of fists flying." He closed his eyes and thought he saw a fist coming at his face.

The chemicals in the drip left him floating in a cloud world. He lay there for a few moments in quiet contemplation listening to both of them talk nothing essential. He shut his eyes. Where was he before his return to the house at midnight?

Disjointed thoughts merged and when his eyes next opened, déjà vu, there stood the Mayor looking down on his battered body.

"This had to be my fault," the Mayor said. "You're lucky you're not totally bandaged and drinking from a straw."

"They said I got mugged, or maybe it was an attempted carjacking."

"The neighborhood is guard gated. They didn't follow you in, they were lying in wait."

"I can't remember a thing. Casey and Theodore said some hefty black guy saved me."

"Police haven't located him is what I've heard."

Owen wondered. A passing neighbor his hero? Any Good Samaritan would've stayed—to call an ambulance—make sure the newspapers spelled his name correctly, took the credit and beamed his face to the news cameras. A black hero, at that. Since his arrival in town only two male African-Americans stood out. One, Detective

Washington, definitely too old for brutal fisticuffs. He would have pulled out his revolver, fired a warning shot and made an arrest. The only other person that crossed his mind was what's his name, Derek Shelly, who worked for Jackson Flynn. He spotted him in the crowd at the top of the garage when Chunky D's body was discovered. Young black man, sporting a light tan cotton jacket and paisley tie, styled and cool in the middle of summer. Was it him last night? But what was he doing in the neighborhood?

The Mayor kept jawboning an apology of sorts.

"Why is my accident your fault?"

"Something I said during our meeting got you excited, and you excused yourself in a rush. Something about setting up an appointment."

"What happened at that meeting?"

"*Your attorney*," The Mayor emphasized, "straightened me out as to your delicate position, as if I shouldn't have seen the conflict of interest. Clay gave us some clues, said they fell under client-attorney privilege, so he could not reveal the source. I guessed that these might be Morrie's last words. None of us could figure out what the words meant. Even Kathleen said it was all gibberish."

"Kathleen?"

"She was there with Clay. She wants to be part of our team. Fine by me. Getting her involved keeps it in the family. She said you gave her and her girlfriends a tour of the Magnum site. I didn't know you had invited her."

"She showed up unannounced."

The Mayor shrugged.

"Probably through Flynn and company. Her dad met Flynn several years before he was killed. The Grayson Estate was the land seller to Flynn, and Kathleen Grayson Sawyer sits as a trustee on the Grayson Foundation board and as Vice President of the real estate operations. She's sharp as a tack."

Closing his eyes Owen could feel her hug and double cheek kiss at the construction site tour. That memory had not evaporated.

"What do we do next?"

"Being stomped says we may be getting warm."

"Meaning what?"

"Two murders are connected, and maybe a third."

"A third? And why weren't we on the scene?" The Mayor laughed. Owen's attempt at laughing brought spasms to his stomach muscles. He choked out a weak smile.

"I don't know why I said three deaths. What do I know that I can't recall? There must be a pattern. What do the two dead men have in common?"

"Outside of being cold stiff, they were partners in crime, in the Wrecking Crew gang."

"And what do four of the five members have in common?"

The Mayor understood. "Cold stiff."

"Yes, but aren't all the deaths recent?"

"Are you suggesting they were all murdered? No, it can't be. Campi died of a heart attack."

"Yeah, but I'm thinking more Scarpetti by fire in a gang killing." Owen had heard the details, was it from Kane? Was it yesterday?

"That shocked me. Scarpetti's death only a week ago. From what Byron told us, it was a gang attack in the prison."

"I don't believe in coincidences. All deaths, whether murder or heart attack, happened recently. They're all retired gangsters from the same gang. What's another tie-in?"

The Mayor pondered. His internal light bulb clicked.

"The Cassandra jewels. Got it. Somebody has a major clue to where they are and is making sure the other gang members don't get there first."

"I agree." Owen shifted, searching for a less painful bed position. "Maybe they've already been found and cashed out."

"No," said the Mayor. "Finding the jewels is the motive, they're still out there. Chunky D and Morrie being tortured demonstrates that theory. Another fact speaks against the search being over. Your getting beaten up was a warning. Maybe you got the searchers riled."

Yes, winced Owen, this made sense. "Maybe we got too close to an answer. And they can't beat you up."

Signaling his departure, the Mayor patted Owen's arm. "When you get out of here in a few days let's get this mess solved." A small chill went up his spine when Owen saw Byron Kane, investigator ex cop, standing in the open doorway, listening, making no effort to announce his presence. Kane not only functioned as an information gatherer he served the Mayor as a low-key, de-facto bodyguard. As much as he tried, as much as he wanted to, digging into last night's mayhem he could not put Kane's face on any of the attackers. Kane's attitude bristled mean spirited, however, Owen could not see him as an enforcer. He could have hired some of his buddies to do his dirty work. For what purpose? Territorial encroachment and jealousy? The lost jewels and antique coins?

Owen mulled over the Mayor's comment that he should spend a few days in the hospital? No way. His job at this point dangled tenuous, not a worrisome peep from his employer. No vase of get-well flowers, no fruit basket, no cheery cards. As news traveled by gossip, certainly the higher ups, perhaps Mr. Flynn himself, granted the infirmed some leave of absence to recuperate. Owen willed himself well, to get out and find out what happened in the dead zone of time, between the late afternoon meeting with Melissa Steele, then the Mayor and the midnight madness in front of the Silver Avenue home.

His hospital visitors would not let him alone.

Detective Chase Taggart smiled at him. That alone, worth a ton in medicinal supplies, he felt new blood congealing in the injuries.

Detective Ray Washington stood next to her. His personality glowered a gruff edge. Chase set the tone of the visit.

"I heard you're the favorite punching bag of the week."

"I hear Mike Tyson lives in Vegas. Has he been questioned?"

"You would have gone all the rounds if it had been him. Plus, he leaves bite marks as evidence." She pulled out her notebook. "Detective Washington and I want to take your statement when you are fully conscious."

"I'm less than helpful. Most of yesterday went missing."

"All of yesterday?" Chase seemed perplexed.

"Tell me what you do remember," asked Washington.

Owen seemed confused. Detective Taggart nose twitched him. Like a bunny. Like Sabrina the witch. Some joke she knows that I don't? Maybe, it's only the prescribed drugs mellowing out his bruises and his mind.

To the detectives, displaying his lethargic cooperation, Owen recounted working at the job site giving tours, going to meet with Ms. Steele in marketing, then *kerplow!*—he found himself in the hospital.

"Have you found the man who jumped my attackers?"

"No," said Washington.

"I find that curious."

"So do we," the senior detective acceded to that mystery. "You'd think he wouldn't mind being called a hero. Maybe he worried over outstanding traffic tickets and didn't want to stick around."

Detective Taggart asked, "Do you remember our meeting yesterday? We discussed your coming to meet with Detective Washington and myself to give a formal statement?"

"No, I'm sorry."

"Can you account for where you were, say from 6:00 p.m. last night until you drove up to your house?"

"No." He could not, as hard as he tried. He knew that time gap was critical.

The two detectives left as Clay Stokes and Kathleen Sawyer walked in.

Kathleen responded to his wounds with soothing coos that Detective Taggart heard as the door shut.

"Oh, Owen, you poor baby." He got a face peck. Clay said, "Sorry, my friend, the neighborhood's going to crap. Back in the old days, we kids used to run around with no fears." Clay and Kathleen filled in blank details on his presence at the Mayor's task force.

"No one can figure out those words you uncovered," said Kathleen. "Do you have any idea?"

He recalled Morrie's death scene. No idea of the dead man's words, Owen told them.

Clay gave disturbing news. "You missed the press conference this morning. The District Attorney and the U.S. Attorney are doing a positioning dance to see which one has enough to open a Grand Jury investigation. You don't need case evidence, and you can keep a grand jury working on gathering evidence and roll in the public limelight though testimony is behind closed doors. D.A. Lattemore is after the Mayor's job, as good as running. The Federal U.S. Attorney, employing the FBI's resources to gain an indictment, is looking for his life-time retirement to the cushy bench of the Appeals Court."

"How long before the dance ends and a Grand Jury empaneled?"

"The Feds have an ongoing Grand Jury, they're one leap ahead, but they don't know if any federal criminal act has been committed outside of violating the civil rights of two known smash and rob crooks. They've allowed the FBI to go sniffing. That may not play too well to the press. I'd say we have less than a week before one or the other acts, and my money is on our own D.A. pandering to press grandstanding." The Mayor had not mentioned this new wrinkle to Owen.

Here it was, cut simple. They had a deadline; two, or was it three murders to be solved in a week or less.

Kathleen gave his hurt hand a tender pat and read his mind.

"Now, Owen, you stay right here in this bed and heal. Don't go playing sleuth. Let the police do their job." And then she gave him a look which Clay could not see, just an instant, the way she caressed his hand, pain and tenderness trying to offset each other. Maybe it was only his befuddled mind creating wet nuances.

Clay supported Kathleen's suggestion that the patient stay patient.

"I'll send that paperwork over if I can find it. The Mayor said he gave it to me." In his tiredness, Owen nodded an affirmation, not knowing what Clay was talking about.

Kathleen said. "Oh, and I'm sending a little get well present to you later. So you make sure you stay put." She still had that first impression of him, he thought, a lummox. If a dangerous one, as she once joked, with his bruised wounds and throbbing head, he knew he had to fear only himself.

8. Connecting Points

Owen slept into the early evening and awoke to more tolerable aches. Each breath suggested a bruised rib. Scabs across his face and body were scattered like confetti where he had been squashed against the asphalt street. From his chest to his legs, blue-black bruises made him look like an abstract painting, or swirled mulatto. After a slow shuffle to the bathroom, the yellow stream, lacking blood, told him he would recover.

His mind started recapturing snatches of the lost day. Two images stood out. Lying on the ground, fighting going on above him, he could see the unmarked car at the end of the block, two figures inside. They made no move to interfere. Who were they? His newest memory befuddled him. More recollections drifted back into his frontal lobe. He remembered being with Chase Taggart and her family, having dinner, having a good time. For some time he lingered on the memory of that rare domestic tranquility, enjoying the awkwardness of his reluctant hostess, circumstances almost making her less cop, more human, more woman.

Within an hour his hospital room door swung open for two candy striped nurse's aides carrying in his food tray. Hunger replaced a few pain cells for equal demand. The food lid removed revealed Dungeness crab soufflé, peppered Ahi tuna salad, and a Coors Light. Not the ordinary hospital meal.

He looked at his nurses.

"It's those damn ears that give you away. They stick out, not natural. And really, which one are you?" He said this to the brunette nurse and she answered, "I'm Hi, and hi again." She readjusted her ears.

The red-haired nurse accompanying her said, "I'm Jinx. I guess I missed a swell tour and a better mosh fight last night. You look horrible."

Blaze, their protector, stared at him from the doorway. He wondered if the bodyguard could have inflicted as much damage as the thugs he had faced. Did she know Byron Kane? They would make a great his/her hit team. Blaze, her steel trap eyes glaring at him, shut the door. Hi and Jinx held his hands. With this surprise, healing juices flowed.

Whether the drip of drugs or the gourmet food he wolfed down, Owen energized and the three of them gabbed like long lost comrades. The girls were news junkies and wanted to know all details about the murders, the investigation, who's doing what about it. He told them all he knew. His story became a self-test to determine what new memory links might resurface.

The other topic of discussion which got them animated involved what they could do with the Magnum Theatre Showroom if put under their contractual control and how it should be customized to fit their personalities. Here, Owen, in his enthusiasm of being a fan, may have represented their interests more than Mr. Flynn's. He scored when he said they needed to capture the charisma of last fall's MTV special that had won them an Emmy and that Broadway type musical video with the signature torch song, "Love Us Two," they had created that went double platinum. *Don't make a choice, rejoice, to love us two.*

He imparted his showmanship wisdom from out of his social days in Denver throwing singles parties with the TDO bachelor club, and later marketing special events down in Biloxi.

"Use Magnum Theatre as your testing ground," he said to them both, alternating in hand holding, "Keep the showroom a knockout Vegas style of glitz and costumes, while the concert road tour and the videos should be your youth market pumping up the latest hits."

Hi-Jinx reciprocated his drugged insight. They helped him escape.

Hospital escapes, if one is planning such a thing, are best executed at shift changes. Blaze revved the getaway Hummer. (Owen found out later that Hi-Jinx would get their own limousine from Mr. Flynn—an outright gift if they signed up to be the anchor residence stars to the new casino. A minor trinket since any contract would mean multi millions). Next, make the bed as if vacated. Leave a note at the closed Accounting Office, so they would guess that the doctor released the patient. His two accomplices ran the gauntlet of nurses and security guards at the doors and shuffled him out in a discharge wheelchair. Hi pushed his wheelchair down the corridor, Jinx led, her petite butt, shake bouncing down the hospital corridors, her gait very un-RN. It reminded him of that ass-wiggling nurse at Bluestein's hospice; when was that?

Blaze drove the Hummer escape vehicle, a race course expert in avoiding kidnappers and paparazzi ambush. The girls paid no notice, taking the rough speed and tight corners as the career norm. They chatted and gossiped to Owen's amusement, texted a few messages without comment, and with coaxing launched into an acappella rendition of their latest ballad, not yet released, "Cosmic Love".

Find my heart lost among the stars
Kiss my tears of silver moonbeams
Take me beyond Orion's belt
And rocket hard your dreams
While you lay me gentle on the sands of Mars.

He could only marvel at their talent. How do you explain such 'cosmic' moments as these, never to be repeated, hardly believed?

The limo brought him to the Silver Avenue house. Like the young girls with giggles they still were, he received stereo Hi-Jinx kisses. In waving good-byes, they pledged to keep tabs on him and rescue him from any future violent misadventures. Limping with pain into the house, he thought, *They know me too well. No doubt, I'll see them again.*

Owen hibernated into a new morning, waking to find fresh orange juice and the morning newspaper by his bed.

No good news. On the front page the Mayor bled, mauled in ink. The rumor about the turf battles between the prosecutors led one story. In an above the fold headline, the Sheriff announced new evidence surfacing and an arrest imminent in both cases. In his column, Pegler revealed the gruesome details of Bluestein's death, news not earlier released. This creep, Owen sensed, could get under your skin like a tick with Rocky Mountain Spotted Fever. Something about Pegler dogged Owen's mind, a piece for that gobblydegook puzzle in a pounding head. Owen went cold turkey to let the drug effects dissipate. A courageous and dumb move since pain filled in the numbing gaps, brutal hurt-to-move pain.

"The Hospital called looking for you," said Casey, helping him to the couch, her wet hair tied up, smelling coconut fresh. "They said you forgot to sign some double digit form for release."

Theodore played with his backpack, securing his ever present computer, ready to shove off.

"We've decided to spend the day as your ambo-care chauffeurs."

"Recuperating at home sounds better."

"What and let the killers escape?"

"Besides, I have the night off," explained Casey, "and I have my outpatient needlework this afternoon at 4. They told me to rest after that. So we need to take care of business this morning."

"Hey, gang, this isn't a television shoot'em up. True nosing around is usually boring."

"You coulda fooled us," grinned Casey.

Owen recalled Clay's comments about his dad and the Grand Juries. If they went after the Mayor, Owen himself would be pressured with legal threats laced with hints of immunity. In other words, rat out the Mayor.

He gave in a little. "But eventually we do need to find a way to interview senior Corallo without Junior butting in."

"The game's afoot," said Theodore, happy to be at play.

"Hold on. I don't know this town, and I've got to get up to speed with the history and the players. Maybe go to the library for the day. Find some old news stories that would make good bedside reading."

"Let me throw on some sleuthing clothes and let's get going," smiled Casey, affirming to Owen he had been hooked and reeled in by experts.

As he waited for his posse the doorbell rang. What now? The stranger at the front door greeted Owen with a manufactured smile that most salesmen fix into their personalities. The man dressed natty, casual yet sharp threads, a folder under his arm.

"I heard you're newly arrived. I specialize in this part of town. My firm assists executives in locating residences that meet all your required comfort needs, yet affordable to your budget. Apartments, Condos, Homes." A real estate salesman on the prowl. Owen didn't brush him off with a 'not interested'. He accepted the man's business card and matched smile to smile.

"Perhaps in a week you could drop by again."

"Excellent. Once we become better acquainted, I'll understand your housing goals." When the salesman left, Owen glanced at the man's card: *Roger Kinkaid*. Soon the time must arrive when he should find his own digs, not be beholding to the Mayor's hospitality. Giving no more thought to that future task the business card slid into Owen's sparse wallet.

The trio agreed on their first stop, to hit the archives at the Las Vegas *Review Journal* where past newspaper copies were retrievable by computer. Since the murders centered around the Wrecking Crew, there might be other associated murders of gang members, even rivals.

Owen told his junior detectives, Hardy Boy and Nancy Drew, to crosslink any connection, however remote, to the Crew and to anyone else that might be involved with the Mayor, the jewel robberies and who might be active and alive today.

To the cross links Owen added shots-in-the-dark: Tony Spilotro of the Hole-in-the-Wall Gang; the Mayor; Jackson Flynn; and, Donald G. Grayson. The charge to Theodore and his computer: create a multidimensional matrix with all the connecting points.

Casey took on the first group of deceased: Mario Scarpetti and Bobby Campi. Theodore charged after Morris Bluestein, weirded out by the old gangster's ant chewing. Owen settled on DiManna and Corallo. Two hours of grunt work found their eyes crossing at computer screen small print.

Theodore pointed out the first connection. "Look at the check out logs for some of the twenty-five year old papers still on microfiche." They saw the sign out sheets where West Pegler dug into the archives researching his book. "I bet he interviewed all the Wrecking Crew he could get to, probably all the other key players. He's probably done our work for us."

The manuscript. *Wise Guys of Vegas.* That rang a bell. Owen wanted to see a copy; asked, the answer 'no'. Who told him he could not see it?

"After we finish here, let's pay Mr. Pegler a visit in his office."

"Here's something interesting," said Theodore pointing to his screen. "Morrie 'Shuga' Bluestein's name appears about twenty places dealing with Vegas crime. There is a cross reference to Horizon Helicopters. He has ten references with that company. It was a charter company for Grand Canyon tours and I guess it was his employment front 'cause it says he was head mechanic. It cratered in bankruptcy after he was indicted in 1987. Guess he had been its front for capital, too. Here might be a 'connecting point'. The reference line reads: 'Also contributing volunteers in the recovery of victims was Horizon Heli-copters'."

"Victims?"

"Victims, plural, as in bodies. The Donald G. Grayson plane ex-plosion. Big headlines in 1986. And look at this old photo. Can you see who that is?"

Owen and Casey leaned over Theodore's shoulder and squinted at the old black and white with its grainy dots. At the plane wreck they could see a torn metal debris field on the tarmac, and a helicopter off to the side with workers loading what looked to be a body in a white plastic sheet. In the front of the photo one worker looked to be a young Pauli DiManna in similarity, but in age, that far back, the fig-ure had to be Pauli's Father.

"Chunky D," confirmed Theodore. "Even if he and Morrie are fellow crooks, what's he doing at the explosion site?"

Owen studied the gruesome page one photo.

"Another connecting point. Look in this second photo."

The pseudo detectives strained to see the significance.

"I see a group of cops standing around. That seems typical," Casey said.

Owen tapped the dark face in a montage of white faces within black and white newsprint. One could see the bare outline of the face.

"In 1986 how many black police officers do you think Las Vegas had on payroll? Not that many. I bet that's a young Ray Washington as a beat cop. He's now chief detective looking into the deaths of the Wrecking Crew. Being there, you'd think he would've come into contact with at least Bluestein, if not DiManna."

Washington's name was added to Theodore's matrix, in a column with a line from Washington's name to Horizon Helicopters to Bluestein to Donald Grayson to a new subtitle, "Plane Explosion Investigation".

"We'll have to talk to Detective Washington."

They kept searching the newspaper's archives. Owen, for his own curiosity, typed in 'Kathleen Grayson Sawyer' and hit Search. Not as much as he expected. True, she had been absent from the city for twenty plus years. He found the front page story tied to her father's death and a paparazzi intrusive photo shot through a car window of a sweet young child, a bandage on her forehead, clutching a flat rectangular gift box. Owen recalled what Kathleen had told him that day in the casino garden, her father's going away present. Other hits on her name produced a few blurbs of executive appointments as she rose in the Grayson Empire back east. Six months ago, the press release of her new position with Grayson Real Estate for the Western

Division, based in Las Vegas; and finally, the society photo of her and Clay Stokes, four months back, coiffed and bejeweled, dressed to impress. Gone for so long and suddenly at the top of the social lists. Money buys access.

Owen did not offer Kathleen's name to the matrix grid. He went back to the Wrecking Crew. His search came up with this fact: the Mayor's track record of legal representation had him defending three of the Wrecking Crew: DiManna, Bluestein, and Corallo.

Casey hovered over his shoulder. "I'm surprised that old man Corallo didn't boast about his tie with the Mayor."

"He wouldn't. According to the news story, that was one of the few cases Mayor Goodfella lost. Corallo was sentenced to four years; he did two years in maximum security."

"That's why," concurred Casey still digging, "at the Pussy Galore on their wall of fame there's no photo of him with the Mayor."

Theodore typed in the clients' names with a line to the Mayor.

"Corallo has a good reason to frame the Mayor," he said.

"And to beat up anyone who's trying to help him," added Casey.

Owen could not see Corallo the Elder taking a chance of getting caught up in a revenge beating for bad legal representation. Maybe Angelo, the son, wanted to step in to clean up old scores.

"Add Angelo 'the Angel' Corallo." Theodore went to work on the son's history but came up empty handed.

"One or two juvie infractions expunged. He's down here for holding the liquor license at the Pussy Galore, along with his sister, Gabriella Corallo. Couple of old stories on him as president of the local photography club. Hey, this is interesting. As a kid, he lived in the same neighborhood where we're living now. And look," Theodore scrolled through the records. "The DiMannas lived two blocks away from the Mayor's old house, our current residence, in the early 1980s into the 1990s."

The street name linked to Corallo's old address, aptly, 4-22-8-7 *Pine Circle*. They ran the other names off the list and made links: Donald G. Grayson lived outside the neighborhood in Rancho Bel Air Estates, within eight blocks. The three of them discovered that the DiMannas lived three blocks from Bluestein, two blocks from Corallos, and five blocks from the Graysons. Old home week. Campi, the noted exception, lived in a condo complex out on Flamingo Boulevard, nevertheless back then, in less traffic, easy driving access to visit buddies. They could find no home address for Scarpetti.

After two hours the three investigators were data-frazzled. They went looking for West Pegler.

"He's not in," explained a busy secretary.

"When do you expect him?"

"Mr. Pegler has a noon deadline on a feature story he's writing, an exposé on city corruption."

The trio saw it was past 1:00 p.m.

"I bet his editor is having a major epileptic melt down." Casey gave the secretary a little female empathy, and the woman nodded.

"Have you called him at home, or his favorite watering spot?" Little signals began to pop up on Owen's warning antennae.

"No response. They have some cub reporter out looking for him," she whispered to Casey, ignoring the men. "He does take a long lunch hour. He likes a couple casino sports books and their bars." She glanced at her computer screen. "Oh damn." The screen emitted wormhole blackness and her button pushing accomplished no reboot.

"Hold on," said Theodore, jumping around her desk as a would-be Mighty Mouse to the rescue. "I graduated in computer science. Be careful you may have blown the mainframe and crashed the hard drive into the flux capacitor. Mind if I give it a try?" The secretary hesitated, then moved from her desk, glad for help from white knight Theodore of Linnux. Casey chatted up the secretary.

He hit buttons on the computer and moments later said with triumph, "all fixed."

As they walked away the computer guru commented, "Basic logic. Computers don't work if their plugs are pulled from the wall. Want to know where West Pegler lives?"

"Yes," Owen said, feeling the aching outline of a large bruise. "And I have this sudden fear we should hurry."

10. One Beat Behind

They rushed to Pegler's apartment. It was the same complex Owen had walked away from when voiding his lease. Cool Sands Apartments. When was that? He tested his mental capacity, only four days back. Living up to its reputation, the Las Vegas scene was moving faster than he would prefer. He had shown up to take possession of his apartment only to find the drifter in squatter residence. Damn Homeless Bob! If only…

When they pressed the entry code to the Cool Sands gate buzzing Pegler's apartment, they received no response. Owen remembered his past visit and told the squawk box he had an appointment to view an apartment. The gate clicked opened.

"You can be devious when you want to be." Casey's intuitive judgment.

Owen moved quick as he could, limping through the complex with his sidekicks following. He punched the elevator for the second floor.

The door to Pegler's apartment was ajar and they saw the interior trashed. Shouts of 'hello' got no response.

Owen whispered, "Don't touch anything." The scene was wanton destruction. Tables overturned, couches slashed, the refrigerator contents flung and slopped around the kitchen. He called the reporter's name. Silence, no they heard a scratching, like cat clawing. Owen walked through trash to Pegler's second bedroom which doubled as his work office. *How did Owen know that?* A body lay on the floor. A breathing form not entirely human, West Pegler lay, or rather crawled. What seemed to be broken hands tried to grasp, scratching, a vain attempt at escape.

"Don't move." The body tensed at the sound of Owen's voice then the living corpse collapsed.

"Casey, call 911. Ask for an ambulance, life or death. Then call Detective Taggart. I've her number in my wallet." He handed over his cell phone and the police officer's card to a hesitant Casey. When she saw what was left of Pegler's face, a pulp of red gore, she fled the room. Owen sent Theodore to pull some wet towels to sponge off the bloody face in an attempt to comfort the beaten newspaperman. He surveyed the office damage. Mustard and syrup had been dumped and stirred into a glop on the floor. Pegler's computer lay destroyed in scattered circuit boards and shards of plastic and glass. An empty CD rack lay on the floor. His writings, his work stolen or trashed? For what purpose? Why? His manuscript of mob history in Vegas, if that's what caused the beating, had little value. His publisher held a copy for editing. Several drafts were circulating for correcting errors and omissions, that much Owen recalled…told by someone, sometime nights ago, on the tip of his mind.

Would Pegler's exposé uncover corruption in the city, a tie to mafioso resurgence, a tie to the Mayor? Instead of hurting the Mayor, who might go to any lengths to protect the Mayor? Owen brought up images of Byron Kane and Harmon Hartley. Together, would they orchestrate this? Could Hartley be vicious under his folds of flab?

Discarded wadded paper lay in the columnist's wastebasket and Owen rooted the trash with a pencil. What he had in his hands were a few pages of a draft of what seemed to be the latest article Pegler was working on. Some draft about audit discrepancies in the City's Housing Authority, a quasi-private agency within the city bureaucracy. What was going on? Not enough to warrant a savage beating.

The discards looked like statistical rehashing, mild plagiarism perhaps, a cut and paste of a government study. Still, in the hand of a muckraker, articles like this could do the Mayor further damage.

One of the pixie leasing agents walked in with a superior air of "What are y'all doing here?" She viewed the damage and stared at Theodore kneeling beside a blood spattered victim, holding in his hands crimson soaked towels. West Pegler moaned a kicked puppy wail. She set off a gurgling scream, fleeing with yells of 'help!', 'murder'! The police would be receiving a second emergency call and more officers would be dispatched. Owen left Theodore to take care of Pegler, and he and Casey retreated onto the outside corridor. How many times was this, awaiting the arrival of the authorities?

"They tried to kill him," said Casey.

"Both arms look broken. His jaws caved in. If he survives, his mouth will be wired shut for months. No talk shows for him." Owen put a comforting arm around Casey and she leaned her head on his shoulder.

"I think whatever we're all doing, including Pegler, we're going in the right direction, but we're bumping along without a roadmap."

"Like toward the source of the Cassandra diamonds?"

"I guess that would be the strongest assumption we have to work with. We're on a timetable not of our choosing. Perhaps we are just one beat behind."

"One beating behind," said Casey, sad and fearful at the same time, seeking reassurance in an injured man's embrace.

The police and ambulance crew arrived to gather up the smashed husk of the writer.

The three of them gave statements corresponding to their arrival, discovery of the brutality, and their few steps into the apartment.

Facts that only a few items like towels were touched. The apartment guide backed up at least their time of arrival for she had taken off after the trespassers in hot pursuit. Strangers are required to sign in at the office, she said, and looked totally stupid when a police officer asked if the criminals who had beaten up her tenant by chance had signed the registry.

Detectives Taggart and Washington showed up. They weren't leads on this case so they took their time. Theodore, in a chipper mood of being the center of attention repeated his story to the police working the crime scene. To Owen's surprise, Chase took Casey aside, for a private talk. Detective Washington caught Owen alone. Owen gave his alibi again, his reasoning for the visit, and offered his spin on a developing theory.

"I think Pegler's attack is related to everything going back to Chunky D, if not to Scarpetti being burned up, but I can't tell you why. That's what I hoped Pegler might tell us. That's the reason for our visit. Pegler did the research on all of them. The Wrecking Crew. "

"Detective Taggart told me you thought as much. Killing off a bunch of felon geezers seems a stretch for a conspiracy." McCombs was surprised. Detective Taggart, Chase, gave his analysis credence?

"Detective, don't you believe these strange coincidences, the similar homicides, two beatings?"

"We're still processing."

"Talking about coincidences I have a history question." Owen went on a blind fishing expedition. "Horizon Helicopters. Was that a mob front run by Morrie Bluestein?" Detective Washington pulled a toothpick from his pocket and poked it in his mouth.

"Yeah, Bluestein worked there. Back before my time."

"You were a patrol cop?"

Washington took the question as accusatory. Owen could give a shit.

"You were new on the police force, handling the petty tasks like traffic citations and such?"

"Yeah, so what?"

"You knew them, didn't you?"

"If you're implying I was hanging around Bluestein or DiManna and the Wrecking Crew, you're barking up the wrong tree. And you can go fuck yourself."

"Let's talk about the Grayson plane explosion. You were there, and so was DiManna, and I'm guessing likewise Bluestein." The detective's eyes blinked a surprise at this trivia and Owen saw he had engaged Washington's memory. He had him hooked. "I'm just sorting facts. Give me a quick history." Their eyes locked. Washington blinked first.

"Pretty miserable. Body parts scattered over the runway. I did nothing more than crowd control."

"The FAA never uncovered the reason for the plane blowing up?"

"Too many fragments. Never solved. Grayson family sued the airplane charter company and the plane manufacturer. Heard it settled out of court.

"Horizon Helicopters was there?"

He eyed Owen, a deeper, careful appraisal to this suspect's agenda.

"Well, yes, the FAA subcontracted out to several helicopter companies to fly the wreckage to a re-assembly hanger for the investigation. Besides, their offices were next to the private aviation terminal."

"I saw old newspaper photos of the plane wreckage. You were in the background in one photo. DiManna in another shot. Bluestein and

DiManna acting as crew personnel under the auspices of Horizon Helicopters to get them past police security. Any reason they'd want to be at such a grisly scene? With all those cops, detectives, FAA investigators poking their noses under wing fragments? Pretty risky, considering what just happened at a particular jewelry store." Washington stood silent, a sphinx with a soggy toothpick in his mouth. Owen grew his theory, a work in progress.

His verbal guesswork went no further, Casey and Chase returned. Theodore finished telling the first group of detectives what they could visibly see themselves, that the reporter's computer could not be salvaged.

Owen and Detective Taggart exchanged eye contact and Owen, when he thought they went unobserved, said, "We do need to talk." Chase could only look at the apartment destruction and then search his face. So, he added, "I'll call. Let's do a little quid pro quo."

One element was certain and Theodore pointed this out as they left the apartment complex. They were being followed. A black Cadillac Escalade with tinted dark windows driven by a professional who knew how to stay several car lengths back. Had they been shadowed from the Silver Avenue house? Owen could not afford another bruise on his flimsy body, nor risk his passengers' safety. A fear of the unknown kept them silent. Owen reaffirmed the car doors were locked.

Casey put their thoughts into words: "Mr. Corallo will be next. He's the only one left."

11. Smelling Their Own Blood

Chase fumed as Owen walked away. Of course, this case was too big not to see what he had to say. She faced another reality, Owen McCombs, the most intriguing man she had ever met, fell back into this strange mix as a suspect, a definite person of interest. Trouble becomes him.

She turned back to the crime scene. Malicious people just don't beat up a newspaper columnist from the most powerful media voice in the city and expect to get away with it. The police kept the unruly behind the yellow tape where they yelled a mixture of annoying questions and in-the-dark accusations. Chase realized the media's urge to avenge one of their own meant they would launch a witch hunt, themselves doomed to be hypocrites to fair play. The Mayor would be further damaged. The police she knew would catch the brunt of the McCarthyistic hunt. Journalistic anarchy would soon reign. Like animals sensing an impending earthquake the police working the apartment were on edge. The best example, the shouting match between Washington and newly arrived Fetters.

"I thought I told you to interview Pegler yesterday!"

"He was dodging my calls."

"You made no effort, did you?"

"Hell, yes, but you wanted to check out the Wrecking Crew. That's what I concentrated on. Don't Monday morning quarterback me!"

Into their midst marched the hierarchy of the-buck-stops-here power, true or not. Commander Stevens, Sheriff Phillips, and District Attorney Lattemore.

The Sheriff lashed out, "I just heard this McCombs character was here? Again, at a crime scene? Goddamn it, why don't you just arrest him and we'll sort it out later?"

The District Attorney, said, "Don't we have any tie-in to the two dead gangsters and Pegler? The common thread is the Mayor. And what about this casino executive, McCombs? Something smells rotten."

Divisional Commander Stevens said, "We need a press release and fast. The media is out in force. I don't think this is the place where we do a live on camera interview."

The Sheriff and D.A., elected politicians, could smell blood, and in this maelstrom, it could be theirs.

"I'll have my office start working on something," said the Sheriff.

"Pegler's attack is all I need to convene a Grand Jury," the D.A. spoke with his own game plan in play.

"Hey!" The shout came from the apartment walkway. A police officer approached with his walkie-talkie. "I think we might have a witness. One of the tenants thought he saw a guy at the victim's door. Someone he had seen before."

"Thank God," breathed Detective Washington aloud. "Finally, a legitimate break."

"God delivers to the just," intoned the D.A.

"Oh, my God, no," said Detective Taggart.

Homeless Bob was brought before them.

Owen dropped off Casey and Theodore back at the house. They would track down Larry Corallo. Owen said he had to run by the Magnum offices. Not true. Among the Egyptian chevrons he stopped to valet at the pyramid Luxor Casino. He limped through the gaming throngs to the convention center and found the Cleopatra meeting room. The meeting in progress sign read: "International Elvi Expo, Executive Board Meeting."

He tapped and opened the door to a businesslike setting. Ten men seated around a conference table with several men and women in the few chairs making up the audience. No white sequin jump suits, no black leather, everyone dressed casual. Three of the men sported bushy black sideburns and dyed black pompadours. Behind them on the wall a large blowup of the King, reminding them all upon whom they depended for their good fortune.

"May we help you? This is a private meeting." The man speaking did not look like an Elvi but a retired auto dealer, older, gray hair, definitely a chairman in charge.

"I apologize for the interruption, and won't take more than a minute of your time. I'm from the Magnum Casino Hotel Las Vegas. You may know that we are building a $2 billion entertainment center on the Strip." He had their attention. Owen's research discovered their regional Elvi conventions were usually held in casinos nationwide to capture flair of the King in concert. Vegas, by Casey's comment, in the running for a future national show. Owen wondered. Had he been hired to run the Magnum Convention Center? This opportunity arose to show his boss, the General Manager, whoever that might be, that even in the midst of personal crises (his own--being beaten, finding dead bodies) the loyal employee could still produce positive results for the Magnum Casino organization. Play it the company way.

Magnum, he proposed to the Elvi people, wanted to host their convention. The casino hotel would bend over backwards to make their stay welcome, the casino providing special amenities to stage an unbelievable event. Think of the press coverage garnered. The Elvi Expo, one of the first at Magnum's new convention center. International notice, Owen stressed.

He rolled on to their rapt attention, hitting all his bullet points. The Magnum would provide a venue the King himself might want to be seen in, and sing in, if he were alive today. "And you may not know this but Mr. Flynn does have one of Mr. Presley's Cadillacs in his auto collection. The first car Elvis ever bought, for Gladys, his dear mamma." He could see pairs of black dyed eyebrows arch in surprise.

"Well, yes," said the Chairman, "We do have this coming year's exposition and convention planned, and how ever you guessed it, yes, this interim meeting was to select the site for next year. I'm afraid we have chosen New Orleans. We don't plan more than a year at a time. Our staff is mostly made up of volunteers. Perhaps the year after."

"Whatever your wishes, as long as we lock in the dates as soon as possible. However, you might want to check with the Weather Channel. I hear there is a storm heading towards the Gulf Coast. Variable weather is a hazard to convention planning. Air traffic delays, who knows, more flooding."

The Elvi Chairman looked to his board. "We'll certainly consider the Magnum's generous offer. I don't think any of us thought an upscale casino like the Magnum would want us parading down your corridors." Owen smiled as the man's voice slipped into a religious homage.

True, Owen agreed to himself. Many casino managers would not welcome garish Elvis costumes running through a casino contrasting against an expensive décor as seen at the Venetian or the Wynn casino hotels. But in Vegas, money is the spoken dialect, even from bumpus-rumpus celebrity impersonators. He knew Magnum's Grand Opening Week required flash, publicity to attract the world, drawing in those with set images of crazy, wild Viva Las Vegas.

"Of course, the Magnum would be honored to maintain the high standards of the King."

His small audience glowed and Owen expected at any moment they might burst out into a group sing-along of "Forbidden Eyes".

Now came the zing; his hope, he wouldn't blow it.

"The only small issue that might be a hindrance, of course, I am sure you could make allowances for ..." he paused. "Magnum is big on equality, diversity. Federal laws are quite strict these days. We would want to make sure that that your Best Elvi Award would be open to all applicants, whether they are handicapped, little people, or even women impersonators. Magnum has to uphold a credo of impartiality. I never heard from the lips of Elvis one word of bias against his fellow man or woman. I hope that won't be a problem." He rushed on to offer having the Flying Elvi parachute team land at Magnum's new Speed Lake onto a floating barge. Finally, Magnum Casinos might even be willing to help underwrite a national television special on the Elvi acts at convention time.

The executive committee sat stunned. One member started clapping, leading to a round of mild applause. The chairman could only stammer his repetition, "Well, we-we certainly will take your gener-ous offer under consideration."

"I would hope you could give us a decision before you adjourn your meetings this week. We will be having a formal press conference concerning the casino in a week or so. That might make a great an-nouncement for all of us." He passed around the same business cards the Chinese received, the last of them. He needed more cards with a real title, defined responsibilities. Only after he left the meeting room did he drawl an Elvis, 'thank you, thank you very much'.

13. Reality Check

Detective Chase Taggart busted her butt to climb out of sexist pigeonholing, rising through the Burglary/Robbery Division to this new job in Homicide, the stuff of field action. She knew on her first homicide case, rather, two related cases, all her actions were being viewed under the microscope. Fail here and she would be shunted aside to some nominal posting. This mood dominated her emotional frame of mind since she left the Pegler apartment and made it back to her cubicle to find the clerical world of forms and reports poured in to smother her.

Chase seethed, finding herself the clerical feeder of messages, recipient of phone tips including a good many who swore Area 51 was the demon source of unearthly, unsolved murders. When she could come up for air she started on her own list of telephone calls. The first to Nanna left her troubled.

"Eric was in a playground fight."

"Is he okay?"

"He's doing fine. He had been invited into a pickup game of soccer. He got too wound up in a goal dispute and got in a push-shove match. By the time I got there the ruckus was over. Eric held his own. He's a little rattled."

"What's he doing now?"

"He's unwinding. I went out to the bookstore and bought him that art book Mr. McCombs mentioned. *Frazetta*. There are several of them. Be assured I did not get him any Frazetta girl drawings. He's tracing the art, and then trying it free hand. I gave him half a pill."

Chase flinched. The need to sedate Eric bothered her tremendously.

"Should I come home?"

"No, we're fine. Someday, though, he needs a whole family in his life."

Chase accepted Nanna's concerns as well meaning. No surprise when Nanna asked, "How's Mr. McCombs doing? Did they ever find the scum who beat the poor man? Have you seen him?"

"I've been busy." She would take the flak later when Nanna saw on the evening news Mr. McCombs at another crime scene, an event that seemed relevant to the Chunky D investigation. She rang off with the promise to get home early. She knew the lack of a big brother or a father figure undermined her child's self-esteem. He required male nurturing and she pled guilty to sheltering Eric from a manipulative and self-serving father. Her private life had been burned by betrayal, heartache, and divorce. Why go seeking a repeat performance?

More telephone calls. She gave off several 'thanks—we'll look into it' canned responses to the tipsters who had seen AK 47s poking out windows or who identified certain fringe groups as the culprits. Each call was logged and someone would have to go chasing dead ends.

A fellow detective waved at her. "A Mrs. Garcia, on line five."

"Get a number. I'll call her back."

Chase spent the rest of the afternoon wading through paperwork. Fetters was due back to interview Homeless Bob, now in custody for breaking into empty apartments. When Ray returned they could push the case detectives for forensics gathered in Pegler's apartment. Lost in thought, she heard the words, "Quid pro Quo", and looked up to see Owen McCombs standing before her. Smiling. Damn this boy scout! She had him in her domain and wasn't going to waste a moment.

14. The Wary Dance

"We're on the same team." He sought to have Detective Chase Taggart see him in a better light.

"Not the way you seem to play the game." She wore reading glasses making her look studious while thumbing through the autopsy photos of Morrie Bluestein. "And who let you in, anyway?"

"The Mayor asked a friend who asked a friend. He said it was okay to meet because we are newfound cooperating associates."

"Don't push your luck, McCombs." She sat at a metal desk in an office grouping of four desks and the only one working there at the moment. Her desk piled high with folders on either side of her working space. He noted the photo of her son, and more important to him, she had a computer which he hoped had access to some of his dangling questions.

"Are you following up on this Grayson plane explosion? I mentioned that to Detective Washington."

"He thinks you're going back into ancient history on a wild goose chase. We don't have the time. It's more productive to look closer to the actions of several days ago."

"You mean how the Mayor fits your bill of particulars? Do you think you're going to find a smoking gun?

She smiled. "This is an ongoing investigation."

"I would like to see the construction video tapes."

"That's police evidence."

"Wouldn't it help you if I could identify some of the players? You already have me on camera driving my rental truck in."

"That's all? Think you can spot the murder in progress?"

"How would it hurt your investigation if I viewed the tapes?"

"Helping is not one of your fortes. Having you around germinates mayhem." Chase liked this Dragnet bantering. She might as well see what cards he might deal to the table. After all, this was Vegas.

"I'd also like to find the files on the Cassandra jewelry store heist, especially the list of what was stolen."

"If you have one smidgen of knowledge where that stolen jewelry is, and don't tell me right now--."

"My dear Detective Taggart, I haven't the faintest clue where the shiny loot is. If anyone would listen to me, I'm certain there's a hard-rock treasure hunt going on by someone else and the only clues seem to be dead people left behind."

"Yeah, McCombs, you'd better be careful. You screw with Metro, and we have an entire police community that can make your crossing the street a nightmare hassle."

"That includes you?"

"With you, I would make it my personal crusade. Police brutality would look like patty-cake."

"When you play tough you're quite alluring."

That did it, mad or floored, she stalked away returning a few minutes later with three compact disks and pointed him to a T.V. and DVD recorder in a small conference room.

"There were three cameras. One was a high building shot from across the street on the Stratosphere, shooting down; the second on top of the parking garage taking in the front entrance, the office trailers and part of the construction side. The third placed to show vehicles entering the construction site. The camera thought to be operating in the garage, disconnected years ago. Let me know if you find Colonel Mustard near the Parking Garage with the knife and gun." She left him to his entertainment.

For over an hour he watched trucks and dust, rewound and slow forward. Nothing stood out, at least to begin with. Construction people came to work, executives parked in the garage. The Stratosphere cam was too far away. With the front gate camera there just were too many vehicles for anything unique to register. The 180 degree camera off the top of the garage had the most promise. There was no car exiting from the garage after 1:45 p.m., until the police arrived. Before that, cars came in the morning and ran out and back for lunch hour.

On about the twentieth viewing he thought he saw something, perhaps nothing. A concrete truck pulled into the construction site. The time about thirty minutes before Owen and the Mayor arrived. Instead of being waved in, the truck driver uses up thirty seconds talking with the guard at the gate. About what? The weather? Hot, more hot? No other truck paused that long. The stop sign traffic controller motioned the truck over to the side and a person exited from the cab on the passenger side. Concrete trucks don't usually carry passengers. That passenger wore jeans and short sleeve shirt, a hard hat, and carried a golf bag; maybe more like a thin duffel bag, perhaps for a surveyor's transom tripod. The bag man said a few words to the traffic director, probably explanation of his job presence, and went into the garage.

Owen guessed the new arrival might be a surveyor who had been outside the gate doing boundary measurements. Or a construction supervisor for the hotel's basement wet cement pourings. Okay, except that the concrete truck moved off to make its dump and returned to a parking spot near the garage, engine idling. Owen saw no car departing with the surveyor. The next sequences show Owen arriving in the construction yard with the rental truck and towed Corvette. He parked and entered the Marketing Office. Minutes go by, five to be exact, and the man with the bag moves out of the garage, a swift pace, and jumped in the waiting cement truck. The truck then drove out through the main gate, followed out by another cement truck in the conga line procession. The Mayor's car drives into view and out of sight into the garage. The Mayor is seen walking to the trailer where he and Melissa are waiting.

Nothing else stands out and he can fast forward to the rushed arrival of the security cops, the body having been discovered.

Owen invited Detective Taggart into his private screening.

"Could your Tech people get a close-up of the passenger in this truck. Or the driver." He pointed to the screen. "See here, where the truck occupants spend time talking to the front gate guard. Was the guard questioning them or just shooting the breeze? You can't see any faces in the gate camera but perhaps you can identify the concrete truck. Maybe there's some other camera in the general vicinity from another location like a fast food store."

"We interviewed the gate guards, took statements; they said they saw nothing unusual."

"I'm not here to tell you how to run your investigation."

"Good. Something we both agree on."

"Find this gate guard. If he doesn't remember a passenger, you've tripped him up.

"And where and when did DiManna come in? We now know he arrived alive, walking or alive and bound in a trunk. The tapes are 24/7. I'm wondering if there is a dead spot at the edge of the garage entrance. I just don't see DiManna's arrival, if on foot. And I hear you found his car nearby."

Where was he getting his information? She pondered his observations. The detectives gathered up the camera footage assumed relevant, focusing on the times close to the Mayor's entrance. She accepted that other theories did not exist. Events moved too quickly and no one had yet reviewed each time stamped recording of the construction yard.

When she did not respond he added, "There's the nonunion gate. The way it works, union and nonunion are required to use separate gates. DiManna could have entered through the nonunion gate. I don't think there is a formal guard shack there, maybe just one of those rent-a-cops. And that traffic control cop, someone needs to get a statement from her."

Chase felt exasperated. McCombs was trying to direct the police on his hunches. "We've interviewed everyone. We got an employee list from the CM and took statements the next day."

"Check on Wayne Hollister, he's Construction Manager. I don't know how helpful he would be. Anything that might slow his construction down-- he'd probably throw it into the trash."

"But he's one of yours?"

"Greed in the form of construction bonuses is a good motive.

"What about the killing dagger? It looked expensive, jewel encrusted. Is it a fake?"

As if Homicide could clone detectives to follow every lead, she thought. In her huffy attitude she gave small credit to his civilian thinking. Still nothing he asked opened the skies to the answers. But their uneasy pact was quid pro quo.

"The lab said the knife's expensive, no cheap knock off." She threw down a folder on the table. "I made copies." Five pages. The list of the Cassandra stolen jewelry, and newspaper clippings of the robbery.

"Thanks." He paused, gave a light smile. "Maybe, we could grab a bite, compare notes. I think the Cassandra robbery is the tie-in. I believe someone is after the jewels and wiping out possible competition, or people who get too close."

"Like you? I am surprised you can walk around." Amazing, he thought, her closest attempt at being kind since first meeting. How many days ago? He plunged.

"So, dinner tonight? We can talk about all this, or do you have plans with Eric and Nanna?"

Mentioning her family by name again spoiled the possibilities. She might have, just might have said yes. Her new job, her success at it, took precedent.

"I am sorry, it can't work." She blustered back to her new investigatory position. "Quid pro quo. Detective Washington…and I…still want a formal sit down and recorded session with you; your beating and now Pegler's attack." His reply, a snappy comeback, she sensed, hid his disappointment.

"Well then, we're on for dinner after we catch the bad guys. And by the way, I now recall I had a great dinner at your house. All I'm asking for is a repeat performance. Nothing more."

Chase watched Owen walk down the hall and disappear. She enjoyed this ritual dance, bantering in a two-step promenade of wariness.

Part III

"For a loser, Vegas is the meanest town on earth."

— Hunter S. Thompson, *Fear and Loathing in Las Vegas*

"Vaquero" by Luis Jiménez

1. Gobbledegook of Law

His cell phone sang out. Claiborne Stokes tracked him down. Meet him at his law office. On the drive over Owen furtively glanced behind. His quiet shadow trailed at a discreet distance, not hiding, which suggested an implied warning; 'we're here, be nervous'. In this borrowed antique T-bird he wasn't ready to swerve through any movie Bullitt-type chase scene or chance a ticket. He tried sleight-of-hand. Near downtown, not far from Clay's office, he pulled into the valet of a Victorian style casino, went inside, found the men's room and did his thing in front of a concrete wall of German graffiti. Exiting a few minutes later, he sought out any beady eyed face throwing stares back at him. No one lethal. He walked past some gaudy, turn of the century train cars to the side casino entrance and caught a cab. No one followed. For the moment Owen thought he was a hot shit James Bond clone.

His lawyer's office, with a view of the old core downtown, smelled of success and higher fees, highlighted by rich woods and plenty of shmantzy leather legal texts in the bookcases. Photos of famous people, business or charity events, from Mr. Las Vegas to Tiger at Tiger Jam, to shots only insiders would know. One could track Clay's age and fame. Several prominent photos were of his Father the Mayor with honored guests and Clay at the edge as tag along. Framed newspaper clippings attested to important public victories of Clay following in his father's criminal defense footsteps.

"I heard you were an escapee from a medical ward. Come over here, I want you to watch this — today's 1:00 p.m. press conference."

Turning on the T.V., Clay hit a play button. A balding scarecrow, floppy in his loose fitting business suit, stood before microphones surrounded by a suited gaggle of frowning underlings, positioned in their pecking order, all ice sober around their boss. Owen could guess: the District Attorney, Arthur Lattemore.

"It is our intention to empanel a formal grand jury to investigate a string of unsolved murders, now being called the 'Chain of Death' that have overtones of organized criminal conspiracy in this city, and may have unknown implications into our political system. These monstrous crimes cannot go unanswered by our justice system." He went on to hit a few high notes of moral indignation. Mob influence was returning and he would not tolerate it. In subsequent questioning by the press, the obvious was asked: "Was the Mayor going to be called to testify?" The District Attorney said it was too premature and that it would be up to the will of the grand jury. Bullshit, thought Owen. District Attorneys before grand juries are directors in the evidence presentation; many Officers of the Court hand-held jurors toward the indictments they sought. The press asked, "Do you think you've evidence enough leading to any sort of criminal prosecution?"

The District Attorney replied with the smarts of a future candidate, "The evidence needs to be processed through the system, and yes, there is concern that a flagrant conspiracy operates and certain laws violated." What equivocation!

A television reporter with her hovering cameraman asked if the brutal beating of news columnist West Pegler had anything to do with the two recent mobster murders.

"Nothing at this time seems to be a link," answered the District Attorney. "However, the police are pursuing that heinous assault with all dispatch. They should have some initial test results on the crime scene evidence by tomorrow morning. The Police Chief will inform you at that time."

Attorney Stokes clicked off the television.

"As you can see we are running out of time. Sooner than later, I expect to have a subpoena to testify delivered to my father. I'm sure you will likewise be on their list."

"Me?"

"You discovered West Pegler beaten in his apartment?"

"Theodore, Casey, and I. We called the police immediately."

"Why did you go there?"

"Questions on his research dealing with early gangster history in Vegas. We discovered he interviewed members of the Wrecking Crew."

"And you now think Pegler's assault is related to the killings?"

"Yes, I do, but why, I don't know. My mind is still reeling. Punishment or revenge? Pegler in the hospital slows the book from reaching the public. It doesn't stop a release date. My way of thinking, his manuscript holds the clues."

"Why didn't you just come by for this?" He plopped down a bulky mailing envelope on his desk. "You asked the Mayor at our last meeting if he'd seen a rough copy of Wise Guys in Vegas. He told you that Pegler sent him a copy of the manuscript. He didn't even glance at it. Dad sent it over to me to review for slander. He wanted nothing to do with even a back handed endorsement of the book. Chapter 9 is the story of the Hole-in-the-Wall gang run by the Spilotro brothers. Chapter 10 concerns the crimes of the Wrecking Crew. Quite a family feud between the gangs. I found the thing this morning. Thought I'd lost it at home. I glanced, saw nothing significant. I'll give you my original for your read. I want it back. I made a copy of Chapter 10 for Byron Kane. Let you both develop independent lines of ideas."

"I don't recall asking for the book, or for that matter, very much of what happened at the meeting, before or after. I've been having this selective memory lapse from my own beating. There is a total blank hole, though once in a while — zip — across my eyesight, flashback snapshots, nothing solid." Owen picked up the heavy tome of Mr. Pegler's fertile night soil mind. Read it tonight and give full concentration. He did have a few sobering questions for his attorney.

"Am I a liability to the Mayor? I seem to be attracting all this crap. Bluestein's murder, Pegler's face kicking? Magnum Casinos doesn't seem to want me around the building project and the police have me on their Most Favorite suspect List."

"My father would have told me if he felt you were not wanted around. He's very blunt."

"What's your opinion?"

"My father has a clean reputation, if not somewhat controversial. Since you and he did not shove Chunky D into the Mercedes, I would say you are both in it together. This grand jury is nothing more than a witch hunt and will damage his chances at re-election. Anyone who threatens my father is my enemy, and I will not represent anyone who is going to besmirch his rep, understand?"

"You'll be there with me before the grand jury?"

"I can't go in with you, but I will be outside and remain as your counsel. You realize that this activity goes beyond our $1.00 fee."

Owen shrugged acknowledgment. As he mounted the gallows the attorney wanted to check his pants pockets for any last spare change.

"No problemo." No problem to add expense to debt. How in the hell was he going to pay this off? On top of his car damage and the recent deductible gap on his hospital stay? He could lose his job at any moment. Any other boss would have cut his losses by now, and flung him to the wolves. Along with a growing specter of future insolvency something else gnawed within, and he had to ask.

"Tell me about the Scotch Eighties neighborhood, where I'm staying now, at Silver and Birch?"

"What's there to know? The place was one of the first upscale real estate developments in the founding years of Las Vegas. First mayor of Vegas put together an investment consortium with a group of Scottish investors. Bought eighty acres of a dairy farm.

"How about more recent? Is the house I'm staying in, was that the house where you grew up?"

"Yes, fun times, my brother and I."

"Who else lived in the neighborhood?"

"Lawyers, judges, and with the University Hospital nearby, several doctors. Steve and Elaine Wynn lived on Silver Avenue at the start of the Golden Nugget days. Comedian Jerry Lewis had a house near the highway. Lounge comedian Shecky Greene's old house is off Waldman Street. I heard Howard Hughes bought a home in the area for one of his actress girlfriends."

"How about gangsters?"

Stokes gave him a look of surprise.

"I don't know about criminals being next door neighbors. A few casino managers lived around the neighborhood when their places were under mob control. And yeah, I see where you're going. One of Sam Giancana's bodyguard drivers built a home in the Scotch Eighties. The Lorenzo Corallo and Charles DiManna families lived a few blocks away, only into the 1990s. Moved when the suburbs started expanding. In the eighties, our neighborhood was one of the safest in the city. FBI agents put suspected wise guys under surveillance. They'd spot any strangers in the area. Most daylight burglaries were thwarted before they even got started. I remember hearing about one where the thief came out carrying a T.V., heavy in those days, and there were five or six Fibbies with their guns pointing right at him. Wet his pants."

"Did you and your brother play with the kids in the neighborhood. Like Angelo Corallo and Pauli DiManna?"

The attorney still regarded him and his answers slowed in coming.

"Yeah, we used to hang around a bit, played touch football in the vacant sand lots. Played music over at my house or at Pauli's. They had a great stereo system, first multi-cassette deck, even speakers out by the pool. Went to the normal kid parties. You know, for birthdays, Halloween, stuff like that. I met Kathleen for the first time at a birthday party. I can't remember which one that was. She was fun; she liked the swim parties, every house with a pool. I didn't know her that well back then. She had her own set of friends. Her father, a successful realtor doing housing tracts. They always lived first class, upscale. Before her dad's death they lived in Rancho Bel Air, one of the first gated communities in the valley. One of the McGuire Sisters lives there."

"Do you think Chunky D and Donald Grayson knew each other?"

"I don't know about socially, they were probably in different circles. Maybe seeing each other at local restaurants, maybe through the kid inner action. Yeah, a good chance they all met."

"How about Angelo Corallo, did you know him well?"

"As well as young children might know each other. We weren't close. I met him at these parties. He always had the latest in new toys and bikes, went for the hot brands. He ran with Pauli. Both very competitive, who could out do the other, sometimes mean spirited. As we grew up, we went different directions. I became more debate club; Angel tried to be a goody-good, became president of the school Photography Club. Pauli put pressure on him. Both spent time behind the school trying out Marlboros they bought from the Paiute Smoke Shop, acting tough, living at the Vice Principal's office for truancy or being smart alecks in class.

"You know I represent Angelo's place, The Pussy Galore, on their liquor license? As an old favor to Angelo and his sister, Gabriella. I never worked for Lorenzo. Still do regulatory matters for brother and sister before the Liquor Board." Sons who follow their fathers. Owen learned that tidbit in the newspaper research. It did bode well that Attorney Stokes was forthcoming.

"How about Campi, Bluestein, or Scarpetti? Did you ever meet them as a kid, or did they have kids, did they live nearby?"

Used to absorbing lots of evidentiary data, Clay processed the question. He stood and began pacing. Owen saw where his queries bothered his attorney, a realization on how old relationships might have new meanings. "I don't recall meeting Campi or Scarpetti, or any children by that name. I do have a vision of seeing old man Corallo and Bluestein sitting around the DiManna's pool in the summer while the kids swam. Maybe the others were there. I played, paid little attention to grown-ups. Looking back, what a good cover to have an underworld conference; yakking away while being parental protective. I know Bluestein in a bathing suit showed a scar on his neck down his back. Kids called him 'Scarback', definitely not to his face. This is not all sharp in my memory. I think I goofed off mostly, and at the pool parties, spent time watching the girls swimming. They were showing off their two pieces with little nubile nipples under the tops. I have vivid flashbacks about that; maybe a little more fantasy than reality. Sometimes all of us ended up at my house. Mom or Dad would chaperone, serve lemonade and hot dogs. I lived the innocence of my youth in that house."

"And this, this kid buddy-buddy stuff, all ended when?"

"Before entering high school. I think those guys, Pauli and Angel, probably were sent to parochial schools as if that would teach them right from wrong. We drifted apart."

"Kathleen Grayson, did she go to high school with you or them?" Clay Stokes, the boyfriend, became cautious. Owen sought to give him comfort. "I'm just trying to understand the dynamics of who knew whom. Did DiManna know Grayson? Did the kids know each other, pal around?"

"Not high school, much earlier. Maybe two years, as pre-teens, a lot of us, maybe ten or so, ran in a pack. Very Mickey Mouse, not Rat Pack. 1985-1986 sounds about right. Yeah, for sure those two summers we ran together. I recall the DiMannas' had a big blowout swim party, end of summer. All the kids were there, some of the grownups. Going from 7th grade into 8th grade we were acting like it was mini adult-hood."

Clay rattled on, excited to be talking about her. "Kathleen left town around then, immediately after her Dad died, as I remember it.

"Graycie—we all carried nicknames, hers off of Grayson. 'Graycie'. No one calls her that today. She didn't come back to Las Vegas until about six months ago. She skied Lake Tahoe after college where she met her future husband. Married into the Nevada pioneer Sawyer clan. He was a State Legislator. The winters and social scene at Carson City were both frigid and they divorced after two years, no kids. She went back to New York to learn her dad's business, handling the East coast interests for the Grayson Real Estate Trusts and the Grayson Foundation. She's one smart cookie in mortgage banking."

"How did you two 'hookup'?" Owen asked.

"Kismet. She'd just returned to Las Vegas. Within a week I met her at an after party at the Billboard Awards. She introduced herself." He pointed to the couple's photo displayed prominently on his desk.

"There's the picture of us they put in the papers. We weren't a couple then. Just my good fortune it's worked out so well."

Owen knew the photo, from the newspaper research. Two young scions of society did look like a match preordained, Clay in tux, Kathleen formalized in the latest fashion. Owen gave closer inspection, offering open admiration. She beamed gorgeous in a low cut gown revealing demur cleavage, blue sapphires, and yellow diamonds wrapping her neck. Some people have their act together.

Clay continued. "She's not ostentatious, has a small house, a former model home in one of the Grayson real estate projects in Summerlin. Is this all going anywhere?"

"I keep coming back to how small this town once was, maybe in the power circles it still is. Six Separations of Mayor Goodfella. Seems everyone up in the higher rungs of the economic ladder, whether a good guy or bad dude, knew each other, even on a first name basis. What that means, I don't know."

Something like a riddle nagged him. A game played? Ah, his memory nudged a few cells awake.

"And one final question, a Magnum Casino question, for our master database, for the public relations department, what are the birthdates of all the Stokes family?"

2. A Softer Side of Steele

Owen caught a cab back to retrieve his car. Later, looking over his shoulder he did not see the black Cadillac tailing him. No, another car, a green-blue Chevy sedan, the standard type registered to government law enforcement types. Whoopee-de-do, grimaced Owen. Everything is going to shit.

To confirm that opinion his cell phone warbled again.

"Can we meet for a drink?" An uncharacteristic Melissa Steele caught Owen off guard. She sounded pleasant.

"Why, of course. Where?"

"Somewhere public and noisy; do you know where the restaurant Spago is? It's located in the Forum Shops at Caesars."

"I'll find the place."

His stomach gurgled. He'd missed lunch. The Pegler manuscript sat beside him in the T-bird. A diversion with her could shake loose his morbid anxieties. Curiosity piqued. No one from Magnum made any effort to contact him. Melissa Steele might bear important corporate news.

He must be popular. A glance in the rear-view mirror revealed two vehicles, secretive persons unknown, tagging along. Hey, join the parade. He'd try his basic Ditch Tactics 101. Valet at The Mirage. Walked in the front door, patting the bronze Mermaid's breast for good luck (that's what he'd heard), and hurried through the slot machines, past the white tiger exhibit (*poor Roy*).

From the Mirage, he took a moving walkway to the street and deposited himself within a few steps of the new and expanded Forum Shops. With skill in people dodging under the ever-changing sky of the inside mall, he crossed the Flamingo overpass, eventually walking into the Bellagio to locate one of Wolfgang's restaurants, *Spago*.

Melissa sat at a table for two. Tourists and shoppers noisily made their way gawking or complaining about the heavy shopping bags. It would be hard for anyone to overhear them, like maybe eavesdroppers. Perhaps that was her plan.

"Thanks for coming." She held a glass of wine. He did not expect that of the efficient marketing director. Strange, stressful, and unusual times.

"It's my pleasure. How goes the work? I was trying to get over there today." Owen ordered one of the Mayor's trademarked blue Margaritas, whatever that concoction held. They exchanged fake smiles.

"I hear you got banged up bad." Her sympathy was unexpected, though not unwelcomed.

"I walk with a few chafing bruises. Whoever did this was going for incapacitation, not a fatality."

"Did they catch them? Did you get a look at them?"

"No, and that's the problem. Memory snafu."

"Forgetfulness?"

"Yeah, like I can't remember what we talked about when I met with you."

"What, nothing at all?"

"Nada."

Melissa created a pause with a wine sip, reflecting. Owen did not want her to build a wall of silence so he sought to coax. "The Doctor says it'll all come back and it's now popping in and out. I just got to piece it all together. Wasn't the construction manager at that meeting?"

Her smile went coy. "Wayne Hollister. He huffed in, did a tirade on both of us, yelling at me for our tours interfering with his work crews, causing dangerous conditions. He started cursing, and surprising, you told him to shut up."

"I did?" Where did that manliness come from?

"In fact, it was kinda refreshing. You were defending my virtue, not that I couldn't handle an obnoxious man. Then he went into you and it got nasty."

She took another sip of her wine and Owen did likewise to his Smurf-colored margarita. He said nothing, just looked at her. Two casino executives, man and woman, as if this was, could he say it, like a date. I don't think so, he decided. She had freshened up from her business day with a little stronger application of lipstick and blush and a heavy dollop of that fruity perfume, more than she would have worn in the office. He wondered if his superman antics changed her perception, or this her normal after work transfiguration. She looked good, sharply dressed. Work clothes to black dress, comfortable tennis shoes of office attire switched to black flats. Dressed up, he concluded she would be a knockout for the club party scene. Night cruising would not be her style. No, not, Melissa Steele. Chances are her personality is like mine, he mulled over, a classic workaholic. Eye on the prize.

"Why was Mr. Hollister angry at me?"

"I think all the attention drawn to your DiManna murder. He's under a lot of pressure, you know, his bonus will be for an on time completion schedule. The police and morbid curious are interference."

"I'm not the cause of that."

Melissa ordered another wine. He sensed her wine glass a prop, any sipping a safety-valve release. Both let the crowd noise mask their silence. She toyed with the glass stem of her new drink. She leaned towards him as if there was someone at the next table who might overhear.

"The unions," she whispered.

"What?"

She forced her voice up an octave.

"The rumor is floating around that Jackson Flynn brought you in to run the anti-union campaign. If he announces that the casino operations are going to be nonunion all hell will break loose." She looked at him expecting Owen to confirm or deny. He denied.

"That's ridiculous."

"But why are you here? I don't want to make an assumption or speak unkind, but with all these shenanigans you've been involved in, I'm surprised you're still working here."

"Believe me, so am I."

"I haven't heard from anyone around Mr. Flynn on what you're supposed to do. They just told me to let you handle some basic stuff for familiarization, like site tours."

"Honestly, I don't know either. I'm awaiting orders, if that's what one says. You say Wayne Hollister blew his top at me about this. As far as I know, I am in no way involved with the union issue." Maybe it's true and he, not yet informed. He should be able to handle that challenge, if Mr. Flynn said so.

"The Magnum construction job, you probably know, is a type of open shop," she explained. "Certain crafts are union. We have a nonunion gate to keep the sides legally separate, working together. Everything's kosher. So far, so good. If, before it opens, the casino decides to have day-to-day worker operations go nonunion or to have union cards signed up and ask for an NRLB vote, then the Culinary Union and the other unions, like Teamsters, are going to jump in, swinging for their piece of turf. That could mean informational pickets outside the gates. In itself that might have the building trades not wanting to cross a picket line, even a non-sanctioned one."

Owen saw the big picture. "And that would cause a work slow-down, and Hollister and his management cronies stand to lose a substantial bonus."

"Pissed off would be a mild statement. Ready to punch you out, there and then. You stood up to him."

A motive arose. "He might not beat me up in front of a witness when there's a pool of strong and burly laborers to do his dirty work. Those who get a little something extra in their paycheck if Mr. Flynn received a warning through my battered body."

"One scenario," she said, sipping. "Another possibility is the mobsters who killed Chunky DiManna. They're trying to scare you and the Mayor away from all this amateur detective work we've heard you've been initiating."

Owen soaked in her hypothesis and asked himself: Who is this'we' she's talking about? Great, I have two evil forces after me, pissed off contractors, maybe even some union members, and of course, unknown criminal elements.

To his surprise, a tantalizing shaken-not-stirred moment: Melissa Steele leaned over and put her hand on top of his. He felt her warmth and sought out her eyes. Eyes could tell you a lot.

"Owen, I came from back East and my first job was entry level marketing with an Atlantic City casino. I know from the history the New Jersey Gaming Commission made extreme efforts to keep out the mob. Made it tough on people wanting to hold gaming licenses. They did a great job, to what advantage? The mobsters infiltrated the linen and food suppliers, the delivery trucking to the casinos, even the local political system. That could be happening here. This District Attorney could be right; Mayor Stokes may not be the one you want to be hanging around. You need to separate from him and tell the authorities all you know about what's happening. Isn't it obvious that you are getting yourself in deeper?"

Looking into her eyes, Owen realized Melissa Steele had been compromised. Her smile and warmth set him up, and like any dummkopf male, down fell his defenses, a zipper yank away. Owen wanted to yell at her 'how much did they pay you!' Too movie cliché. He believed a few redeeming qualities might exist outside of her being a basic bitch and ass kisser.

"Is this meeting being recorded or are we in a public place because your basic paranoid neurosis is that Jackson Flynn and Metro will think you and I are in some diabolical plot." So much for tact.

"What?" Her eyes widened. He knew it was an act. What spin would she put to her being outted? "Owen, that's not it at all. It's just that you seem to be in with what's going on and I want to know what's happening. I could help protect you."

"As in a deal, sacrifice me to the authorities?"

Redness pushed its way through her makeup. Her eyes narrowed to piercing slits.

"Your mix-up in two murders and the West Pegler beating is going to hurt Magnum Casinos." It boiled down to the truth he did not want to accept: she was right, he was in too deep.

"So my protecting you against the verbal bashing by Hollister, that's all a fake story to build my ego?"

"No," she said, her voice dropping in partial surrender, "that's what happened. I'm appreciative that you stood up for me."

"Who is the black executive at our site? Isn't his name Derek Shelly? Who does he work for?"

She stumbled. "Why, Derek works for Magnum."

He took his best shot. "Security, right. He's one of Magnum's senior go-to agents in the Security Department. Jackson Flynn is only bringing the best to Vegas for this place, right?"

"Yes, yes, that's true. I heard Derek worked with the government, some hush-hush agency, so says the office scuttlebutt. I've met him a couple of times." She hid her nervous voice behind a chardonnay sip.

"Then what's he doing sitting over there licking an ice cream cone. Is he spying on us? Or is he your personal protector? Who else is here that's on your support team and not mine." Owen took her hand with a flashy all-teeth smile to show the world that they were very close friends, intimate, and placed his lips on her fingers with a slow lingering kiss.

"Miss Steele, learn who the good guys are before you join the lynching party." He left her there. As he passed through the crowds looking for a safe exit, he shaped his hand as a gun and finger triggered Mr. Derek Shelley to let him know his cover was blown. He also mouthed a 'thank you', believing this paid Magnum employee to be the martial arts hero who saved his life from two merciless thugs. Looking back several days later on his cutesy flip off towards Mr. Shelley of Magnum Security, he wondered who else saw him make that stupid little gesture.

3. Casey Corrals Corallo

A tight afternoon schedule. Theodore, adept at his role ferreting out of the unobtainable learned the senior Corallo would be at the Italian American Supper Club from 2:00 p.m. where long time paisanos would gather in a backroom and play penny ante card games and drink campari and ginger ale. Casey's schedule required being at the hospital for her lip surgery by 4:00 p.m.. Theodore's blackjack tournament 6 p.m. at the Wynn Casino. Owen's night dedicated to reading a manuscript on early Las Vegas. He glanced at the package in the back seat of the T-bird. He hoped for value within those pages.

Theodore, dressed as a Fed Ex delivery man, entered the Italian American Club and exited with the last survivor of the Wrecking Crew.

"This jerk said Elvis wanted to see me," grumbled Mr. Corallo. "My friends laughing. I shut them up--'You oughtta see her tits.' And look at you now, Missy, those jugs hanging in the suit. Elvis didn't have no titties like you do."

Casey wore her white rhinestone studded jumpsuit.

Owen completed the ambush. "The Cassandra diamonds are still in Las Vegas, aren't they? Chunky D had to fence them out of town because all your Vegas contacts were under police pressure, roadblocks, random searches. He found a way. Smuggle them on board a private jet going back East that would be above suspicion. Donald Grayson's jet. Something went wrong and the diamonds never made it." Owen paused for breath. Six separations of Mayor Goodfella meant there were no coincidences. Mobsters at the airport spoke volumes. *The day of Grayson's death was the day of the Cassandra robbery.*

Corallo squinted at Owen. He recognized him, then he pulled the FedX hat off of Theodore's head and saw he knew the FedX man, too. Only to Casey did he smile. To the rest he said: "I can't hear you, sweetums." He walked back toward the Club.

They followed Corallo back inside. Theodore carried Casey's boom box as the strategy's next phase. The feeling a door cracked open. Larry Corallo never told them to fuck off.

Owen continued speed talking. "Bluestein, as the Horizon mechanic, worked next door to the accident site. He got DiManna access, for what purpose? Diamond jewelry gone astray."

Larry Corallo looked at the three bothersome nuisances, gave them a weak evil eye, more benign bushy eyebrow twitching than all out of spite. A tired man, an aged gangster whose time had run its course, living on his memories, exaggerated ones. Memories keep life flowing.

"McGiver, you still sore from the other night? I heard you welched on a sports bet maybe and the bookies didn't take too kindly. You gotta learn to stay healthy."

He was not going to give Owen the runaround or intimidate him.

"You're the Last of the Mohicans, Mr. Corallo, the senior statesman of the Vegas capos. Don't you understand the old gang of yours is being systematically wiped out? Someone is killing off you Wise Guys. I think you're the one who should be very careful."

His shoulders shrugged indifference or senile defiance. He turned to Casey, "You gotta come and show the fellas. They think I've gotta few screws loose upstairs, anyway."

"Sure. Would love to, Mr. Corallo." She gave him that butter-melt smile. He belonged to her. She added. "You gotta help us, Mr. Corallo. I wouldn't want to see you hurt. Really." Eyelashes fluttered.

"For you, I've heard it's just about who put Chunky D in Stokes's Mercedes. Big Fucking Deal! I didn't do it. That's a mystery to us all. You want the rest of the history, go read a book."

Book meant Pegler's book. Progress. With a manuscript copy in his possession, solutions might be forthcoming.

Corallo continued his ramble. "Maybe another day I'll be in one of those slobbery mouthy moods and I'll tell you something interesting. Maybe like when one damn asshole has a brain fart and screws up everything."

Owen pinched the bridge of his nose, concentrating. Pegler had said to Owen: "I gave five copies of the Chapter Ten draft to the Wrecking Crew. They were supposed to make changes and return them to me, and I'd see if I'd do corrections. If they gave no comment, like the Mayor, I would do what I like and consider they had their chance."

Strange. Owen talked to West Pegler, but when?

Casey set up her boombox in the card room on a small stage they used for polka night or whatever Italian-Americans did for weekend song and drink. Fed Ex Theodore and Owen took seats behind the card players. Lorenzo Corallo rose to sainthood in the eyes of his fellow card sharks as he returned with a vestal virgin in an outfit with the front zipper down below her breasts. Stimulating, on purpose. Knew her audience, gave them what they wanted. She flipped on the Sony player and the familiar music came out strong with a heavy beat. From her mouth, the singing drawl of the King. Syncopated, her pelvic gyrations annunciated the song, 'Heartbreak Hotel'. With a portable microphone she walked into the small audience, shaking her boom-booms right in Corallo's face. The ancient men, leering and laughing with gurgling emphysema coughs, shifted happy in their seats, enjoying a wrinkled hardness requiring no blue pills. Theodore cringed as he watched. All the men applauded, including Owen. They begged for more. Instead, she handed out her business cards and joked about her calendar availability for Columbus Day. Several of the men swore they would talk to the Club's entertainment director.

Back in the car, Owen marveled aloud.

"You are good. I enjoy how you can get into character so extemporaneous." His casino marketing mind spotted talent. He wanted to tell Casey about his visit to the Elvi Expo overlords. He held quiet. What if his good deed backfired? Owen committed in silence to help her in subtle ways without discovery. She's a nice kid.

"But Casey," Theodore protested. "do you have to bump and grind?"

"Oh, Theodore. I'll never compromise my talent or the King's reputation," she paused with a sigh of real life... "Well, if Playboy calls and the money's good." Giggling, she toyed with his heart strings.

Owen said, "The King would be proud of you. Can I be your Colonel Parker?" She stuck her tongue out at him, an imp in the King's clothing.

While Owen drove, Theodore in the back seat, lap-topped connecting points into their matrix board. They reviewed and discussed their accumulated data, sifting info, garbage in-out. Owen presented his case that everything pointed to the Cassandra jewels. Something, probably Pegler's Wise Guy manuscript, revived a search by persons unknown for the still missing gems. First, a connecting point between Chunky D being dead at a property formerly owned by realtor Donald Grayson, who twenty years before died in a plane explosion where the newspaper photo showed a young Chunky D. Looking, to find what? The Cassandra diamonds? That could be the answer if one tried to digest senior Corallo's vague answers that acknowledged DiManna's blunder. What failing?

Casey said, "I want to know when Campi and Scarpetti died and more details on their deaths."

Owen saw her connecting point and finished her thought. "If it's before the manuscript's finished, then those men dying are not associated to all these recent events. But if they died after the manuscript went out for review, I would say there's cause and effect. Somebody willing to kill to silence the other Crew members. There are hard clues in the manuscript."

Theodore concurred, tapping in a computer note. "I bet Pegler interviewed each gang member. Maybe one's throw-away gossip added to another's mutterings became important when spliced together."

"We don't have very much time if Mayor Goodfella is going to have to testify before this grand jury." Casey gave this slow speech as she changed back into her street clothes. In the mirror, Owen watched her wiggle and jiggle into her jeans. "What about your mumbo jumbo of the 'Aunts lost the fortune' and the 'Sight Station'. What's that all mean?"

"I think I typed it in as 'Damn Sight Nation', three separate words," said Theodore.

Casey sing-songed to no revelation of an answer and Theodore joined in on her frivolity. "Damn. Damn. Slambam. Sight Nation. Palace Station. Sunset Station. Fight Station. Damn. Damn. Frustration." A release of tension. They all laughed. Owen felt good; here were friends to depend on, to help.

Owen dropped Casey at the University Hospital outpatient clinic for her ultimate lip-synch-glossing. Theodore volunteered to later pick up Casey the Lip, he teased her. Get her home to sleep off painkillers and anticipated recovery pain of post cosmetic surgery. Owen didn't want to see Casey's facial features change. Her face beamed without blemish. Body tampering ought never to be done without concern for the consequences.

Theodore jumped off at the Wynn Casino to play his tournament. Owen, left to his own devices, took the T-bird for a highway run to cool down his damaged mind. I-15 to the 95. He exited into suburban neighborhoods, to side streets, to ditch any would-be pursuers. Left, right, left. Past housing developments with names suggesting desert bliss, oasis paradise. No one seemed to be matching his maneuvers. He needed think time and hoped flying wind and auto power would rev back those misplaced brain cells. His hair was stuck under a Vegas ball cap Theodore had given him. An embossed slogan read: "Trespassers will be (given a) shot."

His theories of book clues and a jeweled treasure hunt sounded plausible. Using Detective Taggart as a sounding board had not fared well. He failed to gain her support. This negative flourished and joined the others, of his life, his job, of relationships. All these minuses tumbled together. The Blue Funk took over. He began to shake, tears in his eyes.

Owen drove his car to a side street with an expanding view of a major housing development. The house address read 8-6-14 Inspirada Overlook, the city, Henderson. At least those here and those living below in his vista had a home life, a semblance of normalcy. Overwhelmed by emptiness his demons returned. A sickness, not of the body physical, of the spiritual mind, when a soul lacks purpose. He reached in his pocket, pulling out pills, and dry popped two. They would take a while to kick in. Until then his body locked up and for the next hour he could not move, his eyes staring without response.

4. Artistic Differences

Pavi 165 triumphs! The night did well to hide him. He had swung on a rope over the overpass to the sign below and tagged the lighted directional that read *Highway 95 Summerlin Parkway Exit*. Ten seconds of paint spray with the cars hurtling fifty feet under his hanging form, hoping no one spied him scrawling his initials, or could react fast enough to call the police before he made his escape. Quite full of himself, his tenth tag of the month, a reputation building. Tomorrow, he'd drive by, photograph his work, and post it online. Someday soon he'd find a wall on the freeway and take his time, do a wicked style bubble piece, real art.

Zap shock!

The 50,000 volt charge of the taser hit him in the side, his body collapsing to the pavement, the spray can falling from his backpack. Lacking motor control Pavi 165 could not stop the handcuff snapped on his wrist, his shaking body dragged to the viaduct, both hands secured through the metal bar guard rail. His sweatshirt yanked over his head, his baggy pants ripped to his ankles. A cold wetness over his butt sent chills through him to take the place of the shock pain. He felt the urge to pee, and minutes later his functions returning, Pavi 165 soiled himself.

Cameramen came first, not speaking to his begging to help hide his naked embarassment. The uncaring shutterbugs were the tabloid free-lancers, responsible to no one except their pocket books. They put on bright lights and took flash photos of him from several angles. The television trucks arrived next and began their filming. Soon after, the patrol car and Pavi 165 with his odors gained a ride to central booking, wearing a new set of handcuffs.

Ah, sweet Posturepedic. The same night, Owen laid his weary body down, the aches of his beating diffused to muted pain. He sensed a creak pop in his spine. A gulp of painkillers kicked in and calmness returned. He set his bedtime goal: regroup, refocus, sift what had so far been gleaned from kernels of truth to separate empty chaff from the more outright 'shaft'. He sipped hot tea. Theodore, out in search of the perfect score, left a note: *Casey in her room – will sleep the night. Doctor said the procedure went fine, as expected.*

Silence pervaded the house as Owen pulled to his side the envelope packet from Clay Stokes and unfastened the flap. Let's read about gangsters.

A shadow moved past his window.

He tensed to the gut. Instinctive, he turned off the light next to the bed. The backyard absorbed an adjacent street light with weak orange illumination. *Nothing unusual.* No priority given to his personal safety within his own residence. He dismissed his beating as being a one-time event: that was that. Why should he be at further risk, staying in a guard gated community, protection from an unmarked car parked a couple of houses down, which he had spied on his return.

He identified the night noises of the city. Owen started to turn the light switch back on when he heard the click of the door to the kitchen, off the pool. In the quiet of the house the lock turn resonated like a gunshot. Owen flexed in sudden fear.

Somebody entered the house. Not Theodore returning. He possessed a front door key, his parking place in the driveway. Not Theodore, who? A form appeared silhouetted in his door, a thin form.

"Hello, Owen," said Kathleen Grayson Sawyer, smooth and graceful. She closed the door to his room and walked over to his bed. He was too dumbfounded to move or speak coherently.

"How-- How did you...?"

"I used to play here, when Clay and I ran around as children. I guessed the key under the flower pot at the back door would never change as the backup system. The Stokes' were too predictable to change habits. Why modernize the good old-fashioned security options?"

She wore gym togs, dark clothing for night maneuvers. She moved to the other side of the bed. He could make out her outline against the dim back yard lighting. He should have said something profound, yet accepted he was not in charge. Kathleen opened the sliding door to the patio, sweeping in a breeze of warm night air. Owen realized he lay on top of the bed sheets in his boxer shorts, and as if she sensed that he could be embarrassed or that he might jump and run, she kicked off her shoes. In the darkness, she took off her running shirt, scurried out of her satin shorts, leaving only a hot pink thong, a string away from being a single thread. Laying down beside him she kissed his lips, hesitant, brushing, tender pressing, her taste lingering. She propped herself up on an elbow.

"We should talk," she whispered, sexuality languid on her lips.

Owen cleared his throat, wetting the dryness of an open mouth.

"That would be the best idea, I think."

Her hand rubbed his shoulder, not caressing, more a light finger-nail massage. Undeniably attractive, a desirable woman. Her flesh touch cauterized his bruised pain.

"From our first meeting, I felt drawn to you," she said as she rubbed. "Call it charisma. The Mayor thinks you are going places, that your insight could help solve his problems."

Two things happened, arousal being the easiest found him first. The press of flesh against flesh was firing up the ol' front burner. He did have self-control, unfortunately failing. The second, her mention of the Mayor made him remember the son.

"Clay--."

"Yes, we'll have to deal with that later. I can't spend a lot of time here tonight. I'm on an evening run. 2 K. That gives us about fifty-five minutes." Her fingers traced his face, down to his chest hairs, making curling circles, wandering down to his hip, to his Joe Boxers. She deftly moved her hand to rub his butt and scooted closer, her leg thrown across his.

He did one of the dumbest, stupidest, craziest things ever in his entire sordid base life. He said, "Whoa."

She did not take the 'whoa' to heart and laughed and kissed his forehead, eyelids and nose. Nerve endings electric, extremely erotic, no doubt about it.

"Kathleen, this is about the most dangerous thing I've ever done."

"Okay, maybe this is a rush, besides, I didn't bring any protection. Do you have anything?"

"No. You weren't on the agenda." Damn. His unopened box of condoms lay packed somewhere in buried luggage.

"Let's cuddle then." She took off her sports bra and pushed pliable Owen over on his side, spooning her body up against his back, wrapping her arms around him, hot breath near his ear. That warmth gave sin a new meaning. It did feel wonderful. Medicinal. If he turned for the other 'cuddling' direction, he would have poked her. He sensed the friggin' snake raise its head out of his underwear.

"I will be back tomorrow night, same time, and the night after. You must tell me what you want us to do. And how we might...learn to experiment."

Screwing the Mayor's son's girlfriend sounded like a program to lose-friends-and-influence animosity. In an effort to prevent premature ejaculation just by thinking of her future plans for him, Owen grabbed at the quickest fire quencher in his repertoire.

"How old were you when your father died?"

She ceased the rubbing friction. A period of silence before she spoke, a sad weariness. "Too young." A nerve hit, her taut breasts a lie detector machine, her shallow breath in the night spoke volumes. If he only could look through the darkness into her eyes, he would see raw truth.

"That was tough. You left town right afterward?

"Within two weeks of his death. I ran away from all the bad karma and went back to Illinois to a Sacred Heart school, later, east to Smith College. Finally, a graduate finance degree at Wharton. Educational avoidance, I guess. I knew someday I'd come back, face my nightmares."

"Claiborne Stokes, your childhood playmate?"

"Yeah, a brainiac, not a geek. Swim club. Debate team. We were neighbor kids back then. He's grown into a successful man, still the kid lives within."

Clay carried the credentials, political connections, a successful career, perfect for a social marriage. Owen saw that within Kathleen she lacked something, perhaps a fresh buzz, a re-charging of batteries. Owen now assumed she selected him to be her Energizer Bunny.

"And how about Paulio DiManna and Angel Corallo, also playmates and classmates?"

Again, a thinking silence, her body tensing, this time she covered her tightness by pushing against him, rubbing her breasts against his back. A massage treatment, he thought, that needs to be added to all Vegas spas.

"You're sure changing the subject from what I came here for; to soothe your aching body. You know they have medical studies that say fucking is good for the health? Don't you want to be cured?" Her playing hot nympho a mere façade. Owen saw his questioning move her from being the she-tigress aggressor to being what she least wanted to be—vulnerable.

"I am guessing that your father met and knew Chunky D?"

She pulled him over to face her, breasts to chest, nose to nose. Point on.

"Owen, my father met a lot of influential interesting people. He knew those in the neighborhood. A great man. His only fault, his life cut too short. Now it's time for your medicine."

She forced her tongue into his mouth, wet him over with a long kiss that slipped down to his chest, and bit at his nipples. She rolled over like a gymnast and crawled on top. Straddling him, her back arched, underwear to underwear, the friction preordained to explode. The undulating movement started, he felt her moistness, felt his fingers edging to her underwear ready to pull it to the side for an awkward yet sliding thrust. He was doomed, and not complaining, damn cad that he was.

The bedroom door opened. He felt a jolt of panic, expecting to be shot dead by Clay Stokes or construction unionists or mob hit men. Take a number, stand in line.

Instead, there stood Casey, in a satin teddy, leaning against the door frame, her lower mouth bandaged.

"Owen, I don't feel so well." She collapsed.

6. Hospital-ity

Though he regretted the pre coitus interruptus, Owen thanked the angels that he was morally saved by an allergic reaction. Casey's. He sat at her bedside at the University Hospital, arriving at the same emergency door where he checked in the night before. His illness being an allergy to fists.

The shots administered to her during the operation, explained the nurse, were made from rooster coxcombs. Casey reacted with a chemical imbalance. Not life threatening, still a scary incident for all concerned.

Owen's immediate response, jumping to her side, not knowing her ailment, fearing the worst. Kathleen, poised almost indifferent, pulled on her running shirt and shorts, and ever efficient, directed Owen to drive Casey to the hospital, by himself. Certainly, Kathleen did not want to post their sexual escapades in the public limelight. Kathleen slipped out the glass door and disappeared. Lost opportunity left him confused. Didn't he long for sweat humping sex with this gorgeous temptress? Why this under current emotion, half-glad intervening luck saved the sex-starved from an 'illicit' tryst?

Casey rested, allowing medicine to flush her system. Her lower lip, from what Owen could see under the bandage, resembled a purple eggplant. The doctor on call said everything is fine, full recovery expected, including her lip, more pronounced and jutting than before. Which is all the poor girl wanted — a career enhancing makeover.

She groaned and opened her eyes, focusing on ceiling tiles before she saw Owen. He held her hand in silent concern.

"Sorry," Casey mumbled, barely able to speak through the swollen lip.

"Sorry for what?"

"Didn't I interrupt? You had company, a lady?"

"No, it was your imagination." And he thought, mine also.

"I don't think so."

He fed her ice chips, spooning them over her numbed lip, telling her to suck the coolness.

"I've been thinking," she mumbled. Owen expected a lecture about his licentious behavior, though he did think of Kathleen's warm breasts fondly.

"Maybe you've just been saying the words wrong 'cause you wouldn't know how Morrie Bluestein spoke about Vegas things."

"What?"

"What if *Aunts* meant *Ant* as in *The Ant*. I saw it in our newspaper research. Didn't click until they sedated me and I went max relax. The Ant is the nickname for gangster Tony Spilotro. I got thinking, Bluestein made references to one particular event, so if The Ant meant Spilotro, could 'C' be a nickname for Chunky D?"

"Spilotro and DiManna going to 'hell'?"

"That's where they went."

Owen gave her a kindly smile. "Okay, miss smarty pants, what about this 'Site Nation' or whatever I heard."

She let go with a head shake. Drowsy. Dopey. "I couldn't think of anything."

Theodore walked in, eyes bloodshot, hair askew, movements jumpy. He looked at her with tears in his eyes.

"I'll be okay, T. I'll have the lips of The King."

Theodore saw Owen holding her hand and offered to watch Casey the rest of the night. Owen relinquished his seat. "The doctors plan to discharge her in the morning." Owen promised Casey, on full recovery, a pineapple peanut butter sandwich, one of the King's favorites. Stars need their caloric substance for the big shows. She gave

Owen a weak farewell smile. Theodore nodded somber. Owen wondered if Casey would tell Theodore about his almost fling of night passion.

He made his exit treading among the melting pot of humanity, the emergency ward unfortunates. Babies with 103 degree temperatures. Domestic disputes displaying head wounds. His being bruised seemed insignificant to the afflicted around him. Life could be so delicate, so unforgiving. The emergency ward was not as frantic as an ER television episode, instead, a place of dreary inactivity as people waited untreated in various forms of distress. As he passed by, an ambulance pulled to the emergency entry doors, a gurney with a patient, face covered by an oxygen mask. He wore the grimy, yellow coverall uniform of a fireman.

"Smoke inhalation. Signs stabilized," the paramedic yelled out.

"Room 6," shouted a nurse in return, and a crash crew of nurses and interns took over and pushed the injured fireman down the hall.

The paramedic, catching his breath, gossiped with another nurse at the admitting counter.

"Hellish fire. Five truck response. Three more men treated for smoke at the scene. Most of the building gone. Fire and smoke damage will make the furniture a total loss."

"Where was this again?"

"You know, what's the name? Crestview Furniture. Owned by the DiMannas, the mobster who got wasted over at Magnum."

"Oh yeah," said the nurse filling out paperwork. "The Mayor's involved."

Things are heating up.

It was well past 2:00 a.m. when he returned home. He put a chair at an angle against the back kitchen door, locked his sliding door, and placed a broom handle to block any jimmying. He locked the bedroom door and, likewise, shoved a cumbersome sofa chair against the door. Now secure, yet exhausted in his fortress, he would sleep the sleep of the dead; not the best metaphor, and read West Pegler's manuscript in the morning. He thumbed its length as he started to put it down, and noticed something he had not spotted before, torn pages from the middle. When inspected and compared, it was apparent that Chapter Ten had been ripped out, the section specific about The Wrecking Crew. What the hell? What was going on? His eyes drooped shut, weighted down by fitful exhaustion.

Bam. Bam. Bam.

Owen did not wake easily.

Bam. Bam. Bam.

With restive annoyance he shook fatigue and soreness off. Someone pounded on his bedroom door. His name shouted. He was waking up to a day of hell.

Bam. Bam. Bam.

"Who's there?"

"It's Theodore and you've got a problem." He opened the door to the young man in a state of hyper anxiety. Theodore spoke at a rapid clip. "I brought Casey home this morning and we saw the police down the block. I know they're coming for you."

"Could be a summons to the grand jury." He jumped back in bed and pulled the sheets up to his neck. "Kinda expected to hear from them. Don't they do business hours? Not early, not on the weekend." A glance at the clock showed he had slept to 8:30 a.m. Delightful sleep.

"No, listen, there are four squad cars and a couple of unmarked vehicles, and Casey thought she saw your lady cop friend."

He rose, cracked his back of old pains. He threw on casual clothes for the day, nothing in particular as he had no real plans. "Detective Taggart? If she's out there, I can talk to her to find out what's going on."

"I think they're here to arrest you. We need to get you out of here."

"Arrest?" For what? For whatever reason, his feet began a quickening pace, as he followed Theodore out the sliding patio door into the backyard. They ran around the pool into the corner of the yard, hidden by evergreen bushes and low pine trees to a break in the fencing. Theodore pointed.

"Through that fence in the gap and we'll meet you on the other block."

"I don't have a reason to run. I've done nothing wrong."

Theodore reproached, wise beyond years.

"How can you save yourself and the Mayor from a jail cell?"

Theodore rushed back into the house. Owen hesitated. *Why should I run?* Two moments later the decision became apparent. A police officer with a flak jacket and a drawn sidearm, serious and threatening, came around the corner of the house. He could not see Owen in the needle undergrowth and the policeman silently entered the back door of the garage. A Metro swat team slipped in from the other direction, Delta Force style, to the corner of the house, awaiting a signal. He heard Theodore's car move onto the street. No sudden rush of sirens signaled the target was the house, and thereby, the remaining occupant.

Owen did not need armed confrontation this early in the morning, and before his coffee jolt. Any arrest or whatever would be immediate grounds for Magnum taking the safe road and firing his sorry ass. He could barely squeeze through the fence break. The aches and pains returned. His was not a body up to par.

Damn and damn again. He gave himself a mental kick. He left Pegler's manuscript on the bed. Unread. He must read that as soon as possible. More than the rest of the manuscript, he wanted to devour in deep study Chapter Ten. Misplaced or rather stolen.

On the next street, Theodore's Toyota idled for him and he slumped into the back seat, ducking down to hide. Casey sat in the front seat. Her face swollen and bandaged, she hid it behind a white dust mask like one sees on anti-germ Asians or the late Michael Jackson when he slummed amongst the common folk.

Owen and Casey exchanged sad glances in understanding the other's pain. The trio drove around the corner to make a getaway, and Owen stole a peek down the block as they passed. To any neighbor glancing out the window this morning, it resembled a raid on a terrorist hideout. Right in the middle of the official hordes, the silver SUV of Detectives Washington and Taggart. So much for any spark of kindness that might have led to a heads-up warning.

His cell buzzed in his pants pocket. Melissa Steele.

"The authorities were by here this morning looking for you."

"And you told the police right where I lived, no doubt."

"No, I just said you were not in and I didn't know where you were. And they weren't really police, but I think Sheriff's deputies. They had papers to serve. I wouldn't accept them. When will you be in?"

Ah, that girl, working for the Magnum cause on the weekend. He'd convince her of his better qualities when and if ever paroled. If the papers were from the Sheriff's office, they function as officers of the Court. This means service of the grand jury invitation. Then what's the convention of cops doing in the front yard of the Silver Avenue house, by now inside the premises? Owen found himself distinguished, sought by various law enforcement agencies. Great, just great.

Owen needed all the resources possible. Regardless.

"Melissa, do me a favor, I need a few addresses and telephone numbers."

"What?"

"Wayne Hollister's for one. He can locate his employees, ones the police should talk to. Like whoever manned the gate the day the Mayor and I were there. And a construction traffic cop might have seen the killer arrive, carrying a golf bag type case."

"You got to be kidding." He hoped not. Any lead would do at the moment.

"I'll call in later. Thanks for your concern." He could not tell if her call came as a friendly warning, a thawing on her part. Or to suggest by implication, do your civic duty, McCombs, turn yourself in and face the consequences. Well, Melissa Steele can kiss --

"Where to, what next?" Casey sounded tired. She should be home, resting. Owen couldn't ask them to hang with him, to put themselves at risk as accomplices. He told them they could drop him off somewhere and he would fend for himself. They both exchanged hurt looks and ignored him.

His phone again. Get ready 'cause here I come.

"And where might you be, Mr. McCombs?" Detective Chase T. Taggart's hard voice stressed they were no longer on first name basis. Now, how did she get this number? Oh, yeah, in a fit of decency, he had offered.

"Touring your fine city. What's the pleasure of your jingle this fine, beautiful morning? Social, perhaps?"

"I'd like you to meet us down at police headquarters. I have a few more questions."

"What? Missed giving me a personal wake-up call? By ambush, that is."

She had battery acid in her voice. "Ah, Mr. McCombs, you were at home. Sorry you left in such a hurry with your friends. We have their plate number if you want to turn this into an O.J. driving day."

"Am I missing something? How serious is all this?"

A moment of silence. He understood.

"If the shoot-now-and-ask-questions-later Starskys and Hutches are hovering around, say I hung up on you, walk away, and call me right back," he said.

The line went dead. He told Theodore to get them like a bat-out-of-hell, to a car rental company. They had to affect a car switch. The cell sang. Detective Taggart did want to talk in private.

"Better?"

"Yes. I'm serious. You need to come in."

"Is there an arrest warrant out for me?"

"Not yet, but a search warrant of the house has been issued. We're looking for the murder weapons, gun and knife, and evidence taken from Pegler's residence. We've been authorized to bring you in for questioning. And if you don't show up, the Sheriff and the D.A. will drop the hammer."

"Where's this all coming from?"

"West Pegler's name ring a bell?"

"How's he doing?"

"Semi-comatose, not coherent. Prognosis is he'll survive to sleaze another day."

"And Pegler and I have what in common?"

"Your fingerprints were found in the living room and on a drinking glass in the kitchen."

"I don't think so. I didn't touch anything or go in those rooms."

"That's what you told us. That flies out the window if in fact you were there earlier, returning to the crime scene with your buddies for a built-in alibi. There's the final nail. A transient we arrested picked you out of a photo lineup. Saw you several days earlier and again the evening before last at Pegler's apartment." She gave him an evil pause. "Probably after you left my house."

"Homeless Bob?"

"One and the same. If you don't have a solid explanation, the D.A. could file for aggravated battery, maybe even attempted murder. Owen, come in."

So, he went to Pegler's apartment twice. That explains a vacancy in the evening timeline lost from the beating. What did Pegler and he talk about? Whatever, he could not admit his previous visit. This police woman would take a giant leap to his guilt.

Wait. Detective Taggart called him by his first name. Very interesting, bridges lay unburned. It was his turn to weigh her reaction.

"Chase, there's a book in my bedroom. It's Pegler's book, his manuscript on the Vegas mob. No, before you guess, I got it from Clay Stokes. The answer is in there, or was. Somehow, some way Chapter Ten has gone missing." He heard her silence, wondering about the first name basis. How personal was this? He tried to make light of his day so far. "Hey, if you look around you might find some of my dirty clothes again."

"I've just been in there. At least, you throw your dirty clothes in a laundry hamper. That's a good habit. Only the bra on the floor by your bed seemed out of place, Mr. McCombs." A sports bra, no doubt, he realized.

"The police on stakeout had a woman leaving your premises last night just after you rushed out with another woman in your arms! None of this is relevant."

He shook his head in defeat. A story he could not win in the telling. He stood on a moral gallows, lynched with a bra strap. All he could say, "Read the book. Find Chapter Ten. It's the common thread. The killer read this manuscript, that's why the killings started."

"What's in it?"

"I'm not sure. Chapter Ten is the key. Do me a big favor and check with your Fed friends and see about the relationship between Tony 'The Ant' Spilotro and his Hole-in-The-Wall Gang, and Chunky D and the Wrecking Crew, specific, for the years 1985 and 1986. "

"What do *you* think is going on?" He heard a skeptical voice.

"I'm sure this whole mess is in one boiling pot; the murders, the manuscript, and the diamonds. I'll try and contact my attorney and have him set up a negotiated appointment with your office. Would that make everyone happy? And it'll be voluntary, not a public guillotining with the press corps en masse."

Silence on her end of the phone. "Owen, I shouldn't do this, but here is my cell number: 867-5309. Emergency only, but knowing you…it may come in handy." She repeated again slowly: "Eight six seven five three oh nine."

"Thanks.

"See you this afternoon. Don't be late."

Finished with his call he had only two seconds before the editorial comments began.

"Is that the lady from last night?" asked Casey.

"Are you sleeping with the enemy?" asked Theodore.

"I need to find Pegler's book. Chapter Ten specifically."

8. Insiteful

Her call to him finished she stepped from the patio back into his bedroom, uninvited.

Fetters held up the bra.

"I'd bet our guy is a cross-dresser."

Fetters would think that.

The raid checked out a total bust. No one at home. No stolen Pegler computer files. No weapons. No knife. No .22 caliber revolver.

She walked the house, explored the individual bedrooms. The interior of the house time-warped back into the Seventies, minimalist art deco. She walked the house, explored the individual bedrooms. The police popped the locks of the bedrooms, except for Theodore's. Here, when they could not snap off the bolt or decipher the multi-sequence combination lock, they smashed in the door. Each room told a tale. She saw Owen yet to put character into his room; living nomadic, out of his suitcase. The bed in disarray. Well, of course, a man of action. She picked up one of his shirts, held it, and when not noticed, as a detective might be curious, smelled for female fragrances. His only, a musk fragrance. Making sure, she smelled again.

The other two rooms drew her attention. One seemed a religious shrine to Elvis Presley. A wall poster of the Memphis crooner. Not the room of a mere fan with a crush. Bookcases spoke volumes, neatly shelved, even a catalogue tray. Like a research library. Videos and DVDs of performances and movies, screen magazines in plastic covers, shelves of books on Elvis, shelves of Elvis memorabilia. A closet full of male clothes, Elvis costumes, only two dresses. Who lived here?

Chase recalled meeting this girl called Casey. At Pegler's apartment she pulled the girl aside. What did she know of the beating? Did she know West Pegler? Yes, Casey said, he had written a review about her participation in a local Elvi talent contest. Wrote she lacked professional talent. The young entertainer admitted she was no admirer of Pegler. How about Owen McCombs, queried the detective. The pretty girl gushed and blushed: he's so nice. Touring the celebrity impersonator's room, Chase found Owen's photo from one of the recent news stories pasted on the young girl's wall, next to a Presley montage. A red lipstick kiss planted on the faces of both men. Childish hero worship, Chase concluded. For a young woman, is that healthy?

Detective Washington searched the other room, "My God, look here. I don't know what I am looking at, has to be illegal."

Theodore's room. Top to bottom in the most sophisticated computer, recording and sound system equipment, light years beyond Radio Shack and probably on par with the CIA.

Detective Washington fingered through a bookshelf of casino how-to books, many titles technical on operations, several on gaming machine repair manuals. "We need to forward the information on to the Nevada Gaming Control Board, if he's not already on their radar."

Detective Washington made another telling comment: "And make sure you don't break anything in here. You may not notice, he has us under surveillance. There's a miniature camera in that corner and see that poster of Bill Gates. Look at the pinprick hole in his nose. Another camera. I'd expect more hidden cameras taping our every move."

When they left the room, Chase glimpsed Detective Fetters slip a purloined iPod from his pocket back to a nearby desk. It figured.

On their way back to the office, Chase questioned Washington on the theory that the mobster killings might have a tie-in to the book Pegler was writing.

"Doesn't it now seem logical that all these murders might be tied to a robbery that took place twenty plus years ago?"

Detective Washington flinched. "It's possible. Never recovered the jewelry. All the players in the crime are dying off, with a little outside help."

"How about the Hole-in-the-Wall-Gang? They were competitors. Any of those gang members still around? Would they get an inside track on the Cassandra jewels?"

"I haven't heard any of those guys making waves. We can check them out, the ones still living. Spilotro was whacked mid '86. There was no love lost between the gangs. Spilotro said to have a spy inside the Wrecking Crew. Stole heists from them. That's a rumor from the normal snitch gristmill. Twenty years ago? I just can't see all this resurfacing and leading to the current killings."

"Pegler's book could be the catalyst." She patted the plastic evidence bag holding the manila envelope with the manuscript. Pages, this Chapter Ten, definitely missing.

"And this manuscript handed to McCombs by his attorney? Why not stolen from Pegler's place? I think that gives us enough to go for an arrest warrant."

"But if Clay Stokes' fingerprints are on the pages, maybe with the Mayor's, that would support McCombs's statement?"

Detective Washington mulled over the dilemma of a rush to judgment. "I don't want the police to look like fools. This has to be the D.A.'s call and I know that man wants action."

"If you don't mind, Ray, I'll get the lab to dust the manuscript. I want to spend some time reading and on locating Pegler's lost Chapter Ten. Today."

He pulled a toothpick from his desk drawer, tore off the plastic wrapper, and went digging for unseen irritation.

"Go ahead. Give it to me, afterward. I might as well take a look, too."

Chase wondered, as Owen had suggested the coincidences. Why did her partner want to see the manuscript? Because he knew the players? Personally? History he could recall, identify with? Or more seriously, had Pegler named which cops the gangs had co-opted within Metro? Several police officers snitched out went to prison. She didn't want to believe it true. Ray Washington, his personnel jacket full of commendations, bravery in the line of duty, dirty. No, she believed in her gut feelings.

Owen McCombs? What did her gut say of him? Her stomach grumbled to bad fast food and gave no other insight.

An awkward call to his attorney. To his relief Clay Stokes did not answer. Normal people, even attorneys, must take the weekend off. Owen held the subconscious fear that if and when the Clay conversation took place, the first blurt out of his mouth, 'Oh, by the way, on top of all my other problems I'm planning on sleeping with your girl-friend, your almost fiancée'. Owen faced Kathleen's return tonight, around 9:00 p.m., she said. Do I call and fend her off or not show up? Do we meet in the bedroom with the inevitable climax, or climaxes? He left a message for Clay Stokes to call ASAP, life-or-death situation. He sensed fatalism around the next corner.

Likewise, he dropped into the Mayor's voice mail. The grand jury tried serving him, so went his message and, therefore, he assumed the Mayor on the same subpoena list. He knew if they were trolling for the big fish, entrapment of the Mayor, they were going to use him as the chum bait.

"Where to, what next?" Casey asked, confident in her leader. Up-beat, her white surgical mask added to the desperado aura. What to do? First steps first, covering tracks.

They signed up a rental car guaranteed by Casey's credit card, with Owen fronting the bill in cash up-front. They would not hit her credit card until the car was returned, so any police tracking would be thwarted. This transaction left him broke until his next paycheck, if there was going to be one. They parked Theodore's Toyota in the lot. He did not expect the police to jump quickly at an all-points bul-letin for Theodore's car since Owen said he would show up at police headquarters. Only six hours left before they might lock him away. He needed time to find the final connecting points. To rally the troops, he congratulated Casey on last night's riddle solved: the Ant. What significance it held he could not fathom.

"That only leaves 'Site Nation' and this 'C or hell'." Theodore said.

They sat at the car rental agency staring at the street. Turn right. Turn left. Choices.

"Let's take a run by Crestview Furniture." Too many damn coincidences.

On the way up to 14-22-9 Town Center, Owen constructed the scenario he thought most plausible, the hypothesis to sell the police on his innocence. He offered a test run to his companions:

"Pegler circulated his final draft manuscript to certain key people, those previously interviewed. He wanted them to check for accuracy, giving them a chance for further embellishment. I'm guessing he parceled out only certain chapters. The Mayor might get a full manuscript because he figured prominently in several chapters. The Wrecking Crew would only see Chapter Ten. The old codgers let something slip. Perhaps separate stories told, but when pieced together, a revelation. I'm guessing it concerned the Cassandra jewels. "

"Chapter Ten is what we need to find," affirmed Theodore.

"But why tear out Chapter Ten, why not just steal the manuscript?" The simplistic question by Casey summed up the depth of the mystery.

Owen mulled over who had taken out specific manuscript pages. Not the Mayor if he wanted his son to check for libelous statements. Clay would have no need to destroy. He would need all the pages, the whole book, for evidence in any defamation suit. Opportunity existed? When? In valet during his meeting with Melissa. Maybe she set him up with the aid of an accomplice. Like Derek Shelly. He shook his head of that suspicion. He did not see a reason for Magnum employees to be involved. Someone else following him? The book left in the car, the doors locked. What did that mean? An antique car and the old coat hanger trick could gain quick entrance.

"Try this on," he told his stalwart gumshoe companions, "and this seems right out of left field, so bear with me. Someone, person or persons unknown, ripped out Chapter Ten of the Wise Guys manuscript. What if the Chapter Ten theft, like my beating, wasn't to make a point or steal clues. Instead, misdirection, wishing to slow me down in our private investigation. Whoever is doing the killing knows we are out snooping."

"You're right, the chapter is not lost, others have it," said Casey. "You'll eventually read it."

Theodore saw it more succinct. "After twenty years, time suddenly matters. What is putting a rush on the killer's timetable?"

Not a pretty scene. Half the building resembled the black ribs of a putrid skeleton. What was left sent odd puffs of white smoke upward overseen by a backup fire crew wetting down hot spots. Inside, furniture resembled burnt embers, black ash or soaked grey gunk. Ironic, a singed window sign announced 'Fire Sale'.

Police kept the curious at a safe distance. Owen surveyed the scene and identified a target.

"Wait here." Owen hoped his handsome mug failed to be digitized into the police central database as a person to 'detain and hold'.

"Hello, Kane." The private investigator sat in his car writing notes. When he recognized Owen his expression went grim, a nasty twitch to his mouth.

"Hear the police are looking for you, McCombs."

"Only to answer a few questions."

"Wonder if they've posted a Crime Stoppers alert yet. I'll keep my eyes open. They give rewards for that."

"Why have you been following me? And don't use that 'it's a free country to drive anywhere' crap."

"Hey, watch your paranoia. Who'd want to see what you're up to? All you're doing is making the police look harder at the Mayor and not at the real killers."

"Any ideas? I am not playing Hercule Poirot the Detective. You solve these murders, I'll put up a statue of you in front of the Magnum." Did he still have a job with Magnum? Owen's mental radar suggested this might be the day that decided his future. "And what about this little weenie roast?"

"The arson investigator says 'suspicious in nature'." Kane could not let some flake out cop him.

"Torched for insurance?"

"From what I hear, Chunky D and family were making good coin furnishing all the new homes being thrown up. You don't kill the golden goose."

Owen found himself agreeing. Why burn the store now; Chunky D's dead? What's the point? "And for my own edification, Kane, where were you when West Pegler's face got rearranged?"

"You adding me to a suspect list? You wouldn't have the slightest idea how to ask a clock the time of day."

"Just curious. I heard the Wrecking Crew gang paid informers inside Metro. Around your time on the force, right? Maybe DiManna of the Wrecking Crew, ready to see his name in a wannabe best seller, revealed his inside police contact. If you, then good-bye any relationship with the Stokes family. You're off the money train." Owen could see a scenario fitting. Kane had the ability to track the Mayor's daily routine. Knew he'd be at the Magnum building site. Maybe DiManna showed up thinking he's going to receive hush money?

Owen hit an unknown nerve. Kane bristled.

"McCombs, stick to being a casino shill. It suits you. So far, all your questions lead you to being beaten. You can see that's not healthy. Here comes an example of what I'm saying. You're your own worst enemy."

Owen turned to find Pauli DiManna rushing into his face, accompanied by a bouncer goon from the Carnivale.

"What the fuck are you two doing here?"

"I'm with him, he's in charge." Kane passed the torch with sadistic pleasure, rolled up his car window and drove off.

"What the fuck do you know about this?" He pointed to the store ruins.

"Nothing. Your dad is killed and this happens. For me to help the Mayor means finding out who torched your parents' store."

"Screw you. This was an electrical accident, nothing else."

"Do you think the Cassandra jewels were in the store? That they were found and the fire was a cover-up?"

That stopped Pauli for a quick two seconds before he pushed hard and Owen went sprawling to the ground. Old hurts resurfaced.

"You got your head up your ass." Pauli's heavy stepped up to do a facial tap dance. The man flexed WWF wrestler bulk.

"Hold on, I'm a reporter from the *R-J*. What's going on?" Theodore appeared with notepad and pencil in hand.

"He tripped over his tongue." Pauli stalked off with his goon. Owen saw the departing glare, understood the menace as a threat unsatisfied.

"Nice seeing you." Owen glanced up and actually saw a smile on the face of Detective Taggart. She had walked away from her partner while they were talking with a fire captain near the store.

"You mean seeing me on my butt." Theodore helped Owen to his feet. He grimaced with continuing pain.

"You have this effect on everyone you meet?" She was enjoying this.

"Mr. DiManna seemed to be upset before he got to me."

"Well, his family store did just burn down. He wants entry into the store to see if any records are salvageable. Arson squad won't let anybody on premises."

"Did it cross your mind that he might be looking for something else?"

"Like diamonds," added Theodore.

Detective Taggart focused on Owen. "Aren't you supposed to be down at police headquarters for questioning?"

"My attorney scheduled me for voluntary compliance later this afternoon." Owen knew this to be an untruth. He had not yet reached Clay.

"I could take you in now, save us all some trouble."

"I appreciate the kind offer, but I think my attorney wants to choreograph by innocence."

"As I said, don't be late."

Casey walked up to them, her mouth lay hidden behind her white gauze mask. Chase saw her leaving the house this morning. What's going on? Could it be, Owen beat her? The Detective took a mental step back to study the twosome, a strange cadre of followers. Is McCombs that mesmerizing?

"If you gain access to the building, mind if I tag along?"

"I don't think so," said Detective Taggart, both firm and snide. "We do have an investigation going on here--."

"Give me credit for trying. Just take a serious look inside Chapter Ten and this building." The trio departed. Chase watched them go and wrote down the license plate of their car.

When Ray Washington walked up to her, he was shaking his head.

"Don't firebugs like to watch their creations, even return to the scene of the crime?" He looked toward Owen. "Weren't we told to arrest him?"

Chase wondered if she had blundered, let a person of interest just walk away. She couldn't have doubts.

"The warrant this morning limited to house premises. He's showing up for questioning this afternoon with his attorney." Chase could not believe she jumped to the casino executive's defense.

"That guy is too everywhere. That means he's involved. Just how, I don't know."

"Ray, do you think we could walk around with the arson folks, see what maybe survived the heat. Pauli DiManna seemed antsy to get inside and that makes me curious."

"I don't have the urge. If you want to end up with ash-mud makeup and ruined shoes, that's up to you. They're pretty sure it's arson. Amateurish. An accelerant, a Moltov cocktail through a window."

"That would take Pauli DiManna off the hook for insurance fraud? He'd have his daddy's smarts to make the fire source unrecognizable."

"Yeah, except we're not talking like father like son. You can't remake the old school with young punks."

10. Owen Someone

Chase felt like a sludge slug.

Detective Washington knew the score. Touring the scene of a fire meant playing in a mud bog. Her shoes of the day ruined, water logged. Her clothes smoke saturated. The arson inspector stopped ever so often to snap photos and make statements into his tape recorder. At one point the fire investigator became distracted. Chase took the opportunity to splash down a corridor that housed the executive offices. Ax chopped holes in the roof illuminated the hallway, black grime shadows offset by bright spears of sunlight. Spooky. Several sodden offices seemed to have escaped the flames.

Finding the old gangster's nameplate on a door, she found the late Chunky D's office devoid of the luxury the showrooms displayed. Spartan like, as if he did not spend much time here. A few heat crinkled photos twisted on the wall, most showcasing community service. Sponsored soccer teams. Heart Health walk-a-thons. No snapshots of the Fraternal Order of the Cosa Nostra. In one corner of the room, the fire hose water cascading from the roof between the joists and wall panels buckled a wall outward. It revealed a sliding panel door, designed to go unnoticed, now wet warped and sprung. She tugged the door fully open and found in a closet size space a small safe and a four drawer filing cabinet, both fireproof, both locked.

She came out of the closet into the snarl of Pauli DiManna. Her heart skipped and fluttered. Off guard, she jumped back and yelled, "What are you doing here?"

He was not at all pleasant. "This is our property. Sticky fingers might pick up what doesn't belong to them."

"This is a crime scene. Get off the premises."

"My attorney is on the way. We want to legally secure this place, especially my dad's office." He stepped forward and she felt pure malice as his face breathed close to hers. Her hand dropped to her holster. At this distance of inches, if he went crazy and made a lunge at her, she knew she could not react in time. Her voice pushed out squeaky, and they both recognized her loss of power.

"Mr. DiManna, leave now or I will put you under arrest for obstructing our investigation."

His stare tore at her. Moments of silence passed where she watched facial tics of Pauli DiManna, arteries in his neck pulsating. She wondered, if he acted, would anyone hear her screams.

Worse than cursing her, he laughed in her face. Triumphant to their standoff, he turned, plodding hard into the cave dripping shadows.

Chase relaxed her confrontational posture and breathed an audible sigh of relief. Nerves askew, her body shook at her inadequacies. Never again would she let herself be so vulnerable.

"Hey, there you are." She jumped again. Detective Washington tiptoed the puddles with little success. "We wondered where you had strolled off to."

"Did you see Pauli DiManna leave a minute ago?"

"No one passed me."

"He knows this place, all the different exits. He found a way in here hoping no one would see him. Probably surprised to find me."

"Wha'd he want?"

"I'm not sure." She looked at the office. "He might have wanted to get into his dad's safe before anyone else could. Get in and out quick. Could we secure the safe as evidence to a potential arson?"

"Yeah, through a court order. I could get the fireboys to do us a favor. Yeah, they'd be for it."

She tugged on the filing cabinet drawer. "Locked files interest me." What Owen McCombs told her gained credence with DiManna the Younger on the scene.

"Hey, you're starting to sound like the lead honcho around here."

"Sorry, enthusiastic."

"I want to show you what I can dig up, that I haven't lost my touch." Washington smiled at her, holding up a dagger-like knife with a braided rope attached to either end of the scabbard.

"It's a knockoff," said Washington. He dropped the faux dagger on an ash-mud desk and tried to wipe his hands of the smoky grime. "Not even close to our evidence knife. Interior decorators use stuff like this as shlock wall décor. I wonder if we can find a furniture catalogue here to locate a more expensive brand."

"Similarity to what sliced and diced Chunky D?"

"Exactly. Chunky D perhaps killed by a blade bought at his own store. Irony of justice?"

Her partner could browse any mushy catalogues ever dried out. Weeks away. Detective Taggart's goal to hustle and view the contents of the safe, the filing cabinet for good measure. Maybe the Cassandra diamonds lay within. Maybe Owen McCombs was right after all. That thought bothered her.

11. "Wise Guys of Las Vegas"

Chase sat at her desk immersed, yellow pad and pen at the ready. She skipped early Nevada history of cowboy desperados and frontier lawmen. Las Vegas, she read, is a new city, founded as a railroad promotion in 1905, helping ship refrigerated produce, Salt Lake to California. The building of Boulder Dam, now Hoover Dam, in the 1930s, brought workers. The legalization of gambling by the legislature in 1931 established the rough and tumble pioneer gamblers, Bugsy Siegel being the most famous. A small monument of Bugsy at the Flamingo Casino remains his historical epitaph.

Chapters Four thru Eight dealt with the mob influence in Las Vegas from the 40s thru 1970s.

Chapter Nine focused on the antics of Spilotro's "Hole in the Wall Gang", made famous by Nicolas Pilagi's book Casino, and later movie with Robert DeNiro, Joe Pesci, and Sharon Stone. The police, Chase read, dubbed them the Hole-in-the-Wall Gang. Outlaws like Butch and Sundance they were not. Their nickname from breaking through store walls to gain after hour access. The only reference to the Wrecking Crew in Chapter Nine, a story on their bitter rivalry.

Pegler wrote:

Late night drinking at the bar at Piero's, Tony heard about the estate jewelry at Fourth Street Pawn. Actress Joanne Holiday had died a month earlier at her ranch near Pahrump, Nevada. To cover medical bills for breast cancer, the cause of her death, she had been pawning her jewelry, gifts from boyfriends and several ex-husbands. Her attorney planned to move the remaining jewelry from Fourth Street Pawn to San Francisco to sell at the Butterfield auction house on Thursday of that week. Spilotro pulled together his outfit and sent his best flying squad donned in KKK burlap hoods into the pawn shop on Monday morning, July 10, 1985.

The Wrecking Crew led by Charles "Chunky D" DiManna must have been privy to the same loose-lip gossip since four members of his gang, in rubber Halloween masks, were already at the counter covering the shop employees when Spilotro's boys came in with weapons drawn. A hood stand-off. They knew who was who. Waving guns, cursing, yelling, they argued about who had the valid claim to knock over the pawn shop. Witnesses outside saw two men arguing in front of the pawn shop. No witnesses came forward but the police guessed one robber probably was Spilotro, identified by his short stature. The other man in the argument should have been Lorenzo Corallo, more brains of the crew than brawn, the rough stuff title going to Chunky D.

In the end, two bags were produced, and the thieves stood there, taking their time, arguing over the division of spoils, nitpicking over choice items before each gang exited, running in separate directions, still shouting obscenities at each other. No one was ever apprehended, though the Fourth Street Pawn jewelry started popping up across the country in stores that bought what they thought were discounted family heirlooms.

It was said, thereafter, that Spilotro's Hole-in-the-Wall gang had it in for the Wrecking Crew and vice versa, and that The Ant tried several hits on them, including a drive-by shooting on the Las Vegas Country Club golf links, hole eight, and an airplane sabotage. Each attempt failed. The Ant's crazy efforts at eliminating rival gangs plus his own legal troubles might have been his undoing. The Kansas City dons asked the Chicago family to remove this thorn in their side.

In June, 1986, Spilotro and his brother were found, battered to death and left as fertilizer in an Indiana cornfield. Mob peace, shaky and uncertain, descended on Las Vegas.

She let her eyes rest. Nothing more in Chapter Nine on the Wrecking Crew. Chapter Ten torn paper stubs, missing. She thumbed the manuscript and her eyes fell on the Acknowledgment page. Pegler listed Sheriff Randall as one of his 'thanked' sources. The Sheriff might have a complete manuscript. There's the answer. She wanted to be one step ahead of Mr. McCombs. Her own mission drove her to quick action: to out-best them all.

Frontal approach thought best and she found herself parked, in a wait mode, adjusting skirt and blouse in the outer reception area of Sheriff Randall's office.

"He's been in a meeting for awhile," said his secretary when Detective Taggart arrived, explaining she required five quick minutes. Official business, and she said nothing more. While waiting, Chase made notes on her yellow pad, highlighting all the key points McCombs had uttered since she had met him. She put aside her annoyance at the man. A good detective listens, does not let personal prejudices block facts. 'Personal'? How did that apply to McCombs? She knew that he put her off balance whenever he swaggered through her life.

The door opened and a group of men exited. Chase noticed them carefully, as they did her, their chatter going silent. They presented the bearing of law enforcement, three of the men older and she guessed job retired. One official was the Federal officer that she had first seen at the Magnum construction site in the shouting face-off with Mayor Stokes. A crewcut of yesteryear set him apart. The last to leave, 'Little Mikey' Fetters. She saw his surprise to see her sitting there, a buddy smile changed to a sneer that seemed to say, 'I'm part of the Insiders and you're not'. He walked past without a word.

As the secretary ushered her in, Sheriff Randall concentrated on checking his phone messages. He looked beat down as if the previous meeting drained his strength. Chase sat across from him, seeking his attention. Finally, he looked up and gave her an uncomfortable once-over before speaking.

"Detective Taggart, I hear you just moved over to Homicide when these murders got dumped in Ray Washington's and your laps. If you feel it's too much for you, let me know, and we'll make adjustments."

"No, sir. I'm fine." She bit her tongue downplaying her worth, not being weak, merely playing 'boy club' politics. "Ray Washington is the lead, and doing an excellent job. I am supporting where he directs me."

The Sheriff nodded his satisfaction. The Good Ol' Boy Club lived and breathed.

"So, what can I do for you?"

"Just background. Sir, you recall columnist West Pegler writing a book on Vegas mobsters?"

"Yeah, sent my office a copy, wanted the department to review the law enforcement side for accuracy."

"Detective Washington thought it would be a good idea if we took a look at Pegler's work to see if it had any clues to his attackers."

Sheriff Randall didn't think much of that idea.

"Waste of time."

She gave him a demure smile. "Yes, sir, I would tend to agree, but Detective Washington asked me to follow up. If you don't mind I can have it right back to you."

"No, what I mean is the D.A. has it all wrapped up. They're putting out an arrest warrant for this McCombs character. Think he might be a hit man. Using a casino as a cover."

"What?" She caught herself. "I don't know if Detective Washington has his case built. Lots of unanswered questions."

"The D.A. thinks the evidence will fall into place once this killer is off the streets." He moved some papers off his back desk credenza. "Here it is. Never got around to reading it though he put my name down as a 'background contributor'. History never excited me. It's all about people long gone, not the excitement of here and now."

That's limp reasoning, Chase considered. History is our only immortality.

She thumbed the manuscript open and saw Chapter Ten.

"Thank you, Sheriff. Maybe this will help."

The Sheriff dismissed her with a wave of the hand, as if she were wasting his time.

She returned to the department and her desk. Before she could sit down and sift through the pages, her schedule called for another appointment. She dropped the manuscript on her desk. Besides, after this next meeting she might not need to read it.

12. Crime within Crime

It was her show. Chase coordinated and assembled the small group as they met in the investigation garage of Metro Police. There were no expectations about where this might lead. Even her partner absent to what he considered more important possibilities.

The safe and the filing cabinet were surrounded by two arson investigators, the attorney for Crestview Furniture, who was indirectly the executor for the Charles DiManna estate and a locksmith, just finishing drilling the safe and popping the locked cabinet. The DiManna family refused cooperation, or rather, said the late Charles DiManna controlled personally the access key and combination.

Chase harbored mixed feelings about Pauli DiManna failing to show. If anything came out of this, she wanted to wave it in his face.

The safe door opened. Chase, wearing gloves, knelt and began to remove contents, while an arson investigator snapped away with a digital camera and the DiManna family attorney began to inventory the contents. Carefully, she reviewed each paper. Contracts for furniture purchases. Mortgage papers. $2,000 in cash. Two checkbooks. A pile of checks for the next payroll period. No stash of stolen gems. Chase felt her face dissolve in disappointment.

A small jewel box marked with the label of a store in the Fashion Show Mall: a pair of ruby earrings and an unsent card reading, "To Candy, Happy Birthday, My best, C.D."

Chase had this distinct feeling Mrs. DiManna's nickname would not be 'Candy'. All the safe contents went into plastic evidence bags.

She would glance through them later. Best to turn them over to the arson folks, let them unravel a link. She saw nothing probative.

The sprung-lock filing cabinet likewise gave her a sinking feeling. The first drawer held furniture vendor file folders. Orders made, bills of lading, invoices paid, all alphabetical. The next drawer consisted of store inventory. Third drawer, furniture catalogues. One catalogue had the title 'Mystic and Ancient Weapons'. She thumbed the pages and saw a Persian-type dagger, similar to the one discovered in the rental truck of Owen McCombs. The catalogue photos the cheap variety, exactly like Ray's discovery in the burned-out store. Except for vague similarity, no correlation direct to the murder weapon. Still, as a detective, she'd show this catalogue to Ray and let him run with the inferences.

Drawer four of the filing cabinet housed the basic file folders of customers; two sections, one representing hotel buyers, the other, area home builders who bought furniture in discounted large bulk packages to furnish their model homes.

She stood back. Not what she had expected. The DiManna attorney suggested this was a waste of his time. The arson investigators were deflated not to find a Molotov cocktail mixer in the locked compartments. With the evidence packaged and inventoried, the group began to go their separate ways. The door of the empty safe was shut. The filing cabinet containing the normal course of business would be returned to its rightful owners.

Chase felt gut empty. No smoking gun, jewels, rare collectibles, or clues, anything. And she called herself a detective. Goddammit, start thinking like one. Nothing …something…paper work…filed in order…to a purpose beyond the obvious? The safe and filing cabinet were both fireproofed and hidden. Yes, protect the store cash, protect customer records. Still... her fault, she saw that now. She put the goal first, believing too quickly there would be hidden diamonds. If the diamonds or another killing knife were not apparent, and she purged them from her mind, what did she see before her? Why had Pauli Di-Manna felt the urgency to come to this particular office? The safe and file. Okay, to remove what? An object that could be tied to a fire or murder... or...? What other crime might fit with... furniture?

"Wait." The small group near the exit stopped and she waved them back. She went to her cell.

"Marcella, where are you? Drop everything. Drop it. Find for me files YX-1980 all the way through GML-1834. I know; it's impressed on my brain. Yes, that whole section, plus from Southern Highlands, GS-1947. I don't care whose desk they're sitting on. And locate Detective Martinez. Bring him and the files. I'm in the Homicide garage across the parking lot. Pronto, por favor. Gracias." Marcella Espinoza worked as a squad secretary, still did, during Chase's years in Burglary/Robbery.

The group stared at her. The attorney huffed and stomped his foot.

"Give me five minutes. Meanwhile, let's go through the safe evidence once more." As expected, reviewing the safe contents did not garner any clues to the fire's culprit, but bought her time. On cue, Tech Secretary Marcella Espinoza and Detective Jose Martinez of Robbery/Burglary Division appeared. Martinez, being the solid Latino gentleman, carried a medium size stack of file folders. Chase always worked well with Martinez, a conscientious, by-the-book officer. Plus, Chase knew that Marcella had a hidden crush on the young detective.

"What's going on?" demanded the DiManna attorney. He had not taken off his suit jacket since his arrival, wanting to maintain his holier-than-thou respectability, and in a garage with weak swamp coolers, he bore the punishment of drenching sweat.

"I wanted you to see how Chunky D, your client, is, was, the crook behind most of the recent valley home break-ins — unless you're already aware of the fact."

The attorney snorted, "I don't believe this."

The arson investigators mumbled to say burglary cases held no interest to them, only fire bugs.

"Just watch. Bear with me."

She went to the bottom drawer of the file cabinet and pulled out a marked section she had noticed: 'Model Home Sales', twenty five folders thereabouts.

On the floor of the garage, she laid them out in a long rectangular shape, each folder separated. She took her time in doing so as if creating a pattern, a geographical compass to various valley neighborhoods. Several crime scene techs working on impounded cars strolled over to watch the strange garage mosaic.

"Marcie, help me. Read an address off a folder and then hand it to me."

"9-6-13 West Festival Pines."

Chase glanced in the folder. She considered the address location, walked over to a folder on the floor, and laid it halfway on the name, the Crestview Furniture folder marked: Diamond Hills Models. She spoke each model name as she laid the folder down. Robbery/Burglary Division folders were color coded so they stood out from the manila file folders from the furniture store. Chase and Marcie repeated the process until Marcie caught on and she went ahead and started doing the searches herself, like a card game of 'Concentration'. This gave Chase the ability to tell her theory of the crime.

"As you will note, the Crestview Furniture folders represent all the model homes where they supplied top-of-the-line furniture. Multi developer projects, at least twenty or so, scattered all over the valley so there did not seem to be a pattern.

"Six months ago, there seemed to be an unusual number of new homes being hit."

Detective Martinez nodded. "We thought workers at the construction sites."

She wanted Martinez as an ally. "Construction workers nearby, daytime burglaries, the suspicion is logical. These break-ins required sophistication, burglaries never leaving physical damage unless locked jewelry drawers."

"And you say Crestview Furniture, the deceased, Charles Di-Manna, was behind this?" the attorney asked. Less huffy in defense, curious as the rest.

"I think if Robbery Division is now focused, they'll discover that Crestview Furniture probably employs ex-cons with burglary records. They are the break-in team. They install the model home furniture, and while doing it, maybe dummy up a window or a sliding door to give them easy access at a later date. Most of the thefts have been small valuables and loose cash. Jewelry, by the way, was Chunky D's specialty. Crestwood's trucks with a logo sign are not out of place in the new neighborhoods. A construction worker as the thief would be tempted to lug away stereo equipment or a flat screen T.V. Not this modus operandi."

"That's the way most all went down," agreed Martinez.

Chase continued her theory.

"With further research, an inordinate high percentage of these home burglaries in new construction subdivisions will be these model homes."

"What about burglar alarms in former model homes skewing your data?" asked one of the arson investigators. She could see him caught up in a growing fervor, excited to be present when a case broke.

She smiled, "I'd bet most robberies occurred soon after the model home sold and occupied, too soon for the new buyer to put in an alarm system. Or if they did, and this is more a guess, a home buyer might for a discount package buy out all the model home furniture as furnished. Crestview would make an excuse to come back for a repair and then tamper with any new alarm system. With these models being closed out and then sold to third parties all over the valley, you had plenty of locations that could be staggered not to look like a pattern. Even if Robbery Division caught on model homes were a main target, the police could not sit on every model home at every new development in the Valley.

"Watch how Marcie is laying out the folders. It looks like most of these developments were hit three or four times, all model homes. I'd stake my career on it that they will have been originally furnished by Crestview Furniture."

Marcie finished her placement, standing back with a grin. The preponderance of suburban burglary locations fit next to or on top of a model home customer file folder of Crestview Furniture. Only five folders fell into the miscellaneous pile, and Chase guessed, those would be random burglars, not of model homes and not part of the DiManna crew. The Crestview Furniture attorney said nothing.

Knowing the history of his former client the attorney said nothing, tantamount to conceding the truth of the accusation, literally laid before his feet.

Detective Taggart wondered how much Pauli knew of the thefts? He could not have been ignorant. She surmised he showed up at the burned out store to destroy evidence of his and his father's culpability? Like father like son. Chase wanted more than anything to nail Pauli DiManna.

13. The Sting

"Modification of plans," said Theodore. "Before we go after your elusive Chapter Ten, The Merry Pranksters are having a raid at the Carnivale Casino. I gotta get right over there." His whole demeanor oozed kinetic rush.

"Carnivale? What raid are you talking about?"

Theodore did roller derby driving, near hits on several honking vehicles, in one tire squeal, missing a statue of a glazed rainbow bucking bronco, rearing in arch, ready to airborne a shoot 'em up cowboy. Owen cringed at the near miss. I fear I'm reliving an olden times: *'I'm like that statue, a crazed rider thrown, in midair, hard ground and pain coming on fast'*.

"Well, in a way," Theodore started his story, "Owen, you gave us the idea."

"What?"

"Remember telling us about Pauli's slot scam at the Carnivale. Well, to us, the Pranksters, this meant other flaws existed in the casino's operations."

Owen knew Theodore's computer geek skill made him a valuable 'advantage player'. That is, he and his buddies went looking for advantages that gave them an edge over casino odds. Instead of independent competition, they worked better in teams, packs, and Theodore ran with card counters known as the Merry Pranksters. The trio was back at Theodore's car at the auto rental. He rummaged in his trunk and arose as a new man. Of course, a cowboy. They were off again.

"Here's what was happening at the Carnivale," he explained. "The Carnivale launched a new marketing promotion called 'Caribbean Fun Party'. The Carnivale ranks card players by a time bet formula, giving you perks for how long you are at the table gambling. Their math says they will come out the winners. Not in this promotion. They will give a player a $1 commemorative chip for each black jack won. Plus, and this is the kicker, thirty extra minutes will be posed onto your time of play sheet, which the pit bosses keep track of. Depending on house rules blackjack has a house advantage of 5.9%, but if you're a better than average blackjack player using what's called 'basic strategy', then you can bring the house advantage to a break-even and that's an advantage to the player. On top of that, if you can handle the mental gymnastics of card counting a multi deck shoe of cards, that's a big score."

"And I assume you excel at that," Owen asked knowing the answer.

"Theodore has recall memory," beamed Casey. "He can code up to six decks, assigning values for the face cards, and never look like he's concentrating on the game play." Once again Theodore basked in the warmth of Casey's notice.

"Anyway, they have made this particular promotion a fun pit of three tables, and by some crazy internal management decision, they're playing with a two deck shoe, instead of the usual six decks.

"It'll be like taking candy from a baby," Theodore said and wah-wahed like an infant. "Now add in the cash value of the player points put into the computer system and one could actually take the house by winning player card points. On a table game the player points are given by length of play, not so much if you are a winner or loser. If you stay at the table playing, you get points, and now additional points for each blackjack. Granted, in a card program, you ended up with points that could go for buffets and discounted hotel rooms; by fate, the Carnivale in another gaffe has a bonus program in their Caribbean promotion. For certain levels of points a winner could exchange Caribbean Fun points for other prizes such as travel vouchers to an island destination and show tickets. Those benefits, once awarded, could be converted back to cash. That's a costly mistake for the Carnivale. How long before they notice means we got to hit them now."

Theodore went on to explain the raid team consisted of twenty players organized to simultaneous attack the Carnivale until the tired bookkeepers in the casino accounting back office spotted the anomaly. Theodore grinned at the chance that this could be an exciting and lucrative one to two day run.

At the Carnivale, Theodore stepped from the car as an all American Cowboy. Hat sunglasses, leather vest, even a large silver belt buckle. "This week there's the Bull Durham Bull Riding competition at Thomas & Mack Center, and a lot of the outlying hotels like the Carnivale with cheaper room rates are packed with budget cowboys."

Late morning and the three black jack tables in the Caribbean promotion party pit had a good crowd. Theodore whispered that not all twenty of the raiding gang were there, they would run shifts. Owen spotted obvious costumes of disguise, the goal to fool the eye-in-the-sky cameras and their facial recognition software. These men and women were in security casino data bases, with standing orders to escort off premises immediately. A player can win in casinos with luck, not smarts.

Owen knew he better not partake in the raid. With enough problems he did not need to find himself in cahoots with ethically challenged sleight-of-hand gamers.

"While you have fun, I have an idea of what we can do, especially since I just left Pauli at the furniture store."

It did not take Owen and Casey long to locate their target.

"What's wrong with your face?" she asked of the young girl wearing the surgical mask.

"I had an operation, Mrs. DiManna."

"Do you mind if we join you for a moment?" Owen sat down anyway, without invitation, and Casey followed suit.

He thought he would find Mrs. DiManna pushing buttons at another rigged slot machine. This time her comp power pushed her to the head of the buffet line. Her plate piled full with goodies, they sat with her at a table.

"How well did Ch—." He caught himself. "How well did Mr. DiManna know Donald Grayson, the Realtor?"

Mrs. D. had a system, as Owen viewed her piled plate. Start with the shrimp and snow crab, prime rib next, salad munchies last.

"You mean the Mr. Grayson killed in the airplane explosion?" When Owen nodded, she said: "A little, I guess. He lived in the neighborhood next to ours. We might run into him at the store. Never the wife, she had a cook buying groceries, buying a lot of liquor bottles, if you know what I mean. Poor woman. The kids played together, a couple of times, we Moms would do carpool favors for each other. What's this have to do with you police catching my husband's killer?"

She misidentified him, but Owen let that slide to his advantage.

"Do you recall your husband saying anything about a new book coming out..." He was careful here. "About the history of Las Vegas, maybe about the era when Mayor Goodfella was practicing law?"

She sucked her fingers from the crab claws and chomped away at the prime rib. "Yeah, book, yeah, he mentioned that, one of the things that upset him over the last month."

"One of the things?"

Her mouth full, she spoke in slow motion gasps.

"He was mad at Morrie, real mad. Maybe because of the book, I don't know. Called him foul names at home and then he went to see him at the hospice."

"When was this?"

"About a week before Morrie died. I read how he was murdered, poor soul. They can't blame Morrie's death on Charlie." What a lady, thought Owen, as if her husband's death would improve his wayward record.

"And what happened after that meeting?"

"Well, he didn't say much to me. He talked to Pauli, my son. I heard snatches of conversation. Like I guess Morrie gave a deathbed confession. He asked my husband's forgiveness."

"Forgiveness for what?" Casey entered the discussion.

"I didn't hear that. Only Pauli saying to Charlie, 'Well, if he doesn't have them, I have an idea who might'."

"Did you know what they were talking about, 'them'?"

Shellfish made way for prime rib. "No, not really."

Owen stretched. "It could've been about the Cassandra diamonds."

Mrs. DiManna paused, her fork raised.

"Is that what killed Charlie? Knowing about the diamonds? Has anyone found them?"

"No, not yet, soon we hope," said Casey. Mrs. DiManna resumed wolfing down her meal.

"Coulda been that. A couple of days back Pauli comes over to dinner. Went to the den for a talk with Charlie. Maybe about the diamonds. I'll ask Pauli."

Owen gave her a sympathetic smile.

"I think your husband might have figured out where the Cassandra jewels were, and he might have been killed because of that knowledge."

"No shit, Sherlock. I wouldn't have thought it would be Charlie figuring that out. After so many years, I knew it bugged him---even if he had nothing to do with it—. So, our friend Sweets finally 'fessed up? I would have laid you two to one that Scarpetti had been the one."

"Mario Scarpetti?"

"The same. He was the fink."

"'Fink'?" Casey asked.

"That's what Charlie said he discovered. A turncoat among his own friends. He was in cahoots with The Ant."

"The Ant?" Bluestein's death rattle came back to Owen.

"Tony Spilotro," said Casey. Her guess had been correct.

"Yeah, Charlie said he learned from Bluestein that Scarpetti, on the sly, worked for Tony. Did him odd favors. I guess, years later, Bluestein picked up on Scarpetti-Spilotro connection. Those betrayed hold long grudges. They might do something bad."

"I think that came true."

Before Mrs. DiManna could ask what Owen meant or make another run to the buffet line, her cell phone rang. "Oh, hello, Pauli. No, I am here with that nice policeman. Who? The detectives working on your father's case. They say they're getting close to locating those diamonds. You know from the Cassandra robbery. Yeah, that's what he looks like. Okay. Let me put him on." But the two young people were gone from her table.

They pried Theodore away from the gaming table.

"Okay, I can break from here, but not long."

"I need to find Clay Stokes," said Owen moving swiftly outside for the requisite fresh air; hot air would have to do. He knew by now Pauli DiManna in talking to his mom would be homicidal. "You can drop me off. I think some pieces to the puzzle are falling into place."

"A clear picture to the stolen jewels?" asked Casey.

"Or the killers of old fogies?" questioned Theodore, stuffing casino chips into his pockets. The colors identical, all high denomination.

"They are one and the same. Problem I have is: I am out of time. Clay and I have a date with the police inquisition in one hour."

14. The Neon Graveyard

Damn!

Owen caught up with Stokes having a late luncheon rendezvous at Gordon Biersch brewpub at the Howard Hughes Center. Clay's companion none other than Kathleen. They were eating outside under water misters in the shade. Owen noticed again, they made a perfect couple.

"What are you doing here?" asked Clay, surprised. Good question. Theodore dropped them off. They had tracked down Clay's romantic interlude pleading with one of his legal associates, intoning the Mayor's name as subterfuge.

"And who's your friend," came Kathleen's polite question, extending her hand. Casey decided to go with Owen since her place of work, the Montecito Casino, nearby. Owen had never seen women take appraisal of each other so blatant. Fast introductions were made but Owen knew a façade farce when he saw one: Kathleen knew Casey from the bedroom melodrama, and he feared, Casey likewise had put a name to a straddling naked woman in the same darkness, mounted and ready to ride.

"I've been trying to reach you. It's a matter of life or life without parole." Owen explained the police demand for his presence, his fingerprints found in Pegler's apartment, and Sheriff deputies roaming the city with a grand jury subpoena. Owen skipped the part about Clay's girlfriend crawling into his bed. He avoided glancing her way and when he did he saw an odd smile on her face. He saw Casey eyeing the society realtor with recognition. He could not worry about Casey's opinion of him. Above all, his information critical to impart to Clay. His interpretation of 'Wise Guys of Vegas'. Even without reading Chapter Ten, from what he learned so far, his discovery a sad truth he could not say in front of Kathleen: someone twenty years back murdered her Father and that someone probably a mobster.

He held his tongue as Attorney Stokes provided, as Owen came to expect, the level headed answers to each crisis: "On the Pegler questioning, I'll clear off the afternoon and go with you, or maybe we can reschedule the police for tomorrow morning. On the subpoena, you can't avoid them. From what I hear from Harmon Hartley, he has a source in the D.A.'s office, my dad's papers will be served next week. I'll call the court and take service on your behalf. Don't worry. They're groping in the dark."

Owen heard that allusion before, and with Kathleen sitting there, the expression compounded his elevating stress. Owen had a rendez-vous with her for 9:00 p.m. tonight. Would anything save him? Did he want to be saved from this 'rush to lust?

"When you read West Pegler's manuscript, the one your father gave you, did you find anything unusual, anything that might shed light on all our present difficulties?"

"I didn't really focus except for those parts where Dad's name was mentioned, scattered all through the last part of the book. I didn't really read in depth."

"Anything in Chapter Ten? Do you remember Chapter Ten?"

"Vaguely. As I told you, I thought I lost the damn thing, couldn't find it. When you mentioned it and I went looking, Kathleen found it under a dresser in the bedroom."

Owen swallowed hard. 'Kathleen' and 'bedroom' mentioned in the same sentence. Jeez--. He hoped Clay did not see him wince. He didn't want to be the one to break up Clay and Kathleen's happiness. Clay really needed to find a way to rein in his hot-to-trot girlfriend.

"You know, all this is coming together. I just may know where the Cassandra diamonds are."

"Really?" Kathleen spoke up. "Please let us know; it's all so…spicy." Owen wanted to tell all, including the part about Kathleen's father and how he died. All still supposition, the book holding the answer. What he thought Morrie had said in his interview to Pegler, not realizing Scarpetti and DiManna both had added to the telling: Grayson's plane tampered with, by Scarpetti under the direction of The Ant, Tony Spilotro. Scarpetti didn't know the stolen loot would be aboard — but it wasn't — by design, and not the design of the gang members. Owen wanted to be right about this.

Did anyone else, meaning the killer, read between the same written lines? The diamonds have been missing since the Grayson plane explosion; DiManna and Corallo both thought the gems were on the plane and went looking for them. *Conclusion: Donald Grayson was the person last holding the Cassandra diamonds.*

Speaking up now would be inappropriate. On the way to the police interview he would bounce his ideas off Clay. Perhaps let Clay dole out the bad news to his girlfriend.

A dark blue Lincoln Continental with tinted dark windows screeched to the curb. A crate-built man in a strange tropical shirt and wearing a ski mask rushed out and grabbed Owen by the arm. He yanked him over the outside railing of the restaurant. Owen shocked, connected with one punch, and the man faltered. A shot rang out, fired from the car's driver. People dove for cover. Owen felt his head sideswiped with the muzzle of a gun barrel. The car's driver waved his gun in wild gestures, aiming indiscriminate at the cowering patrons of the restaurant. Casey jumped the railing and flung herself on the man who thrust Owen into the car's backseat. The attacker flicked her off like a troublesome gnat. The driver pointed the gun at her. Owen yelled 'No!' and kicked the front seat, throwing off the driver's aim, the shot shattering a restaurant window. The car squealed back into horn blaring traffic. Owen glanced back and saw deer-in-the-headlight numbness on the faces of the restaurant patrons. Some probably believed it some sort of reality punk'd contest, nevertheless, taking no chances, cowering under tables. Only Kathleen Grayson, he could see, seemed unruffled, having the presence to pick up her phone and dial for help. Before the backseat goon shoved his head down, Owen thought he saw a familiar car trailing behind them, trying to catch up.

The kidnapper's car turned a corner and rushed down a side street.

What was going on? His kidnappers weren't pulling a bag over his head to hide their destination. Was he on a one-way ride to a hole in the desert? Uneasiness crept over him. Three blocks down, a few rushed sliding corners taken to throw off pursuers, they stopped. Grabbed and pushed roughly, they hustled him to another auto, racing off again. Switcheroo slick. So much for any restaurant patron noticing car description and license plate. In the bum's rush, Owen glanced back, the car he saw earlier, nowhere to be seen. Another five blocks and they stopped again. The car acquired a new passenger. There were now three kidnappers in the car. Smells of gun cordite and sweat from ski masked thugs was overpowered by a strong odor of a man's aftershave. Scents of musk lay heavy. Owen's side view of the back seat kidnapper's Hawaiian shirt created a vacation atmosphere not real. Ski masks were removed and the most recent occupant sitting in the front seat grabbed at Owen's shirt pulling him forward. He saw his fate. This will be a one-way ride.

Angelo Corallo. Angel. No Shadow of Death dispensing momentary darkness but the real Angel of Death.

Angel delivered a slap across Owen's face.

"Where's my Papa, you fucker?!"

"What?"

"You and your goonies were the last to be seen with my father yesterday and today he never shows at the club. Where the shit is he?!" A fist slam to the jaw and Owen collapsed backward in the seat.

The hoodlum in the back seat gave him a sideways elbow crunch to the ribs. Owen's head hit the car seat in front as he rediscovered old bruises. This ugly mug in the back seat had fuzzy baldness, a three day old beard, and two scars on one cheek that crossed to make an X. He resembled a Gestapo tourist or a neo-Nazi skinhead. His Hawaiian shirt with the floral pattern matched his colored skin tattoos. The freak was a definite candidate for a GQ makeover, beginning with manners. He saw Owen staring and Owen's head and shoulder were shoved hard against the window. Moist warmth from the top of his scalp ran down his cheek. He wiped at the discomfort to find his hand bloodied.

"I've nothing to do with your father."

"You may not be the mother fuckers who grabbed him, but you and your snooping started all this. And if he's in anyway hurt, I'll...." He searched for the appropriate threat. "I'll split open your body and put your guts on your chest and you can watch your heart have its last beat." That was colorful. Owen could visualize that very well, indeed.

"Angelo, I swear, I know nothing. I have this crazy idea that someone is out killing off all of your father's old Wrecking Crew. He's the last one. Yesterday, I told him his life could be in danger. He didn't seem worried."

"My Papa's afraid of no one. The papers keep saying DiManna's the Wrecking Crew boss. Bullshit! DiManna flexed only muscle, weak like a mad cow. Lorenzo Corallo, my father, was the real brains and smart enough not to boast about it."

If Owen faced death, as he sincerely believed was going to occur, he wanted questions answered. "They both screwed up, right? The Cassandra diamonds? Did Grayson steal the Cassandra diamonds from the thieves who first stole them?" That mystery solved might piece the entire tapestry together.

"Who told you this?" He didn't deny Owen's patchwork plot.

"*Wise Guys of Vegas* gives all the hints." A book he had yet to read.

"Pegler's a piece of crap, and his book is shitty toilet paper."

The driver snickered and the back seat Nazi oaf laughed and Owen figured these two goons of Angel's had paid Pegler a brutal visit. "You got your facts all wrong, like Pegler. Grayson's Citation jet didn't have the diamonds on board. None of the Wrecking Crew ended up with the diamonds." Angel laughed, more a grunt of disgust.

Citation. Owen sing-songed, "Site Nation. Citation." Morrie's last words.

"Okay, Angelo, tell me. I deserve at least that."

"They all fucked up. Morrie with airport access. He let Scarpetti in through security, not knowing Scarpetti was working both sides, moonlighting. Spilotro asked Scarpetti to do him a favor. Seemed Spilotro's bosses out of Detroit thought Grayson, in raising the money to open the El Morocco, would do so without them as silent partners. Grayson making speeches, a convert to clean government. Told everyone he'd kick the bad influences out of the casinos. The capos decided to kill him. The Ant saw where he could get back into the good graces of his bosses."

Owen pictured sweet little Kathleen holding the last gift from her father, waving good-bye at the airport, only to be thrown to the ground moments later, feeling the searing heat of the plane burning, the smell of charred flesh.

Owen joined the story.

"So the brains, your father, and DiManna, the muscles, didn't know there's a hit out on Grayson?"

"Old School Dago Schmucks."

"The deal had the diamonds with Grayson on the Citation. They were never found because they weren't on the plane."

The car took a sharp turn. A wave of dizziness swept over him.

"The newspapers reported twenty years ago that after his death, Grayson's office and home were burglarized. The Wrecking Crew on a rampage to find the lost diamonds. Today, is someone that close in finding them?"

"So I've been told. But not you, McGyver."

They drove north into a warehouse district, the driver peering in his rear view mirror. Owen glanced out, lost to location. Without the Strip casinos as landmarks, he did not know where they were. The car entered a large construction yard, a junk yard of old Las Vegas casino signs. A few names he remembered from old 1960s movies with the Rat Pack. Hacienda. The Mint. The Dunes. A small sign promised: *Future Neon Museum.* This place he had heard about — dare he say it — a neon and light bulb graveyard, a bone yard of relic signs. The significance not lost on him.

The driver dragged him from the car, and the beach bum Nazi sucker punched out Owen's air, bringing him to his knees. A rib kick sent him sprawling. Owen accepted this gutter rat must have been his attacker of the other night. No hero to save him, the hula Nazi wanted to finish his stomping footwork.

With his face in the dirt, Owen caught the glimpse of a rusted sign with broken light bulbs: 'El Morocco Oasis'. Into view walked two spit polished ostrich loafers, legs attached and upward, Corallo Junior standing over him, the hate of a thousand torturers spread on his face, fists clenched, murder in his eyes.

His henchmen propped Owen's body against an old faded sign, a tall cowboy with a cigarette. At one time the arm might have waved along Fremont Street, and perhaps the cigarette once spouted real smoke. The first jab found his stomach and Angelo whose hands remained to his side, again asked, "Where's my Papa?!"

"I don't know. I don't know."

"Let's try it another way." Another punch found Owen, this blow to his back and kidneys. He'd piss blood if they hit him there again. "I want to hear about everyone you've talked to in the last two days. From the top. What you said. What they said. No mistakes. Capiche?"

As best as his broken mind could tabulate, he gave names and a brief one sentence synopsis of contact.

Melissa Steele. The Mayor. Hartley Harmon, Byron Kane, Clay Stokes. West Pegler. He mentioned the card room at the Italian-American Restaurant, could not recall names and threw in Morrie Bluestein's name as an afterthought. He left out secretary Frieda's name and those of Casey and Theodore praying Angelo didn't care about any bit players in this fatal drama.

Owen thought he got them all, but a nod from Angelo and a fist to his crotch in an upper cut keeled him over. Angelo was a sadistic son-of-a-bitch and like his dad let others do the smashing grunt work.

"You left a few persons off your list. How about Ray Washington and his girl sidekick?"

Owen wondered: why mention Washington? Did the Corallos' know the detective?

"And there's another lady, a very pretty rich bitch. Mr. McGyver, I don't think you are having much luck at Questions and Answers today."

"Kathleen Grayson Sawyer." How did Angelo know about her? Did he have paid informants in the police department? Washington? Someone else? Detectives Taggart and Washington knew Kathleen had found the knife at the Gold Avenue house. That would be in their reports. Then, last night, Kathleen and Owen together. Could Angelo have known that? Maybe someone other than the police watched his house. If the police department leaked worse than a rainstorm, sooner or later the Mayor would get word and believe Owen was making gooey eyes at his future daughter-in-law. And Clay Stokes would hear of it and Owen would be a pariah in town, leading to certain, permanent unemployment. If he lived that long.

He recalled another name.

"Pauli DiManna. I saw him twice. He says as a kid he played with Clay Stokes and Kathleen Grayson around the neighborhood. Did you? Is that how your dad met Mr. Grayson?"

Angel chuckled, a devil's smile of having an answer that Owen didn't.

"We knew each other." His laugh at an old insider joke. Owen grew tired of the games, even with him being the game ball they kicked around.

"Angelo, if you and your dad are so bright, why don't you have the Cassandra diamonds in your greedy little paws. I'm guessing the DiManna clan is going to get to them first."

Angel looked to the Nazi and nodded.

Owen agreed he deserved that knuckle punch. Why did he ask for it? He often thought that one day his internal turbulent nightmares would lead him to an overdose or a diver from the top of a Magnum hotel. Now he was facing death, a mobster Dr. Kevorkian to do his self-destructive bidding. In learning about the jet sabotage, Grayson's Citation jet, and about the kidnapping of Angelo's father, Owen suspected, this wannabe gangster was not going to leave behind a living witness. His tongue tasting blood and dirt, he groaned and sought the strength to accept the next blow.

Angelo's cell played a tune. Of course, "The Godfather Theme."

"Yeah?" Angelo listened.

"Wha'd you hear?" He listened to the caller.

"Fuck, I should have guessed." Owen could see Angelo's head shaking in agreement, his agitation calming.

"What time? Yeah, I can be there. We're having a social visit with your friend, Mr. McGyver. Oh, right, McCombs." He listened for a moment. "Aw come on, let us boys have some fun? Yeah, yeah. If I know what's good for me. How about for you? Yeah, he could know. Given a day I could get it out of him. Okay, we'll leave him alone. For later, right? Okay, see you there. Yes, I'll have the package with me. " Owen collapsed, believing he had gained a momentary reprieve. Thank God, thought Owen, praising with gritted hallelujahs the unknown, merciful godfather. Thankful praise too soon.

They scraped his body along the dirt and gravel. He heard a creaking noise, a metal scraping and felt his limp form picked up and heaved up and over a steel container side, onto glass and metal. His scream real; cut in several places. Before Angelo Corallo closed and locked the trash dumpster he let Owen in on a few secrets, none he really wished to hear.

"I think I got it figured it out, and you did show me the way. I know where my Papa is or at least will be. And if you thought I was going to leave you alive I am, I made a promise. You'll die nevertheless. I've recently found a bullet is too simple of an ending. Suffering a slow death is crème de la crème. It tortures the soul, knowing you are going to die, having a day or two to understand you have no hope. Yours will be dehydration and the shutdown of your body's systems. No one comes here. Their Neon Museum won't open for another year. No one picks up the trash. If they find you even next week, they'll have to crane out the bloated carcass. Cook well." His laugh enjoyed smug pleasure.

The lid shut. Clanking reverberated on the dumpster, sounding like a metal rod jammed in to secure the contents. Owen heard the car drive away on the loose gravel. No highway sounds. In the distance, occasional jet plane noises, fading in and out. An urban silence of loneliness and that feeling of doom began to fester within.

In less than a minute, he knew the sun and its radiance, barely tolerated since his arrival in Las Vegas reached its zenith of baking mode. The smells of his cooking were of blood and perspiration, oil rags, dried out garbage, metallic grease. This is the end. He could sink no further in his life. His demons recognized his flawed weakness, a man living without value to himself, and before he could find his pills, the banshees flew around him, screaming and his mind flatlined.

Neon Museum & Boneyard

Part IV

The Devil is in the dice

— Old English proverb

Clark County Library

1. Raid Galore

The telephone rang.

"The whole fuckin' world is falling apart," said Washington, pissed and exasperated.

"What's up?"

"Broad daylight kidnapping. Two of them. Both tied to our investigation."

"They kidnapped two people?"

"More insane. Two separate kidnappings."

Chase could not believe what she heard. *Damn McCombs. Damn him.*

Chase knew that Owen McCombs' life was forfeit. She went back over everything he told her, one of his ideas might trigger the right answer to his rescue. To avoid distractions, she found a stall in the ladies' room and began to read Chapter Ten. The most viable clue.

Five minutes later, she heard a persistent knock on her cloistered throne and a man's voice.

"Detective Taggart?"

Mayor Goodfella. What the ---?

Debating whether she was embarrassed or not she escorted him from her hiding place. Chase mulled what to say. He spoke first. "How do we find our missing Mr. McCombs?"

Our?

"Missing Persons is working on it." What could she say?

"Come off of it, Detective, you know his kidnapping is tied to your homicides. The police need to produce results. They'll kill our boy. You've seen how they've killed before."

He was right, she realized. Chase offered the Mayor a seat in her phone booth sized cubicle. The Homicide office buzzed with this visitor's appearance, the nefarious defender of guilty criminals. A collective dislike smoldered the air. Across the room, Chase could see Detective Fetters steaming hatred. The Mayor saw Chase's copy of Pegler's book.

"I had my son's investigator, Byron Kane, check out all the Spilotro's Hole-in-the-Wall survivors. None are active, most are deceased. We can rule out current rivalries among the over-the-hill gangs."

Chase thumbed the book's pages. She needed time to digest her recent readings.

"Owen was right that Chapter Ten draws attention to the Cassandra Diamonds."

"My bet would've been Lorenzo Corallo, the only one left. Now, he's kidnapped. His daughter even called me."

"His daughter?"

"Gabriella. She runs the Italian steakhouse at the Pussy Galore. I hadn't talked to her in years. She cried for me to push the police. She's afraid you guys will let him stay missing. Owen kidnapped off the streets and Corallo gone missing is tied together."

"I agree, the mystery is why now? Why together?"

A new voice and not a welcome one: Detective Michael Fetters.

"I heard someone mention Gabriella Corallo. That's a real coincidence. Ray, Detective Washington, is headed over there to interview her as part of his investigation. I guess sooner than later because her daddy's gone missing." He looked to Chase. "Maybe a woman-to-woman coffee klatch might work better than a male third degree?"

Chase wanted to tell Fetters where to stick his advice. The Mayor thought otherwise.

"That's not a bad idea, at least we can see if she can shed some light on her father's recent activities. I heard a couple of weeks ago Lorenzo visited Scarpetti in prison."

Detective Taggart digested the word 'we'. The Mayor of Las Vegas could not tag along on a murder investigation. Fetters disagreed.

"That's a good idea, Mayor." The detective said with a smile. "I'll meet you there and see if I can be of service."

Kane as chauffer waited in the police parking lot. Detective Taggart in her unmarked led the procession, very reluctant to the events unfolding. She saw Little Mikey bring up the rear of their convoy. Chase tried one last time to dissuade the Mayor from visiting a strip club, but he remained adamant. To aid his friend, McCombs, interviewing Corallo's daughter sounded promising.

As she drove up into the self-park at the Pussy Galore, Chase marveled at the millions of dollars poured into the Grecian temple façade, a gilded box to sell the female box. At the door she turned to see Fetters pull up his car across the street, not in the club's parking lot or valet. Smart move, she considered, act the role of respectable cop, not associated with a bunch of strippers or the Mayor.

Mayor Goodfella, on the other hand, the political animal, could justify his civic morality. He informed her that his son was attorney for several of the strip clubs, handling their liquor licenses.

"They pay a city tax to do business. If it is legal to disrobe on stage in Nevada, then they have their right to tout their products."

Chase's eyes adjusted to the darkness. The Mayor's investigator followed them saying little, unless into the Mayor's ear. Detective Taggart asked for Gabriella Corallo and they were pointed towards the restaurant entrance. Chase saw men drinking and gawking, and the women strutting on stage or swiveling on laps. What disturbed her? The women were gorgeous. Her own taut body paled in comparison. Prowling men who glanced at the fresh morsel dismissed her, leaving her to feel unattractive.

One man at the bar looked familiar. A sense she met him earlier, but where? He picked at a beer bottle label, not looking at the women. That seemed out of the ordinary.

They entered the restaurant, to the side of the dance floor. One lone blonde danced at a center pole for the few early evening dining customers. Her swaying flaunted the biggest breasts Chase had ever seen, even 'watermelon size' did not seem an apt description.

Mind games nagged Chase. That man outside at the bar. His hair, a burr close trim, shaved close to bald, something about him. From where?

Detective Washington entered behind them, jaw-drop surprised by the Mayor and his partner together.

"What's going on?"

"You have a meeting with Gabriella Corallo," said the Mayor. "We wanted to join in."

"I just got word myself. Someone called and left me a message to meet her on the Corallo kidnapping. Nothing formal was arranged."

Bells and whistles clanged and tooted in Chase's brain. That man at the bar…

Gabriella Corallo walked into the room, a striking beauty, not styled as an exotic dancer. Slim, tall, dark haired, and well formed. Sicilian traits of her father were in her face and mannerisms. She dressed as a professional businesswoman.

"Miss Corallo," Chase jumped in flashing her badge. "Did you know we were coming over to interview you?"

"No. I did call Mayor Stokes. And if you are here to help find my Papa, God bless you all."

"What's more important," Chase spoke with haste. "Do you have a back way out of here? I think this place is about to be raided and we need to get the Mayor out."

"This way," Gabriella Corallo motioned toward the kitchen, and the cops, ex-cop, and the politician followed her at a rapid pace, everyone tensed. At the receiving back door, they paused, wary.

"Is there a more secure exit? I'm sure the Feds have all visible building entrances covered." The two women took measure of each other. Chase presumed that if you were in this business, meaning tits and ass and other nefarious enterprises, and you want to really hide things, or escape, you had methods.

Chase played her trump card. "I believe we've been set up. Maybe the Feds don't want your father found. Maybe they want to hurt the Mayor. I don't know. The Mayor, without hesitating, walked into your place for all to see, willing to help find your father. Believe me, we can't help you if we're embroiled in more front page controversy."

Another detour into a walk-in freezer. A push to the back wall revealed the ice box held a hidden door at the back, behind a sliding pallet shelf of frozen steaks. The door opened into a narrow empty corridor, and crouching, they descended steps. Chase guessed they were underneath the club's parking lot, following electrical conduits in a small tunnel. Climbing stairs at the other end of the tunnel, they walked into a storage room full of medical and hospital supplies. Through another door they entered the front office of a medical supply company. A salesman and his secretary, at first glancing up, startled, went back to working as usual, heads down, seeing nothing. From their vantage point at the street-side window the five escapees had a front row view as the bust went down. Federal agents stormed in.

"Look," said Kane, "it's an alphabet buffet of Kevlar vests. FBI – DEA – ATF. The shirt and tie officials I bet are from the U.S. Attorney's office. If a full bureaucratic assault, I'm sure the IRS will make an appearance."

The Mayor showed his disgust. "The press, as usual, has been tipped off." Camera trucks were positioning their remotes.

"Chase, how did you know this was happening?" Ray Washington gave her a skeptical look.

"Two small items; when I went in I saw a nervous man at the bar, disinterested in the dancers, and I finally recognized him as a federal agent that I saw coming out of Sheriff Randall's office. The other fact, Detective Fetters acted too nice. You can see him over there leaning on his car. He attended the same meeting. He's supposed to be coordinating with the Feds on the DiManna investigation. FBI probably told him they were running their own investigation on the surviving

Wrecking Crew member, giving him the day and hour they were going to hit Corallo's establishment. Fetters took advantage of it for his own purposes. I hear he's not a fan of the Mayor's."

"I'll ring Fetters' neck." Washington, balling his fists, seethed with righteous indignation.

"Aren't you near retirement, Ray?" Kane asked. "Take it easy, I'm sure Mike will see the error of his ways." Detective Washington studied Kane's passive face and nodded.

"I'll go get my car and get the Mayor out of here." Kane, the silent cowboy, exited toward the back door.

Chase had a thought.

"Mayor, is there some public event you could get to right away? Offset any rumors saying you were at a strip club during a raid?"

"Well, yes, I turned down an invitation to give a speech to our local Korean Chamber of Commerce. They'd be happy to still see me show up, even unannounced." He paused and gave her the once over. "You sure you aren't related to Owen McCombs?"

"What?"

"You both seem to shine when in difficult situations. You'd make a great team."

A minute later, Kane honked a signal from the back of the supply building and the Mayor departed, just in time to avoid seeing Chase blush. Over his shoulder, at the back door, he called out, "I haven't stopped helping McCombs. I'm going to call Jackson Flynn. See if he can marshal his troops to help in the search."

Gabriella Corallo waited until the Mayor left before she placed a cell call. "Clay, the Feds just hit my place. Yeah, I'm sure for all our records. Can you get over here right away to see if they trip up on the search warrant. Thanks, tiger."

The two women exchanged glances. "Clay?" Chase knew that name.

"The Mayor's son. We used to know each other when we were young. I was Angelo's invisible little sister. Yeah, call it puppy love for Clay. I don't think he ever knew."

"They're not just going for your records," said Washington. "I can see Jack Plummer from Vice." They watched as the Feds brought out four dancers, draped in coats and jackets, still in costumes. In front of the club they were handed over to another group of suited men and put in a Metro police van.

"Who's the blonde bombshell?" questioned Chase wondering how the top ballasted stripper the police were escorting out of the club could stand and not keel over.

Gabriella cursed under her breath, her face frowned displeasure.

"That's Papa's new girlfriend, Miss Candy Land."

Candy. The name written on a birthday card. Well, well, Chase might meet a stripper up close after all.

An hour later, Chase walked past Detective Fetters' desk.

"Oh, Mike, sorry we missed you. Something came up. Ray and I never made it over to that strip club. Hope that didn't put you out any?"

His face looked dumb and questioning.

Asshole. She would like to be there when Mike Fetters and Byron Kane had a private talk.

2. Sauna – Vegas Style

When his brain acknowledged reality, Owen realized darkness lay inside and outside his dumpster prison. His catatonic departure must have lasted hours. His clothing drenched with salty sweat. Each shift of his weight brought anguish. His legs had bled and crusted from landing on top of sharp metal and broken neon tubing. He smelled his body odor mixed with smells of discarded oil cans. By tomorrow he knew he would be semi-comatose from lack of water. The day after, dead, murdered their preferred old-fashioned way, torturous.

Owen could take minor satisfaction. His killers were not as smart as they thought. With all the pushing and pounding they had not searched him. Rescue would be simple. Owen pulled out his cell phone. He punched 911.

Dammit, no signal.

Either because the dumpster was located against a building or because he was trapped in a metal container, he saw the red light indicating no reception. Eyes open in utter darkness pushed him to act. The dumpster lacked a tight clasp and the bent rod lock allowed the top to be moved up about an inch, so he could bring the red neon evening sky into his execution chamber. He wedged it a couple more inches with a rod shank of discarded steel. His attempts at prying off the lid were futile. Sin City has found me, used me, and discarded me. Trapped in this sauna death box he began to shake. For that brief momentary flash, his illness peaked. A detached debate raged among his demons trying to tell him to search for any discarded object sharp enough to slit his wrists. He argued back; why speed up death? Why go that extra step?

After another hour, even his demons became bored at the uselessness of it all and flittered away. For nothing better to do he let his mind dwell on all issues unsolved.

Angel Corallo's father kidnapped. For what reason? To gain information most likely, since the lost diamonds were in play and someone knew or thought they knew that the Wrecking Crew had the answers. The tally of death bore out his assumption, the Wrecking Crew alumni eradicated, with the exception of the elder Corallo.

One answer came out of Owen's brutal interrogation. Angel Corallo thought he knew where his father might be and who might be holding him. Under the duress of being stomped into the dirt Owen in compliance rattled off everyone met since arriving in Vegas. Angelo knew the kidnapper. The telephone call from the anonymous 'Mr. Big' confirmed it.

What triggered the renewal of the diamond search twenty some years later? Owen readjusted both body and mind, and the revelation came to him. How simple.

A new generation: Angel Corallo and Pauli DiManna. The old geezers over time understood the diamonds were lost when Grayson died. They went on to other crimes and eventual retirement. When the new breed read Pegler's book excerpts, Angel and Pauli realized the diamonds were still out there. They each fostered an idea where the glittering baubles might be hidden or the person holding the final piece to the puzzle: a quest and a mystery.

Trying to digest all that he knew, Owen worked on varied hypotheses with his scattered facts. Slowly, his spirits began to lift. Optimism to believe he stood a chance, curiosity to see how the rest of his dissolute life would turn out. Out loud he told his imaginary goblins and specters, "If I escape, I'll write a book. My opening sentence: 'In the summer of his nervous breakdown, he went to live in Las Vegas.'"

His lips parched dry. He faced another physical crisis. In another hour or less, the need to piss. That smell in the mix would gag him to barf. And then, that mix…

Considering his iron coffin, he wondered if the opening was wide enough to thrust his cell phone out, and dial. If he got a signal, who would he call? Who would actually come to his rescue?

He thought of all the people met in the last week, those he could now call friends. One person not yet a friend came to mind. He punched in her speed dial number as his fingertips held the phone outside of the dumpster. He could not see if there had been a connection, thought he heard a voice, maybe her recorded voice mailbox and Owen began shouting her name and where he thought he was. The signal blinked to red, and disconnected.

911 was his next crapshoot chance. They had to respond. He would tell them he was a terrorist and they would hear the airplanes overhead. He would yell for Detective Taggart. He had no other choice in his thoughts. He punched the three numbers and carefully wriggled the phone back through the small opening. When he thought he might have a connection he started shouting his name, Detective Taggart's name, and desperate, ready to give them his terrorist threat to bomb Las Vegas out of existence when the cell phone, slippery in his hand, fell to the ground, outside the dumpster.

3. Candy Landed

"You sure this has something to do with one of your homicides."

"Most definitely," stressed Ray giving his and his partner's visit high importance, all based on Chase's hunch. "You saw where the two old gangsters, past clients of the Mayor, got themselves diced up?"

"Yeah. So?" said Metro Vice detective, Jack Plummer.

"Well, both of those guys used to partner up with Lorenzo Corallo, who today went missing, and Corallo's girlfriend is the blonde you're holding, a Miss Land."

"Candy Land," smiled Plummer. "A sweet woman of untold bounty."

"Wha'd you tag her for?" queried Chase, knowing the obvious.

"Solicitation. Four of them have been running a prostitution ring out of the Pussy Galore. Targeting customers who flirt heavy, who spend a lot of money. They make dates to meet later."

Chase voiced her suspicions. "I can't see the Corallos taking a hooker risk with a multi-million dollar business. Not that I care. Seems too risky. If the women are independent sub-contractors, or are doing it without management's knowledge, it could be argued the Pussy Galore might be the aggrieved party."

Washington wondered aloud.

"What with today's Federal splash and trash?"

"You know what it's like, Ray, they got wind of it, thought something bigger might be under the rug, and stepped in. We get the little fish and the Fed auditors will start digging for corruption, tax evasion, you know the drill."

Ray knew how the Feds loved conspiracy theories.

"Kinda rushing to judgment, it seems to me."

Chase's honest question.

"Can the sin industry ever be innocent?" Ray's response.

"We got the girls dead on, ran undercover on them. Might have kept it in play to help the Feds on building a RICO corruption case. Sting folded. Last night we got an anonymous tip the girls were shutting down operations. Move our ass time. Our friends at the Federal Building have a bigger manpower budget than we do. Say, didn't I hear you were at the bust today, that's why you're here, right?"

"Naw, I couldn't make it," deadpanned Ray. "We got these other cases, dead gomers by knife."

Plummer laughed. "So you tell me." They stopped in front of a door, in a hallway full of doors and one-way glass.

"There's your lady. She might be good for a few years turning tricks. Down the road she's going to have serious back problems when she hits thirty and starts saggin'. Mind if I listen in from outside? We've finished our prelim. She'll give you the same story, a lot of mea culpa."

"Listen all you want. We won't be long. Mostly background to Corallo's disappearance."

Ray and Chase entered the interrogation room. Miss Candy Land was sipping coffee from a Styrofoam cup. A long white plastic coat, in the middle of summer, covered her skimpy outfit.

"Hey, you don't need to roust me. They played the tape, I'll pay the fine, do the time, maybe." Facing the law and consequences nothing new to her.

Washington put on his 'Big Daddy' compassion costume.

"We're here to talk about Lorenzo. You heard he went missing?"

She actually choked a sob.

"Yeah, I hope my baby is okay; he was snatched right? He was a big man just a few years back. He's harmless now."

"Know anyone who had it in for him? Did he talk about his enemies?"

"Only in the past tense; his old stories, how all his friends have died off."

Chase asked, "Did he talk about Charles 'Chunky D' DiManna after he got murdered?"

Candy Land paused to eye the woman cop. "Like he was trying to figure out who might have shot his old friend. Last couple of days, he made a couple of comments about going to see where Charlie met the grim reaper.

"You mean at the Magnum Casino construction site?"

"The old El Morocco. In their glory, he told me that's where the Wrecking Crew used to go crazy. Held fond memories for him."

Chase pulled on a slim thread to follow.

"You called him 'Charlie', an endearment. You and Charles Di-Manna had a thing going? Something behind Larry's back?" The accusation caught the stripper in mid coffee sip.

"No, you got that wrong. My main man, even in my business, is Larry. He treats me the best."

"You did see Chunky D on the side. He gave you presents."

The stripper, alleged working girl, blinked her spidery eyebrows.

"It wasn't my doing, it was kinda like I was asked to go and be bosom buddies with him." She gave a half giggle at her joke.

"What?" Ray shook his head at imponderables. Another conspiracy.

"Who asked you?"

"Mr. Corallo."

"Lorenzo"? Ray asked. Chase considered a different slant.

"Angelo Corallo?"

"Yeah, he said he wanted to know what Chunky was up to."

"How long ago was this?"

"About a month," said Miss Candy Land, very unlady-like chewing on a torn fingernail.

Her answer bristled Ray's moral standards. "And Larry Corallo didn't mind your sharing your party favors with his buddy?"

She stiffed her back and looked at him indignantly. "Hey, I didn't tell Lorenzo. Chunky D knew about me and Lorenzo. Think he was more excited, if you know what I mean, that he was pulling one over on Mr. Corallo. Angel paid me to keep my ears and eyes open. I didn't get paid from Chunky, just gifts."

Detective Washington plugged a toothpick into his mouth and questioned without tact.

"Any juicy pillow talk?"

"Nothing important. Over the phone about furniture deliveries to model home clients." Chase masked her pleasure in hearing that.

"So, Corallos put you into doing tricks. Did they get a kickback?" Ray's toothpick rolled across his teeth.

"I'm not sure. That's what I told the other cop."

"Wha'd you mean? You either know or you don't know." Miss Candy Land watched the cop's toothpick clinch, pointed at her.

"It's like I was working up north, Reno and Lake Tahoe, and from nowhere I get this money in the mail, $3,000 and a plane ticket, asking me to come down and run a few girls. I thought I'd have a partner, maybe the Corallos. No one ever contacted me except I got another $3,000 and a note that told me go apply for a job with the Pussy Galore, and quietly do some side work. As you can see…" and she exhaled and puffed her chest, "I could get a job anywhere. But Pussy Galore has classy women and then I met Mr. Corallo."

"Met him at the club?"

She shook her head no.

"That's funny too. Right after they hired me, I got a message to go over to this other club and sing happy birthday to Mr. Corallo."

"Another club?"

"The wops."

Chase was puzzled, so Ray took a stab.

"The Italian-American Social Club?"

"Yeah, that was the joke. Whoever sent me got the date wrong. Wasn't his birthday, but Mr. Corallo, like he didn't complain, if you know what I mean?"

"So you have no idea where Mr. Corallo is at this moment?"

"No, but please find him, I miss him something horrible." Miss Candy Land started small sniff crying, her chest heaving, like the Sierra Nevadas rolling from a 6.9 quake.

Outside the interrogation room the detectives compared notes.

"Do you believe that crap where she says she's not paying off anyone? She has to give, pardon the expression, a piece off the top to management."

Chase wasn't so sure.

"Unless the Corallos didn't know Candy and her girls were hustling jobs using the club as their front."

"But who set her up in business?" Washington didn't buy her story.

"All I know," laughed Detective Plummer, "Candy is stuck."

Chase didn't want to say anymore until they returned to their office, then she laid out all the scattered accumulation. She closed Ray's office door.

"We have been looking at the killers of the old gangsters as something dealing with the olden days."

"Yeah, the misplaced Cassandra diamonds."

"I now believe we have a gang war on our hands."

"Gang war? What gang?"

"The DiMannas and the Corallos."

"They're dead, one for sure, one possible."

"No, I mean Pauli DiManna versus Angel Corallo. I don't know what triggered the explosion, could have been a rivalry to find the diamonds. It got out of hand. The DiManna furniture store is torched and by luck we fall into the model home burglary ring."

"You uncovered that. Word's getting around. Pretty sharp conclusions."

Chase let the compliment pass, glad it came from Ray.

"And in the Corallo column, their liquor license is at risk from a prostitution ring run out of the club. I'm guessing Angelo set the match to the furniture store. He was prepared to find a way to get us to notice the suburb break-ins. Pauli, from his side, put a sleeper hooker cell into the Pussy Galore. And waits for an excuse. When his family's store is torched, he rats the girls out in the strip club as revenge to have the Feds close the place.

"A modern turf war? More smarts, less gunplay."

"In gangland wars you take over the businesses. This is more like a scorched earth policy, no building left standing. Seems more nuclear option than economic gain."

"And this led to the Corallo kidnapping? Why?"

"Senior Corallo is revenge for Senior DiManna."

"So Pauli grabbed Lorenzo which means Angel killed Chunky D."

"I think so. The diamonds for all the hype may play little or not at all in this drama."

"How about Owen McCombs?"

At the mention of his name Chase felt her body skin tingling, flushed cheeks. It was unsettling.

"Maybe just unlucky. From the beginning he got too close to the right answer? I don't know."

"Who has him?"

"Pauli has Lorenzo, my guess is Angel went after Owen. I just checked my voice mail. I think he tried to call me an hour ago. I couldn't understand — did he escape? — was it ransom? — calling for help? Sounded like a bad connection."

"If it was him, it means he's still alive. Your hunch could have merit. We should go look for Angel and Pauli."

But Chase had another idea, something buxom Candy mentioned. Something she would check out on her own. A long shot.

When she returned to her desk a woman sat in the guest chair, gripping her purse, slump shouldered, shriveled lines in her Hispanic features, crow's feet around the eyes. Young, looking aged. The only thing certain: she shifted in the chair, uncomfortable in her surroundings.

"May I help you?"

"You are Detective Taggart?"

"Yes."

"I always try to talk to Detective Lange. He says I talk to you now."

One of Chase's cold cases, one she knew lay somewhere on her desk, overlooked in this last hurried week, no opportunity to review in detail.

"I'm sorry, they have just assigned these cases to me."

"I call you."

"Yes, and this concerns…?"

"Hector Garcia."

So, this is Mrs. Garcia. Chase had not returned the woman's calls. Distractions. Hector Garcia, the unsolved drive-by shooting. Two years ago.

"He my only boy. His father in Mexico. He cried too when he heard."

"I'm so sorry."

"Have the police found anything? My son never in a gang, he assistant manager at McDonalds. They said he might go to that hamburger school, be manager someday. He had big dreams."

Beyond a heart that stops beating, violent death destroys those still living. The guilt Chase felt, overwhelming. Caught up in the ego of fame, drawn to a high profile case that would make the front page, she gave little shrift to the mundane cases. How wrong of her, she conceded to herself. Have them spell her name right, run her photo. If she were to be a homicide detective, a good one, and she wanted to be, her true job in Homicide she meant, the reality of the day-to-day grunge. In Chase's work, the detective accepted that some crimes might never be solved. But how would she know if she didn't do her job in the first place.

"I will look at your son's file tonight and I'll ask the other detectives, talk to those in the Gang Unit and see if we have anything new." She paused, wondering what would give this woman comfort. What if the victim had been Eric? What would her life be like now? She shuddered to even think such a horror.

"I will *definitely* call you tomorrow." A sworn pledge, more to herself than to the still grieving woman sitting in front of her.

After the woman departed Chase realized the mother did not cry once. No more tears left to shed.

What next?

"Detective Taggart?" She looked up to see one of the young ladies who worked the Tech side of Investigations.

"They had a 911 call about thirty minutes ago. From a cell phone."

Chase sat upright.

"Very muffled yelling for about one minute, then a minute of static noise, then the signal went dead. We filtered out static and heightened the analog. We isolated a few random words. Your name was definitely shouted, several times."

McCombs. Her life brightened. He's alive.

"The phone call is from a kidnap victim. Please give it top priority."

"We could hear a faint airplane noise. By configuring noise levels of take offs and landings we might gain a pretty accurate idea on distance from the airport, gain a perpendicular cross street to the plane's landing or take-off trajectory. Interesting, the planes sounded propeller-driven. Might not be McCarren with their jet traffic, but North Las Vegas airport. If he stayed on the line we could have triangulated his location by cell towers."

"His cell phone is from Mississippi."

"We should be able to figure it out. Our software is pretty unbelievable. Why didn't he leave his cell on?" Not a good question to ask, Chase feared. Perhaps someone else shut the phone off.

"You do your magic. I'll head toward North Las Vegas. Call me when you get anything, including estimated distance. I'll have a couple of patrol cars start cruising." Finding McCombs trumped any other priorities.

"We isolated a bunch of curse words and also got a couple of strange words isolated."

"Yeah?"

"He was shouting something... 'dead signs'. Your name and 'dead signs'."

What did that mean? Chase had no clue.

4. Reskewed

Owen heard a noise, a car crunching across gravel, driving into the yard, not directly to him. He took that to mean Angelo was not returning to make his stay permanent. It made wide circles as if lost or searching. Police? Quick response he grabbed a piece of metal tubing, ripped his shirt, tied it on, sticking out and waving it, not surrender but seeking rescue. He yelled and kicked his feet against the dumpster walls creating metallic thunder. The car stopped, a car door slammed. Silence, he yelled, then approaching steps.

The dumpster lid flew back with a clanking bang. His sweat-filled eyes adjusted to the Savior he would kiss, regardless.

The Mayor of Las Vegas.

"My God, you're alive! I even got the Highway Department doing an Amber Alert on the highways. Told them you were an abused child. Looks like you've been abused for sure."

"We don't have much time." Owen's faith, reconstituted in miracles, considered his next destination.

"Let's get you out of here. All hell's breaking loose."

He could barely crawl out. His bent legs had fallen asleep. As the Mayor hauled him from the dumpster his eyes adjusted to the headlight beams of the Mayor's car.

"What is that?"

It was not the Mayor's Mercedes. It seemed to be an old Cadillac convertible. Mid-1940s. A classic. Where did he—? The Mayor retrieved from the Caddy a bottle of water, and a tourist t-shirt. The water Owen gulped down with religious fervor and poured the rest over his body stink, cleansing the gutter smells. The t-shirt replaced his bloody, torn shirt, even if the writing when held up to the car's headlights said "Magnum Casino & Resort Las Vegas", and on the reverse, the fateful wording: "At the Speed of Fun!" He edged around the dumpster, and took a relieving leak, humoring himself to be pissing on his abandoned grave.

The Mayor helped him stagger on his wobbly legs, and eased Owen into the passenger side of the car. It was beautiful, red leather inside, with sleek traditional lines. The convertible top was down, the Mayor started raising the soft top. Owen protested, the night air rushing over his body would be soothing.

"The Caddy has air conditioning. Besides, we don't want people staring too close into the car, there's an arrest warrant out for you."

"What?"

"Clay called them to say that some gorillas kidnapped you. The police weren't buying and when the District Attorney's office found out, they went ballistic. Said it was just an excuse for ditching their investigation, and they now had probable cause, either as a suspect or a material witness in Pegler's beating and a suspect in the DiManna and Bluestein murders. They even think you might have had a hand in Lorenzo Corallo's disappearance." The Mayor laughed. "It seems like I have been associated once again with disreputable individuals, meaning you. You seem to have this acquired taste for continual manhandling."

"Wait, my phone fell out of the dumpster." Owen pointed it out and the Mayor retrieved it.

"Here, take my rag shirt," said Owen, "you got some gunk on your hand from getting me out of there." The Mayor looked to his right hand and wiped his fingers, removing most of a blue paint color.

"Yeech. I don't think you'd ever want to really know what was in that dumpster."

"Outside the broken glass tubing, yeah, paint and motor oil and old fast food to begin with; don't remind me."

Owen examined his phone. "I think my call went through, but then it slipped out of my fingers."

Owen shut off the phone because of low battery. Had the 911 call been made? The police wouldn't believe his kidnapping story, even the injuries. One beating could mean a crime, but two beatings suggested he got what he deserved.

Owen started in on a second bottle of aqua manna. "Let's blow this party." He knew the answer, asked anyway. "This car?"

"Isn't it spiffy?" The Mayor had the same gleam in his eye as Owen saw on the first day he met him. Like the teenager with his first set of wheels. "1947 Cadillac. I saw one like this up in Reno in the Harrah's Auto Museum. This one, are you ready for this, once owned by Marilyn Monroe." Owen gave him a tired, beat-up look.

"This is a Magnum car for the 'Transportation of Speed' exhibit?"

The Mayor smiled as they sped out onto the roadway and into the night.

"The Temple of Zoom. I got a call late this afternoon, from that Melissa Steele at Magnum. She said that Jackson Flynn wanted me to have use of this car before it had to be returned to the construction site tonight and placed on the storage floor. They said the car was outside my house. If this is favoritism, so be it. It drives heavy, brakes are loose, you have to pump them. I've been waving a lot. It's a vote getter. Melissa says Mr. Flynn has no problem if I ever want to use one of his cars in a city parade. Isn't that kind of Jackson?"

The Mayor calling her 'Melissa' and his boss, 'Jackson'. And Flynn letting his prize cars out on crash prone streets. Crazy times and he's in the midst.

"How did you find me?"

"Ah, the mystery starts. Freida received a call after I'd left my office. Supposedly, a message for a last minute cameo on a 'see Las Vegas' tourist commercial. I'm a sucker for any camera I can control. I am here driving around looking for the film crew, and see waving fingers. Someone is using us."

"Everyone's using us."

"Okay, what's the plan?"

"You're returning the car to the Magnum Casino site? Good as place as any for a first stop." He hurt, he ached, and his mind had been beaten back into some semblance of intelligence. "I know who killed Chunky D."

"Don't leave me hanging."

"Angel Corallo. He was after the diamonds. He knew the general location. He thought maybe Chunky D knew the specific location. After torturing the old man, he killed him."

"There's not a formalized Mafia in town anymore. Maybe he's trying to start a new crime syndicate?"

"Maybe. Pure and simple I think Angel is just evil, excited to have made his first 'bones'."

"This is probably news to you, but Larry Corallo's been kidnapped. You mean the kidnapper is—"

"Pauli DiManna. I—You—we have fallen into a blood feud. The winner is last man standing and maybe with $7 million in precious stones. One answer might be back at the construction site."

"Why back to the Magnum site?"

"No, back to the El Morroco. That's where I got misled. I could tie the Wrecking Crew into knowing Grayson, and yeah, maybe Scarpetti along with Spilotro were responsible for Grayson's death. The other tie-in was the El Morocco building itself. When Grayson bought the El Morocco he ended up selling off a lot of the old fixtures, and surprise, I'm guessing Charles DiManna owned a used furniture business back then, his sideline front before going upscale. I bet Grayson turned to DiManna, knowing him as a neighbor, and asked his help in liquidating the El Morocco inventory."

"And what are you saying? In turn, maybe, DiManna one day asked Grayson, 'Say, I heard from my friend Bluestein, the mechanic at the airport that you're flying back east. Could you take this duffle bag back to friends of mine as a favor?'"

Owen could see that scenario play out. "Maybe Grayson invited them along. Maybe another reason for The Ant to try and kill them all. At the last moment, for whatever reason, the stolen gems never were put on the plane. DiManna and Corallo chose not to fly.

"You have to look at it this way, the diamonds disappeared the day Grayson died. What does that tell you?"

"Grayson had the diamonds. So where are they?"

"In the Garden of Allah."

"What?"

"Kathleen Grayson told me."

"She did?" The Mayor's suspicions heightened, protective feelings for his son.

"At the tour I gave. Her father gave her a farewell gift and a note mentioning the Garden of Allah. Maybe he had a premonition, maybe playful teasing. If Grayson had the diamonds, the best hiding spot would be on his own property, in a place with few visitors. The El Morocco once called 'the El', in its heyday a wise guy hangout."

"That I know. I saw them there." Owen momentarily forgot the historical figure sitting next to him.

"What Morrie Bluestein mumbled finally caught up to my mind while vacationing amongst the trash. His last words were, "C or hell'. what if he actually whispered, 'See or L', 'See Orr at the L'. There's a statue of Frederick Orr in the Garden of Allah. Morrie, lying on his death bed, divined the location. After the realtor died, the newspapers reported both Grayson's home and office were burglarized. The Wrecking Crew went looking for their misplaced loot. Somehow, years later it clicked for Morrie the only other valued property Grayson owned in Vegas at the time, the El Morocco. Maybe it was Grayson's idea of an inside joke to hide the mob diamonds in an old mob hotel. The diamonds are buried somewhere in the Garden of Allah."

"We should call the police."

"And what would they do? We're the targets. I thought for a while that Detective Taggart might listen."

"She might."

"I don't know."

"Call her. Tell her about your theory on the two boys."

"Two hoodlums. Two killers. Young Corallo whacks elder DiManna and I now believe young DiManna is going to take revenge on the senior Corallo."

"Who killed the others? Who burned down Crestview furniture?"

"Hey, it took me several sweltering hours in a dumpster to get this far."

"Call your friend Detective Taggart, give it your best shot. I'll call Clay to pick us up. We have to negotiate your turning yourself into the police. The longer you stay out, the worse it will be."

Owen leaned his aching head and sore back against the leather seat of the classic auto and smiled through his pains that he had two excellent defense attorneys looking after his welfare.

The Mayor suddenly slowed the car and pulled to the side, driving into a restaurant parking lot.

Up ahead a group of people milled around the front gate at the Magnum construction site. They were protesting, marching in short circles and waving signs.

"That's a wildcat picket line. I can't drive across. All the Unions are my supporters."

An imaginary line was drawn in the desert sand, testing their budding friendship. Owen knew he represented management, while the Mayor went where the votes were. Workers were voters.

The Mayor got out of the car.

"You drive the car in. I'll walk over, press a little flesh and find out what's going on. I'll catch a cab. I'll get Clay to pick you up. Let him deal with your surrender to the police. This thing is blowing up, and I am out of alternatives and ideas."

Owen slid into the driver's seat and held out his damaged hand.

"We will prevail."

"Good luck, Owen."

"You, too, Mayor." Owen drove the last block and watched in the rear view mirror as the most powerful man in Las Vegas walked down the sidewalk into yet another controversy.

5. Garden of Good and Evil

The shouting demonstrators didn't have their act together. Their protest looked sloppy, an impromptu last minute throw together. If there was an official union sanction behind the protest, Owen thought, the professionals would have had more people screaming and chanting at any worker scabs. Construction on the Magnum Casino Resort would grind to a halt.

Thank God for the 1947 Cadillac convertible and all its grandeur. The unionists were ready to hurl themselves under concrete trucks. A beautiful car caught them off guard. The hired security who knew Mr. Flynn owned antique cars, threw open the construction gates and waved Owen inside.

He stopped inside the gate, past the crowd's view. A few of them hurled epithets insinuating Owen a ranking member of the ruling class. He opened the car door and faced the strained and serious face of Melissa Steele.

"I thought the Mayor was driving this car?"

"He wanted to return it safe to us before somebody sideswiped him. He wouldn't want to be seen with us with that crowd parading around. What goes? You're working late hours?"

"Didn't you hear?" Her face bore a tiredness of the job. The crisis of the moment wore her best features to putty.

"No, I've been out of circulation." She stared at the Magnum t-shirt, several blood splotches leaking through the whiteness. She made no comment. Nothing about him would surprise her.

"Rumor is out that we are going nonunion. A couple of construction locals walked off the job today. They'll be under court order by tomorrow or face financial sanctions. Didn't stop the Teamsters from throwing up informational pickets. The Culinary Union, so far, has not made a political statement. The Teamsters want to gain control over the hotel service people. We'll be facing jurisdictional in fighting between unions."

The entire project faced closure. Owen knew the score. "This would make the Venetian and the Magnum the largest non-union shops on the Strip. Have you ever been through an organizing attempt?"

In the darkness, with pale lighting, Melissa Steele looked older than her years, slump-shouldered, weighted down from chains of stress. For a moment she seemed to suggest they were on the same side. "I told you I worked Atlantic City for awhile. All union, except executives were exempt, including myself in the marketing department. At Magnum Cherokee the Indians avoided unions by their sovereign nation status."

"I agree this won't be pretty. Maybe Mr. Flynn is using it just for a bargaining position. By doing it before we start the major employee hiring, he gains leverage chips in his pile."

"Maybe, but it didn't help that the Magnum issued a press release today where they're moving up the timetable on imploding the El Morocco casino building and garage."

Owen saw another puzzle piece fall into place. His eyes fell on the parking garage and the old casino building.

"How long has casino management known about the implosion?"

"Let's see. The word started circulating a few days before you arrived. The demolition people arrive on site tomorrow. Like all implosions it will be a major press event."

The last time Owen saw the name "El Morocco Casino" it was a dead neon and he was face down in the dirt with a shoe in the ribs. They could blow the whole thing up as far as he was concerned. Her comment let him know that the killers discovered they had limited time to find the diamonds. Torture, under a deadline, became necessary. DiManna, Bluestein, and now Corallo.

"Strikes and buildings being blown up," said Owen. "This all falls on you. Bummer. Let me know if I can help." He voiced sincerity.

"Yeah." She forced a pursed lip smile which turned quizzical. "Aren't the police looking for you?"

"Among others. Soon as I drop off this car my attorney is picking me up. He'll get it all straightened out." Owen didn't think that true; what the heck.

Two or three mini-busses drove up with their cargo of protestors on a shift change. Melissa turned back and returned to her office. Nothing more to say. They were two separate corporate beings in this time and space, he thought, nothing else.

Owen drove the car up to the second story ramp of the parking garage. This garage is where it all started, and how long ago was that? A week, and the results? Wanted by the Metro Police, the Sheriff's Office, the D.A., and assorted ruffians who have no regard for human life. On the second floor, other antique cars added since his last visit. About a dozen cars, various shapes and sizes, stuffed under car covers. When he had time, when he got out of jail, if his destiny, he promised himself to browse this million dollar plus car lot.

Exiting the Cadillac, he noticed the leather briefcase in the back of the Cadillac. There are no coincidences. The Mayor is not that forgetful. Owen felt the satisfaction like a gambler who knew Lady Luck was blowing in his ear. He pulled out the case, laid it flat, and entered three separate digits to each combination. He pulled at the slide levers. The locks clicked open. How simple: the birthdays of the Mayor's two grandchildren. He had gleaned those kernels from Clay Stokes. Somehow, he just knew. He did not open the lid and look inside. Random thoughts floated. He fastened the locks and set the digits, one number off the birth date opening sequence. The Mayor would know Owen knew. He beamed fresh confidence like a student knowing most of the answers to a class test. He would get an A before the night ended. Unfortunately, such assuredness can create over zeal, false confidence.

Owen headed for the Garden of Allah. He limped down the stairs instead of the garage ramp. He nearly stepped on a body in the stairwell.

The man face down, thank God, was alive, unconscious. He recognized the silent form as he turned him over, Derek Shelly, bodyguard to Jackson Flynn, and most certain the person following him after his kidnapping. Shelly's breathing labored erratic and shallow. The back of his head dripped slow droplets, the wound coagulating. Later he would admit at this moment he snapped, tired of people taking advantage of him.

Faced with a choice to flee and retreat, he moved forward. Slowly he opened the first floor stairway door and walked passed the elevators to the doors which led to the garden, toward the El's old main casino, toward Jackson Flynn's penthouse hideout. Before he entered the garden, he halted and faced the camera at the ceiling corner, the one everyone thought did not work, and mouthed: "Call the police." If in fact, no one upstairs watched the security monitor in the penthouse, he had another choice. He pulled out his battered cell phone. Not good, still low battery.

"Owen, where the fuck are you?" Chase's voice sounded to him more like a yell of relief than anger. "They tracked your 911 call to that Neon Sign Yard. There's blood in a dumpster, blood on the ground."

"The blood's mine."

"What's going on?"

"The kidnapper is Angel Corallo."

"I knew it!"

"I'm at the parking garage at the Magnum. In the Garden of Allah."

"Good Lord, I'm heading that way. Donald Grayson might have had something to do with the diamonds. The El served as the meeting house for the Wrecking Crew."

"Great minds think alike, Chase. Come quietly, and come armed. Bring an ambulance, there's already one person injured. And remember I'm one of the good guys." He heard her plea not to hang up. He did. His steps led to answers hidden in the Garden of Allah.

Spotlights from the old casino building gave off a gray-blue tinge. Yellow lights led into the garden's interior, the other path into the El Morocco Casino Building. Shadows danced on either side of each building. Owen sought to be the stealthy hunter not the unaware prey. Somebody did a better job at stalking. He felt a hard thrust to his back, which he interpreted to be a gun barrel and the voice attached, lethal.

"Keep walking, or they'll find a hole in both sides." Quaint dialogue from Angel Corallo.

"Didn't we just meet?"

"Yeah, and didn't I leave you to rot forever?"

The push of the gun prodded Owen into the clearing near where benches defined the garden opening. In front of the Frederick Orr aka Freddy Bandini statue he could see the other people. He was afraid it might be like this.

Instead of a malicious slur, Angel Corallo said only one thing in a loud wailing voice.

"Papa!"

6. Shoot Out in the Garden of Allah

Blood dripping from both sides of his head, the old man brought his anguished gaze to his son. Both ears had been severed. Lorenzo Corallo sat sprawled and tied at the base of the Frederick Orr statue. Angel's cry and the old man's movement made his torturer turn, going for a gun on the statue's pedestal. Pauli DiManna.

"Pauli, let Papa go."

DiManna's drawn pistol aimed at the senior Corallo.

"He isn't finished telling us where the diamonds are."

'Us', wondered Owen, who's 'us'?

"Do you think he knows? I've spent 15 years working on him. My own Father. He knows nothing. Let him go."

"He knows who has the diamonds. Bluestein told him it was Grayson, and they're somewhere here at the L."

The boys each understood Pegler's manuscript pages.

In the midst of this standoff, Owen heard a beeping noise. Out of the shadows walked Kathleen Grayson Sawyer. She looked out of place, ridiculous, wearing earphones and swinging a stick by her arm in a sweeping motion.

A treasure hunter with a metal detector. Owen held forth with guesses and confusion. The metal detector in the bag brought in the day of Chunky D's killing. Angel did that killing. Why did DiManna's camp, if Kathleen a willing participant with Pauli, now have control over the ground search wand?

Kathleen looked at the four men and said nothing. She leaned to the ground and with a dandelion digger poked and prodded and picked at the garden soil.

"A lousy slot token," she said standing up and removing the headphones. "Well, the diamonds have to be here. Mr. Corallo said as much."

Her presence added to the firecracker frayed nerves of the two young gangsters. Angelo maneuvered behind Owen for a better position. Owen could see Pauli woodpecker tapping his finger on his gun's trigger. Any slight burning flicker could set this whole powder keg off.

The senior Corallo spoke, groggy with excruciating pain.

"Grayson had the diamonds. He was the fence. He needed money for his casino project, and Chunky said he could have a fee to be the courier. He said he would take them on his next trip. After the crash, they weren't on the plane. We searched."

"That's not true! You used him!" Kathleen looked like she wanted to spit at him. "Liar!" She made a wild throw. The dandelion digging blade stuck like mumbley-peg next to the old man's leg. She threw down the treasure hunting equipment and ran to the bound mobster, dropped to her knees, and whispered into the bloody gash where his ear used to be.

"No, no!" cried the elder Corallo his face grimaced, eyes shocked. He tried to push her away, to shake himself free.

Angel stepped to Owen's side trying to go to his father's aid, and in that physical body shift Owen dove over a hedge. Pauli took a wild shot at Angel, and Angel returned fire, and everyone fled for cover.

More shots rang out. Owen moved lateral, trying to get away from the thicket he entered for limited protection. He pushed away some palm fronds, and with a crack and a ricochet, a bullet thudded into the tree inches above his head. He belly crawled, dragging his fresh bruised legs, seeking better safety.

A hand went over his mouth. Momentarily, he expected a bullet impact or his neck to spew blood with a jugular knife slice. Kathleen pushed him down, laying next to him. In a heavy-breath hushed tone, she whispered, "Stay still, they're both crazy!"

"How'd you get here?" Owen trying to figure out the Pauli and Kathleen partnership.

"DiManna grabbed me after he got Lorenzo. He did the torturing and made me go looking for the diamonds."

They shut up when they heard Angel call out.

"Pauli, why don't we back off, come back another day. We split the diamonds when we find them. We don't have much time. Someone must have heard these shots. Just let Papa go."

Another voice, Pauli's, from an unknown direction. "We don't have any time left, Angel baby. They're going to start loading explosives in here tomorrow for the demolition. Tonight's the only night."

Owen squinted through the foliage, only spying the senior Corallo, dazed, looking one way then the other.

Kathleen shouted, "Call a truce, guys. For old times sake. Remember your father's memory, Pauli."

A moment of silence, and then from Chunky D's son.

"That reminds me, Angelo." He heard Pauli's voice loud and panting, out there somewhere. "I found out the other day from a little bird that you burned down our furniture store."

"That's a lie." Angel spoke up from a different location.

"Bullshit. And then I put it together that my father died by your fuckin' hand. You knew the diamonds were here at the El, but you didn't get that from my father. He'd never squeal, not like your *precious papa*."

A shot rang out and the old man slumped. There would be no partnership, no split in any found diamonds. Owen was terrified. He knew there would be no witnesses. He leaned back to protect Kathleen. Gone. Like a ghost.

Wild gunshots, ricocheting, signaled Angel's mad response to his slain father. Owen hunkered down behind a protecting pine tree. He heard a scream and Angel went sailing into the open space, falling, stumbling, crawling to his feet, looking for the gun that had fumbled from his hand. He grabbed it and Pauli DiManna shot him twice in the chest. Angel fell at the feet of his father, and DiManna, the avenger, rose from his hiding place and stood over the bodies of his adversaries. Owen could see the wild ferocity in his face. With a coup d'grace he fired a bullet into Angel Corallo's brain.

"Mr. McCombs. Let's not make this too difficult." It was Owen's turn. "And Kathleen, others might have liked you better, unfortunately I feel it's time we ended our relationship, whatever it was, for old time's sake." He laughed in high pitch relief and started walking a straight line toward Owen's hiding spot.

"Come out, Mr. McCombs. You won't feel a thing."

This was it. He would not be shot dead lying on the ground. He could run, however, a bullet in the back makes a bad obituary. Awkward, no need to rush, Owen rose. No Hollywood sound stage. No re-edit in the cutting room. In real life, he mused, they shoot you. No time to make dying scene soliloquies or talk your way out of impossible dilemmas.

But he would try.

"I know where the Cassandra diamonds are." He walked into the open to face the leveled gun.

"Screw you! None of the old goombas knew."

"Bluestein knew. He told me."

"Screw you."

"Bluestein said the words: 'C or hell'."

"So what?"

"He slurred. He was trying to say Frederick Orr at the El Morocco. *See Orr at the El. Orr-L.*" Owen pointed. "The statue. It's in the statue." He didn't really know. His unknown faith told him the diamonds were here, somewhere. He prayed for those rare oddities called miracles.

Owen and Pauli DiManna exchanged telling stares, one of last chance hope, the other of insanity of armed power. Owen held his breath. DiManna turned to look at the statue. Owen could live a few more seconds and he exhaled his precious breath through clenched teeth. It came to him, the revelation perhaps too late: life was indeed precious. Pauli kept an eye on Owen as he walked to the statue and with one hand tried to push at the bronze bust. The head did not come off the pedestal. He turned with menace, the gun poised.

Owen could only guess. He motioned.

"In the base." This was it. Last of his last chances.

Pauli saw the wisdom. With one hand he untied the dead senior Corallo and dragged the body away from the monument. He then kept one hand with the gun aimed, and with the other, pushed with might and force. It did not move. He placed the gun in his pocket and used two hands with forced anger. The statue and pedestal rocked, swayed, and toppled. Within the base an empty core revealed a place for hiding valuables.

Sudden, searing pain. Owen's eyes went wide. He screamed in agony. Staggering, awkward, his hand sought to reach the middle of his back, only to come away filled with blood. Owen stumbled to the middle of the garden and fell to his knees. He looked back to see Kathleen holding a sharp curved knife. A jeweled killing dagger. *Why*, he asked himself. "*Why?*" he asked her.

Pauli DiManna started laughing at Owen's bloody predicament. Owen saw quick movements from his slasher. She darted to Angelo's body, kneeling, retrieving an envelope and stuffed it in her back pocket. Pauli made the mistake of believing he controlled, that he had an ally. The killer of the Corallos, turned his back, and reached up into the statue base, a smile of discovery to his face. Kathleen threw herself at him, knife poised. She hit him with a flying crash and both went tumbling. They struggled, she flailing away. Pauli cried out to a painful slash, the gun he had pulled from his pocket dropped from his grasp while Kathleen kept up frantic blade plunging, missing his vital body parts.

Owen crawled to Angel's revolver. Pauli punched Kathleen and sent her sprawling against the fallen statue. The knife flew to the ground. Pauli grabbed it with a wolf like snarl and Kathleen rolled to retrieve Pauli's gun, aiming it with both of her trembling hands. Owen stood, shaking, unsure if he could raise Corallo's weapon.

"Drop it, or I'll shoot!" Owen heard the heavenly commanding voice of Detective Chase T. Taggert. She swung a service revolver at them, back and forth as she walked out from the dark undergrowth.

Owen, blood covering his entire back, straddled Angelo Corallo's body a pistol in hand. Kathleen Grayson, hair askew like a wild Medusa, weaving with Pauli's own revolver aimed at Pauli. Pauli DiManna held the curved knife, the symbol of all viciousness, of the strange deaths of his father, Bluestein and Larry Corallo.

"Drop the weapons." She shouted the command once more. For a second the three froze in stride, and then for some dumb reason, all three made a move of response. Owen dazed, stumbled forward. Kathleen chose to focus her aim at Pauli, whose madness coalesced and he lunged at her with the knife, close enough to reach her heart. Detective Taggart blew him away. A good choice Owen told her later. Chase gave him a twist of her nose and said he had been next on her list of targets.

Kathleen dropped her weapon and ran to Owen, noticing his slow motion collapse. She caught him and eased him to the ground, holding him in her warm arms, his blood staining her blouse and slacks. A Kodak moment.

Owen could only say under this panting breath, mystified, "You stabbed me."

"Hush," she cooed. "It was a diversion. It saved our lives."

He did not believe her.

Detective Taggart made a quick formal pulse check of the dead on the ground. They were dead as in stone dead. She walked over to the two living souls and Kathleen poured out dramatic anguish.

"Owen saved my life. Pauli DiManna kidnapped me and Larry Corallo. He killed both of the Corallos because he found out Angelo killed his father. I heard him say that. Owen tried to intervene. Angelo slashed him like he cut Chunky D. Oh, you poor baby."

Something rang true to Owen. He bit his lip feeling his parted skin burn. For now, he would go with Kathleen's version, his thoughts too jumbled. Her arms bore him in tender rapture.

Chase rolled her eyes. Her report would have to reflect the society woman's story--and it did make a good story.

The three of them heard a loud metallic sounding *thunk*. From the bushes staggered another hoodlum, the Nazi boxer from the neon boneyard who used Owen's body as his personal punching bag. He was armed, strange though, the weapon pointed at the ground. His face waffled peculiar.

Chase, moments before, had holstered her weapon. Fearing she would be too late for all of them, she dropped to her knee in a stance for clear fire. Before she could fire, the skinhead Nazi collapsed to his knees, shaking his lummox head, his pistol falling with him. Behind him Mayor Aurlieus "Goodfella" Stokes of Las Vegas entered the clearing with a shovel, and taking no chances at the hood's early recovery, hit the Nazi again. The thug ate the ground face first.

"I guess he was the back door lookout. I followed him in when I didn't see Owen leave." The Mayor surveyed the carnage. "Shit. What have you done, Owen?" Of course, he would think that. Everyone thinks that.

Owen lay in the lap of the beautiful damsel. He must be in the dying scene where the movie cowboy moseys toward the last round-up-in-the-sky and speaks in his dying breath. "Before I pass out there's a Magnum employee, Derek Shelly, on the stairs in the parking garage. Probably, he saw DiManna arrive and went to investigate and got clobbered." Owen looked up into Kathleen's hazel eyes, seeing for the first time clarity from all his mauling and told her: "I think I see the light." Kathleen put her fingers to his lips with a 'hush'.

Detective Taggart interrupted.

"Give me a break," she scoffed. Chase had this sixth sense that Owen McCombs would live to stumble another day.

Kathleen remembered. "The Cassandra diamonds. They're in the statue base." The Mayor walked over and, to his amazement, pulled out a long thin black box, like a safe deposit box.

"They're not there," said a new voice.

Smiling, the man in the wheelchair rolled himself into the Garden of Allah. Jackson Flynn. Owen's boss.

The Mayor opened the box. Empty.

7. New Meds

Bedlam. Sirens. Police roamed the construction site, helter-skelter into the garage and garden. Emergency floodlights. Investigators everywhere, charged up that they were on the scene of one of the biggest shootouts in recent Vegas history. Owen heard later that the lead union cheerleader at the outside fence on hearing the gunfire thought one of his protestors had gone berserk and pulled his crowd away from the site and set up his picket line across the street. This allowed the Mayor to walk in, unchallenged, politically correct. The press, inept behind barriers, shouted and made threats to scale the fence, to break into the perimeter. Two TV helicopters, as well as the Metro police chopper, circled the crime scene, their searchlights beaming blue staccato bursts, a night surreal.

Owen lay near the casino building wall propped on his side with several bandage compresses placed by the medics over the knife wound. As if to cheer him up, they said the blade scrawling looked like a 'happy face' half-moon. Gee, thanks. He waited for them to return with the stretcher. The interim drugs given for pain started to make him loopy. He was getting used to numbness.

No one approached him for his side of the story, so he watched as Kathleen talked to the investigators. At one point she walked over to see how he was faring, and to suggest he should wait to tell his version after *his* attorney, Clay Stokes, arrived. Owen made the point of telling her: "We need to visit, privately," and, he thought, in a well-lit and public place.

Jackson Flynn, anchored in his wheelchair, watched the proceedings, conferring with the police hierarchy and with Melissa Steele. Owen knew they were choreographing how to present the casino's public spin of events. Melissa looked in a state of semi shock and made no effort to come Owen's way. What would she say? He learned they rushed Derek Shelley to the hospital, regaining consciousness with concussion lucidity, a good sign.

The black box hidden in the statue base was a downer, totally anti-climactic. Flynn had Shelley put the box back empty for no better reason than if discovered, the finders would go away, disappointed.

"One of my gardeners found this box with a lock on it about a month ago. Dumb clod knocked over the pedestal and the box fell out. He was either honest enough to bring it to our attention or thought I might be watching from above. No idea that it figured in this whole affair or I would have come forward earlier."

'Affair'? Owen scoffed to himself. Calling this an 'affair' like it was an intimate catered party, I don't think so. One does not call days of trepidation and brutalization an 'affair'.

"Where are the diamonds?" Detective Taggart hovered at the side of Detective Washington and tapped with a nervous hand on her empty holster. Internal Affairs had confiscated her sidearm in the anticipated review of an officer involved shooting.

"The diamonds are with my attorneys," answered Jackson Flynn, "and locked up under their supervision."

"Those diamonds were 'found' by Donald Grayson," Kathleen's voice strained. "He hid them for safe keeping. He was murdered before he could retrieve them. They belong to the Grayson Family."

"Those diamonds are stolen property," said Detective Washington with the official opinion. "And evidence in a multi homicide investigation."

Jackson Flynn smiled. Owen knew from company lore the casino owner basked as ranking executive in negotiated confrontation.

"I assume the insurance company for the Cassandra Jewelry store will have the final say." An answer that mollified no one present.

Owen wanted to see the gems sparkle, to understand the value of shiny stones against human life.

As Flynn watched the police at their tasks, Owen paid attention to his boss. Flynn held youth in his face and seemed to wear a life of tragedy well. A tan marked where he had worn sunglasses. So, he did get out and about. He was not an invalid, except for his legs. His upper body looked healthy. He finally glanced Owen's way and wheeled in that direction.

"Good job, McCombs." Flynn held his hand up halting any pandering response to the praise. "Wonder why I kept you around? For what you've gone through one would think sadistic entertainment. No, it's the eternal wonderment on how an unassuming man can survive what the world throws at him. Colorado. Mississippi. Now, Vegas. Gives vicarious spice to my dull, confined existence. And somehow, in the end, you get the job done.

"Anyway, I want you in San Diego in two weeks. There's an auto auction and I need you to coordinate some bidding. I have a shopping list. While you're down there, a Native American tribe is seeking a casino management team. Check them out."

Owen accepted his assignments, not smiling.

"The camera in the parking garage, the one focused on the elevators, that works, doesn't it?"

Flynn stared ahead, silently watching the comings and goings of officialdom. Owen continued, the drugs doing the talking.

"You could review the tapes. You would have seen who came through the garage, past the elevators into the garden. Pauli DiManna said Angel killed his father. He's the most likely candidate and that would put revenge in motion. Were others in on this? You'd have seen them on tape, at least entering the garage."

The camera would have shown the arrival and departure of the guilty parties. That's why Derek Shelley was there. Jackson Flynn probably had his own plan to catch the killer but something went wrong after DiManna's arrival. They weren't expecting Angel and his neo-Nazi and they jumped Flynn's private security man.

Jackson Flynn spoke, not looking at Owen, "Donald Grayson was a good friend of mine," and wheeled himself back to the casino door, back to the protection of his office. "After all those years, his killers have been brought to justice." The police paid him no notice, they saw only the handicap, not the strength he masked and the power he could wield. At the door he turned to Owen.

"The camera will be dismantled tomorrow as part of the building demolition. That blowup and formal groundbreaking dedication for the Magnum Showroom is in one week, so when you get out of the hospital, help coordinate the Magnum festivities with Miss Steele."

At the hospital, one hundred plus stitches sewed up his veg-o-matic back, and various anti-bacterial shots for infection and more needle insertions provided his final fade-out. He slept in spurts until the late afternoon when the nurse said he had visitors, his mother and his son.

8. Recovering Reality

Internal Affairs was no walk in the park.

"It's their job to be pricks." Detective Washington knew. Been there, done that. He sat outside the interview room along with Chase's assigned rep from the Las Vegas Police Protective Association.

"They questioned everything I did. Asked the same questions over and over, trying to trip me up." She did not tell her two supporters how she squirmed or how well she knew the kidnap victims, Ms. Sawyer and Mr. McCombs. They met, she testified, in her official capacity investigating the Chunky D murder, and that was the truth. She did not know McCombs, not really, not yet.

Her lawyer gave her some comfort.

"Short interview, Detective, you'll come out okay. I expect the D.A. will have the grand jury issue a quick no bill. Pardon my bluntness, they seldom get any women police heroes. What with the political hay of eradicating some bad seed mobsters, be prepared to become a poster child as the modern crime fighter."

The LVPPA lawyer sat with her because of the case's high profile. Chase was surprised that her fellow workers in Homicide had passed the hat to defer any incidental legal costs. She had made them look good. People in the office smiled at her, threw small office chitchat her way. She had gained provisional acceptance. A new era dawned.

While climbing through a mountain of incident paperwork, Commander Stevens summoned her to his office. He told her what 'Paid Administrative Leave' meant, summarizing:

"Take a week off, but don't stray too far."

"I'll concentrate on being a Mom." Strange circumstances that killing a man gave her quality parenting time for Eric. Chase knew the more the press milked the story with her as community heroine, the less likely Rodger the Dodger had a chance in hell to prevail with his bogus legal claim for child custody. That man with another failure would go crazy.

"Take a few files home with you. Don't go stale on me," said Commander Stevens.

"Yes, sir. We have one cold case: Hector Garcia. I'd like to re-activate that."

"Fine, whatever. I assume you've heard we found another headless conventioneer?"

"Yes, sir. Heard it might be a gay thrill killing."

"That'll be one of your new cases when you return. See if you can hit another home run." Chase hated baseball analogies.

"Detective Washington and I could do that."

"I had in mind you and Fetters to head up a sub task force. Any problem with that?"

Oh, no. Her sense of euphoria that things were going in the right direction took a misstep.

"No, sir. But…Washington, he'll still be my partner?"

"Yeah, no change there. Let's meet as soon as you get cleared to work and Fetters gets out of the hospital."

"Hospital?"

"Yeah, this morning, on the headless conventioneer case, he was canvassing a gay bar following up on a tip. Got himself ambushed in the men's room. Two guys did a number on him, bruised ribs, compound fracture to his leg, and broke his nose."

Chase bit her tongue to keep from laughing aloud. Commander Stevens, as the boss, did not have to restrain himself. Widening to a grin, making her finally feel one of the team, he said, "Poor Mike, that'll be a hard one to live down, beaten by a couple of sissies."

Chase thought back to Byron Kane's promise to Ray that day at The Pussy Galore raid. She joked to herself, *What goes around returns to be slapped around.*

When she arrived home at day's end expecting hugs and kisses as the returning heroine, there was only a note: "Had to run an errand of mercy, Love, Nanna and Eric." She could smell the lingering odors of fried chicken. They had left her a wing and drumstick. Chase could almost guess what they were up to, after all, she was the current *number one homicide detective*. She thought well of their mission.

"Outstanding. That looks great." Owen on his stomach in the hospital bed had to glance to the side to view the greasy bag of homemade goodies. "I will munch now and take the rest home. They should release me this afternoon." He had slept little. The stitch work artistry came painfully alive as the drugs dissipated. Any distraction to his 'Happy Face' etched back was welcomed.

"I made you a comic book." Eric handed over his hard scribbled graphic drawings, stapled together into a pamphlet. Owen thumbed the pages. Spaceships and horrible alien creatures, laser blasting through a recognizable plot. This boy had a creative mind. He wondered if he and Eric were similar, their realities not like those normal people faced. Owen might have found a simpatico buddy.

"Gee, thanks Eric. From this position, reading is about all I can do." That had been the prognosis from the doctors with the good news he could do his recovery from his residence, wherever that was going to be.

No one from the Mayor's office had called. The Mayor's handlers were keeping His Honor on a short leash. No more association with threats to his political future. No calls either transmitted from the Magnum offices, nothing more from Jackson Flynn. The press tried to sneak in with no success, his hospital floor guarded and he incognito, growing quickly bored.

Nanna told Owen she heard the awful news when Chase arrived home at dawn from the Magnum crime scene. What Nanna did not tell the injured young man was Chase sitting like a lump on the couch, gushing waterfall tears, as she had unburdened what had happened in the Garden of Allah. Her first shooting, a required death, in the line of duty. Chase might see her emotions as weakness. Nanna saw a young woman retaining her humanity. Calming her, listening to the story of the shootings, Nanna knew in turn she needed to comfort the only man who had treated them well in years.

"I promise I'll make you some more chicken, but you have to come and visit us." Nanna said.

"Whenever I'm healthy I'd enjoy that."

Owen for the benefit of a young boy gave the shoot 'em rendition of the kidnapping and shootings, like a glossy comic book, void of real hurt. At the end, he emphasized that Eric's mom saved his life.

After Eric and Nanna left, two surgeons in masks arrived, wheeling an operating bed. A quick hit of fear. Had he relapsed and didn't even know it?

"You're driving us crazy," said Hi, or was it Jinx?

9. The Shallow End

Three days later, he lay wrapped in towels by the pool, the sun once his enemy radiated his body with healing powers.

Kathleen Grayson, dressed in summer white, her makeup shielded by the scorching sun under a broad brimmed hat, sat next to Owen, sipping ice water brought by Casey who frowned dislike toward this high society visitor. What lessened Casey's fretting about this turf trespasser was Kathleen's boyfriend, Clay Stokes, who sat in the living room trying to entertain himself. Casey promised to babysit him until the outside private conversation had concluded.

Kathleen reviewed her statement to the police.

Pauli DiManna kidnapped her at gunpoint; that they drove to the construction site with some sort of pass, letting Pauli in the back gate. There she discovered Lorenzo Corallo gagged and tied in the trunk of Pauli's car. DiManna forced them into the garden, tied up the elder gangster to the base of the statue just as his father had been only a few days earlier and forced her to look for the diamonds using a metal detector, while he tortured the elder Corallo with a razor blade dagger. Dicing the old man's ears off. Kathleen informed the police it was apparent her captor showed signs of being mentally unstable and that when Angel, she called him Angelo, showed up with Owen at gunpoint, all the gunfire started, and she thought she saw Angelo stab Owen. Pauli shot Angelo's father, then Pauli shot Angelo, and the police woman shot Pauli.

Owen could see her at police headquarters playing the part masterfully with sobbing enunciation eliciting official sympathy. Kathleen Grayson Sawyer ought to be awarded an Academy Award. Owen wanted one of the Mayor's signature double blue Margaritas.

"I can live with Angel slashing me," Owen gave her tale a basic credence. "After all, your knife swipe action was not an attempt at being lethal, was it? You weren't trying to kill me, right, just trying to distract Pauli? Correct?"

"Of course, Owen, a quick reaction. A rock tossed might have done the trick." Then bitch, why not pick up a rock and throw it, he yelled to himself, itching from stitches, under his shoulder blade, out of reach.

Okay, he heard her story. His turn. "Kathleen, are we going to be friends?"

"Owen, you're my hero." And she gave him a sexy wink. "And more if we can work it out."

"Cut the crap, Kathleen. You are one of the best manipulators I've ever run across. I need to have the total truth or I will tell my interpretation of events, first to Clay, then to the Mayor, and finally to the police."

"What're you saying?" Her mood went from coquette to cautious, a darkness appearing beneath her brimmed designer hat.

"Your expertise with a knife comes from some practice. You intentionally put that blade across my back, just as you were the one who sliced up Chunky D in the garden one week earlier. It's become a familiar signature."

He saw her face tighten. What she had expected as a tête à tête poolside among survivors became a patio stage for indictment. He continued.

"I believe there were two knife attacks on Mr. Corallo, two separate perpetrators. Mr. Corallo's autopsy showed a few amateurish razor cuts. Pauli beginning to practice, Pauli building up the courage to do his own torturing. The ear-ectomy was your skill, not Pauli's. Just like on Chunky D--."

A sharp interruption. "I did not kill Chunky D."

Owen saw the two-sided truth.

"Yes, you could say that. You tortured while Angelo did the deed with a .22. You were there the day Chunky D bought the big cannoli. I saw you. You were the lady construction worker all masked up waving with the stop sign. When I talked to our people, to our Construction Manager Hollister, he could find no record of a woman working site traffic control. Your Angelo buddy had construction contacts. He set you up on the inside and somehow you baited Chunky D to the garden. Maybe your sexy sighs or an anonymous tip to where the diamonds were buried, whatever the bait. You tied him up to the statue base and started your torturing to find where the diamonds were and then Angel showed up, maybe by conspiracy or by invitation. He arrived in a concrete truck looking too dapper to be a construction worker. The cameras caught his arrival. You directed him down to the garden, and he brought down his, or is it your metal detector, in the golf bag, the same one you loaned Pauli last night?"

"Your imagination is rampant, Owen. What kind of pain killers are they giving you?"

"Oh, I'm just warming up. I could even go so far as to suggest it was your idea to snatch the senior Corallo? Somewhere along the way you hinted to Pauli that you thought Angelo killed his dad. And the night in the garden what did I hear but you, with subtlety, baiting Pauli to shoot Larry Corallo. Whether it's Capulets or Montigues, or Eastwood mimicing Kurosowa's *Joyjimbo*, you are the Fate Fulcrum in this tragedy. You have put everyone into motion and I think it all began when you picked up West Pegler's manuscript at your boyfriend's house and read *Wiseguys of Vegas*."

"And what gives you this great insight?"

"Because Chapter Nine and Ten confirmed what you always suspected, that your Dad was 'assassinated' by the Mob. Your total motive was revenge."

Kathleen sought to brush him off.

"I'm listening to your fairy tale. It does have some elements of imagination. Have you ever considered noir writing?"

"I can visualize a tragedy. The little girl who has her father kissing her with all his love, and minutes later his plane is blown up. You lived years with that nightmare, but during that time you started guessing that it might not have been an accident. You knew about your Dad's personal interest in the diamonds long before anyone else might have guessed."

"My father never had any dealings with stolen diamonds. He was a gracious and wonderful human being."

"A mistake or error, he did know mobsters. He was the last to handle the diamonds. Perhaps he was going to turn in the thieves. That's why the stolen gems weren't on the plane." He saw her hesitant nod to the bittersweet possibility.

There was no reason to demolish her father's unsullied memory. The bereaved must believe the best of the departed. This was one part of Owen's story that would have been pure guesswork and did not require a solution. Leave Donald Grayson's motive as the unresolved mystery. Full truth would not satisfy the simple truth.

"One thing we know for certain, he had this lovely preteen daughter, pre debutante. She was growing into a beautiful woman, and as a proud father he desired to enhance her radiance. Look at the newspaper photos of you learning of your Father's death at the airport. You're wearing a small pendant. A diamond. And at the social function last week with Clay and the Mayor, a more stunning necklace. The same necklace that you wore on your first social outing in Vegas the night you met Claiborne Stokes. The photo in the Society column.

"Kathleen, I saw the stolen property list from the police. I would bet you a pile of Magnum casino chips that those two jewelry pieces will be on the police list of stolen items from the Cassandra heist. Your dad set aside a few baubles just for his darling princess.

"More than anyone else, you knew if your father had hidden the jewelry you had a pretty good idea where. Kathleen, it will go no farther than poolside, but as they say, 'the truth will set you free'."

10. The Deep End

Kathleen, a problem he could not ignore, leaned towards him as if not to be overheard.

"It became a race to the diamonds."

Owen mulled over various scenarios. "You wore the necklace prior to Pegler's book being passed around. By doing that, the old gangsters took notice, and likewise, the sons. You put the search for the diamonds into play. You baited the gangsters."

"You're perceptive, Owen. Through Angelo, being that we were such good old friends" (she said this with cold sarcasm). "I got a call from him asking if I knew anything more about where the diamonds were."

"But you didn't have to join the search? Did Pauli or Angel have something on you? Something from your childhood that made you an unwilling player in the diamond quest?"

"You might say that." Her reply could have put frost on the lawn.

Kathleen, to calm her nerves, pulled a pen from her purse and started doodling on a napkin. Owen could see she drew small daggers with numbers beside them. He saw Casey eyeing them from the living room, keeping tabs, assured there was a minimum three feet of separation.

"It was sexual," Owen decided. "Maybe playing doctor with a threesome. The nurse, the doctor and the anesthesiologist—you and Angel and Pauli."

She sparked in anger. Opening her purse she placed it on the table before him. Inside, he could see a sheathed dagger. Another, the third in play. Owen had hit close to home, he thought, in the old neighborhood at least.

"Your stretching, aren't you, McCombs? What's your big clue?"

"Your bedroom antics for me were too calculating."

"If I recall you were enjoying the passion."

"I wouldn't disagree, but the spell was broken. When I reviewed that night, if not for self-improvement, I realized that your come-on instead of being part slut and part nympho, seemed contrived. Your body, how can I say this, ambivalent! Your kind of fucking was a means to an end. You had a plan."

Her laugh was weak. "My screwing you, a conspiracy?"

"The demolition of the El Morocco. You and your cohorts had a limited window of opportunity. The Mayor and I were running around demanding to see Pegler's book. Reading Chapter Ten might eventually lead to the Garden of Allah. You were the one who stole Chapter Ten from the book, in my bedroom, after I rushed Casey to the hospital. Delay was your sole purpose, not to be in my arms."

She put her hand on his leg.

"Owen, how can you say that? We'll have time to ourselves… ahead."

"Kathleen, there's something wrong with you. Like your spirit inside has been trampled on. I'm an expert on that trait. If I were to guess, maybe by your father's untimely exit from your life, your mother's alcoholism, the lost parental love; and then perhaps a body betrayed."

He saw a rigid flex, her body tensed. The Ice Maiden Cometh.

"Where's this guesswork going?"

"What do you mean?"

"Do you like hurting people?"

"Hey, Miss Kathleen Grayson Sawyer, I'm trying to get to my second week on the job. And as far as I can guess the outcome, two young hoodlums with the bad genes of their fathers went on a murderous rampage after diamond loot their parents had themselves stolen. I think the case, at least for the police, is pretty well closed. The bad guys bite the dust, end of story."

"Why should I trust you?"

"Kathleen, of all my failings, lack of honor is not one of them."

Her silence showed her borderline indecision.

"Let me do some storytelling, as I might guess it happened. I think something sexual occurred, something you could be blackmailed for to go look for the diamonds. Perhaps, in your youth, Pauli took advantage of you, whether consensual or otherwise, maybe more date rape than anything. At the age of, when was it, 15 or 16, that's pretty traumatic for any woman to bottle up inside. Between you and I, and it goes no further, is that what happened?"

Their eyes met, but hers lay obscured behind sunglasses.

"The Wrecking Crew," she said finally.

"What?"

"They raped me."

"The Wrecking Crew? All of them?"

"You guys call it a 'gang bang'. And I was thirteen years old. I had been drinking wine that day. Chunky D had some family medication in his house. Pauli might have slipped a pill or two in one of the drinks. I was bug-eyed high, but very, very conscious. An easy

mark, but I remember every waking moment of the sweat and pene-
trations, some awkward, some brutal, painful tearing. Campi could
never have an erection, he used his two fingers for the pleasure. Large
fingers to probe a virgin."

So abhorrent, Owen tried to visualize the source of her nightmare
madness.

*A young girl in a growing woman's body, looking older than her age,
running around the DiManna swimming pool, splashing water, chasing,
giggling in kid's play with her two boy playmates. Maybe some adolescent
jesting, catching the attention of the adult men sitting poolside, drinking.
Her small body, those child's tender breasts, one mouthful each. The boys
grab some beer or wine from the grown-ups, and force her to sip in tease,
larger gulps in dares. The men watch this, watch the girl reel to tipsy, the
sun beating the alcohol fast into her system. Into theirs. She is dizzy, wandering to the bedroom, dazed. Angelo had pulled off the top off her bathing
suit, feeling her breasts. Pauli, yanked her suit down to her ankles, staring.
An adult appeared in the doorway. Who was the first? The more violent probably, the one who liked beating up women. Scarpetti. Then the others at the
door egging on, waiting their turns, lust animals without morality; and a
young girl, hands clamped to her mouth, smoky tongues forced on her, eventually staring with vacant eyes, dilated head turned to the wall, faces obscured by her own tears.*

"Shit." Owen whistled. "And Angel and Pauli?"

"They were the cleverest of them all. Pauli stood lookout. Angelo
took Polaroids when the men were otherwise distracted, too excited
to catch on that they were the patsies.

"Angel and Pauli told me I was going to be their fuck slave or
they'd send dad an anonymous letter with a photo of me sprawled
naked on the bed and say that I was fucking my way through school.

I felt dirty, forever washing unseen filth. I hid it all, the shame, the vaginal tears. It was a miracle I didn't get pregnant. A few days later I went to the airport to see my father off with tissue stuffed in my panties to staunch the bleeding.

"Pauli and Angelo were as good as their fathers in their own vicious ways. With their packet of Polaroids, they blackmailed the Wrecking Crew for occasional 'loans'. I was underage and most of them were ex-felons. That meant thirty to life for them."

"You could have gone to the police?"

"My life was forfeit to them. I would have never reached trial as a witness. You know their past. I had a cigarette burn under my breast, a threat to keep silence from Scarpetti the Torch. Then there was my father. Did I want to be the public center of this ultimate humiliation? Destroy my life, my father's belief in his pure little girl?"

"After he died, that's why you went back East?"

She nodded slowly, raised her head to the sun, closed her eyes, and accepted the day's warmth, purging. "My father died never knowing. Thank God for that small blessing."

This shell of beauty concealed a disturbed woman. Owen blinked wide to the bigger picture.

"You killed them all?!"

Kathleen looked away at a leaf floating in the pool. Owen's eyes followed her gaze, the leaf sucked into the pool skimmer, crammed in with the other trapped plant material. Drowned.

She pulled out a Kleenex from her Gucci shoulder bag. Owen once more saw the sheathed dagger. She dabbed away perspiration beneath her eyes, not tears, and he got the message: what is said poolside, stays poolside. The fresh, unconsecrated blade in her purse, the bible upon which they were sworn in this confessional pact. Owen started down the list.

"Bobby Campi, heart attack. The Mayor joked about Campi's heart attack in bed with a hooker. You were the hooker. I bet if I could find the medical report, the evidence would show that he had no semen ejaculation. You said he couldn't get it up. No penetration. He died from being humped to death. I think I caught a preview on how the action might cause an adrenalin rush, over stimulate a heart muscle." He recalled her attempted seduction on his own weak-willed body. "His death occurred before Pegler passed around his manuscript with Chapter Ten. No one even considered his death as a possible homicide, actually, an execution."

"Beautiful day," she said, sucking on an ice cube from her glass.

"Then, Scarpetti the Torch. You couldn't reach him because he was in prison, but someone with connections could. That's when you renewed your old acquaintance with Angel. He knew how to get rid of jail scum. The police would think it 'ironic' because of Scarpetti's arson history, but he burned your breast. Okay, I see each revenge had a personal touch to fit their style of rape. Campi's death by non-penetration, Scarpetti because he burned you."

"They all knew at the very end why they were being punished. Scarpetti must have read at the last moment that his funeral pyre was courtesy of a girl nicknamed 'Graycee.'" He knew who Graycee was. *'You won't tell, will you Graycee? A cigarette like this could leave your face so ugly. Feel that burn. You're not going to tell, are you, Graycee?'*

"How far did you go with *dear* 'Angelo' to get his participation?"

"Angelo wanted the diamonds more than sex. Greed was his obsession, like his old man. The fewer the old timers who might start searching, the better for him. They were eager to see me as one of their old playmates. Keep in mind Angelo still held the old Polaroids."

That is what Owen had heard in the signyard.

"That's what you took from Angel's body. I heard him on the phone: 'Yes, I'll have the package.' I saw that move before you attacked Pauli. You tricked Angel into bringing the photos to the garden, in exchange for what? His father's freedom, the diamonds?"

"Guy was never that smart, never made copies of those Polaroids. Kept them in a shoebox like a sex magazine collection."

"What was Pauli's excuse to play games with you?"

"Pauli only required an occasional feminine hand down his pants, grabbing his balls to give him a direction to follow."

"Yes, you're good at the tease. I see, with the boys, you made them the gangsters they wanted to be. Angelo probably wanted to make his 'bones', prove he could be like his papa. You used the knife in the Garden of Allah on Chunky but you let Angel finish the job. Nice setup. An easy kill for a nouveau gangsta. Your plan was the same for Pauli and Lorenzo. No one knew they were being played. I'm impressed."

She accepted the compliment with silence.

"And why the knife?"

"I would not look into their faces, rape shames you, then and for-ever after. The angered madness only comes later. Lying on the bed in DiManna's house, I turned my head to the wall and there was an odd assortment of weapons, cheap costume props, hung up as wall decoration. I focused on the dagger, and as they took turns, I mentally gripped that knife. About three years ago, I'm paging through a Christie's auction catalogue and there were four Persian 17th century dirks, almost identical to what Crestview Furniture sells as cheap Asian knockoffs. Seeing them up for bid, remembering the dagger on the wall, set my plan in action."

"You used one of those daggers on Morrie Bluestein."

"I saw you there."

Owen thought back, amazed at her cunning.

"Yes, I recall."

"I almost bumped into you and the Mayor. I like costumes. Construction worker. Hooker. Hospice nurse. You only saw a nurse going down the hallway."

Yes, Owen saw the image, a thin body with a bounce that no nurse with years on her feet could likewise emulate.

"And Bluestein's calling card. The ants? The severed penis?"

"Bluestein, slobbering with is candy sticky mouth, couldn't crawl on top of me, didn't want to see my face. He flipped me over and found a new orifice. Torn, that took the longest to heal. I felt he should die the slowest."

"And his dick, being the most offensive, I assume had to go."

"Bluestein gave me some useful information, after some encouragement. He confirmed that Scarpetti had killed my father on orders from Tony Spilotro. He told me the diamonds, after all their searches, must be in the Garden of Allah. It confirmed my own guesswork. With the demolition schedule on short notice, I hustled, forming alliances where required, fulfilling my own obligation."

"The avenging angel, for yourself, your father."

"And the final curtain." She spoke with mild release and he took his cue.

"Chunky D and Larry Corolla?"

"Chunky D's weight nearly suffocated me. Trying to breathe, with one hand, I scratched his face, and he slapped me several times."

"The knife flourishes on his cheeks. Fingernail scratches. Yes, he would remember you well."

"Larry Corallo?"

"I tried screaming and Larry stuffed my bathing suit in my mouth. He kept saying, "I can't hear you, sweetums. I can't hear you, sweetums."

"Yes, I can see where the ears would have to go.

"You pitted everyone against everyone, looking for the diamonds, it was father against son, but the ultimate payback would be for sons to slay each other's fathers. That happened. But were you going to then kill Angel and Pauli?"

"I wanted them to live to suffer daily as I do. I had other plans. This outcome was chance, poetic justice. They wanted to grow up to be like their fathers, and they did, just dead a lot earlier. It could have gone either way. If Pauli killed me, after he killed you, it would have been a release."

"Random circumstances and we both survive, the bad guys perish."

She glanced behind him, and Owen turned with pain and saw Clay Stokes standing in the house doorway. He was being sensitive to the private talk, wondering.

"Final questions: The fire at Crestview Furniture and a call girl ring in The Pussy Galore? I can't see our boy gangsters being that smart to torch one establishment and corrupt another."

Her smile, her lip turned at the corner, confirmed the depth of Kathleen's malicious revenge.

"How about Chunky D in the Mayor's car? It had to be you. Angel killed Chunky with a bullet, even though you were going to let him bleed out. I saw the tapes. He exited and you went back in."

"Dumb luck the trunk was opened by you and the Mayor. Angel had run out, shitless at his first killing. I needed to get the body out of the garden. If I could do that, the garden wouldn't be a police focus of a search. I could keep looking in the garden. Surprised, I recognized it was the Mayor's Mercedes. Blind luck opportunity. Why would he look in the trunk? And I could dump the body later."

Owen wanted to believe it was pure coincidence. But was it, really? Kathleen ought to be as angry at the Mayor, being the defense attorney, who indirectly kept her rapists out of jail. Owen wondered if the Mayor, maybe even his progeny, was on her eradication list. Destroying the Mayor's career was as good as death for a politician. And breaking a man's heart, as she could do to her boyfriend at anytime, would move beyond cruelty to diabolical. Owen could only pray her blood taste had been sated.

She looked to Clay, standing in the back window, and threw him a cheery smile, her wave to him, a come hither. Her backyard confessional at its conclusion.

"Is this all over with? In Vegas, the bad guys crapped out?"

"Mr. McCombs, Owen, I'm not proud of what I've done. There's no salvation for my soul. My life will remain in torment, but at least, there has been a hollow victory of sorts. Old fashioned Bible justice is the code of the West."

Owen did not hesitate. "Deserved fate, but my dear, you need deep therapy."

Kathleen closed her purse and the antique dagger disappeared. She left the napkin under her empty glass, eight scrawled daggers, from a green ink pen, next to each seeming random numbers. As she rose, she stretched to her full stature, the sophisticated beautiful woman he had seen the first day of his arrival. That's what Clay Stokes would see in her, and Owen had no desire to change the perception. Kathleen's half grin to him revealed her protective covering re-established.

"I guess I won't see you around as much in the days ahead."

"Oh, I'm sure as Magnum cranks out its social entry into Las Vegas, you and your boyfriend will be on the guest lists."

"Until then?"

"You are a remarkable woman, Kathleen. Please find a less vigorous challenge to undertake. Start by burying your dagger collection where no one, including you, can find them."

She blew Clay a kiss as she walked toward him. Clay gave Owen one of those 'what was that all about?' shrugs. Owen smiled back and gave him a thumbs up, all is right with the world. Why not, options were not his choice to make. Casey strolled out of the house toward them both, and as the two women passed each other with their eyes straight ahead at their intended targets, Kathleen said to Casey, "He's all yours."

Casey, not missing a beat, replied, "Yes, he will be."

11. Premature Epilogue

Elvis was finishing her routine. She wiggled her butt in those tight black leather pants, slow gyrating as she belted out "Mean Woman Blues". The temporary stage was covered with red, white, and blue bunting, the crowd handclapping the rhythm with enthusiasm. They were the handpicked elite of Las Vegas, invited by the embossed invitation of Mr. Jackson Flynn, Chairman and CEO of Magnum Casinos & Resorts, and its premiere, in development property, Magnum Las Vegas. The press corps and television cameras were set off as the unwashed behind velvet ropes.

Owen McCombs rejuvenated in his element. Just don't slap him on the back. Into his second week of employment in Las Vegas, to anyone who asked what he did for Magnum he handed them a business card smelling of fresh ink but no title. On the reverse side of his business card were corporate name and address, his name and company quotation: 'At the Speed of Fun', in both Japanese and Chinese. The Chinese delegation, huddled in their tight group, boogied to the party festivities, this being their last night in Vegas. Standing in their midst Miss Candy Land beamed all headlights, excited to be the center of so much close-up camera snapping.

Owen, over the last week, saw all loose ends tied into neat bundles, palatable to all but a very few.

The District Attorney, grumbling, postponed his grand jury investigation. You could not indict a folk hero like Mayor Goodfella. A few posters have already appeared with him holding a shovel with the caption, "Love Las Vegas or I'll Whack You." Owen knew such sentiment would be the next election's political slogan. Harmon Hartley, political operative, worked the elite crowd with handshakes, back slapping and guffaws, the campaign underway though a year off. Hartley, Owen saw, even glad-handed Homeless Bob, a gate crasher, munching off a plate of complimentary hors d'oeuvres.

He scanned the crowd for Chase. He heard she went back into the field, the heroine and rightly so. Owen himself could have been a local public hero from Kathleen's testimony, but he pushed for a low profile. Melissa Steele acted as guardian of Owen's privacy, handling all inquisitive press calls.

The show today the majority of her creation, yet the female Elvis in the talent lineup only by Owen's subterfuge. He went out on a limb to promote Casey as a future star and one of the hotel's primary celebrity greeters. Melissa loved the idea, as her own, since the first expo to be held in the Magnum Convention Center would be the International Elvi Expo. Melissa had lost a bet on that one. She swore the Elvis impersonators would pick the Rio, or Hooters.

Among the gathering were the wounded warriors, but not a band of brothers. West Pegler sat in a wheelchair, two arms in plaster, his face still swollen. He accepted the sympathy of well-wishers with wired jaw mumbles as he basked in being center stage of controversy. His book's contents, now acknowledged as the reasons for multiple murders, had him on the cusp of the bestseller's list. From his hospital bed, Pegler blamed his beating on the neo-Nazi that the mayor beaned with the shovel.

Casey took her bow to audience applause and stepped to the side of the stage. Theodore clapped the loudest. Owen didn't know where this trinity of relationships was going. Casey broke the news to Theodore that she had the hots for her other roommate, which Owen of course swore in front of them both could not be reciprocally returned. Casey ignored this affirmation and Theodore dismissed Owen as an old man who would always end up bloody and bruised. The fact Theodore cleared twenty thousand dollars against the Carnivale raid eased the boy's lovesick pain. The Carnivale reeling from the unexpected demise of Pauli DiManna, their Slot Manager, meant Theodore and his team would continue to hang around, as math vultures, ready to pounce.

Owen, in turn, prepared the worst for the Magnum gaming floor by introducing Theodore to Derek Shelly, Head of Security, the Good Samaritan, a bandage across the back of his head. Theodore and Shelly circled each other, taking measurements. Owen finally had the chance to thank Derek for beating up his attackers that night. What caught Owen off guard was that Derek told him he didn't believe the hoods savaging Owen in front of the Silver Avenue house were either from the DiManna or the Corallo outfits. They have to be, Owen prayed, or there's an unnamed menace still at large. It was Derek Shelly who followed Angelo and his henchmen when they dumpster dumped Owen, and through Mr. Flynn's direction, Shelly anonymously directed the Mayor to the neon graveyard for Owen's rescue. None of them anticipated the later confrontation in the Garden of Allah, and were caught off guard, especially Derek Shelly.

After Casey took her final bow, on stage strutted a covey of Vegas showgirls in their high feathered bonnets and skimpy sequin outfits. Next entered the Mayor who pushed wheelchair bound Jackson Flynn to center stage. The spin was in. Mayor Goodfella came out of last week smelling like a rose. The press even wove the tale that the Mayor might have had a hand in locating the lost diamonds and the Mayor would do nothing to stifle such printable gossip. Earlier this week he had agreed to broker peace talks between the Magnum management and the Culinary Union and the Teamsters. Owen could see no protestors at the gate or along the sidewalks.

An enormous, one story gift box was rolled out onto the stage. Owen stood at the fringe of the crowd. He held in his hand the script of the day's festivities which he had played a small part in drafting. Melissa Steele was at the microphone as the voice of Magnum. Mr. Flynn gave her his beaming endorsement.

"Ladies and Gentlemen," said the lovely Marketing Director, "distinguished guests and members of the press. Mr. Jackson Flynn of Magnum Casino Resorts Las Vegas is pleased you have joined us today as we unveil certain attractions for our new casino. First, of course, is our celebration of transportation." Owen could see the Mayor mouth the words, 'Temple of Zoom'. "And so we present the first of our speed fleets!"

With this, a cluster of fireworks hit the sky with multiple bangs, and from the parking garage exited a fleet of the most expensive antique cars ever assembled, nearly $28 million in value. The vehicles made a half circle convoy around the audience, halting in military formation, parking on putting green astroturf. Owen had seen the cars arrive in the last few days, rushed in for this specific occasion, secreted to the L parking garage. The last cars to be housed in that structure as demolition was on today's program. He glanced at his script. Twenty elegant cars to arrive from the parking garage at 2:05 p.m.. As an auto aficionado (his Corvette was finally back from the shop) Owen planned someday to sit in the Duesenberg, turn on the engine, let it idle and dream dreams of the contented voyeur.

Owen recognized Wayne Hollister, the project contractor's manager, standing on the steps of his trailer office. Still not happy, another day shot, his completion bonus in jeopardy. Tough luck, buddy. Near him, two hardhat construction workers stared at Owen, likewise not happy campers. Hey guys, Flynn gave you the day off with full pay. They probably have not been told Owen was not a hired union buster. One of them was pounding his fist into his palm. Was he…?

Fifteen minutes until the demolition charges both in the casino and parking structures would be detonated. In between was the Mayor's speech of welcome, the Governor's remarks, and a special treat for the guests, public, and press. No later than 2:25 p.m.

Twenty cars. Owen had made a passing visual count deciding which, beyond the Duesenberg would be his second favorite.

The Mayor stood at the podium to speak.

Nineteen cars. Owen counted only nineteen cars, lined up on the Astro turf to be viewed at the ceremony's end. He recounted.

One car was missing. Had it broken down and pulled from the caravan? Possible. But the script was hard wired to accuracy. He would have heard. Something in the back of his mind began to fester, and he started a fast walk to the garage.

"You can't go beyond the tape," said a rent-a-cop. "They're blowing up the buildings soon."

"No, it's okay," Owen flashed his new calling card. "They've postponed it for a half an hour. Some glitch. I'll take a quick look. Back in five minutes." Insisted authority will always trump.

He picked up his pace. He had fifteen minutes.

"Ladies and Gentlemen," intoned the Mayor. "Governor, Mr. Flynn, what a beautiful day for the City of Las Vegas…"

The El parking garage. For a whole week, it had been like a mesmerizing vamp pulling him back, always into trouble. A haunting of all that is old, the tarnished, trying with futility to hold onto memories before becoming pulverized concrete dust.

His pace increased to running. His back ached with each stretched step. Bandages on his back rubbed against his shirt.

No autos on the first level where they all had been lined up for their announced exits. If there was a car left in here, where would it be? Intentionally left? If so, it would have to have been the last one in the parade. Not on the roof. It would have been too visible from those on the outside. They would see it make the turns to go up to the upper levels and halt the demolition. The basement parking had to be the likely place to hide a car. If there was a car at all? Maybe Mr. Flynn pulled it out himself from the showing, and had not told anyone. Power trumps mid-level authority.

The darkness of the basement parking garage brought bad vibes. Even the emergency exit signs with glimmer lighting were removed. Creepy things only happened within shadows. At first glance he saw nothing but then it was pitch black in the further recesses of the lower garage. He shuffled downward, his own scraping footsteps, creating an atmosphere of emptiness. That's when his squinting eyes saw the shape, obscured. Running up to the vehicle, he felt its sides, sensing it was the 1948 Mercury, he had seen arrive days earlier. This indeed had been on the show list. But why would anyone want to destroy one car as pure meaningless vandalism? What did they have against Jackson Flynn and the Magnum?

He opened the car door and the interior lights showed no keys in the ignition. He searched the visor and on the floor. Nothing. And then a cold chill came over him. Déjà vu. Two weeks ago to this moment...no, no, it could not be. He worked his way back to the car's trunk. It was locked and he did not have a key. He had to leave, he was running out of time.

He saw the empty liquor bottle in the auto's back shelf. Strange? He had not looked in the back seat, and there he found a body.

The body of a woman lay, thank God, still breathing. She reeked of spilled liquor, her blouse wet. He turned her over. God Almighty! Chase Taggart! Unconscious. He heard applauding over the loudspeakers. The Mayor had finished, next the Governor. He had less than ten minutes to clear the garage.

He lifted her out and placed her against the side of the car. In doing so, he smelled a deeper odor of chemicals, perhaps chloroform, he guessed.

And that's when he screamed as the fist slammed into his back. The attacker knew who he was and where he was most vulnerable. He felt stitches ripping. Instead of falling to his knees and expecting the next hit to be a kick—had he already done this dance before? He stumbled to the side, and turned to face his assailant.

Owen at first could not identify who was taking the next swing, but he had had enough. He was not a wuss, pussy, or wimp, all previous actions to the contrary. Enough was enough. He parried the man's arm, and drove his fist into his stomach. He felt strength surge from unknown regions, and as his attacker doubled over, he slammed his fist with an uppercut into the man's jaw. The crunching noise of breaking bones crushed any smile his foe might ever have again. He yanked him up and thrust the man's back to the car's front seat, into the small beam of light.

Owen's mind muddled for answers. *The realtor. What's his name?* Two days ago, this man had dropped by and introduced himself and said he would be glad to find him a home, and left his business card.

Now a realtor was trying to kill him? No, he was trying to murder Chase. But why? No, that would not happen, to her, or to him. Anger surged from wanting to protect someone he cared about, led him to yank and spin the realtor and slam him into the concrete wall of the garage. The realtor collapsed into the darkness.

He gathered Chase up in his arms and began his plodding, painful ascent from the garage.

When he reached the light, the Governor had turned the show back to Melissa Steele. The Show must always go on, thought Owen, as he brought he and Chase to safety, and carried her over to the standby emergency shade tent the Magnum had on hand for victims of sunstroke, too much alcohol, and in case of accidents, this incident such a case.

"She's fainted," he lied to the nurse. Let her think a drunk had passed out. He helped to lay Chase onto a cot in the shaded tent, a wet cloth on her face. An older woman sat in a chair, fanning herself, drinking liquids. The scorcher day had its victims. He took in Chase's peaceful gaze and saw what he had been looking for, lost for so many years. A kindred spirit. He kissed her eyelids. "I'll be back," he whispered.

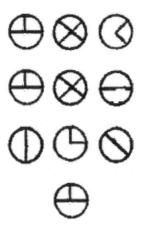

Melissa recaptured the crowd's attention.

"We are here today to say goodbye to the old and reconstitute our visions with the new; today we break ground on our Magnum Theatre Showroom and introduce you to the loveliest jewels in our Magnum crown — she hit the huckster scream — "Here they are: 'Hi-Jinx!'" The giant gift box fell open to reveal through the stage fog and released balloons, those two vixen super stars. Their hit song set the crowd into cheering. The girls romped and pranced the stage singing and waving to the crowd. But what Owen noticed most as he made his way through the crowd, were their diamond necklaces sparkling from the bouncing sun rays. Owen was privy to this secret. Jackson Flynn, promoter that he is, had settled on the Cassandra insurance claim and had bought the found loot. Owen could guess on opening day of the casino-hotel that a black box with diamonds oozing out and surrounded by security guards would be part of a future Magnum lobby display. Perhaps even a plaque someday: "The History of the Shootout in the Magnum Garden." (Note the El Morroco name disappeared from all vocabularies.) He could see a diorama, or perhaps even a musical skit in some Magnum Vegas show act. Today was the day the mythology begins. Vegas is like that, glamorize half-truths and publish them in a tourist brochure.

Owen was in search of help. He passed by Nanna and Eric near the stage, both fascinated with the super stars. He had promised them, in a few days, a behind-the-scene tour of the construction site. When they'd reach the casino model room, Eric would receive a set of the metal show cars in miniature reproduction like those to be sold at high prices as collector's items in the casino gift shop.

From the crowd, Owen located Detective Washington and went to his side. One minute into explaining the attack in the garage and discovering Chase he found himself hustling after the police officer over to the first aid station. Detective Washington wasted no time in telling a volunteer doctor the seriousness of the chemicals she might have inhaled. The doctor gave an odd stare and went to work checking Chase's vital signs, and preparing a glucose drip. Only then, did the detective say to the doctor, "And you might also see to our friend's back. He seems to be bleeding through his shirt." A nurse tended to Owen and placed gauze and a new dressing.

The detective began his investigation of events but stopped with a shock when Owen showed him the business card of the attacker's identity. Washington gave him this dumb struck look.

"You know who Kinkaid is, don't you?"

"A realtor, crazy for sure."

"Roger Kinkaid is Chase's ex-husband."

"Ex? You mean…Kinkaid is Eric's father?"

Washington nodded.

Owen absorbed the shock like a shotgun blast to his heart. Holy Shit! He had left the boy's father to die in the garage. He took off running. Not in time.

With the Mayor on one side, Jackson Flynn on the other, assisting the duo superstars to a large, gaudy ribbon plunger. The twins pushed down the plunger setting off deafening explosions in a series of staggered blasts, as the old El Morocco Casino building and parking garage imploded. More aerial fireworks. Pure Vegas.

Owen found himself leaning against the Duesenberg. He was sick to his stomach. In an act of pure vengeance, even if protecting some-one he now cared about, he had killed. Eric would never forgive him and that would doom his relationship with Chase. Depressive fluids sought their old niches. As he buried his head in his arms, aching throughout body and soul, Owen did not see a grey silt encrusted form, an apparition bent and wounded, stumble through the dust clouds of vaporized buildings, tripping across the strewn rubble to exit and disappear onto a side street, away from the crowd of onlook-ers awed at the explosive power of man's desire to create new edifices.

Owen wanted to use this celebratory day to start to absorb Las Vegas. The effused life, not only for the tourists, but a vibrancy of its citizens, swirling in exciting motion. He pulled from his pocket a busi-ness card. Roger Kinkaid, Realtor. He tore it up and littered the wind.

The Mayor approached, admiring the line of antique classic cars.

"I am glad you're back on the mend. You realize I had to keep everything at arms-length until all the investigations were con-cluded."

"Yes, no problem." He tried to put on his public relations face. Owen knew the dark forces of Byron Kane and Harmon Hartley were working their magic, putting the correct spin in place. Protecting the Mayor, thereby, protecting their jobs.

"I'm also glad," said the Mayor, "that Kathleen came out un-scathed, though Clay tells me she's off in the next few days to Europe for a month, maybe longer, take in some spa treatments."

"I think that's for the best, it was an ordeal." The Mayor searched Owen's face for further answers. That woman was disturbed. If her dagger doodling on that napkin by the Silver House pool signified body count, then she had one extra inked knife. He hoped not. The numbers he had yet to decipher. Would she rid herself of the killing instruments and her compulsion to use them? If the couple does settle down together Owen wanted to give friendly advice to Clay Stokes, as the new husband, *'don't piss her off.'* Still, that whole consummating relationship may not come to pass. Earlier, Owen spotted Clay laughing, at ease, with Gabriella Corallo. Well, certainly she needed comfort for losing two family members and she was Clay's client, and the new heir in the skin trade business. Solving the issues from the Fed raid at The Pussy Galore would require Clay and Gabriella to work closely together. Interesting times ahead, if he could only hang around to watch.

Owen gave the Mayor the verbal assurance he was looking for, "I think Kathleen and Clay, down the road, will each find their happiness. She just needs time alone. This entire bloodbath resurrected memories of her father's death, and her discovery that he was murdered. You can understand she has yet to deal with that."

The Mayor affirmed this observation with an agreeing nod. He gave a harsh look cutting deep into the casino executive.

"What about us?"

"Us?"

"The briefcase. You figured out the lock combinations. You could have looked inside, and put the numbers back as they were and I would've never guessed. But you left your own code in place. 911 and 411. Emergency and information. Important that I knew you knew. Did you look inside?"

"No, it's your privacy. I honored that. Odd you'd forgotten the briefcase with me on two occasions. I guessed it was your litmus test, a search for honesty, more important, seeking loyalty. If opened, I'm sure you had some gizmo that would've made you aware the case had been tampered with and the contents viewed. I had no need. I already had a good idea at what's inside."

"And that is?"

"Not municipal papers but tools of justice. I came to the conclusion when I noticed at the sign yard your right fingertip with paint on it. At the time I thought it was from the dumpster. But that was blue and when we first met it was a brown color like liver spots. I noted an entirely different color when I drove you to the shopping center opening. Slightly visible but oil base paint is hard to remove even with thinner. Each time on the right hand, predominantly on the right index finger where one might pick up residue paint from pushing the tab on a spray can in the dark.

"I can sympathize with a frustrated politician who can't speed along the process to right wrongs. That you felt impotent about one particular crime spree: the spray painting of the town you love so much. No one listened to you, and criminal mischief not a high priority for police crime fighting. You needed to make the issue national, create a political groundswell, to target the crime, force the state legislature to act with stiffer penalties. Who would guess if they saw the Mayor at night that instead of his normal duties he stalked urban scum with a stun gun, mask, and handcuffs, all hidden in his 24/7 briefcase. Who would ever challenge the Mayor and demand to see what's inside? Wouldn't you say your goals are accomplished? By the latest polls the political pump is primed for you to demand legal changes, short of cutting off the perpetrator's hand. My personal advice: the Graffiti Vigilante should retire before he starts another political scandal, or worse, that he gets himself hurt. You have your own political campaign to launch. The City of Las Vegas would be far less fun if a Goodfella wasn't at the municipal helm."

"I shoulda had you back in the good old days." Owen finally knew the Mayor was serious and not in jest.

The Mayor returned to viewing the antique cars.

"Owen, when you have a chance, come and visit me. Las Vegas has a lot to offer. Let's see if I can be of help." They exchanged meaningful smiles, male bonding at its best.

"Mayor, let me have a rain check. Jackson Flynn has my travel agenda planned and all of a sudden I feel the urge to travel and find some personal sanctuary." He could not tell the Mayor moments earlier he allowed a man to die. His mind ached from his shortcomings, his frailties. He was not yet cured.

"Here's our traveling chariot." The Mayor had picked out a 1957 green Chevy with white fins.

Owen, weak in spirit, half-dazed from the back wound reopened, followed the Mayor as the politician circled this classic car, admiring the lines, reliving his youth. Owen could see Chase across the way, with the assistance of the nurse and her stalwart partner, sitting up, wobbling, her hands pressed to her head, holding a massive headache. Detective Washington could break the bad news of Kinkaid's infamy and death. Maybe someday Chase, Nanna, and Eric would forgive him. He made up his mind to leave this day, without good-byes. He required a time-out from Las Vegas. Since his arrival two weeks ago, the dice rolls of his life showed only snake eyes staring back. Could it get any worse?

"Hey, this has been jimmied," said the Mayor of Las Vegas, opening the car trunk.

Finis

Return of the Questors…Again

Over 20 years ago, I started toying with the concept of hiding clues, not too apparent on book pages, within the writing itself, obscured within the story. This evolved into the Quest Mystery™ concept, resulting in what is now referred to as, *Vegas Die* 1.0 (published in 2008). This novel was a best seller, won a prize and illuminated a new niche in the fiction world. Flash forward into the midst of a pandemic, into the economic recession-depression of the tourist dependent Las Vegas. I now set a goal to revise the Quest Mystery within *Vegas Die* 2.0 in a good faith effort to publicize the re-opened town as well as the book.

I have many to thank for the continued interest and support in *Vegas Die*. Treasure hunters Mike Cowlazars and Kristie Thor (hintofriches.com) who through their website, podcasts, YouTube programs were in the forefront as search leaders on the Forrest Finn Treasure Hunt (now discovered) and have decided that this Quest Mystery will be their next worthwhile challenge. Such people are called 'Questors'. Mike was active in the Vegas Die 1.0 hunt, and got so close to discovery. Others to thank are Histria Books, which under the imprint of Addison & Highsmith, has made the decision to republish all of the Author's past works, most recently the coming-of-age story, *Lafayette: Courtier to Crown Fugitive* (see HistriaBooks.com). Thanks also to Seva Kalashinikov who over the years has been instrumental in website and social media services; Author Katie Salidas for editing support; artist Jerry Blank, seven year friend M. Mantle, handling the Prize Pool, and longtime friend, Michael McCombs, who heroically offered his name to Owen, with the hope there might be more Owen McCombs and Chase Taggart adventures in the future. Prize and hunt rules of the Quest Mystery are to be found at the author's webpage, www.spgrogan.com/treasure-hunt. And I hope to hear from those who enjoy historical novels with a little Quest Mystery hidden within.

[Update: We wish all well in overcoming these pandemic times. For writers it was not 'Love in Time of Cholera' and these times seemed to have quieted treasure hunters from running around outside or in (not there)historic buildings. Then, also, the Forrest Fenn hunt ended with discouraging opinions. Other hunts appeared to act like crowd-funding gimmicks. And, to some Questors, those expecting a constant stream of clues and the immediate answers to all questions became disappointed. Looking for instant gratification hits they moved on, several even accusing me of hiding under a rock. Not true. I want Questors to find the prize but can't be blamed if I must be excellent in secreting strong clues. I believe I am the only long-lasting treasure hunt where the clues are hidden within the book's writing. That has not changed. Clues to *Vegas Die* were even hidden in my novel, **Lafayette: Courtier to Crown Fugitive** but few followed that thread. A Questor needs to know me, understand creative character, the devious clue plotting. Example: Google me and there was a press release several years back of my creative writing and business papers archived for scholastic research (who would believe?). But no one followed that Rebel train of thought.

Lately, I have been working hard to revise the Hawaiian Quest Mystery of *Captain Cooked* into a Las Vegas-Island theme based Quest Mystery hunt which will be soon appearing in fresh paperback. So, there are two Quest Mysteries still out there. Maybe add a few more $5 bills to the prize, hoping there will be a serendipitous Questor who will discover the Spanish pirate coin.

And there is even another book on the horizon, **My Cookbook Passion** by wife Pamela Kure Grogan, and myself as Editor. Who knows what evil lurks in the artichoke hearts of woman?]

SPG

Book Design Title: *Roc Di – 2 Pas Las Thro*

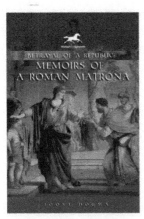